THE
STAR TREK
READER II

Also published by E. P. Dutton
The Star Trek Reader by James Blish

THE STAR TREK READER II

adapted by
James Blish

Based on the Television Series
Created by
Gene Roddenberry

E. P. Dutton
New York

895
9

The nineteen episodes contained in *The Star Trek Reader II* first published in hardcover by E. P. Dutton 1977.

Star Trek 1 copyright © 1967 by Bantam Books, Inc.
and Desilu Productions, Inc.
Star Trek 4 copyright © 1971 by Bantam Books, Inc.
and Paramount Pictures Corporation.
Star Trek 9 copyright © 1973 by Bantam Books, Inc.
and Paramount Pictures Corporation.

To Harlan Ellison
who was right all the time

CONTENTS

Book I
Star Trek 1

CHARLIE'S LAW*
(D. C. Fontana and Gene Roddenberry)

Though as Captain of the starship *Enterprise* James Kirk had the final authority over four hundred officers and crewmen, plus a small and constantly shifting population of passengers, and though in well more than twenty years in space he had had his share of narrow squeaks, he was firmly of the opinion that no single person ever gave him more trouble than one seventeen-year-old boy.

Charles Evans had been picked up from a planet called Thasus after having been marooned there for fourteen years, the sole survivor of the crash of his parents' research vessel. He was rescued by the survey ship *Antares,* a transport about a tenth of the size of the *Enterprise,* and subsequently transferred to Kirk's ship, wearing hand-me-down clothes and carrying all the rest of his possessions in a dufflebag.

The officers of the *Antares* who brought him aboard the *Enterprise* spoke highly of Charlie's intelligence, eagerness to learn, intuitive grasp of engineering matters—"He could run the *Antares* himself if he had to" —and his sweetness of character; but it struck Kirk that they were almost elbowing each other aside to praise him, and that they were in an unprecedented hurry to get back to their own cramped ship, without even so much as begging a bottle of brandy.

Charlie's curiosity had certainly been obvious from those first moments, though he showed some trepidation, too—which was not surprising, considering his long and lonely exile. Kirk assigned Yeoman Rand to take him to his quarters. It was at this point that Charlie stunned her and everyone else present by asking Kirk honestly:

"Is that a girl?"

* Originally "Charlie X"

Leonard McCoy, the ship's surgeon, checked Charlie from top to toe and found him in excellent physical condition: no traces of malnutrition, of exposure, of hardship of any sort; truly remarkable for a boy who'd had to fend for himself on a strange world from the age of three. On the other hand, it was reasonable to suppose that fourteen years later, Charlie would either be in good shape, or dead; he would have had to come to terms with his environment within the first few years.

Charlie was not very communicative about this puzzle, though he asked plenty of questions himself—he seemed earnestly to want to know all the right things to do, and even more urgently, to be liked, but the purport of some of McCoy's questions apparently baffled him.

No, nobody had survived the crash. He had learned English by talking to the memory banks on the ship; they still worked. No, the Thasians hadn't helped him; there were no Thasians. At first he had eaten stores from the wreck; then he had found some other . . . things, growing around.

Charlie then asked to see the ship's rule book. On the *Antares,* he said, he hadn't done or said all the right things. When that happened, people got angry; he got angry, too. He didn't like making the same mistake twice.

"I feel the same way," McCoy told him. "But you can't rush such matters. Just keep your eyes open, and when in doubt, smile and say nothing. It works very nicely."

Charlie returned McCoy's grin, and McCoy dismissed him with a swat on the rump, to Charlie's obvious astonishment.

McCoy brought the problem up again on the bridge with Kirk and his second-in-command, Mr. Spock. Yeoman Rand was there working on a duty roster, and at once volunteered to leave; but since she had seen as much of Charlie as anyone had, Kirk asked her to stay. Besides, Kirk was fond of her, though he fondly imagined that to be a secret even from her.

"Earth history is full of cases where a small child managed to survive in a wilderness," McCoy went on.

"I've read some of your legends," said Spock, who was native to a nonsolar planet confusingly called Vulcan. "They all seem to require a wolf to look after the infants."

"What reason would the boy have to lie, if there *were* Thasians?"

"Nevertheless there's some evidence that there were, at least millennia ago," Spock said. "The first survey reported some highly sophisticated artifacts. And conditions haven't changed on Thasus for at least three million years. There might well be *some* survivors."

"Charlie says there aren't," Kirk said.

"His very survival argues that there are. I've checked the library computer record on Thasus. There isn't much, but one thing it does say: 'No edible plant life.' He simply had to have had some kind of help."

"I think you're giving him less credit than he deserves," McCoy said.

"For the moment let's go on that assumption," Kirk said. "Mr. Spock, work out a briefing program for young Charlie. Give him things to do—places to be. If we keep him busy until we get to Colony Five, experienced educators will take him over, and in the meantime, he should leave us with relative calm aboard . . . Yeoman Rand, what do you think of our problem child?"

"Wellll," she said. "Maybe I'm prejudiced. I wasn't going to mention this, but . . . he followed me down the corridor yesterday and offered me a vial of perfume. My favorite, too; I don't know how he knew it. There's none in the ship's stores, I'm sure of that."

"Hmm," McCoy said.

"I was just going to ask him where he got it, when he swatted me on the rump. After that I made it my business to be someplace else."

There was an outburst of surprised laughter, quickly suppressed.

"Anything else?" Kirk said.

"Nothing important. Did you know that he can do card tricks?"

"Now, where would he have learned that?" Spock demanded.

"I don't know, but he's very good. I was playing solitaire in the rec room when he came in. Lieutenant Uhura was playing 'Charlie is my darling' and singing, and at first he seemed to think she was mocking him. When he saw she didn't mean it personally, he came over to watch me, and he seemed to be puzzled that I couldn't make the game come out. So he made it come out for me—without even touching the cards, I'd swear to that. When I showed I was surprised, he picked up the cards and did a whole series of tricks with them, good ones. The best sleight-of-hand I've ever seen. He said one of the men on the *Antares* taught him how. He was enjoying all the attention, I could tell that, but I didn't want to encourage him too much myself. Not after the swatting incident."

"He got *that* trick from me, I'm afraid," McCoy said.

"No doubt he did," Kirk said. "But I think I'd better talk to him, anyhow."

"Fatherhood becomes you, Jim," McCoy said, grinning.

"Dry up, Bones. I just don't want him getting out of hand, that's all."

Charlie shot to his feet at the moment Kirk entered his cabin; all his fingers, elbows, and knees seemed to bend the wrong way. Kirk had barely managed to nod when he burst out: "I didn't do anything!"

"Relax, Charlie. Just wanted to find out how you're getting along."

"Fine. I . . . I'm supposed to ask you why I shouldn't—I don't know how to explain it."

"Try saying it straight out, Charlie," Kirk said. "That usually works."

"Well, in the corridor . . . I talked to . . . when Janice . . . when Yeoman Rand was . . ." Abruptly, setting his face, he took a quick step forward and slapped Kirk on the seat. "I did that and she didn't like it. She said you'd explain it to me."

"Well," Kirk said, trying hard not to smile, "it's that there are things you can do with a lady, and things you can't. Uh, the fact is, there's no right way to hit a lady. Man to man is one thing, man to woman is something else. Do you understand?"

"I don't know. I guess so."

"If you don't, you'll just have to take my word for it for the time being. In the meantime, I'm having a schedule worked out for you, Charlie. Things to do, to help you learn all the things you missed while you were marooned on Thasus."

"That's very nice, for you to do that for me," Charlie said. He seemed genuinely pleased. "Do you like me?"

That flat question took Kirk off guard. "I don't know," he said equally flatly. "Learning to like people takes time. You have to watch what they do, try to understand them. It doesn't happen all at once."

"Oh," Charlie said.

"Captain Kirk," Lieutenant Uhura's voice broke in over the intercom.

"Excuse me, Charlie . . . Kirk here."

"Captain Ramart of the *Antares* is on D channel. Must speak to you directly."

"Right. I'll come up to the bridge."

"Can I come too?" Charlie said as Kirk switched out.

"I'm afraid not, Charlie. This is strictly ship's business."

"I won't disturb anybody," Charlie said. "I'll stay out of the way."

The boy's need for human company was touching, no matter how awkwardly he went about it. There were many years of solitude to be made up for. "Well, all right," Kirk said. "But only when you have my permission. Agreed?"

"Agreed," Charlie said eagerly. He followed Kirk out like a puppy.

On the bridge, Lieutenant Uhura, her Bantu face intent as a tribal statue's, was asking the microphone: "Can you boost your power, *An- tares?* We are barely reading your transmission."

"We are at full output, *Enterprise,*" Ramart's voice said, very distant and hashy. "I must speak with Captain Kirk at once."

Kirk stepped up to the station and picked up the mike. "Kirk here, Captain Ramart."

"Captain, thank goodness. We're just barely in range. I've got to warn—"

His voice stopped. There was nothing to be heard from the speaker now but stellar static—not even a carrier wave.

"See if you can get them back," Kirk said.

"There's nothing to get, Captain," Lieutenant Uhura said, baffled. "They aren't transmitting any more."

"Keep the channel open."

Behind Kirk, Charlie said quietly: "That was an old ship. It wasn't very well constructed."

Kirk stared at him, and then swung toward Spock's station.

"Mr. Spock, sweep the transmission area with probe sensors."

"I've got it," Spock said promptly. "But it's fuzzy. Unusually so even for this distance."

Kirk turned back to the boy. "What happened, Charlie? Do you know?"

Charlie stared back at him, with what seemed to be uneasy defiance. "I don't know," he said.

"The fuzzy area is spreading out," Spock reported. "I'm getting some distinct pips now along the edges. Debris, undoubtedly."

"But no *Antares?*"

"Captain Kirk, that *is* the *Antares,*" Spock said quietly. "No other interpretation is possible. Clearly, she blew up."

Kirk continued to hold Charlie's eye. The boy looked back.

"I'm sorry it blew up," Charlie said. He seemed uneasy, but nothing more than that. "But I won't miss them. They weren't very nice. They didn't like me. I could tell."

There was a long, terribly tense silence. At last Kirk carefully unclenched his fists.

"Charlie," he said, "one of the first things you're going to have to get rid of is that damned cold-bloodedness. Or self-centeredness, or whatever it is. Until that gets under control, you're going to be less than half human."

And then, he stopped. To his embarrassed amazement, Charlie was crying.

"He what?" Kirk said, looking up from his office chair at Yeoman Rand. She was vastly uncomfortable, but she stuck to her guns.

"He made a pass at me," she repeated. "Not in so many words, no. But he made me a long, stumbling speech. He wants me."

"Yeoman, he's a seventeen-year-old boy."

"Exactly," the girl said.

"All this because of a swat?"

"No, sir," she said. "Because of the speech. Captain, I've seen that look before; *I'm* not seventeen. And if something isn't done, sooner or later I'm going to have to hold Charlie off, maybe even swat him myself, and not on the fanny, either. That wouldn't be good for him. I'm his first love and his first crush and the first woman he ever saw and . . ." She caught her breath. "Captain, that's a great deal for anyone to have to handle, even one item at a time. All at once, it's murder. And he doesn't understand the usual put-offs. If I have to push him off in a way he does understand, there may be trouble. Do you follow me?"

"I think so, Yeoman," Kirk said. He still could not quite take the situation seriously. "Though I never thought I'd wind up explaining the birds and the bees to anybody, not at my age. But I'll send for him right now."

"Thank you, sir." She went out. Kirk buzzed for Charlie. He appeared almost at once, as though he had been expecting something of the sort.

"Come in, Charlie, sit down."

The boy moved to the chair opposite Kirk's desk and sat down, as if settling into a bear trap. As before, he beat Kirk to the opening line.

"Janice," he said. "Yeoman Rand. It's about her, isn't it?"

Damn the kid's quickness! "More or less. Though it's more about you."

"I won't hit her like that any more. I promised."

"There's more to it than that," Kirk said. "You've got some things to learn."

"Everything I do or say is wrong," Charlie said desperately. "I'm in the way. Dr. McCoy won't show me the rules. I don't know what I am or what I'm supposed to be, or even *who*. And I don't know why I hurt so much inside all the time—"

"I do, and you'll live," Kirk said. "There's nothing wrong with you that hasn't gone haywire inside every human male since the model came out. There's no way to get over it, around it, or under it; you just have to live through it, Charlie."

"But, it's like I'm wearing my insides outside. I go around bent over all the time. Janice—Yeoman Rand—she wants to give me away to someone else. Yeoman Lawton. But she's just a, just a, well, she doesn't even smell like a girl. Nobody else on the ship is like Janice. I don't want anybody else."

"It's normal," Kirk said gently. "Charlie, there are a million things in the universe you can have. There are also about a hundred million that you can't. There's no fun in learning to face that, but you've got to do it. That's how things are."

"I don't like it," Charlie said, as if that explained everything.

"I don't blame you. But you have to hang on tight and survive. Which reminds me: the next thing on your schedule is unarmed defense. Come along to the gym with me and we'll try a few falls. Way back in Victorian England, centuries ago, they had a legend that violent exercise helped keep one's mind off women. I've never known it to work, myself, but anyhow let's give it a try."

Charlie was incredibly clumsy, but perhaps no more so than any other beginner. Ship's Officer Sam Ellis, a member of McCoy's staff, clad like Kirk and Charlie in work-out clothes, was patient with him.

"That's better. Slap the mat when you go down, Charlie. It absorbs the shock. Now, again."

Ellis dropped of his own initiative to the mat, slapped it, and rolled gracefully up onto his feet. "Like that."

"I'll never learn," Charlie said.

"Sure you will," Kirk said. "Go ahead."

Charlie managed an awkward drop. He forgot to slap until almost the last minute, so that quite a thud accompanied the slap.

"Well, that's an improvement," Kirk said. "Like everything else, it takes practice. Once more."

This time was better. Kirk said, "That's it. Okay, Sam, show him a shoulder roll."

Ellis hit the mat, and was at once on his feet again, cleanly and easily.

"I don't want to do that," Charlie said.

"It's part of the course," Kirk said. "It's not hard. Look." He did a roll himself. "Try it."

"No. You were going to teach me to fight, not roll around on the floor."

"You have to learn to take falls without hurting yourself before we can do that. Sam, maybe we'd better demonstrate. A couple of easy throws."

"Sure," Ellis said. The two officers grappled, and Ellis, who was in much better shape than the Captain, let Kirk throw him. Then, as Kirk got to his feet, Ellis flipped him like a poker chip. Kirk rolled and bounced, glad of the exercise.

"See what I mean?" Kirk said.

"I guess so," Charlie said. "It doesn't look hard."

He moved in and grappled with Kirk, trying for the hold he had seen Ellis use. He was strong, but he had no leverage. Kirk took a counter-hold and threw him. It was not a hard throw, but Charlie again forgot to slap the mat. He jumped to his feet flaming mad, glaring at Kirk.

"*That* won't do," Ellis said, grinning. "You need a lot more falls, Charlie."

Charlie whirled toward him. In a low, intense voice, he said: "Don't laugh at me."

"Cool off, Charlie," Ellis said, chuckling openly now. "Half the trick is in not losing your temper."

"*Don't laugh at me!*" Charlie said. Ellis spread out his hands, but his grin did not quite go away.

Exactly one second later, there was a pop like the breaking of the world's largest light bulb. Ellis vanished.

Kirk stared stupefied at the spot where Ellis had been. Charlie, too, stood frozen for a moment. Then he began to move tentatively toward the door.

"Hold it," Kirk said. Charlie stopped, but he did not turn to face Kirk.

"He shouldn't have laughed at me," Charlie said. "That's not nice, to laugh at somebody. I was trying."

"Not very hard. Never mind that. What happened? What did you do to my officer?"

"He's gone," Charlie said sullenly.

"That's no answer."

"He's gone," Charlie said. "That's all I know. I didn't want to do it. He made me. He laughed at me."

And suppose Janice has to slap him? And . . . there was the explosion of the *Antares* . . . Kirk stepped quickly to the nearest wall intercom and flicked it on. Charlie turned at last to watch him. "Captain Kirk in the gym," Kirk said. "Two men from security here, on the double."

"What are you going to do with me?" Charlie said.

"I'm sending you to your quarters. And I want you to stay there."

"I won't let them touch me," Charlie said in a low voice. "I'll make them go away too."

"They won't hurt you."

Charlie did not answer, but he had the look of a caged animal just before it turns at last upon its trainer. The door opened and two security guards came in, phaser pistols holstered. They stopped and looked to Kirk.

"Go with them, Charlie. We'll talk about this later, when we've both cooled off. You owe me a long explanation." Kirk jerked his head toward Charlie. The guards stepped to him and took him by the arms.

Or, tried to. Actually, Kirk was sure that they never touched him. One of them simply staggered back, but the other was thrown violently against the wall, as though he had been caught in a sudden hurricane. He managed to hold his footing, however, and clawed for his sidearm.

"No!" Kirk shouted.

But the order was way too late. By the time the guard had his hand levelled at the boy, he no longer had a weapon to hold. It had vanished, just like Sam Ellis. Charlie stared at Kirk, his eyes narrowed and challenging.

"Charlie," Kirk said, "you're showing off. Go to your quarters."

"No."

"Go with the guards, or I'll pick you up and carry you there myself." He began to walk steadily forward. "That's your only choice, Charlie. Either do as I tell you, or send me away to wherever you sent the phaser, and Sam Ellis."

"Oh, all right," Charlie said, wilting. Kirk drew a deep breath. "But tell them to keep their hands to themselves."

"They won't hurt you. Not if you do as I say."

Kirk called a general council on the bridge at once, but Charlie moved faster: by the time Kirk's officers were all present, there wasn't a phaser to be found anywhere aboard ship. Charlie had made them all "go away." Kirk explained what had happened, briefly and grimly.

"Given this development," McCoy said, "it's clear Charlie wouldn't have needed any help from any putative Thasians. He could have magicked up all his needs by himself."

"Not necessarily," Spock said. "All we know is that he can make things vanish—not make them appear. I admit that that alone would have been a big help to him."

"What are the chances," Kirk said, "that he's a Thasian himself? Or at least, something really unprecedented in the way of an alien?"

"The chance is there," McCoy said, "but I'd be inclined to rule it out. Remember I checked him over. He's ostensibly human, down to his last blood type. Of course, I could have missed something, but he was hooked to the body-function panel, too; the machine would have rung sixteen different kinds of alarms at the slightest discrepancy."

"Well, he's inhumanly powerful, in any event," Spock said. "The probability is that he was responsible for the destruction of the *Antares*, too. Over an enormous distance—well beyond phaser range."

"Great," McCoy said. "Under the circumstances, how can we hope to keep him caged up?"

"It goes further than that, Bones," Kirk said. "We can't take him to Colony Five, either. Can you imagine what he'd do in an open, normal environment—in an undisciplined environment?"

Clearly, McCoy hadn't. Kirk got up and began to pace.

"Charlie is an adolescent boy—probably human, but totally inexperienced with other human beings. He's short-tempered because he wants so much and it can't come fast enough for him. He's full of adolescent aches. He wants to be one of us, to be loved, to be useful. But . . . I remember when I was seventeen that I wished for the ability to remove the things and people that annoyed me, neatly and without fuss. It's a power fantasy most boys of that age have. Charlie doesn't have to wish. *He can do it.*

"In other words, in order to stay in existence, gentlemen, we'll have to make damn sure we don't annoy him. Otherwise—pop!"

"Annoyance is relative, Captain," Spock said. "It's all going to depend on how Charlie is feeling minute by minute. And because of his background, or lack of it, we have no ways to guess what little thing might annoy him next, no matter how carefully we try. He's the galaxy's most destructive weapon, and he's on a hair trigger."

"No," Kirk said. "He's not a weapon. He *has* a weapon. That's a difference we can use. Essentially, he's a child, a child in a man's body, trying to be a whole man. His trouble isn't malice. It's innocence."

"And here he is," McCoy said with false heartiness. Kirk swung his chair around to see Charlie approaching from the elevator, smiling cheerfully.

"Hi," said the galaxy's most destructive weapon.

"I thought I confined you to your quarters, Charlie."

"You did," Charlie said, the grin fading. "But I got tired of waiting around down there."

"Oh, all right. You're here. Maybe you can answer a few questions for us. Were you responsible for what happened to the *Antares?*"

"Why?"

"Because I want to know. Answer me, Charlie."

Breaths were held while Charlie thought it over. Finally, he said:

"Yes. There was a warped baffle plate on the shielding of their Nerst generator. I made it go away. It would have given sooner or later anyhow."

"You could have told them that."

"What for?" Charlie said reasonably. "They weren't nice to me. They didn't like me. You saw them when they brought me aboard. They wanted to get rid of me. They don't any more."

"And what about us?" Kirk said.

"Oh, I need you. I have to get to Colony Five. But if you're not nice to me, I'll think of something else." The boy turned abruptly and left, for no visible reason.

McCoy wiped sweat off his forehead. "What a chance you took."

"We can't be walking on eggs every second," Kirk said. "If every act, every question might irritate him, we might as well pretend that none of them will. Otherwise we'll be utterly paralyzed."

"Captain," Spock said slowly, "do you suppose a force field might hold him? He's too smart to allow himself to be lured into a detention cell, but we just might rig up a field at his cabin door. All the lab circuitry runs through the main corridor on deck five, and we could use that. It's a long chance, but—"

"How long would the work take?" Kirk said.

"At a guess, seventy-two hours."

"It's going to be a long seventy-two hours, Mr. Spock. Get on it." Spock nodded and went out.

"Lieutenant Uhura, raise Colony Five for me. I want to speak directly to the Governor. Lieutenant Sulu, lay me a course away from Colony Five—not irrevocably, but enough to buy me some time. Bones—"

He was interrupted by the sound of a fat spark, and a choked scream of pain from Uhura. Her hands were in her lap, writhing together uncontrollably. McCoy leapt to her side, tried to press the clenched fingers apart.

"It's . . . all right," she said. "I think. Just a shock. But there's no reason for the board to be charged like that—"

"Probably a very good reason," Kirk said grimly. "Don't touch it until further orders. How does it look, Bones?"

"Superficial burns," McCoy said. "But who knows what it'll be next time?"

"I can tell you that," Sulu said. "I can't feed new co-ordinates into this panel. It operates, but it rejects the course change. We're locked on Colony Five."

"I'm in a hurry," Charlie's voice said. He was coming out of the elevator again, but he paused as he saw the naked fury on Kirk's face.

"I'm getting tired of this," Kirk said. "What about the transmitter?"

"You don't need all that subspace chatter," Charlie said, a little defensively. "If there's any trouble, I can take care of it myself. I'm learning fast."

"I don't want your help," Kirk said. "Charlie, for the moment there's nothing I can do to prevent your interference. But I'll tell you this: you're quite right, I don't like you. I don't like you at all. Now beat it."

"I'll go," Charlie said, quite coolly. "I don't mind if you don't like me now. You will pretty soon. I'm going to make you."

As he left, McCoy began to swear in a low whisper.

"Belay that, Bones, it won't help. Lieutenant Uhura, is it just outside communications that are shorted, or is the intercom out too?"

"Intercom looks good, Captain."

"All right, get me Yeoman Rand . . . Janice, I have a nasty one for you—maybe the nastiest you've ever been asked to do. I want you to lure Charlie into his cabin. . . . That's right. We'll be watching—but bear in mind that if you make him mad, there won't be much we can do to protect you. You can opt out if you want; it probably won't work anyhow."

"If it doesn't," Yeoman Rand's voice said, "it won't be because *I* didn't try it."

They watched, Spock's hand hovering over the key that would activate the force field. At first, Janice was alone in Charlie's cabin, and the wait seemed very long. Finally, however, the door slid aside, and Charlie came into the field of the hidden camera, his expression a mixture of hope and suspicion.

"It was nice of you to come here," he said. "But I don't trust people any more. They're all so complicated, and full of hate."

"No, they're not," Janice said. "You just don't make enough allowance for how *they* feel. You have to give them time."

"Then . . . you do like me?"

"Yes, I like you. Enough to try to straighten you out, anyhow. Otherwise I wouldn't have asked to come here."

"That was very nice," Charlie said. "I can be nice, too. Look. I have something for you."

From behind his back, where it had already been visible to the camera, he produced the single pink rosebud he had been carrying and held it out. There had been no roses aboard ship, either; judging by that and the perfume, he could indeed make things appear as well as disappear. The omens did not look good.

"Pink *is* your favorite color, isn't it?" Charlie was saying. "The books say all girls like pink. Blue is for boys."

"It was . . . a nice thought, Charlie. But this isn't really the time for courting. I really need to talk to you."

"But you asked to come to my room. The books all say that means something important." He reached out, trying to touch her face. She moved instinctively away, trying to circle for the door, which was now on remote control, the switch for it under Spock's other hand; but she could not see where she was backing and was stopped by a chair.

"No. I said I only wanted to talk and that's what I meant."

"But I only wanted to be nice to you."

She got free of the chair somehow and resumed sidling. "That's a switch on Charlie's Law," she said.

"What do you mean? What's that?"

"Charlie's Law says everybody better be nice to Charlie, or else."

"That's not true!" Charlie said raggedly.

"Isn't it? Where's Sam Ellis, then?"

"I don't know where he is. He's just gone. Janice, I only *want* to be nice. They won't let me. None of you will. I can give you anything you want. Just tell me."

"All right," Janice said. "Then I think you had better let me go. That's what I want now."

"But you said . . ." The boy swallowed and tried again. "Janice, I . . . love you."

"No you don't. You don't know what the word means."

"Then show me," he said, reaching for her.

Her back was to the door now, and Spock hit the switch. The boy's eyes widened as the door slid back, and then Janice was through it. He charged after her, and the other key closed.

The force field flared, and Charlie was flung back into the room. He stood there for a moment like a stabled stallion, nostrils flared, breathing heavily. Then he said:

"All right. All right, then."

He walked slowly forward. Kirk swung the camera to follow him. This time he went through the force field as though it did not exist. He advanced again on Janice.

"Why did you do that?" he said. "You won't even let me try. None of you. All right. From now on I'm not trying. I won't keep any of you but the ones I need. I don't need you."

16

There came the implosion sound again. Janice was gone. Around Kirk, the universe turned a dull, aching gray.

"Charlie," he said hoarsely. The intercom carried his voice to Charlie's cabin. He looked blindly toward the source.

"You too, Captain," he said. "What you did wasn't nice either. I'll keep you awhile. The *Enterprise* isn't quite like the *Antares*. Running the *Antares* was easy. But if you try to hurt me again, I'll make a lot of other people go away . . . I'm coming up to the bridge now."

"I can't stop you," Kirk said.

"I know you can't. Being a man isn't so much. I'm not a man and I can do anything. You can't. Maybe I'm the man and you're not."

Kirk cut out the circuit and looked at Spock. After a while the First Officer said:

"That was the last word, if ever I heard it."

"It's as close as I care to come to it, that's for sure. Did that field react at all, the second time?"

"No. He went through it as easily as a ray of light. Easier—I could have stopped a light ray if I'd known the frequency. There seems to be very little he can't do."

"Except run the ship—and get to Colony Five by himself."

"Small consolation."

They broke off as Charlie entered. He was walking very tall. Without a word to anyone, he went to the helmsman's chair and waved to Sulu to get out of it. After a brief glance at Kirk, Sulu got up obediently, and Charlie sat down and began to play with the controls. The ship lurched, very slightly, and he snatched his hands back.

"Show me what to do," he told Sulu.

"That would take thirty years of training."

"Don't argue with me. Just show me."

"Go ahead, show him," Kirk said. "Maybe he'll blow us up. Better than letting him loose on Colony Five—"

"Captain Kirk," Lieutenant Uhura broke in. "I'm getting something from outside; subspace channel F. Ship to ship, I think. But it's all on instruments; I can't hear it."

"There's nothing there," Charlie said, his voice rough. "Just leave it alone."

"Captain?"

"I am the captain," Charlie said. Yet somehow, Kirk had the sudden conviction that he was frightened. And somehow, equally inexplicably, he knew that the *Enterprise* had to get that call.

"Charlie," he said, "are you creating that message—or are you blocking one that's coming in?"

"It's my game, Mr. Kirk," Charlie said. "You have to find out. Like you said—that's how the game is played." He pushed himself out of the chair and said to Sulu, "You can have it now. I've locked on course for Colony Five again."

He could have done nothing of the sort in that brief period; not, at least, with his few brief stabs at the controls. Probably, his original lock still held unchanged. But either way, it was bad enough; Colony Five was now only twelve hours away.

But Charlie's hands were trembling visibly. Kirk said:

"All right, Charlie, that's the game—and the game is over. I don't think you can handle any more. I think you're at your limit and you can't take on one more thing. But you're going to have to. Me."

"I could have sent you away before," Charlie said. "Don't make me do it now."

"You don't dare. You've got my ship. I want it back. And I want my crew back whole, too—if I have to break your neck to do it."

"Don't push me," Charlie whispered. *"Don't push me."*

At the next step forward, a sleet-storm of pain threw Kirk to the deck. He could not help crying out.

"I'm sorry," Charlie said, sweating. "I'm sorry—"

The subspace unit hummed loudly, suddenly, and then began to chatter in intelligible code. Uhura reached for the unscrambler.

"Stop that!" Charlie screamed, whirling. "I said, stop it!"

The pain stopped; Kirk was free. After a split-second's hesitation to make sure he was all there, he lunged to his feet. Spock and McCoy were also closing in, but Kirk was closer. He drew back a fist.

"Console is clear," Sulu's voice said behind him. "Helm answers."

Charlie dodged away from Kirk's threat, whimpering. He never had looked less like the captain of anything, even his own soul. Kirk held back his blow in wonder.

Pop!

Janice Rand was on the bridge, putting out both hands to steady herself. She was white-faced and shaken, but otherwise unharmed.

Pop!

"That was a hell of a fall, Jim," Sam Ellis' voice said. "Next time, take it a little—hey, what's all this?"

"Message is through," Lieutenant Uhura's voice said dispassionately. "Ship off our starboard bow. Identifies itself as from Thasus."

With a cry of animal panic, Charlie fell to the deck, drumming on it with both fists.

"Don't listen, don't listen!" he wailed. "No, no please! I can't live with them any more."

Kirk watched stolidly, not moving. The boy who had been bullying and manipulating them for so long was falling apart under his eyes.

"You're my friends. You *said* you were my friends. Remember—when I came aboard?" He looked up piteously at Kirk. "Take me home, to Colony Five. That's all I want . . . It's really all I want!"

"Captain," Spock said in an emotionless voice. "Something happening over here. Like a transporter materialization. Look."

Feeling like a man caught in a long fall of dominoes, Kirk jerked his eyes toward Spock. There was indeed something materializing on the bridge, through which Spock himself could now be seen only dimly. It was perhaps two-thirds as tall as a man, roughly oval, and fighting for solidity. It wavered and changed, and colors flowed through it. For a moment it looked like a gigantic human face; then, like nothing even remotely human; then, like a distorted view of a distant but gigantic building. It did not seem able to hold any state very long.

Then it spoke. The voice was deep and resonant. It came, not from the apparition, but from the subspace speaker; but like the apparition, it wavered, blurred, faded, blared, changed color, as if almost out of control.

"We are sorry for this trouble," it said. "We did not realize until too late that the human boy was gone from us. We searched a long time to find him, but space travel is a long-unused skill among us; we are saddened that his escape cost the lives of those aboard the first ship. We could not help them because they were exploded in this frame; but we have returned your people and your weapons to you, since they were only intact in the next frame. Now everything else is as it was. There is nothing to fear; we have him in control."

"No," Charlie said. He was weeping convulsively. Clambering to his knees, he grappled Kirk by a forearm. "I won't do it again. Please, I'll be nice. I won't ever do it again. I'm sorry about the *Antares,* I'm sorry. Please let me go with you, please!"

"Whee-oo," McCoy said gustily. "Talk about the marines landing—!"

"It's not that easy," Kirk said, looking steadily at the strange thing—a Thasian?—before him. "Charlie destroyed the other ship and will have to be punished for it. But thanks to you, all the other damage is repaired —and he is a human being. He belongs with his own people."

"You're out of your mind," McCoy said.

"Shut up, Bones. He's one of us. Rehabilitation might make him really one of us, reunite him to his own people. We owe him that, if he can be taught not to use his power."

"We gave him the power," the apparition said, "so that he could live. It cannot be taken back or forgotten. He will use it; he cannot help himself. He would destroy you and your kind, or you would be forced to destroy him to save yourselves. We alone offer him life."

"Not at all," Kirk said. "You offer him a prison—not even a half-life."

"We know that. But that damage was done long ago; we can do now only what little best is left. Since we are to blame, we must care for him. Come, Charles Evans."

"Don't let them!" Charlie gasped. "Don't let them take me! Captain—*Janice!* Don't you understand, I *can't even touch them*—"

The boy and the Thasian vanished, in utter silence. The only remaining sound was the dim, multifarious humming sound of the *Enterprise*.

And the sound of Janice Rand weeping, as a woman weeps for a lost son.

DAGGER OF THE MIND

(S. Bar-David)

Simon van Gelder came aboard the *Enterprise* from the Tantalus Penal Colony via transporter, inside a box addressed to the Bureau of Penology in Stockholm—a desperate measure, but not a particularly intelligent one, as was inevitable under the circumstances. He had hardly been aboard three minutes before Tristan Adams, the colony's director and chief medic, had alerted Captain Kirk to the escape ("a potentially violent case") and the search was on.

Nevertheless, in this short time van Gelder, who was six feet four and only in his early forties, was able to ambush a crewman, knock him out, and change clothes with him, acquiring a phaser pistol in the process. Thus disguised, he was able to make his way to the bridge, where he demanded asylum and managed to paralyze operations for three more minutes before being dropped from behind by one of Mr. Spock's famous nerve squeezes. He was then hauled off to be confined in sick bay, and that was that.

Or that should have been that. Standard operating procedure would have been to give the captive a routine medical check and then ship him by transporter back to Tantalus and the specialized therapeutic resources of Dr. Adams. Kirk, however, had long been an admirer of Dr. Adams' rehabilitation concepts, and had been disappointed that ship's business had given him no excuse to visit the colony himself; now the irruption of this violent case seemed to offer an ideal opportunity. Besides, there was something about van Gelder himself that intrigued Kirk; in their brief encounter, he had not struck Kirk as a common criminal despite his desperation, and Kirk had not been aware that noncriminal psychiatric cases were ever sent to Tantalus. He went to visit the prisoner in the sick bay.

Dr. McCoy had him under both restraint and sedation while running body function tests. Asleep, his face was relaxed, childlike, vulnerable.

"I'm getting bursts of delta waves from the electroencephalograph," McCoy said, pointing to the body function panel. "Highly abnormal, but not schizophrenia, tissue damage, or any other condition I'm acquainted with. After I got him here, it took a triple dose of sedation to—"

He was interrupted by a sound from the bed, a strange combination of groan and snarl. The patient was coming back to consciousness, struggling against his bonds.

"The report said he was quite talkative," Kirk said.

"But not very informative. He'd claim one thing, seem to forget, then start to claim something else . . . and yet what little I could understand seemed to have the ring of truth to it. Too bad we won't have time to study him."

"So that's the system, is it?" the man on the bed said harshly, still struggling. "Take him back! Wash your hands of him! Let somebody else worry! Damn you—"

"What's your name?" Kirk said.

"My name . . . my name . . ." Suddenly, it seemed to Kirk that he was struggling not against the restraints, but against some kind of pain. "My name is . . . is Simon . . . Simon van Gelder."

He sank back and added almost quietly: "I don't suppose you've heard of me."

"Same name he gave before," McCoy said.

"Did I?" said van Gelder. "I'd forgotten. I was Director of . . . of . . . at the Tantalus Colony. Not a prisoner . . . I was . . . assistant. Graduate of . . . of . . ." His face contorted. "And then at . . . I did graduate studies at . . . studies at . . ."

The harder the man tried to remember, the more pain he seemed to be in. "Never mind," Kirk said gently. "It's all right. We—"

"I know," van Gelder said through clenched teeth. "They erased it . . . edited, adjusted . . . subverted me! I won't . . . I won't forget it! Won't go back there! Die first! Die, die!"

He had suddenly gone wild again, straining and shouting, his face a mask of unseeing passion. McCoy stepped close and there was the hiss of a spray hypo. The shouting died down to a mutter, then stopped altogether.

"Any guesses at all?" Kirk said.

"One point I don't have to guess at," McCoy said. "He doesn't want to go back to that—how did you describe it? 'More like a resort than a prison.' Evidently a cage is still a cage, no matter how you label it."

"Or else there's something drastically wrong down there," Kirk said. "Keep him secure, Bones. I'm going to do a little research."

By the time Kirk returned to the bridge, Spock was already removing a tape cassette from the viewer. "I got this from our library, Captain," he said. "No doubt about it: our captive is Dr. van Gelder."

"Dr.–?"

"That's right. Assigned to Tantalus Colony six months ago as Dr. Adams' assistant. Not committed; assigned. A highly respected man in his field."

Kirk thought about it a moment, then turned to his Communications Officer. "Lieutenant Uhura, get me Dr. Adams on Tantalus . . . Doctor? This is Captain Kirk of the *Enterprise*. Regarding your escapee—"

"Is Dr. van Gelder all right?" Adams' voice cut in with apparent concern. "And your people? No injuries? In the violent state he's in—"

"No harm to him or anyone, sir. But we thought you might be able to enlighten us about his condition. My medical officer is baffled."

"I'm not surprised. He'd been doing some experimental work, Captain. An experimental beam we'd hoped might rehabilitate incorrigibles. Dr. van Gelder felt he hadn't the moral right to expose another man to something he hadn't tried on his own person."

While Adams had been talking, McCoy had entered from the elevator and had crossed to the library-computer station, where he stood listening with Kirk and Spock. Now he caught Kirk's eye and made the immemorial throat-cutting gesture.

"I see," Kirk said into the microphone. "Please stand by a moment, Dr. Adams." Uhura broke contact, and Kirk swung to McCoy. "Explain."

"It doesn't quite ring true, Jim," the medico said. "I don't think whatever's wrong with this patient is something he did to himself. I think it was something that was done to him. I can't defend it, it's just an impression—but a strong one."

"That's not enough to go on," Kirk said, irritated in spite of himself. "You're not dealing with just any ordinary warden here, Bones. In the past twenty years, Adams has done more to revolutionize, to humanize, prisons and the treatment of prisoners than all the rest of humanity had done in forty centuries. I've been to penal colonies since they've begun following his methods. They're not 'cages' any more, they're clean, decent hospitals for sick minds. I'm not about to start throwing unsubstantiated charges against a man like that."

"Who said anything about charges?" McCoy said calmly. "Just ask questions. Propose an investigation. If something's really wrong, Adams will duck. Any harm in trying it?"

"I suppose not." Kirk nodded to Uhura, who closed the circuit again. "Dr. Adams? This is rather embarrassing. One of my officers has just reminded me that by strict interpretation of our starship regulations, I'm required to initiate an investigation of this so that a proper report—"

"No need to apologize, Captain Kirk," Adams' voice said. "In fact, I'd take it as a personal favor if you could beam down personally, look into it yourself. I'm sure you realize that I don't get too many visitors here. Oh—I would appreciate it if you could conduct the tour with a minimum staff. We're forced to limit outside contact as much as possible."

"I understand. I've visited rehab colonies before. Very well. *Enterprise* out . . . Satisfied, McCoy?"

"Temporarily," the medical officer said, unruffled.

"All right. We'll keep van Gelder here until I complete my investigation, anyway. Find me somebody in your department with psychiatric *and* penological experience—both in the same person, if possible."

"Helen Noel should do nicely. She's an M.D., but she's written several papers on rehab problems."

"Very good. We beam down in an hour."

Though there were plenty of women among the *Enterprise's* officers and crew, Helen Noel was a surprise to Kirk. She was young and almost uncomfortably pretty—and furthermore, though Kirk had seen her before, he had not then realized that she was part of the ship's complement. That had been back at the medical lab's Christmas party. He had had the impression then that she was simply a passenger, impressed as female passengers often were to be singled out for conversation by the Captain; and in fact, in the general atmosphere of Holiday he had taken certain small advantages of her impressionability . . . It now turned out that she was, and had then been, the newest addition to the ship's medical staff. Her expression as they met in the transporter room was demure, but he had the distinct impression that she was enjoying his discomfiture.

Tantalus was an eerie world, lifeless, ravaged, and torn by a bitter and blustery climate, its atmosphere mostly nitrogen slightly diluted by some of the noble gasses—a very bad place to try to stage an escape. In this it closely resembled all other penal colonies, enlightened or otherwise. Also as usual, the colony proper was all underground, its location marked on the surface only by a small superstructure containing a transporter room, an elevator head, and a few other service modules.

Dr. Tristan Adams met them in his office: a man in his mid-forties, with broad warm features, a suspicion of old freckles at the nose, and an almost aggressively friendly manner which seemed to promise firm handshakes, humor, an ounce of brandy at the right hour, and complete candor at all times. He hardly seemed to be old enough to have accumulated his massive reputation. The office reflected the man; it was personal, untidy without being littered, furnished with an eye to comfort and the satisfaction of someone perhaps as interested in primitive sculpture as in social medicine.

With him was a young woman, tall and handsome though slightly cadaverous, whom he introduced as "Lethe." There was something odd about her which Kirk could not quite fathom: perhaps a slight lack of normal human spontaneity in both manner and voice. As if expecting just such a reaction, Adams went on:

"Lethe came to us for rehabilitation, and ended up staying on as a therapist. And a very good one."

"I love my work," the girl said, in a flat voice.

With a glance at Adams for permission, Kirk said: "And before you came here?"

"I was another person," Lethe said. "Malignant, hateful."

"May I ask what crime you committed?"

"I don't know," Lethe said. "It doesn't matter. That person no longer exists."

"Part of our treatment, Captain, is to bury the past," Adams said. "If the patient can come to terms with his memories, all well and good. But if they're unbearable, why carry them at all? Sufficient unto the day are the burdens thereof. Shall we begin the tour?"

"I'm afraid we haven't time for a complete tour," Kirk said. "Under the circumstances, I'd primarily like to see the apparatus or experiment that injured Dr. van Gelder. That, after all, is the whole point of our inquiry."

"Yes, quite. One doesn't enjoy talking about failures, but still, negative evidence is also important. If you'll just follow me—"

"One minute," Kirk said, pulling his communicator out of his hip pocket. "I'd best check in with the ship. If you'll pardon me a moment—?"

Adams nodded and Kirk stepped to one side, partly turning his back. In a moment, Spock's voice was saying softly:

"Van Gelder's no better, but Dr. McCoy has pulled a few additional bits and pieces out of his memory. They don't seem to change the situation much. He insists that Adams is malignant, the machine is dangerous. No details."

"All right. I'll check in with you at four-hour intervals. Thus far everything here seems open and aboveboard. Out."

"Ready, Captain?" Adams said pleasantly. "Good. This way, please."

The chamber in which van Gelder had allegedly undergone his mysterious and shattering conversion looked to Kirk's unsophisticated eye exactly like any other treatment room, perhaps most closely resembling a radiology theater. There was a patient on the table as Kirk, Adams, and Helen entered, seemingly unconscious; and from a small, complex device hanging from the ceiling, a narrow, monochromatic beam of light like a laser beam was fixed on the patient's forehead. Near the door, a uniformed therapist stood at a small control panel, unshielded; evidently, the radiation, whatever it was, was not dangerous at even this moderate distance. It all looked quite unalarming.

"This is the device," Adams said softly. "A neural potentiator, or damper. The two terms sound opposite to each other but actually both describe the same effect: an induced increase in neural conductivity, which greatly increases the number of cross-connections in the brain. At a certain point, as we predicted from information theory, increased connectivity actually results in the disappearance of information. We thought it would help the patient to cope better with his most troublesome thoughts and desires. But the effects are only temporary; so, I doubt that it'll be anything like as useful as we'd hoped it would be."

"Hmm," Kirk said. "Then if it's not particularly useful—"

"Why do we use it?" Adams smiled ruefully. "Hope, that's all, Captain. Perhaps we can still get some good out of it, in calming violent cases. But strictly as a palliative."

"Like tranquilizing drugs," Helen Noel suggested. "They do nothing permanent. And to continually be feeding drugs into a man's bloodstream just to keep him under control . . ."

Adams nodded vigorously. "Exactly my point, Doctor."

He turned toward the door, but Kirk was still eyeing the patient on the table. He swung suddenly on the uniformed therapist and said, "How does it operate?"

"Simply enough, it's nonselective," the therapist said. "On and off, and a potentiometer for intensity. We used to try to match the output to the patient's resting delta rhythms, but we found that wasn't critical. The brain seems to do its own monitoring, with some help from outside suggestion. For that, of course, you have to know the patient pretty well; you can't just put him on the table and expect the machine to process him like a computer tape."

"And we shouldn't be talking so much in his presence, for that very reason," Adams said, a faint trace of annoyance in his voice for the first time. "Better if further explanations waited until we're back in the office."

"I'd better ask my questions while they're fresh," Kirk said.

"The Captain," Helen said to Adams, "is an impulsive man."

Adams smiled. "He reminds me a little of the ancient skeptic who demanded to be taught all the world's wisdom while he stood on one foot."

"I simply want to be sure," Kirk said stonily, "that this is in fact where Dr. van Gelder's injury occurred."

"Yes," Adams said, "and it was his own fault, if you must know. I dislike maligning a colleague, but the fact is that Simon is a stubborn man. He could have sat in here for a year with the beam adjusted to this intensity, or even higher. Or if there simply had been someone standing at the panel to cut the power when trouble began. But he tried it alone, at full amplitude. Naturally, it hurt him. Even water can poison a man, in sufficient volume."

"Careless of him," Kirk said, still without expression. "All right, Dr. Adams, let's see the rest."

"Very well. I'd like to have you meet some of our successes, too."

"Lead on."

In the quarters which Adams' staff had assigned him for the night, Kirk called the *Enterprise,* but there was still nothing essentially new. McCoy was still trying to get past the scars in van Gelder's memory, but nothing he had uncovered yet seemed contributory. Van Gelder was exhausted; toward the end, he would say nothing but, "He empties us . . . and then fills us with himself. I ran away before he could fill me. It is so lonely to be empty . . ."

Meaningless; yet somehow it added up to something in Kirk's mind. After a while, he went quietly out into the corridor and padded next door to Helen Noel's room.

"Well!" she said, at the door. "What's this, Captain? Do you think it's Christmas again?"

"Ship's business," Kirk said. "Let me in before somebody spots me. Orders."

She moved aside, hesitantly, and he shut the door behind himself.

"Thanks. Now then, Doctor: What did you think of the inmates we saw this afternoon?"

"Why . . . I was impressed, on the whole. They seemed happy, or at least well-adjusted, making progress—"

"And a bit blank?"

"They weren't normal. I didn't expect them to be."

"All right. I'd like to look at that treatment room again. I'll need you; you must have comprehended far more of the theory than I did."

"Why not ask Dr. Adams?" she said stiffly. "He's the only expert on the subject here."

"And if he's lying about anything, he'll continue to lie and I'll learn nothing. The only way I can be sure is to see the machine work. I'll need an operator; you're the only choice."

"Well . . . all right."

They found the treatment room without difficulty. There was nobody about. Quickly Kirk pointed out the controls the therapist had identified for him, then took up the position that had been occupied by the patient then. He looked ruefully up at the device on the ceiling.

"I'm expecting you to be able to tell if that thing is doing me any harm," he said. "Adams says it's safe; that's what I want to know. Try minimum output; only a second or two."

Nothing happened.

"Well? Any time you're ready."

"I've already given you two seconds."

"Hmm. Nothing happened at all."

"Yes, something did. You were frowning; then your face went blank. When I cut the power, the frown came back."

"I didn't notice a thing. Try it again."

"How do you feel now?"

"Somewhat . . . uh, nothing definite. Just waiting. I thought we were going to try again."

"We did," Helen said. "It looks as though your mind goes so completely blank that you don't even feel the passage of time."

"Well, well," Kirk said drily. "Remarkably effective for a device Adams said he was thinking of abandoning. The technician mentioned that suggestion was involved. Try one—something harmless, please. You know, when we finally get through this, I hope we can raid a kitchen somewhere."

"It works," Helen said in a strained voice. "I gave you two seconds at low intensity and said, 'You're hungry.' And now you are."

"I didn't hear a thing. Let's give it one more try. I don't want to leave any doubt about it."

"Quite right," Adams' voice said. Kirk sat bolt upright, to find himself staring squarely into the business end of a phaser pistol. The therapist was there too, another gun held unwaveringly on Helen.

"Prisons and mental hospitals," Adams went on, smiling, almost tolerantly, "monitor every conversation, every sound—or else they don't last long. So I'm able to satisfy your curiosity, Captain. We'll give you a proper demonstration."

He stepped to the control panel and turned the potentiometer knob. Kirk never saw him hit the on-off button. The room simply vanished in a wave of intolerable pain.

As before, there was no time lapse at all; he only found himself on his feet, handing his phaser to Adams. At the same time, he knew what the pain was: it was love for Helen, and the pain of loneliness, of being without her. She was gone; all he had was the memory of having carried her to her cabin that Christmas, of her protests, of his lies that had turned into truth. Curiously, the memories seemed somewhat colorless, one-dimensional, the voices in them, monotonous; but the longing and the loneliness were real. To assuage it, he would lie, cheat, steal, give up his ship, his reputation . . . He cried out.

"She's not here," Adams said, passing Kirk's phaser to the therapist. "I'll send her back in a while and then things will be better. But first, it's time to call your vessel. It's important that they know all is well. Then perhaps we can see Dr. Noel."

Through a renewed stab of pain, Kirk got out his communicator and snapped it open. "Captain . . . to *Enterprise*," he said. He found it very difficult to speak; the message did not seem to be important.

"*Enterprise* here, Captain," Spock's voice said.

"All is well, Mr. Spock. I'm still with Dr. Adams."

"You sound tired, Captain. No problems?"

"None at all, Mr. Spock. My next call will be in six hours. Kirk out."

He started to pocket the communicator, but Adams held out his hand.

"And that, too, Captain."

Kirk hesitated. Adams reached for the control panel. The pain came back, redoubled, tripled, quadrupled; and now, at last, there came a real and blessed unconsciousness.

He awoke to the murmur of a feminine voice, and the feeling of a damp cloth being smoothed across his forehead. He opened his eyes. He was on his bed in the quarters on Tantalus; he felt as though he had been thrown there. A hand obscured his vision and he felt the cloth again. Helen's voice said:

"Captain . . . Captain. They've taken you out of the treatment room. You're in your own quarters now. Wake up, please, please!"

"Helen," he said. Automatically, he reached for her, but he was very weak; she pushed him back without effort.

"Try to remember. He put all that in your mind. Adams took the controls away from me—do you remember the pain? And then his voice, telling you you love me—"

He lifted himself on one elbow. The pain was there all right, and the desire. He fought them both, sweating.

"Yes . . . I think so," he said. Another wave of pain. "His machine's not perfect. I remember . . . some of it."

"Good. Let me wet this rag again."

As she moved away, Kirk forced himself to his feet, stood dizzily for a moment, and then lurched forward to try the door. Locked, of course. In here, he and Helen were supposed to consolidate the impressed love, make it real . . . and forget the *Enterprise*. Not bloody likely! Looking around, he spotted an air-conditioning grille.

Helen came back, and he beckoned to her, holding his finger to his lips. She followed him curiously. He tested the grille; it gave slightly. Throwing all his back muscles into it, he bent it outward. At the second try, it came free in his hand with a slight shearing sound. He knelt and poked his head into the opening.

The tunnel beyond was not only a duct; it was a crawl-space, intended also for servicing power lines. It could be crawled through easily, at least, as far as he could see down it. He tried it, but his shoulders were too bulky.

He stood up and held out his arms to the girl. She shrank back, but he jerked his head urgently, hoping that there was nothing in his expression which suggested passion. After a moment's more hesitation, she stepped against him.

"He may be watching as well as listening," Kirk whispered. "I'm just hoping he's focused on the bed, in that case. But that tunnel has to connect with a whole complex of others. It probably leads eventually to their power supply. If you can get through it, you can black out the whole place—and cut off their sensors, so Spock could beam us down some help without being caught at it. Game to try?"

"Of course."

"Don't touch any of those power lines. It'll be a bad squeeze."

"Better than Adams' treatment room."

"Good girl."

He looked down at her. The pain was powerful, reinforced by memory and danger, and her eyes were half-closed, her mouth willing. Somehow, all the same, he managed to break away. Dropping to her knees, she squirmed inside the tunnel and vanished, and Kirk began to replace the grille.

It was bent too badly to snap it back into place; he could only force it into reasonable shape and hope that nobody would notice that it wasn't fastened. He was on his feet and pocketing the sheared rivet heads when he heard the tumblers of the door lock clicking. He swung around just in time to see the therapist enter, holding an old-style phaser pistol. The man looked around incuriously.

"Where's the girl?" he said.

"Another of you zombies took her away. If you've hurt her, I'll kill you. Time for another 'treatment'?" He took a step closer, crouching. The pistol snapped up.

"Stand back! Cross in front of me and turn right in the corridor. I won't hesitate to shoot."

"That would be tough to explain to your boss. Oh, all right, I'm going."

Adams was waiting; he gestured curtly toward the table.

"What's the idea?" Kirk said. "I'm co-operating, aren't I?"

"If you were, you wouldn't have asked," Adams said. "However, I've no intention of explaining myself to you, Captain. Lie down. Good. Now."

The potentiator beam stabbed down at Kirk's head. He fought it, feeling the emptiness increase. This time, at least, he was aware of time passing, though he seemed to be accomplishing nothing else. His very will was draining away, as though somebody had opened a petcock on his skull.

"You believe in me completely," Adams said. "You believe in me. You trust me. The thought of distrusting me is intensely painful. You believe."

"I believe," Kirk said. To do anything else was agony. "I believe in you. I trust you, I trust you! Stop, stop!"

Adams shut off the controls. The pain diminished slightly, but it was far from gone.

"I give you credit," Adams said thoughtfully. "Van Gelder was sobbing on his knees by now, and he had a strong will. I'm glad I've had a pair like you; I've learned a great deal."

"But . . . what . . . purpose? Your reputation . . . your . . . work . . ."

"So you can still ask questions? Remarkable. Never mind. I'm tired of doing things for others, that's all. I want a very comfortable old age, on my terms—and I am a most selective man. And you'll help me."

"Of course . . . but so unnecessary . . . just trust . . ."

"Trust you? Naturally. Or, trust mankind to reward me? All they've given me thus far is Tantalus. It's not enough. I know how their minds work. Nobody better."

There was the sound of the door, and then Kirk could see the woman therapist, Lethe. She said:

"Dr. Noel's gone. Nobody took her out. She just vanished."

Adams swung back to the panel and hit the switch. The beam came on, at full amplitude. Kirk's brainpan seemed to empty as if it had been dumped down a drain.

"Where is she?"

"I . . . don't know . . ."

The pain increased. "Where is she? Answer!"

There was no possibility of answering. He simply did not know, and the pain blocked any other answer but the specific one being demanded. As if realizing this, Adams backed the beam down a little.

"Where did you send her? With what instructions? *Answer!*"

The pain soared, almost to ecstasy—and at the same instant, all the lights went out but a dim safe light in the ceiling. Kirk did not have to stop to think what might have happened. Enraged by agony, he acted on reflex and training. A moment later, the therapist was sprawled on the floor and he had Lethe and Adams covered with the old-style phaser.

"No time for you now," he said. Setting the phaser to "stun," he pulled the trigger. Then he was out in the corridor, a solid mass of desire, loneliness, and fright. He had to get to Helen; there was nothing else in his mind at all, except a white line of pain at having betrayed someone he had been told to trust.

Dull-eyed, frightened patients milled about him as he pushed toward the center of the complex, searching for the power room. He shoved them out of the way. The search was like an endless nightmare. Then, somehow, he was with Helen, and they were kissing.

It did not seem to help. He pulled her closer. She yielded, but without any real enthusiasm. A moment later, there was a familiar hum behind

him: the sound of a transporter materialization. Then Spock's voice
said:

"Captain Kirk—what on—"

Helen broke free. "It's not his fault. Quick, Jim, where's Adams?"

"Above," Kirk said dully. "In the treatment room. Helen—"

"Later, Jim. We've got to hurry."

They found Adams sprawled across the table. The machine was still
on. Lethe stood impassively beside the controls; as they entered, backed
by a full force of security guards from the ship, she snapped them off.

McCoy appeared from somewhere and bent over Adams. Then he
straightened.

"Dead."

"I don't understand," Helen said. "The machine wasn't on high
enough to kill. I don't think it could kill."

"He was alone," Lethe said stonily. "That was enough. I did not
speak to him."

Kirk felt his ringing skull. "I think I see."

"I can't say that I do, Jim," McCoy said. "A man has to die of something."

"He died of loneliness," Lethe said. "It's quite enough. I know."

"What do we do now, Captain?" Spock said.

"I don't know . . . let me see . . . get van Gelder down here and
repair him, I guess. He'll have to take charge. And then . . . he'll have
to decondition me. Helen, I don't want that, I want nothing less in the
world; but—"

"I don't want it either," she said softly. "So we'll both have to go
through it. It was nice while it lasted, Jim—awful, but nice."

"It's still hard to believe," McCoy said, much later, "that a man
could die of loneliness."

"No," Kirk said. He was quite all right now; quite all right. Helen
was nothing to him but another female doctor. But—

"No," he said, "it's not hard to believe at all."

THE UNREAL MC COY*
(George Clayton Johnson)

The crater campsite—or the Bierce campsite, as the records called it—on Regulus VIII was the crumbling remains of what might once have been a nested temple, surrounded now by archeological digs, several sheds, and a tumble of tools, tarpaulins, and battered artifacts. Outside the crater proper, the planet was largely barren except for patches of low, thorny vegetation, all the way in any direction to wherever the next crater might be—there were plenty of those, but there'd been no time to investigate them, beyond noting that they had all been inhabited once, unknown millennia ago. There was nothing uncommon about that; the galaxy was strewn with ruins about which nobody knew anything, there were a hundred such planets for every archeologist who could even dream of scratching such a surface. Bierce had just been lucky—fantastically lucky.

All the same, Regulus VIII made Kirk—Capt. James Kirk of the starship *Enterprise,* who had seen more planets than most men knew existed—feel faintly edgy. The *Enterprise* had landed here in conformity to the book; to be specific, to that part of the book which said that research personnel on alien planets must have their health certified by a starship's surgeon at one-year intervals. The *Enterprise* had been in Bierce's vicinity at the statutory time, and Ship's Surgeon McCoy had come down by transporter from the orbiting *Enterprise* to do the job. Utterly, completely routine, except for the fact that McCoy had mentioned that Bierce's wife Nancy had been a serious interest of McCoy's, pre-Bierce, well over ten years ago. And after all, what could be more commonplace than that?

* Originally "The Man Trap"

Then Nancy came out of the temple—if that is what it was—to meet them.

There were only three of them: McCoy and a crewman, Darnell, out of duty, and Kirk, out of curiosity. She came forward with outstretched hands, and after a moment's hesitation, McCoy took them. "Leonard!" she said. "Let me look at you."

"Nancy," McCoy said. "You . . . you haven't aged a year."

Kirk restrained himself from smiling. Nancy Bierce was handsome, but nothing extraordinary: a strongly built woman of about forty, moderately graceful, her hair tinged with gray. It wasn't easy to believe that the hard-bitten medico could have been so smitten, even at thirty or less, as to be unable to see the signs of aging now. Still, she did have a sweet smile.

"This is the Captain of the *Enterprise,* Jim Kirk," McCoy said. "And this is Crewman Darnell."

Nancy turned her smile on the Captain, and then on the crewman. Darnell's reaction was astonishing. His jaw swung open; he was frankly staring. Kirk would have kicked him had he been within reach.

"Come in, come in," she was saying. "We may have to wait a little for Bob; once he starts digging, he forgets time. We've made up some quarters in what seems to have been an old altar chamber—not luxurious, but lots of room. Come on in, Plum."

She ducked inside the low, crumbling stone door.

"Plum?" Kirk said.

"An old pet name," McCoy said, embarrassed. He followed her. Embarrassed himself at his own gaucherie, Kirk swung on the crewman.

"Just what are you goggling at, Mister?"

"Sorry, sir," Darnell said stiffly. "She reminds me of somebody, is all. A girl I knew once on Wrigley's Planet. That is—"

"That's enough," Kirk said drily. "The next thought of that kind you have will probably be in solitary. Maybe you'd better wait outside."

"Yessir. Thanks." Darnell seemed genuinely grateful. "I'll explore a little, if that suits you, Captain."

"Do that. Just stay within call."

Commonplace; Darnell hadn't seen a strange woman since his last landfall. But most peculiar, too.

Bierce did not arrive, and after apologies, Nancy left again to look for him, leaving Kirk and McCoy to examine the stone room, trying not to speak to each other. Kirk could not decide whether he would rather be back on board the *Enterprise,* or just plain dead; his diplomacy had not failed him this badly in he could not think how many years.

Luckily, Bierce showed up before Kirk had to decide whether to run or suicide. He was an unusually tall man, all knuckles, knees, and cheekbones, wearing faded coveralls. Slightly taller than McCoy, his face was as craggy as his body; the glint in the eyes, Kirk thought, was somehow both intelligent and rather bitter. But then, Kirk had never pretended to understand the academic type.

"Dr. Bierce," he said, "I'm Captain Kirk, and this is Ship's Surgeon—"

"I know who you are," Bierce broke in, in a voice with the blaring rasp of a busy signal. "We don't need you here. If you'll just refill us on aspirin, salt tablets, and the like, you needn't trouble yourselves further."

"Sorry, but the law requires an annual checkup," Kirk said. "If you'll co-operate, I'm sure Dr. McCoy will be as quick as possible." McCoy, in fact, already had his instruments out.

"McCoy?" Bierce said. "I've heard that name . . . Ah, yes, Nancy used to talk about you."

"Hands out from your sides, please, and breathe evenly . . . Yes, didn't she mention I'd arrived?"

After the slightest of pauses, Bierce said, "You've . . . seen Nancy?"

"She was here when we arrived," Kirk said. "She went to look for you."

"Oh. Quite so. I'm pleased, of course, that she can meet an old friend, have a chance of some company. I enjoy solitude, but it's difficult for a woman sometimes."

"I understand," Kirk said, but he was none too sure he did. The sudden attempt at cordiality rang false, somehow, after the preceding hostility. At least *that* had sounded genuine.

McCoy had finished his checkup with the tricorder and produced a tongue depressor with a small flourish. "She hasn't changed a bit," he said. "Open your mouth, please."

Reluctantly, Bierce complied. At the same instant, the air was split by a full-throated shriek of horror. For an insane moment Kirk had the impression that the sound had issued from Bierce's mouth. Then another scream ripped the silence, and Kirk realized that it was, of course, a female voice.

They all three bolted out the door. In the open, Kirk and McCoy outdistanced Bierce quickly; for all his outdoor life, he was not a good runner. But they hadn't far to go. Just beyond the rim of the crater,

Nancy, both fists to her mouth, was standing over the body of Darnell. As they came pounding up she moved toward McCoy, but he ignored her and dropped beside the body. It was lying on its face. After checking the pulse, McCoy gently turned the head to one side, grunted, and then turned the body over completely.

It was clear even to Kirk that the crewman was dead. His face was covered with small ringlike red blotches, slowly fading. "What hit him?" Kirk said tensely.

"Don't know. Petachiae a little like vacuum mottling, or maybe some sort of immunological—hullo, what's this?"

Bierce came panting up as McCoy slowly forced open one of Darnell's fists. In it was a twisted, scabrous-looking object of no particular color, like a mummified parsnip. It looked also as though part of it had been bitten away. Now *that* was incredible. Kirk swung on Nancy.

"What happened?" he said tersely.

"Don't snap at my wife, Captain," Bierce said in his busy-signal voice. "Plainly it's not her fault!"

"One of my men is dead. I accuse nobody, but Mrs. Bierce is the only witness."

McCoy rose and said to Nancy, gently: "Just tell us what you saw, Nancy. Take your time."

"I was just . . ." she said, and then had to stop and swallow, as if fighting for control. "I couldn't find Bob, and I'd . . . I'd just started back when I saw your crewman. He had that borgia root in his hand and he was smelling it. I was just going to call out to him when—he bit into it. I had no idea he was going to—and then his face twisted and he fell—"

She broke off and buried her face in her hands. McCoy took her gently by one shoulder. Kirk, feeling no obligation to add one bedside manner more, said evenly: "How'd you know what the root was if you'd just come within calling distance?"

"This cross-examination—" Bierce grated.

"Bob, please. I didn't know, of course. Not until I saw it now. But it's dangerous to handle any plant on a new world."

Certainly true. Equally certainly, it would have been no news to Darnell. His face impassive, Kirk told McCoy: "Pack up, Bones. We can resume the physicals tomorrow."

"I'm sure that won't be necessary," Bierce said. "If you'll just disembark our supplies, Captain—"

"It's not going to be that easy, Dr. Bierce," Kirk said. He snapped open his communicator. "Kirk to Transporter Room. Lock and beam: two transportees and a corpse."

The autopsied body of Darnell lay on a table in the sick bay, unrecognizable now even by his mother, if so veteran a spaceman had ever had one. Kirk, standing near a communicator panel, watched with a faint physical uneasiness as McCoy lowered Darnell's brain into a shallow bowl and then turned and washed his hands until they were paper-white. Kirk had seen corpses in every conceivable state of distortion and age in one battle and another, but this clinical bloodiness was not within his experience.

"I can't rule poison out entirely," McCoy said, in a matter-of-fact voice. "Some of the best-known act just as fast and leave just as little trace: botulinus, for example. But there's no trace of any woody substance in his stomach or even between his teeth. All I can say for sure is that he's got massive capillary damage—which could be due to almost anything, even shock—and those marks on his face."

McCoy covered the ruined body. "I'll be running some blood chemistry tests, but I'd like to know what I'm testing for. I'd also like to know what symptoms that 'borgia root' is *supposed* to produce. Until then, Jim, I'm really rather in the dark."

"Spock's running a library search on the plant," Kirk said. "It shouldn't take him long. But I must confess that what you've said thus far doesn't completely surprise me. Darnell was too old a hand to bite into any old thing he happened to pick up."

"Then what's left? Nancy? Jim, I'm not quite trusting my own eyes lately, but Nancy didn't use to be capable of murder—certainly not of an utter stranger, to boot!"

"It's not only people who kill—hold it, here's the report. Go ahead, Mr. Spock."

"We have nothing on the borgia root but what the Bierces themselves reported in their project request six years ago," Spock's precise voice said. "There they call it an aconite resembling the *Lilium* family. Said to contain some twenty to fifty different alkaloids, none then identifiable specifically with the equipment to hand. The raw root is poisonous to mice. No mention of any human symptoms. Except . . ."

"Except what?" McCoy snapped.

"Well, Dr. McCoy, this isn't a symptom. The report adds that the root has a pleasant perfume, bland but edible-smelling, rather like tapioca. And that's all there is."

"Thanks." Kirk switched off. "Bones, I can't see Darnell having been driven irresistibly to bite into an unknown plant because it smelled like tapioca. He wouldn't have bitten into something that smelled like a brandied peach unless he'd known its pedigree. He was a seasoned hand."

McCoy spread his hands expressively. "You knew your man, Jim—but where does that leave us? The symptoms do vaguely resemble aconite poisoning. Beyond that, we're nowhere."

"Not quite," Kirk said. "We still have to check on the Bierces, I'm afraid, Bones. And for that I'm still going to need your help."

McCoy turned his back and resumed washing his hands. "You'll get it," he said; but his voice was very cold.

Kirk's method of checking on the Bierces was simple but drastic: he ordered them both on board the ship. Bierce raged.

"If you think you can beam down here, bully us, interfere with my work—considering the inescapable fact that you are a trespasser on my planet—"

"Your complaint is noted," Kirk said. "I apologize for the inconvenience. But it's also an inescapable fact that something we don't understand killed one of our men. It could very well be a danger to you, too."

"We've been here almost five years. If there was something hostile here we'd know about it by now, wouldn't we?"

"Not necessarily," Kirk said. "Two people can't know all the ins and outs of a whole planet, not even in five years—or a lifetime. In any event, one of the missions of the *Enterprise* is to protect human life in places like this. Under the circumstances, I'm going to have to be arbitrary and declare the argument closed."

It was shortly after they came aboard that McCoy forwarded his reports on the analyses of Darnell's body. "It was shock, all right," he told Kirk grimly by vidscreen. "But shock of a most peculiar sort. His blood electrolytes were completely deranged: massive salt depletion, hell—there isn't a microgram of salt in his whole body. Not in the blood, the tears, the organs, not anywhere. I can't even begin to guess how that could have happened at all, let alone all at once."

"What about the mottling on his face?"

"Broken capillaries. There are such marks all over the body. They're normal under the circumstances—except that I can't explain why they should be most marked on the face, or why the mottling should be ring-shaped. Clearly, though, he wasn't poisoned."

"Then the bitten plant," Kirk said equally grimly, "was a plant—in the criminal, not the botanical sense. A blind. That implies intelligence. I can't say I like that any better."

"Nor I," McCoy said. His eyes were averted.

"All right. That means we'll have to waste no time grilling the Bierces. I'll take it on. Bones, this has been a tremendous strain on you, I know, and you've been without sleep for two days. Better take a couple of tranquilizers and doss down."

"I'm all right."

"Orders," Kirk said. He turned off the screen and set off for the quarters he had assigned the Bierces.

But there was only one Bierce there. Nancy was missing.

"I expect she's gone below," Bierce said indifferently. "I'd go myself if I could get access to your Transporter for ten seconds. We didn't ask to be imprisoned up here."

"Darnell didn't ask to be killed, either. Your wife may be in serious danger. I must say, you seem singularly unworried."

"She's in no danger. This menace is all in your imagination."

"I suppose the body is imaginary, too?"

Bierce shrugged. "Nobody knows what could have killed him. For all I know, you brought your own menace with you."

There was nothing further to be got out of him. Exasperated, Kirk went back to the bridge and ordered a general search. The results were all negative—including the report from the Transporter Room, which insisted that nobody had used its facilities since the party had returned to the ship from the camp.

But the search, though it did not find Nancy, found something else: Crewman Barnhart, dead on Deck Twelve. The marks on his body were the same as those on Darnell's.

Baffled and furious, Kirk called McCoy. "I'm sorry to bust in on your sleep, Bones, but this has gone far enough. I want Bierce checked out under pentathol."

"Um," McCoy said. His voice sounded fuzzy, as though he had still not quite recovered from his tranquilizer dose. "Pentathol. Truth dope. Narcosynthesis. Um. Takes time. What about the patient's civil rights?"

"He can file a complaint if he wants. Go and get him ready."

An hour later, Bierce was lying on his bunk in half-trance. Kirk bent over him tensely; McCoy and Spock hovered in the background.

"Where's your wife?"

"Don't know . . . Poor Nancy, I loved her . . . The last of its kind . . ."

"Explain, please."

"The passenger pigeon . . . the buffalo . . ." Bierce groaned. "I feel strange."

Kirk beckoned to McCoy, who checked Bierce's pulse and looked under his eyelids. "He's all right," he said. "The transfer of questioner, from me to you, upset him. He's recovering."

"What about buffalo?" Kirk said, feeling absurd.

"Millions of them . . . prairies black with them. One single herd that covered three states. When they moved . . . like thunder. All gone now. Like the creatures here."

"Here? You mean down on the planet?"

"On the planet. Their temples . . . great poetry . . . Millions of them once, and now only one left. Nancy understood."

"Always the past tense," Spock's voice murmured.

"Where is Nancy? Where is she *now?*"

"Dead. Buried up on the hill. It killed her."

"Buried! But—how long ago was this, anyhow?"

"A year . . ." Bierce said. "Or was it two? I don't know. So confusing, Nancy and not Nancy. They needed salt, you see. When it ran out, they died . . . all but one."

The implication stunned Kirk. It was Spock who put the question.

"Is this creature masquerading as your wife?"

"Not a masquerade," Bierce droned. "It can *be* Nancy."

"Or anybody else?"

"Anybody. When it killed Nancy, I almost destroyed it. But I couldn't. It was the last."

The repetition was becoming more irritating every minute. Kirk said stonily: "Is that the only reason, Bierce? Tell me this: When it's with you, is it always Nancy?"

Bierce writhed. There was no answer. McCoy came forward again.

"I wouldn't press that one if I were you, Jim," he said. "You can get the answer if you need it, but not without endangering the patient."

"I don't need any better answer," Kirk said. "So we've intruded here into a little private heaven. The thing can be wife, lover, best friend, idol, slave, wise man, fool—anybody. A great life, having everyone in the universe at your beck and call—and you win all the arguments."

"A one-way road to paranoia," Spock said. Kirk swung back to the drugged man.

"Then can you recognize the creature—no matter what form it takes?"

"Yes . . ."

"Will you help us?"

"No."

Kirk had expected no more. He gestured to McCoy. "I've got to go organize a search. Break down that resistance, Bones, I don't care how you do it or how much you endanger Bierce. In his present state of mind he's as big a danger to us as his 'wife.' Spock, back him up, and be ready to shoot if he should turn violent."

He stalked out. On the bridge, he called a General Quarters Three; that would put pairs of armed men in every corridor, on every deck. "Every man inspect his mate closely," he told the intercom. "There's one extra person aboard, masquerading as one of us. Lieutenant Uhura, make television rounds of all posts and stations. If you see any person twice in different places, sound the alarm. Got it?"

A sound behind him made him swing around. It was Spock. His clothes were torn, and he was breathing heavily.

"Spock! I thought I told you—what happened?"

"It was McCoy," Spock said shakily. "Or rather, it wasn't McCoy. You were barely out of the cabin when it grabbed me. I got away, but it's got my sidearm. No telling where it's off to now."

"McCoy! I *thought* he seemed a little reluctant about the pentathol. Reluctant, and sort of searching his memory, too. No wonder. Well, there's only one place it can have gone to now: right back where it came from."

"The planet? It can't."

"No. McCoy's cabin." He started to get up, but Spock lifted a hand sharply.

"Better look first, Captain. It may not have killed him yet, and if we alarm it—"

"You're right." Quickly, Kirk dialed in the intercom to McCoy's cabin, and after only a slight hesitation, punched the override button which would give him vision without sounding the buzzer on the other end.

McCoy was there. He was there twice: a sleeping McCoy on the bunk, and another one standing just inside the closed doorway, looking across the room. The standing form moved, passing in front of the hidden camera and momentarily blocking the view. Then it came back into the frame—but no longer as McCoy. It was Nancy.

She sat down on the bed and shook the sleeping doctor. He muttered, but refused to wake.

"Leonard," Nancy's voice said. "It's me. Nancy. Wake up. Please wake up. Help me."

Kirk had to admire the performance. What he was seeing was no doubt an alien creature, but its terror was completely convincing. Quite possibly it *was* in terror; in any event, the human form conveyed it as directly as a blow.

She shook McCoy again. He blinked his eyes groggily, and then sat up.

"Nancy! What's this? How long have I been sleeping?"

"Help me, Leonard."

"What's wrong? You're frightened."

"I am, I am," she said. "Please help me. They want to kill me!"

"Who?" McCoy said. "Easy. Nobody's going to hurt you."

"That's enough," Kirk said, unconsciously lowering his voice, though the couple on the screen could not hear him. "Luckily, the thing's trying to persuade him of something instead of killing him. Let's get down there fast, before it changes its mind."

Moments later, they burst into McCoy's cabin. The surgeon and the girl swung toward them. "Nancy" cried out.

"Get away from her, Bones," Kirk said, holding his gun rock steady.

"What? What's going on here, Jim?"

"That isn't Nancy, Bones."

"It isn't? Of course it is. Are you off your rocker?"

"It killed two crewmen."

"Bierce, too," Spock put in, his own gun leveled.

"*It?*"

"It," Kirk said. "Let me show you."

Kirk held out his free hand, unclenching it slowly. In the palm was a little heap of white crystals, diminishing at the edges from perspiration. "Look, Nancy," he said. "Salt. Free for the taking. Pure, concentrated salt."

Nancy took a hesitant step toward him, then stopped.

"Leonard," she said in a low voice. "Send him away. If you love me, make him go away."

"By all means," McCoy said harshly. "This is crazy behavior, Jim. You're frightening her."

"Not fright," Kirk said. "Hunger. Look at her!"

The creature, as if hypnotized, took another step forward. Then, without the slightest warning, there was a hurricane of motion. Kirk had a brief impression of a blocky body, man-sized but not the least like a man, and of suction-cup tentacles reaching for his face. Then there was a blast of sound and he fell.

It took awhile for both Kirk and McCoy to recover—the captain from the nimbus of Spock's close-range phaser bolt, McCoy from emotional shock. By the time they were all back on the bridge, Bierce's planet was receding.

"The salt was an inspiration," Spock said. "Evidently the creature only hunted when it couldn't get the pure stuff; that's how Bierce kept it in control."

"I don't think the salt supply was the only reason why the race died out, though," Kirk said. "It wasn't really very intelligent—didn't use its advantages nearly as well as it might have."

"They could well have been residual," Spock suggested. "We still have teeth and nails, but we don't bite and claw much these days."

"That could well be. There's one thing I don't understand, though. How did it get into your cabin in the first place, Bones? Or don't you want to talk about it?"

"I don't mind," McCoy said. "Though I do feel like six kinds of a fool. It was simple. She came in just after I'd taken the tranquilizer and was feeling a little afloat. She said she didn't love her husband any more —wanted me to take her back to Earth. Well . . . it was a real thing I had with Nancy, long ago. I wasn't hard to tempt, especially with the drug already in my system. And later on, while I was asleep, she must have given me another dose—otherwise I couldn't have slept through all the excitement, the general quarters call and so on. It just goes to prove all over again—never mess with civilians."

"A good principle," Kirk agreed. "Unfortunately, an impossible one to live by."

"There's something *I* don't understand, though," McCoy added. "The creature and Bierce had Spock all alone in Bierce's cabin—and from what I've found during the dissection, it was twice as strong as a man anyhow. How did you get out, Mr. Spock, without losing anything but your gun?"

Spock smiled. "Fortunately, my ancestors spawned in quite another ocean than yours, Dr. McCoy," he said. "My blood salts are quite different from yours. Evidently, I wasn't appetizing enough."

"Of course," McCoy said. He looked over at Kirk. "You still look a little pensive, Jim. Is there still something else wrong?"

"Mmm?" Kirk said. "Wrong? No, not exactly. I was just thinking about the buffalo."

BALANCE OF TERROR
(Paul Schneider)

When the Romulan outbreak began, Capt. James Kirk was in the chapel of the starship *Enterprise,* waiting to perform a wedding.

He could, of course, have declined to do any such thing. Not only was he the only man aboard the starship empowered to perform such a ceremony—and many others even less likely to occur to a civilian—but both the participants were part of the ship's complement: Specialist (phaser) Robert Tomlinson and Spec. 2nd Cl. (phaser) Angela Martine.

Nevertheless, the thought of refusing hadn't occurred to him. Traveling between the stars, even at "relativistic" or near-light speeds, was a long-drawn-out process at best. One couldn't forbid or even ignore normal human relationships over such prolonged hauls, unless one was either a martinet or a fool, and Kirk did not propose to be either.

And in a way, nothing could be more symbolic of his function, and that of the *Enterprise* as a whole, than a marriage. Again because of the vast distances and time lapses involved, the starships were effectively the only fruitful links between the civilized planets. Even interstellar radio, which was necessarily faster, was subject to a dozen different kinds of interruptions, could carry no goods, and in terms of human contact was in every way less satisfactory. On the other hand, the starships were as fructifying as worker bees; they carried supplies, medical help, technical knowledge, news of home, and—above all—the sight and touch of other people.

It was for the same complex of reasons that there was a chapel aboard the *Enterprise.* Designed by some groundlubber in the hope of giving offense to nobody (or, as the official publicity had put it, "to ac-

commodate all faiths of all planets," a task impossible on the face of it),
the chapel was simplified and devoid of symbols to the point of in-
sipidity; but its very existence acknowledged that even the tightly designed *Enterprise* was a world in itself, and as such had to recognize
that human beings often have religious impulses.

The groom was already there when Kirk entered, as were about half a
dozen crew members, speaking *sotto voce*. Nearby, Chief Engineer Scott
was adjusting a small television camera; the ceremony was to be carried
throughout the intramural network, and outside the ship, too, to the observer satellites in the Romulus-Remus neutral zone. Scotty could more
easily have assigned the chore to one of his staff, but doing it himself
was his acknowledgment of the solemnity of the occasion—his gift to the
bride, as it were. Kirk grinned briefly. Ship's air was a solid mass of
symbols today.

"Everything under control, Scotty?"

"Can't speak for the groom, sir, but all's well otherwise."

"Very good."

The smile faded a little, however, as Kirk moved on toward the
blankly nondenominational altar. It bothered him a little—not exactly
consciously, but somewhere at the back of his conscience—to be conducting an exercise like this so close to the neutral zone. The Romulans
had once been the most formidable of enemies. But then, not even a
peep had been heard from them since the neutral zone had been closed
around their system, fifty-odd years ago. Even were they cooking something venomous under there, why should they pick today to try it—and
with a heavily armed starship practically in their back yards?

Scotty, finishing up with the camera, smoothed down his hair self-
consciously; he was to give the bride away. There was a murmur of
music from the intercom—Kirk could only suppose it was something
traditional, since he himself was tune-deaf—and Angela came in, flanked
by her bridesmaid, Yeoman Janice Rand. Scott offered her his arm.
Tomlinson and his best man were already in position. Kirk cleared his
throat experimentally.

And at that moment, the ship's alarm went off.

Angela went white. Since she was new aboard, she might never have
heard the jarring blare before, but she obviously knew what it was.
Then it was replaced by the voice of Communications Officer Uhura:

"Captain Kirk to the bridge! Captain Kirk to the bridge!"

But the erstwhile pastor was already out the door at a dead run.

Spock, the First Officer, was standing beside Lieutenant Uhura's station as Kirk and his engineer burst onto the bridge. Spock, the product of marriage between an earth woman and a father on Vulcan—not the imaginary Solar world of that name, but a planet of 40 Eridani—did not come equipped with Earth-human emotions, and Lieutenant Uhura had the impassivity of most Bantu women; but the air was charged with tension nonetheless. Kirk said: "What's up?"

"It's Commander Hansen, outpost satellite four zero two three," Spock said precisely. "They've picked up clear pips of an intruder in the neutral zone."

"Identification?"

"None yet, but the engine pattern is modern. Not a Romulan vessel, apparently."

"Excuse me, Mr. Spock," a voice said from the comm board. "I'm overhearing you. We have a sighting now. The vessel is modern—but the markings are Romulan."

Kirk shouldered forward and took the microphone from Lieutenant Uhura's hand. "This is Captain Kirk. Have you challenged it, Hansen?"

"Affirmative. No acknowledgment. Can you give us support, Captain? You are the only starship in this sector."

"Affirmative."

"We're clocking their approach visually at . . ." Hansen's voice died for a moment. Then: "Sorry, just lost them. Disappeared from our monitors."

"Better transmit your monitor picture. Lieutenant Uhura, put it on our bridge viewscreen."

For a moment, the screen showed nothing but a scan of stars, fading into faint nebulosity in the background. Then, suddenly, the strange ship was there. Superficially, it looked much like an *Enterprise*-class starship; a domed disc, seemingly coming at the screen nearly edge-on—though of course it was actually approaching the satellite, not the *Enterprise*. Its size, however, was impossible to guess without a distance estimate.

"Full magnification, Lieutenant Uhura."

The stranger seemed to rush closer. Scott pointed mutely, and Kirk nodded. At this magnification, the stripes along the underside were unmistakable: broad shadows suggesting a bird of prey with half-spread wings. Romulan, all right.

From S-4023, Hansen's voice said urgently: "Got it again! Captain Kirk, can you see—"

"We see it."

But even as he spoke, the screen suddenly turned white, then dimmed as Uhura backed it hastily down the intensity scale. Kirk blinked and leaned forward tensely.

The alien vessel had launched a torpedolike bolt of blinding light from its underbelly. Moving with curious deliberateness, as though it were traveling at the speed of light in some other space but was loafing sinfully in this one, the dazzling bolt swelled in S-4023's camera lens, as if it were bound to engulf the *Enterprise* as well.

"She's opened fire!" Hansen's voice shouted. "Our screen's failed—we're—"

The viewscreen of the *Enterprise* spat doomsday light throughout the control room. The speaker squawked desperately and went dead.

"Battle stations," Kirk told Uhura, very quietly. "General alarm. Mr. Spock, full ahead and intercept."

Nobody had ever seen a live Romulan. It was very certain that "Romulan" was not their name for themselves, for such fragmentary evidence as had been pieced together from wrecks, after they had erupted from the Romulus-Remus system so bloodily a good seventy-five years ago, suggested that they'd not even been native to the planet, let alone a race that could have shared Earthly conventions of nomenclature. A very few bloated bodies recovered from space during that war that proved to be humanoid, but of the hawklike Vulcanite type rather than the Earthly anthropoid. The experts had guessed that the Romulans might once have settled on their adopted planet as a splinter group from some mass migration, thrown off, rejected by their less militaristic fellows as they passed to some more peaceful settling, to some less demanding kind of new world. Neither Romulus nor Remus, twin planets whirling around a common center in a Trojan relationship to a white-dwarf sun, could have proved attractive to any race that did not love hardships for their own sakes.

But almost all this was guesswork, unsupported either by history or by interrogation. The Vulcanite races who were part of the Federation claimed to know nothing of the Romulans; and the Romulans themselves had never allowed any prisoners to be taken—suicide, apparently, was a part of their military tradition—nor had they ever taken any. All that was known for sure was that the Romulans had come boiling out of their crazy little planetary system on no apparent provocation, in primitive, clumsy cylindrical ships that should have been clay pigeons for the Federation's navy and yet in fact took twenty-five years to drive back to their home world—twenty-five years of increasingly merciless slaughter on both sides.

The neutral zone, with its sphere of observer satellites, had been set up around the Romulus-Remus system after that, and for years had been policed with the utmost vigilance. But for fifty years nothing had come out of it—not even a signal, let alone a ship. Perhaps the Romulans were still nursing their wounds and perfecting their grievances and their weapons—or perhaps they had learned their lesson and given up—or perhaps they were just tired, or decadent. . . .

Guesswork. One thing was certain now. Today, they had come out again—or one ship had.

The crew of the *Enterprise* moved to battle stations with a smooth efficiency that would hardly have suggested to an outsider that most of them had never heard a shot fired in anger. Even the thwarted bridal couple was at the forward phaser consoles, as tensely ready now to launch destruction as they had been for creation only a few hours before.

But there was nothing to fire at in the phaser sights yet. On the bridge, Kirk was in the captain's chair, Spock and Scott to either side of him. Sulu was piloting; Second Officer Stiles navigating. Lieutenant Uhura, as usual, was at the comm board.

"No response from satellites four zero two three, two four or two five," she said. "No trace to indicate any are still in orbit. Remaining outposts still in position. No sightings of intruding vessel. Sensor readings normal. Neutral zone, zero."

"Tell them to stay alert and report anything abnormal."

"Yes, sir."

"Entering four zero two three's position area," Sulu said.

"Lieutenant Uhura?"

"Nothing, sir. No, I'm getting a halo effect here now. Debris, I'd guess—metallic, finally divided, and still scattering. The radiant point's obviously where the satellite should be; I'm running a computer check now, but—"

"But there can't be much doubt about it," Kirk said heavily. "They pack a lot more punch than they did fifty years ago—which somehow doesn't surprise me much."

"What *was* that weapon, anyhow?" Stiles whispered.

"We'll check before we guess," Kirk said. "Mr. Spock, put out a tractor and bring me in some of that debris. I want a full analysis—spectra, stress tests, X-ray diffusion, micro-chemistry, the works. We know what the hull of that satellite used to be made of. I want to know what it's like *now*—and then I want some guesses from the lab on how it got that way. Follow me?"

"Of course, sir," the First Officer said. From any other man it would have been a brag, and perhaps a faintly insulting one at that. From Spock it was simply an utterly reliable statement of fact. He was already on the intercom to the lab section.

"Captain," Uhura said. Her voice sounded odd.

"What is it?"

"I'm getting something here. A mass in motion. Nothing more. Nothing on visual, no radar pip. And no radiation. Nothing but a De Broglie transform in the computer. It could be something very small and dense nearby, or something very large and diffuse far away, like a comet. But the traces don't match for either."

"Navigator?" Kirk said.

"There's a cold comet in the vicinity, part of the Romulus-Remus system," Stiles said promptly. "Bearing 973 galactic east, distance one point three light hours, course roughly convergent—"

"I'd picked that up long ago," Uhura said. "This is something else. Its relative speed to us is one-half light, in toward the neutral zone. It's an electromagnetic field of some kind . . . but no kind I ever saw before. I'm certain it's not natural."

"No, it isn't," Spock said, with complete calmness. He might have been announcing the weather, had there been any out here. "It's an invisibility screen."

Stiles snorted, but Kirk knew from long experience that his half-Vulcanite First Officer never made such flat statements without data to back them. Spock was very odd by Earth-human standards, but he had a mind like a rapier. "Explain," Kirk said.

"The course matches for the vessel that attacked the last satellite outpost to disappear," Spock said. "Not the one we're tracking now, but four zero two five. The whole orbit feeds in along Hohmann D toward an intercept with Romulus. The computer shows that already."

"Lieutenant Uhura?"

"Check," she said, a little reluctantly.

"Second: Commander Hansen lost sight of the enemy vessel when it was right in front of him. It didn't reappear until it was just about to launch its attack. Then it vanished again, and we haven't seen it since. Third: Theoretically, the thing is possible, for a vessel of the size of the *Enterprise,* if you put almost all the ship's power into it; hence, you must become visible if you need power for your phasers, or any other energy weapon."

"And fourth, baloney," Stiles said.

"Not quite, Mr. Stiles," Kirk said slowly. "This would also explain why just one Romulan vessel might venture through the neutral zone, right under the nose of the *Enterprise*. The Romulans may think they can take us on now, and they've sent out one probe to find out."

"A very long chain of inferences, sir," Stiles said, with marked politeness.

"I'm aware of that. But it's the best we've got at the moment. Mr. Sulu, match course and speed exactly with Lieutenant Uhura's blip, and stick with it move for move. But under no circumstances cross after it into the neutral zone without my direct order. Miss Uhura, check all frequencies for a carrier wave, an engine pattern, any sort of transmission besides this De Broglie wave-front—in particular, see if you can overhear any chit-chat between ship and home planet. Mr. Spock and Mr. Scott, I'll see you both directly in the briefing room; I want to review what we know about Romulus. Better call Dr. McCoy in on it, too. Any questions?"

There were none. Kirk said, "Mark and move."

The meeting in the briefing room was still going on when Spock was called out to the lab section. Once he was gone, the atmosphere promptly became more informal; neither Scott nor McCoy liked the Vulcanite, and even Kirk, much though he valued his First Officer, was not entirely comfortable in his presence.

"Do you want me to go away too, Jim?" McCoy said gently. "It seems to me you could use some time to think."

"I think better with you here, Bones. You too, Scotty. But this could be the big one. We've got people from half the planets of the Federation patrolling the neutral zone. If we cross it with a starship without due cause, we may have more than just the Romulans to worry about. That's how civil wars start, too."

"Isn't the loss of three satellites due cause?" Scott said.

"I'd say so, but precisely what knocked out those satellites? A Romulan ship, we say; but can we prove it? Well, no, we say; the thing's invisible. Even Stiles laughs at that, and he's on our side. The Romulans were far behind us in technology the last we saw of them—they only got as far as they did in the war out of the advantage of surprise, plus a lot of sheer savagery. Now, suddenly, they've got a ship as good as ours, *plus* an invisibility screen. I can hardly believe it myself.

"And on the other hand, gentlemen . . . On the other hand, while we sit here debating the matter, they may be about to knock us right out of the sky. It's the usual verge-of-war situation: we're damned if we do, and damned if we don't."

The elevator door slid open. Spock was back. "Sir—"

"All right, Mr. Spock. Shoot."

Spock was carrying a thick fascicle of papers bound to a clip board, held close to his body under one arm. His other hand swung free, but its fist was clenched. The bony Vulcanite face had no expression and could show none, but there was something in his very posture that telegraphed tension.

"Here are the analyses of the debris," he said in his inhumanly even voice. "I shan't bother you with the details unless you ask. The essence of the matter is that the Romulan weapon we saw used on S-4023 seems to be a molecular implosion field."

"Meaning what?" McCoy said roughly.

Spock raised his right fist over the plot board, still clenched. The knuckles and tendons worked for a moment. A fine metallic glitter sifted down onto the table.

"It fatigues metals," he said. "Instantly. The metal crystals lose cohesion, and collapse into dust—like this. After that, anything contained in the metal blows up of itself, because it isn't contained any more. I trust that's clear, Dr. McCoy. If not, I'll try to explain it again."

"Damn you, Spock—"

"Shut up, Bones," Kirk said tiredly. "Mr. Spock, sit down. Now then. We're in no position to fight among ourselves. Evidently we're even worse off than we thought we were. If the facts we have are to be trusted, the Romulans have, first, a practicable invisibility screen, and second, a weapon at the very least comparable to ours."

"Many times superior," Spock said stolidly. "At least in some situations."

"*Both* of these gadgets," McCoy said, "are Mr. Spock's inventions, very possibly. At least in both cases, it's his interpretation of the facts that's panicking us."

"There are no other interpretations available at the moment," Kirk said through thinned lips. "Any argument about that? All right. Then let's see what we can make of them for our side. Scotty, what have *we* got that we can counter with, given that the Romulan gadgets are real? We can't hit an invisible object, and we can't duck an invisible gunner. Where does that leave us?"

"Fully armed, fast and maneuverable," the engineer said. "Also, they aren't quite invisible; Lieutenant Uhura can pick up their De Broglie waves as they move. That means that they must be operating at nearly full power right now, just running away and staying invisible. We've got the edge on speed, and I'd guess that they don't know that our sensors are picking them up."

"Which means that we can outrun them and know—approximately—what they're doing. But we can't out-gun them or see them."

"That's how it looks at the moment," Scott said. "It's a fair balance of power, I'd say, Jim. Better than most commanders can count on in a battle situation."

"This isn't a battle situation yet," Kirk said. "Nor even a skirmish. It's the thin edge of an interstellar war. We don't dare to be wrong."

"We can't be righter than we are with the facts at hand, sir," Spock said.

McCoy's lips twitched. "You're so damned sure—"

A beep from the intercom stopped him. Way up in the middle of the air, Lieutenant Uhura's voice said:

"Captain Kirk."

"Go ahead, Lieutenant," Kirk said, his palms sweating.

"I've got a fix on the target vessel. Still can't see it—but I'm getting voices."

Even McCoy pounded up with them to the bridge. Up there, from the master speaker on the comm board, a strange, muted gabble was issuing, fading in and out and often hashed with static, but utterly incomprehensible even at its best. The voices sounded harsh and only barely human; but that could have been nothing more than the illusion of strangeness produced by an unknown language.

The Bantu woman paid no attention to anything but her instruments. Both her large hands were resting delicately on dial knobs, following the voices in and out, back and forth, trying to keep them in aural focus. Beside her left elbow a tape deck ran, recording the gabble for whatever use it might be later for the Analysis team.

"This appears to be coming off their intercom system," she said into the tape-recorder's mike. "A weak signal with high impedance, pulse-modulated. Worth checking what kind of field would leak such a signal, what kind of filtration spectrum it shows—oh, damn—no, there it is again. Scotty, is that you breathing down my neck?"

"Sure is, dear. Need help?"

"Get the computer to work out this waver-pattern for me. My wrists are getting tired. If we can nail it down, I might get a picture."

Scott's fingers flew over the computer console. Very shortly, the volume level of the gabble stabilized, and Lieutenant Uhura leaned back in her seat with a sigh, wriggling her fingers in mid-air. She looked far from relaxed, however.

"Lieutenant," Kirk said. "Do you think you can really get a picture out of that transmission?"

"Don't know why not," the Communications Officer said, leaning forward again. "A leak that size should be big enough to peg rocks through, given a little luck. They've got visible light blocked, but they've left a lot of other windows open. Anyhow, let's try . . ."

But nothing happened for a while. Stiles came in quietly and took over the computer from Scott, walking carefully and pointedly around Spock. Spock did not seem to notice.

"This is a funny business entirely," McCoy said almost to himself. "Those critters were a century behind us, back when we drove them back to their kennels. But that ship's almost as good as ours. It even *looks* like ours. And the weapons . . ."

"Shut up a minute, please, Dr. McCoy," Lieutenant Uhura said. "I'm beginning to get something."

"Sulu," Kirk said. "Any change in their course?"

"None, sir. Still heading home."

"Eureka!" Lieutenant Uhura crowed triumphantly. "There it is!"

The master screen lit. Evidently, Kirk judged, the picture was being picked up by some sort of monitor camera in the Romulan's control room. That in itself was odd; though the *Enterprise* had monitor cameras almost everywhere, there was none on the bridge—who, after all, would be empowered to watch the Captain?

Three Romulans were in view across the viewed chamber, sitting at scanners, lights from their hooded viewers playing upon their faces. They looked human, or nearly so: lean men, with almond-colored faces, dressed in military tunics which bore wolf's-head emblems. The severe, reddish tone of the bulkheads seemed to accentuate their impassivity. Their heads were encased in heavy helmets.

In the foreground, a man who seemed to be the commanding officer worked in a cockpit-like well. Compared to the bridge of the *Enterprise,* this control room looked cramped. Heavy conduits snaked overhead, almost within touch.

All this, however, was noted in an instant and forgotten. Kirk's attention was focused at once on the commander. His uniform was white, and oddly less decorated than those of his officers. Even more importantly, however, he wore no helmet. And in his build, his stance, his coloring, even the cant and shape of his ears, he was a dead ringer for Spock.

Without taking his eyes from the screen, Kirk could sense heads turning toward the half-Vulcanite. There was a long silence, except for the hum of the engines and the background gabble of the Romulan's conversation. Then Stiles said, apparently to himself:

"So now we know. They got our ship design from spies. They can pass for us . . . or for some of us."

Kirk took no overt notice of the remark. Possibly it had been intended only for his ears, or for nobody's; until further notice he was tentatively prepared to think so. He said:

"Lieutenant Uhura, I want linguistics and cryptography to go to work on that language. If we can break it—"

There was another mutter from Stiles, not intelligible but a good deal louder than before. It was no longer possible to ignore him.

"I didn't quite hear that, Mr. Stiles."

"Only talking to myself, sir."

"Do it louder. I want to hear it."

"It wasn't—"

"Repeat it," Kirk said, issuing each syllable like a bullet. Everyone was watching Kirk and Stiles now except Spock, as though the scene on the screen was no longer of any interest at all.

"All right," Stiles said. "I was just thinking that Mr. Spock could probably translate for us a lot faster than the analysts or the computer could. After all, they're his kind of people. You have only to look at them to see that. We can all see it."

"Is that an accusation?"

Stiles drew a deep breath. "No, sir," he said evenly. "It's an observation. I hadn't intended to make it public, and if it's not useful, I'll withdraw it. But I think it's an observation most of us have already made."

"Your apology doesn't satisfy me for an instant. However, since the point's now been aired, we'll explore it. Mr. Spock, do you understand the language those people are speaking? Much as I dislike Mr. Stiles' imputation, there is an ethnic resemblance between the Romulans and yourself. Is it meaningful?"

"I don't doubt that it is," Spock said promptly. "Most of the people in this part of space seem to come from the same stock. The observation isn't new. However, Vulcan has had no more contact than Earth has with the Romulans in historical times; and I certainly don't understand the language. There are suggestions of roots in common with my home language—just as English has some Greek roots. That wouldn't help you to understand Greek from a standing start, though it might help you to figure out something about the language, given time. I'm willing to try it —but I don't hold out much hope of its being useful in time to help us out of our present jam."

In the brief silence which followed, Kirk became aware that the muttering from the screen had stopped. Only a second later, the image of the Romulan bridge had dissolved too.

"They've blocked the leak," Uhura reported. "No way to tell whether or not they knew we were tapping it."

"Keep monitoring it and let me know the instant you pick them up again. Make a copy of your tape for Mr. Spock. Dr. McCoy and Mr. Scott, please come with me to my quarters. Everyone else, bear in mind that we're on continuous alert until this thing is over, one way or another."

Kirk stood up, and seemed to turn toward the elevator. Then, after a carefully calculated pause, he swung on Stiles.

"As for you, Mr. Stiles: Your suggestion may indeed be useful. At the moment, however, I think it perilously close to bigotry, which is a sentiment best kept to yourself. Should you have another such notion, be sure I hear it *before* you air it on the bridge. Do I make myself clear?"

White as milk, Stiles said in a thin voice: "You do, sir."

In his office, Kirk put his feet up and looked sourly at the doctor and his engineer. "As if we didn't have enough trouble," he said. "Spock's a funny customer; he gets everybody's back hair up now and then just on ordinary days; and this . . . coincidence . . . is at best a damn bad piece of timing."

"If it is a coincidence," McCoy said.

"I think it is, Bones. I trust Spock; he's a good officer. His manners are bad by Earth standards, but I don't think much of Stiles' manners either at the moment. Let's drop the question for now. I want to know what to do. The Romulan appears to be running. He'll hit the neutral zone in a few hours. Do we keep on chasing him?"

"You've got a war on your hands if you do," McCoy said. "As you very well know. Maybe a civil war."

"Exactly so. On the other hand, we've already lost three outpost satellites. That's sixty lives—besides all that expensive hardware . . . I went to school with Hansen, did you know that? Well, never mind. Scotty, what do you think?"

"I don't want to write off sixty lives," Scott said. "But we've got nearly four hundred on board the *Enterprise,* and I don't want to write them off either. We've got no defense against that Romulan weapon, whatever it is—and the phasers can't hit a target they can't see. It just might be better to let them run back inside the neutral zone, file a complaint with the Federation, and wait for a navy to take over. That would give us more time to analyze these gadgets of theirs, too."

"And the language and visual records," McCoy added. "Invaluable, unique stuff—all of which will be lost if we force an engagement and lose it."

"Prudent and logical," Kirk admitted. "I don't agree with a word of it, but it would certainly look good in the log. Anything else?"

"What else do you need?" McCoy demanded. "Either it makes sense or it doesn't. I trust you're not suddenly going all bloody-minded on me, Jim."

"You know better than that. I told you I went to school with Hansen; and I've got kids on board here who were about to get married when the alarm went off. Glory doesn't interest me, either, *or* the public record. *I want to block this war*. That's the charge that's laid upon me now. The only question is, How?"

He looked gloomily at his toes. After a while he added:

"This Romulan irruption is clearly a test of strength. They have two weapons. They came out of the neutral zone and challenged a starship with them—with enough slaughter and destruction to make sure we couldn't ignore the challenge. It's also a test of our determination. They want to know if we've gone soft since we beat them back the last time. Are we going to allow our friends and property to be destroyed just because the odds seem to be against us? How much peace will the Romulans let us enjoy if we play it safe now—especially if we let them duck back into a neutral zone they've violated themselves? By and large, I don't think there's much future in that, for us, for the Earth, for the Federation—*or even for the Romulans*. The time to pound that lesson home is now."

"You may be right," Scott said. "I never thought I'd say so, but I'm glad it isn't up to me."

"Bones?"

"Let it stand. I've one other suggestion, though. It might improve morale if you'd marry those two youngsters from the phaser deck."

"Do you think this is exactly a good time for that?"

"I'm not sure there's ever a right time. But if you care for your crew—and I know damn well you do—that's precisely the right way to show it at the moment. An instance of love on an eve of battle. I trust I don't embarrass you."

"You do, Doctor," Kirk said, smiling, "but you're right. I'll do it. But it's going to have to be quick."

"Nothing lasts very long," McCoy said enigmatically.

On the bridge, nothing seemed to have happened. It took Kirk a long moment to realize that the conference in his office had hardly taken ten minutes. The Romulan vessel, once more detectable only by the De Broglie waves of its motion, was still apparently fleeing for the neutral zone, but at no great pace.

"It's possible that their sensors can't pick us up either through that screen," Spock said.

"That, or he's trying to draw us into some kind of trap," Kirk said. "Either way, we can't meet him in a head-on battle. We need an edge . . . a diversion. Find me one, Mr. Spock."

"Preferably nonfatal," Stiles added. Sulu half turned to him from the pilot board.

"You're so wrong about this," Sulu said, "you've used up all your mistakes for the rest of your life."

"One of us has," Stiles said stiffly.

"Belay that," Kirk said. "Steady as she goes, Mr. Sulu. The next matter on the agenda is the wedding."

"In accordance with space law," Kirk said, "we are gathered together for the purpose of joining this woman, Angela Martine, and this man, Robert Tomlinson, in the bond of matrimony . . ."

This time there were no interruptions. Kirk closed his book and looked up.

". . . And so, by the powers vested in me as Captain of the U.S.S. *Enterprise,* I now pronounce you man and wife."

He nodded to Tomlinson, who only then remembered to kiss the bride. There was the usual hubbub, not seemingly much muted by the fewness of the spectators. Yeoman Rand rushed up to kiss Angela's cheek; McCoy pumped Tomlinson's hand, slapped him on the shoulder, and prepared to collect his kiss from the bride, but Kirk interposed.

"Captain's privilege, Bones."

But he never made it; the wall speaker checked him. The voice was Spock's.

"Captain—I think I have the diversion you wanted."

"Some days," Kirk said ruefully, "nothing on this ship ever seems to get finished. I'll be right there, Mr. Spock."

Spock's diversion turned out to be the cold comet they had detected earlier—now "cold" no longer, for as it came closer to the central Romulan-Reman sun it had begun to display its plumage. Spock had found it listed in the ephemeris, and a check of its elements with the computer had shown that it would cross between the *Enterprise* and the Romulan 440 seconds from now—not directly between, but close enough to be of possible use.

"We'll use it," Kirk declared promptly. "Mr. Sulu, we'll close at full acceleration at the moment of interposition. Scotty, tell the phaser room we'll want a bracketing salvo; we'll be zeroing on sensors only, and with that chunk of ice nearly in the way, there'll be some dispersion."

"Still, at that range we ought to get at least one hit," Scott said.

"One minute to closing," Spock said.

"Suppose the shot doesn't get through their screen?" Stiles said.

"A distinct possibility," Kirk agreed. "About which we can do exactly nothing."

"Thirty seconds . . . twenty . . . fifteen . . . ten, nine, eight, seven, six, five, four, three, two, one, zero."

The lights dimmed as the ship surged forward and at the same moment, the phaser coils demanded full drain. The comet swelled on the screen.

"All right, Mr. Tomlinson . . . Hit 'em!"

The *Enterprise* roared like a charging lion. An instant later, the lights flashed back to full brightness, and the noise stopped. The phasers had cut out.

"Overload," Spock said emotionlessly. "Main coil burnout." He was already at work, swinging out a panel to check the circuitry. After only a split second of hesitation, Stiles crossed to help him.

"Captain!" Sulu said. "Their ship—it's fading into sight. I think we got a hit—yes, we did!"

"Not good enough," Kirk said grimly, instantly suspecting the real meaning of the Romulan action. "Full retro power! Evasive action!"

But the enemy was still faster. On the screen, a radiant torpedo like the one they had seen destroy Satellite 4023 was scorching toward the *Enterprise*—and this time it was no illusion that the starship was the target.

"No good," Sulu said. "Two minutes to impact."

"Yeoman Rand, jettison recorder buoy in ninety seconds."

"Hold it," Sulu said. "That shot's changing shape—"

Sure enough: the looming bolt seemed to be wavering, flattening.

Parts of it were peeling off in tongues of blue energy; its brilliance was dimming. Did it have a range limit—

The bolt vanished from the screen. The *Enterprise* lurched sharply. Several people fell, including Spock—luckily away from the opened instrument panel, which crackled and spat.

"Scotty! Damage report!"

"One hold compartment breached. Minor damage otherwise. Main phaser battery still out of action, until that coil's replaced."

"I think the enemy got it worse, sir," Lieutenant Uhura said. "I'm picking up debris-scattering ahead. Conduits—castings—plastoform shadows—and an echo like the body of a casualty."

There was a ragged cheer, which Kirk silenced with a quick, savage gesture. "Maintain deceleration. Evidently they have to keep their screen down to launch their weapon—and the screen's still down."

"No, they're fading again, Captain," Sulu said. "Last Doppler reading shows they're decelerating too . . . Now they're gone again."

"Any pickup from their intercom, Lieutenant Uhura?"

"Nothing, sir. Even the De Broglies are fading. I think the comet's working against us now."

Now what in space did that mean? Fighting with an unknown enemy was bad enough, but when the enemy could become invisible at will— And if that ship got back to the home planet with all its data, there might well be nothing further heard from the Romulans until they came swarming out of the neutral zone by the millions, ready for the kill. That ship had to be stopped.

"Their tactics make sense over the short haul," Kirk said thoughtfully. "They feinted us in with an attack on three relatively helpless pieces, retreated across the center of the board to draw out our power, then made a flank attack and went to cover. Clearly the Romulans play some form of chess. If I had their next move, I'd go across the board again. If they did that, they'd be sitting in our ionization wake right now, right behind us—with reinforcements waiting ahead."

"What about the wreckage, sir?" Uhura said.

"Shoved out the evacuation tubes as a blind—an old trick, going all the way back to submarine warfare. The next time they do that, they may push out a nuclear warhead for us to play with. Lieutenant Sulu, I want a turnover maneuver, to bring the main phaser battery aligned directly astern. Mr. Spock, we can't wait for main coil replacement any longer; go to the phaser deck and direct fire manually. Mr. Stiles, go with him and give him a hand. Fire at my command directly the turnover's been completed. All understood?"

Both men nodded and went out, Stiles a little reluctantly. Kirk watched them go for a brief instant—despite himself, Stiles' suspicion of Spock had infected him, just a little—and then forgot them. The turnover had begun. On the screen, space astern, in the *Enterprise's* ionization wake, seemed as blank as space ahead, in the disturbed gasses of the now-dwindling comet's tail.

Then, for the third time, the Romulan ship began to materialize, precisely where Kirk had suspected it would be—and there was precisely nothing they could do about it yet. The bridge was dead silent. Teeth clenched, Kirk watched the cross-hairs on the screen creep with infinite slowness toward the solidifying wraith of the enemy—

"All right, Spock, *fire!*"

Nothing happened. The suspicion that flared now would not be suppressed. With a savage gesture, Kirk cut in the intercom screen to the phaser deck.

For a moment he could make nothing of what he saw. The screen seemed to be billowing with green vapor. Through it, dimly, Kirk could see two figures sprawled on the floor, near where the phaser boards should have been. Then Stiles came into the field of view, one hand clasped over his nose and mouth. He was trying to reach the boards, but he must have already taken in a lungful of the green gas. Halfway there, he clutched at his throat and fell.

"Scotty! What is that stuff—"

"Coolant fluid," Scott's voice said harshly. "Seal must have cracked—look, there's Spock—"

Spock was indeed on the screen now, crawling on his hands and knees toward the boards. Kirk realized belatedly that the figures on the deck had to be Tomlinson and one of his crew, both dead since the seal had been cracked, probably when the Romulan had hit the *Enterprise* before. On the main screen, another of the Romulan energy bolts was bearing down upon them, with the inexorability of a Fury. Everything seemed to be moving with preternatural slowness.

Then Spock somehow reached the controls, dragged himself to his knees, moved nearly paralyzed fingers over the instruments. He hit the firing button twice, with the edge of his hand, and then fell.

The lights dimmed. The Romulan blew up.

On board the *Enterprise,* there were three dead: Tomlinson, his aide, and Stiles. Angela had escaped; she hadn't been on the deck when the coolant had come boiling out. Escaped—a wife of half a day, a widow for all the rest of her days. Stolidly, Kirk entered it all in the log.

The Second Romulan War was over. And never mind the dead; officially, it had never even begun.

THE NAKED TIME
(John D. F. Black)

Nobody, it was clear, was going to miss the planet when it did break up. Nobody had even bothered to name it; on the charts it was just ULAPG42821DB, a coding promptly shorted by some of the *Enterprise's* junior officers to "La Pig."

It was not an especially appropriate nickname. The planet, a rockball about 10,000 miles in diameter, was a frozen, windless wilderness, without so much as a gnarled root or fragment of lichen to relieve the monotony from horizon to purple horizon. But in one way the name fitted: the empty world was too big for its class.

After a relatively short lifetime of a few hundred million years, stresses between its frozen surface and its shrinking core were about to shatter it.

There was an observation station on La Pig, manned by six people. These would have to be got off, and the *Enterprise,* being in the vicinity, got the job. After that, the orders ran, the starship was to hang around and observe the breakup. The data collected would be of great interest to the sliderule boys back on Earth. Maybe some day they would turn the figures into a way to break up a planet at will, people and all.

Captain Kirk, like most line officers, did not have a high opinion of the chairborne arms of his service.

It turned out, however, that there was nobody at all to pick up off La Pig. The observation station was wide open, and the ice had moved inside. Massive coatings of it lay over everything—floors, consoles, even chairs. The doors were frozen open, and all the power was off.

The six members of the station complement were dead. One, in heavy gear, lay bent half over one of the consoles. On the floor at the entrance to one of the corridors was the body of a woman, very lightly clad and more than half iced over. Inspection, however, showed that she had been dead before the cold had got to her; she had been strangled.

In the lower part of the station were the other four. The engineer sat at his post with all the life-support system switches set at OFF, frozen there as though he hadn't given a damn. There was still plenty of power available; he just hadn't wanted it on any more. Two of the others were dead in their beds, which was absolutely normal and expectable considering the temperature. But the sixth and last man had died while taking a shower—fully clothed.

"There wasn't anything else to be seen," Mr. Spock, the officer in charge of the transporter party, later told Captain Kirk. "Except that there were little puddles of water here and there that hadn't frozen, though at that temperature they certainly should have, no matter what they might have held in solution. We brought back a small sample for the lab. The bodies are in our morgue now, still frozen. As for the people, I think maybe this is a job for a playwright, not an official investigation."

"Imagination's a useful talent in a police officer," Kirk commented. "At a venture, I'd guess that something volatile and highly toxic got loose in the station. One of the men got splattered and rushed to the shower hoping to sluice it off, clothes and all. Somebody else opened all the exit ports in an attempt to let the stuff blow out into the outside atmosphere."

"And the strangled woman?"

"Somebody blamed her for the initial accident—which was maybe just the last of a long chain of carelessnesses, and maybe irritating behavior too, on her part. You know how tempers can get frayed in small isolated crews like this."

"Very good, Captain," Spock said. "Now what about the engineer shutting off the life systems?"

Kirk threw up his hands. "I give up. Maybe he saw that nothing was going to work and decided on suicide. Or more likely I'm completely wrong all down the line. We'd better settle in our observation orbit. Whatever happened down there, apparently the books are closed."

For the record, it was just as well that he said "apparently."

Joe Tormolen, the crewman who had accompanied Mr. Spock to the observation station, was the first to show the signs. He had been eating all by himself in the recreation room—not unusual in itself, for though efficient and reliable, Joe was not very sociable. Nearby, Sulu, the chief pilot, and Navigator Kevin Riley were having an argument over the merits of fencing as exercise, with Sulu of course holding the affirmative. At some point in the discussion, Sulu appealed to Joe for support.

For answer, Joe flew into a white fury, babbling disconnectedly but under high pressure about the six people who had died on La Pig, and the unworthiness of human beings in general to be in space at all. At the height of this frenzied oration, Joe attempted to turn a steak knife on himself.

The resulting struggle was protracted, and because Sulu and Riley naturally misread Joe's intentions—they thought he was going to attack one of them with the knife—Joe succeeded in wounding himself badly. All three were bloodsmeared by the time he was subdued and hauled off to sick bay; at first arrival, the security guards couldn't guess which of the three scuffling figures was the hurt one.

There was no time to discuss the case in any detail; La Pig was already beginning to break up, and Sulu and Riley were needed on the bridge as soon as they could wash up. As the breakup proceeded, the planet's effective mass would change, and perhaps even its center of gravity—accompanied by steady, growing distortion of its extensive magnetic field—so that what had been a stable parking orbit for the *Enterprise* at one moment would become unstable and fragment-strewn the next. The changes were nothing the computer could predict except in rather general orders of magnitude; human brains had to watch and compensate, constantly.

Dr. McCoy's report that Joe Tormolen had died consequently did not reach Kirk for twenty-four hours, and it was another four before he could answer McCoy's request for a consultation. By then, however, the breakup process seemed to have reached some sort of inflection point, where it would simply pause for an hour or so; he could leave the vigil to Sulu and Riley for a short visit to McCoy's office.

"I wouldn't have called you if Joe hadn't been one of the two men down on La Pig," McCoy said directly. "But the case is odd and I don't want to overlook the possibility that there's some connection."

"What's odd about it?"

"Well," McCoy said, "the suicide attempt itself was odd. Joe's self-doubt quotient always rated high, and he was rather a brooding, introspective type; but I'm puzzled about what could have brought it to the surface this suddenly and with this much force.

"And Jim, he shouldn't have died. He had intestinal damage, but I closed it all up neatly and cleaned out the peritoneum; there was no secondary infection. He died anyhow, and I don't know of what."

"Maybe he just gave up," Kirk suggested.

"I've seen that happen. But I can't put it on a death certificate. I have to have a proximate cause, like toxemia or a clot in the brain. Joe just seemed to have a generalized circulatory failure, from no proximate cause at all. And those six dead people on La Pig are not reassuring."

"True enough. What about that sample Spock brought back?"

McCoy shrugged. "Anything's possible, I suppose—but as far as we can tell, that stuff's just water, with some trace minerals that lower its freezing point a good deal. We're handling it with every possible precaution, it's bacteriologically clean—which means no viruses, either—and very nearly chemically pure. I've about concluded that it's a blind alley, though of course I'm still trying to think of new checks to run on it; we all are."

"Well, I'll keep an eye on Spock," Kirk said. "He was the only other man who was down there—though his metabolism's so different that I don't know what I'll be looking for. And in the meantime, we'll just have to hope it was a coincidence."

He went out. As he turned from the door, he was startled to see Sulu coming down a side corridor, not yet aware of Kirk. Evidently he had just come from the gym, for his velour shirt was off, revealing a black tee-shirt, and he had a towel around his neck. He was carrying a fencing foil with a tip protector on it under his arm, and he looked quite pleased with himself—certainly nothing like a man who was away from his post in an alert.

He swung the foil so that it pointed to the ceiling, then let it slip down between his hands so that the capped end was directly before his face. After a moment's study, he took the cap off. Then he took the weapon by the hilt and tested its heft.

"Sulu!"

The pilot jumped back and hit lightly in the guard position. The point of the foil described small circles in the air between the two men.

"Aha!" Sulu said, almost gleefully. "Queen's guard or Richelieu's man? Declare yourself!"

"Sulu, what's this? You're supposed to be on station."

Sulu advanced one pace with the crab-step of the fencer.

"You think to outwit me, eh? Unsheathe your weapon!"

"That's enough," Kirk said sharply. "Report yourself to sick bay."

"And leave you the bois? Nay, rather—"

He made a sudden lunge. Kirk jumped back and snatched out his phaser, setting it to "stun" with his thumb in the same motion, but Sulu was too quick for him. He leapt for a recess in the wall where there was an access ladder to the 'tween-hulls catwalks, and vanished up it. From the vacated manhole his voice echoed back:

"Cowarrrrrrrrrrrrrd!"

Kirk made the bridge on the double. As he entered, Uhura was giving up the navigator's position to another crewman and moving back to her communications console. There was already another substitute in Sulu's chair. Kirk said, "Where's Riley?"

"Apparently he just wandered off," Spock said, surrendering the command chair to Kirk in his turn. "Nobody but Yeoman Harris here saw him go."

"Symptoms?" Kirk asked the helmsman.

"He wasn't violent or anything, sir. I asked where Mr. Sulu was and he began to sing, 'Have no fear, Riley's here.' Then he said he was sorry for me that I wasn't an Irishman—in fact I am, sir—and said he was going for a turn on the battlements."

"Sulu's got it too," Kirk said briefly. "Chased me with a sword on level two, corridor three, then bolted between the hulls. Lieutenant Uhura, tell Security to locate and confine them both. I want every crewman who comes in contact with them medically checked."

"Psychiatrically, I would suggest, Captain," Spock said.

"Explain."

"This seizure, whatever it is, seems to force buried self-images to the surface. Tormolen was a depressive; it drove him down to the bottom of his cycle and below it, so he suicided. Riley fancies himself a descendant of his Irish kings. Sulu at heart is an eighteenth-century swashbuckler."

"All right. What's the present condition of the planet?"

"Breaking faster than predicted," Spock said. "As of now we've got a 2 per cent fall increment."

"Stabilize." He turned to his own command board, but the helmsman's voice jerked his attention back.

"Sir, the helm doesn't answer."

"Fire all ventral verniers then. We'll rectify orbit later."

The helmsman hit the switch. Nothing happened.

"Verniers also dead, sir."

"Main engines: warp one!" Kirk rasped.

"That'll throw us right out of the system," Spock observed, as if only stating a mild inconvenience.

"Can't help that."

"No response, sir," the helmsman said.

"Engine room, acknowledge!" Spock said into the intercom. "Give us power. Our controls are dead."

Kirk jerked a thumb at the elevator. "Mr. Spock, find out what's going on down there."

Spock started to move, but at the same time the elevator door slid aside, and Sulu was advancing, foil in hand. "Richelieu!" he said. "At last!"

"Sulu," Kirk said, "put down that damned—"

"For honor, Queen and France!" Sulu lunged directly at Spock, who in sheer unbelief almost let himself be run through. Kirk tried to move in but the needlepoint flicked promptly in his direction. "Now, foul Richelieu—"

He was about to lunge when he saw Uhura trying to circle behind him. He spun; she halted.

"Aha, fair maiden!"

"Sorry, neither," Uhura said. She threw a glance deliberately over Sulu's left shoulder; as he jerked in that direction, Spock's hand caught him on the right shoulder with the Vulcanian nerve pinch. Sulu went down on the deck like a sack of flour.

Forgetting his existence instantly, Kirk whirled on the intercom. "Mr. Scott! We need power! Scott! Engine room, acknowledge!"

In a musical tenor, the intercom said indolently: "You rang?"

"Riley?" Kirk said, trying to repress his fury.

"This is Capt. Kevin Thomas Riley of the Starship *Enterprise*. And who would I have the honor of speakin' to?"

"This is Kirk, dammit."

"Kirk who? Sure and I've got no such officer."

"Riley, this is Captain Kirk. Get out of the engine room, Navigator. Where's Scott?"

"Now hear this, cooks," Riley said. "This is your captain and I'll be wantin' double portions of ice cream for the crew. Captain's compliments, in honor of St. Kevin's Day. And now, your Captain will render an appropriate selection."

Kirk bolted for the elevator. Spock moved automatically to the command chair. "Sir," he said, "at our present rate of descent we have less than twenty minutes before we enter the planet's exosphere."

"All right," Kirk said grimly. "I'll see what I can do about that monkey. Stand by to apply power the instant you get it."

The elevator doors closed on him. Throughout the ship, Riley's voice began to bawl: "I'll take you home again, Kathleen." He was no singer.

It would have been funny, had it not been for the fact that the serenade had the intercom system completely tied up; that the seizure, judging by Joe Tormolen, was followed by a reasonless death; and that the

Enterprise itself was due shortly to become just another battered lump in a whirling, planet-sized mass of cosmic rubble.

Scott and two crewmen were outside the engine room door, running a sensor around its edge, as Kirk arrived. Scott looked quickly at the Captain, and then back at the job.

"Trying to get this open, sir," he said. "Riley ran in, said you wanted us on the bridge, then locked us out. We heard you talking to him on the intercom."

"He's cut off both helm and power," Kirk said. "Can you by-pass him and work from the auxiliary?"

"No, Captain, he's hooked everything through the main panel in there." Scott prodded one of the crewmen. "Get up to my office and pull the plans for this bulkhead here. If we've got to cut, I don't want to go through any circuitry." The crewman nodded and ran.

"Can you give us battery power on the helm, at least?" Kirk said. "It won't check our fall but at least it'll keep us stabilized. We've got maybe nineteen minutes, Scotty."

"I heard. I can try it."

"Good." Kirk started back for the bridge.

"And tears be-dim your loving eyes . . ."

On the bridge, Kirk snapped, "Can't you cut off that noise?"

"No, sir," Lieutenant Uhura said. "He can override any channel from the main power panels there."

"There's one he can't override," Kirk said. "Mr. Spock, seal off all ship sections. If this is a contagion, maybe we can stop it from spreading, and at the same time—"

"I follow you," Spock said. He activated the servos for the sector bulkheads. Automatically, the main alarm went off, drowning Riley out completely. When it quit, there was a brief silence. Then Riley's voice said:

"Lieutenant Uhura, this is Captain Riley. You interrupted my song. That was petty of you. No ice cream for you."

"Seventeen minutes left, sir," Spock said.

"Attention crew," Riley's voice went on. "There will be a formal dance in the ship's bowling alley at 1900 hours. All personnel will have a ball." There was a skirl of gleeful laughter. "For the occasion all female crewmen will be issued one pint of perfume from ship's stores. All male crewmen will be raised one pay grade to compensate. Stand by for further goodies."

"Any report on Sulu before the intercom got blanketed?" Kirk said.

"Dr. McCoy had him in sick bay under heavy tranquilization," Lieutenant Uhura said. "He wasn't any worse then, but all tests were negative . . . I got the impression that the surgeon had some sort of idea, but he was cut off before he could explain it."

"Well, Riley's the immediate problem now."

A runner came in and saluted. "Sir, Mr. Scott's compliments and you have a jump circuit from batteries to helm control now. Mr. Scott has resumed cutting into the engine room. He says he should have access in fourteen minutes, sir."

"Which is just the margin we have left," Kirk said. "And it'll take three minutes to tune the engines to full power again. Captain's compliments to Mr. Scott and tell him to cut in any old way and not worry about cutting any circuits but major leads."

"Now hear this," Riley's voice said. "In future all female crew members will let their hair hang loosely down over their shoulders and will use restraint in putting on make-up. Repeat, women should not look made up."

"Sir," Spock said in a strained voice.

"One second. I want two security guards to join Mr. Scott's party. Riley may be armed."

"I've already done that," Spock said. "Sir—"

". . . Across the ocean wide and deep . . ."

"Sir, I feel ill," Spock said formally. "Request permission to report to sick bay."

Kirk clapped a hand to his forehead. "Symptoms?"

"Just a general malaise, sir. But in view of—"

"Yes, yes. But you can't *get* to sick bay; the sections are all sealed off."

"Request I be locked in my quarters, then, sir. I can reach those."

"Permission granted. Somebody find him a guard." As Spock went out, another dismaying thought struck Kirk. Suppose McCoy had the affliction now, whatever it was? Except for Spock and the now-dead Tormolen, he had been exposed to it longest, and Spock could be supposed to be unusually resistant. "Lieutenant Uhura, you might as well abandon that console, it's doing us no good at the moment. Find yourself a length of telephone cable and an eavesdropper, and go between hulls to the hull above the sick bay. You'll be able to hear McCoy but not talk back; get his attention, and answer him, by prisoners' raps. Relay the conversation to me by pocket transmitter. Mark and move."

"Yes, *sir*."

Her exit left the bridge empty except for Kirk. There was nothing he could do but pace and watch the big screen. Twelve minutes.

Then a buzzer went off in Kirk's back pocket. He yanked out his communicator.

"Kirk here."

"Lieutenant Uhura, sir. I've established contact with Doctor McCoy. He says he believes he has a partial solution, sir."

"Ask him what he means by partial."

There was an agonizing wait while Uhura presumably spelled out this message by banging on the inner hull. The metal was thick; probably she was using a hammer, and even so the raps would come through only faintly.

"Sir, he wants to discharge something—some sort of gas, sir—into the ship's ventilating system. He says he can do it from sick bay and that it will spread rapidly. He says it worked on Lieutenant Sulu and presumably will cure anybody else who's sick—but he won't vouch for its effect on healthy crew members."

"That sounded like typical McCoy caution, but—ask him how he feels himself."

Another long wait. Then: "He says he felt very ill, sir, but is all right now, thanks to the antidote."

That might be true and it might not. If McCoy himself had the illness, there would be no predicting what he might actually be preparing to dump into the ship's air. On the other hand, to refuse him permission wouldn't necessarily stop him, either. If only that damned singing would stop! It made thinking almost impossible.

"Ask him to have Sulu say something; see if he sounds sane to you."

Another wait. Only ten minutes left now—three of which would have to be used for tune-up. And no telling how fast McCoy's antidote would spread, or how long it would need to take hold, either.

"Sir, he says Lieutenant Sulu is exhausted and he won't wake him, under the discretion granted him by his commission."

McCoy had that discretion, to be sure. But it could also be the cunning blind of a deranged mind.

"All right," Kirk said heavily. "Tell him to go ahead with it."

"Aye aye, sir."

Uhura's carrier wave clicked out and Kirk pocketed his transceiver, feeling utterly helpless. Nine minutes.

Then, Riley's voice faltered. He appeared to have forgotten some of the words of his interminable song. Then he dropped a whole line. He tried to go on, singing "La, la, la," instead, but in a moment that died away too.

Silence.

Kirk felt his own pulse, and sounded himself subjectively. Insofar as he could tell, there was nothing the matter with him but a headache which he now realized he had had for more than an hour. He strode quickly to Uhura's console and rang the engine room.

There was a click from the g.c. speakers, and Riley's voice said hesitantly: "Riley here."

"Mr. Riley, this is Kirk. Where are you?"

"Sir, I . . . I seem to be in the engine room. I'm . . . off post, sir."

Kirk drew a deep breath. "Never mind that. Give us power right away. Then open the door and let the chief engineer in. Stand out of the way when you do it, because he's trying to cut in with a phaser at full power. Have you got all that?"

"Yes, sir. Power, then the door—and stand back. Sir, what's this all about?"

"Never mind now, just do it."

"Yes, sir."

Kirk opened the bulkhead override. At once, there was the heavy rolling sound of the emergency doors between the sections opening, like a stone being rolled back from a tomb. Hitting the general alarm button, Kirk bawled: "All officers to the bridge! Crash emergency, six minutes! Mark and move!"

At the same time, the needles on the power board began to stir. Riley had activated the engines. A moment later, his voice, filled with innocent regret, said into the general air:

"Now there won't be a dance in the bowling alley tonight."

Once a new orbit around the disintegrating mass of La Pig had been established, Kirk found time to question McCoy. The medico looked worn down to a nubbin, and small wonder; his had been the longest vigil of all. But he responded with characteristic indirection.

"Know anything about cactuses, Jim?"

"Only what everybody knows. They live in the desert and they stick you. Oh yes, and some of them store water."

"Right, and that last item's the main one. Also, cactuses that have been in museum cases for fifty or even seventy years sometimes astonish the museum curators by sprouting. Egyptian wheat that's been in tombs for thousands of years will sometimes germinate, too."

Kirk waited patiently. McCoy would get to the point in his own good time.

"Both those things happen because of a peculiar form of storage called *bound water*. Ordinary mineral crystals like copper sulfate often have water hitched to their molecules, loosely; that's water-of-crystallization. With it, copper sulfate is a pretty blue gem, though poisonous; without it, it's a poisonous green powder. Well, organic molecules can bind water much more closely, make it really a part of the molecule instead of just loosely hitched to it. Over the course of many years, that water will come out of combination and become available to the cactus or the grain of wheat as a liquid, and then life begins all over again."

"An ingenious arrangement," Kirk said. "But I don't see how it nearly killed us all."

"It was in that sample of liquid Mr. Spock brought back, of course—a catalyst that *promoted* water-binding. If it had nothing else to bind to, it would bind even to itself. Once in the bloodstream, the catalyst began complexing the blood-serum. First it made the blood more difficult to extract nutrients from, beginning with blood sugar, which starved the brain—hence the psychiatric symptoms. As the process continued, it made the blood too thick to pump, especially through the smaller capillaries—hence Joe's death by circulatory collapse.

"Once I realized what was happening, I had to figure out a way to poison the catalysis. The stuff was highly contagious, through the perspiration, or blood, or any other body fluid; and catalysts don't take part in any chemical reaction they promote, so the original amount was always present to be passed on. I think this one may even have multiplied, in some semi-viruslike fashion. Anyhow, the job was to alter the chemical nature of the catalyst—poison it—so it wouldn't promote that reaction any more. I almost didn't find the proper poison in time, and as I told Lieutenant Uhura through the wall, I wasn't sure what effect the poison itself would have on healthy people. Luckily, none."

"Great Galaxy," Kirk said. "That reminds me of something. Spock invalided himself off duty just before the tail end of the crisis and he's not back. Lieutenant Uhura, call Mr. Spock's quarters."

"Yes, sir."

The switch clicked. Out of the intercom came a peculiarly Arabic howl—the noise of the Vulcanian musical instrument Spock liked to practice in his cabin, since nobody else on board could stand to listen to it. Along with the noise, Spock's rough voice was crooning:

"Alab, wes-craunish, sprai pu ristu,
Or en r'ljiik majiir auooo—"

Kirk winced. "I can't tell whether he's all right or not," he said. "Nobody but another Vulcanian could. But since he's not on duty during a crash alert, maybe your antidote did something to him it didn't do to us. Better go check him."

"Soon as I find my earplugs."

McCoy left. From Spock's cabin, the voice went on:

"Rijii, bebe, p'salku pirtu,

Fror om—"

The voice rose toward an impassioned climax and Kirk cut the circuit. Rather than that, he would almost rather have "I'll take you home again, Kathleen," back again.

On the other hand, if Riley had sounded like that to Spock, maybe Spock had needed no other reason for feeling unwell. With a sigh, Kirk settled back to watch the last throes of La Pig. The planet was now little better than an irregularly bulging cloud of dust, looking on the screen remarkably like a swelling and disintegrating human brain.

The resemblance, Kirk thought, was strictly superficial. Once a planet started disintegrating, it was through. But brains weren't like that.

Given half a chance, they pulled themselves together.

Sometimes.

MIRI

(Adrian Spies)

Any SOS commands instant attention in space, but there was very good reason why this one created special interest on the bridge of the *Enterprise.* To begin with, there was no difficulty in pinpointing its source, for it came not from any ship in distress, but from a planet, driven out among the stars at the 21-centimeter frequency by generators far more powerful than even the largest starship could mount.

A whole planet in distress? But there were bigger surprises to come. The world in question was a member of the solar system of 70 Ophiucus, a sun less than fifteen light-years away from Earth, so that in theory the distress signals could have been picked up on Earth not much more than a decade after their launching except for one handicap: From Earth, 70 Ophiucus is seen against the backdrop of the Milky Way, whose massed clouds of excited hydrogen atoms emit 21-centimeter radiation at some forty times the volume of that coming from the rest of the sky. Not even the planet's huge, hard-driven generators could hope to punch through that much stellar static with an intelligible signal, not even so simple a one as an SOS. Lieutenant Uhura, the communications officer of the *Enterprise,* picked up the signal only because the starship was at the time approaching the "local group"—an arbitrary sphere 100 light-years in diameter with Earth at its center—nearly at right angles to the plane of the galaxy.

All this, however, paled beside the facts about the region dug up by the ship's library computer. For the fourth planet of 70 Ophiucus, the computer said, had been the first extrasolar planet ever colonized by man—by a small but well-equipped group of refugees from the political disaster called the Cold Peace, more than five hundred years ago. It had been visited only once since then. The settlers, their past wrongs unforgotten, had fired on the visitors, and the hint had been taken; after all, the galaxy was full of places more interesting than a backwater like the 70 Ophiucus system, which the first gigantic comber of full-scale exploration had long since passed. The refugees were left alone to enjoy their sullen isolation.

But now they were calling for help.

On close approach it was easy to see why the colonists, despite having been in flight, had settled for a world which might have been thought dangerously close to home. The planet was remarkably Earth-like, with enormous seas covering much of it, stippled and striped with clouds. One hemisphere held a large, roughly lozenge-shaped continent, green and mountainous; the other, two smaller triangular ones, linked by a long archipelago including several islands bigger than Borneo. Under higher magnification, the ship's screen showed the gridworks of numerous cities, and, surprisingly more faintly, the checkerboarding of cultivation.

But no lights showed on the night side, nor did the radio pick up any broadcasts nor any of the hum of a high-energy civilization going full blast. Attempts to communicate, once the *Enterprise* was in orbit, brought no response—only that constantly repeated SOS, which now was beginning to sound suspiciously mechanical.

"Whatever the trouble was," Mr. Spock deduced, "we are evidently too late."

"It looks like it," Captain Kirk agreed. "But we'll go down and see. Mr. Spock, Dr. McCoy, Yeoman Rand, and two security guards, pick up your gear and report to me in the transporter room."

The landing party materialized by choice in the central plaza of the largest city the screen had shown—but there was no one there. Not entirely surprised, Kirk looked around.

The architecture was roughly like that of the early 2100s, when the colonists had first fled, and apparently had stood unoccupied for almost that long a period. Evidences of the erosion of time were everywhere, in the broken pavements, the towering weeds, the gaping windows, the windrows of dirt and dust. Here and there on the plaza were squat sculptures of flaking rust which had perhaps been vehicles.

"No signs of war," Spock said.

"Pestilence?" McCoy suggested. As if by agreement, both were whispering.

By the dust-choked fountain near which Kirk stood, another antique object lay on its side: a child's tricycle. It too was rusty, but still functional, as though it had been indoors during much of the passage of time which had worn away the larger vehicles. There was a bell attached to the handlebar, and moved by some obscure impulse, Kirk pressed his thumb down on its lever.

It rang with a kind of dull sputter in the still air. The plaintive sound was answered instantly, from behind them, by an almost inhuman scream of rage and anguish.

"Mine! *Mine!*"

They whirled to face the terrible clamor. A humanoid creature was plunging toward them from the shell of the nearest building, flailing its arms and screaming murderously. It was moving too fast for Kirk to make out details. He had only an impression of dirt, tatters, and considerable age, and then the thing had leapt upon McCoy and knocked him down.

Everyone waded in to help, but the creature had the incredible strength of the utterly mad. For a moment Kirk was face to face with it —an ancient face, teeth gone in a reeking mouth, contorted with wildness and hate, tears brimming from the eyes. Kirk struck, almost at random.

The blow hardly seemed to connect at all, but the creature sobbed and fell to the pocked pavement. He was indeed an old man, clad only in sneakers, shorts, and a ripped and filthy shirt. His skin was covered with multi-colored blotches. There was something else odd about it, too—but what? Was it as wrinkled as it should be?

Still sobbing, the old head turned and looked toward the tricycle, and an old man's shaking hand stretched out toward it. "Fix," the creature said, between sobs. "Somebody fix."

"Sure," Kirk said, watching intently. "We'll fix it."

The creature giggled. "Fibber," it said. The voice gradually rose to the old scream of rage. "You bustud it! Fibber, fibber!"

The clawing hand grasped the tricycle as if to use it as a weapon, but at the same time the creature seemed to catch sight of the blotches on its own naked arm. The scream died back to a whimper. "Fix it—please fix it—"

The eyes bulged, the chest heaved, and then the creature fell back to the pavement. Clearly, it was dead. McCoy knelt beside it, running a tricorder over the body.

"Impossible," he muttered.

"That it's dead?" Kirk said.

"No, that it could have lived at all. Its body temperature is over one-fifty. It must have been burning itself up. Nobody can live at that temperature."

Kirk's head snapped up suddenly. There had been another sound, coming from an alley to the left.

"Another one?" he whispered tensely. "Somebody stalking us . . . over there. Let's see if we can grab him and get some information . . . Now!"

They broke for the alley. Ahead of them they could hear the stalker running.

The alley was blind, ending in the rear of what seemed to be a small apartment house. There was no place else that the stalker could have gone. They entered cautiously, phasers ready.

The search led them eventually to what had once been a living room. There was a dusty piano in it, a child's exercise book on the music rack. Over one brittle brown page was scribbled, "Practice, practice, practice!" But there was no place to hide but a closet. Listening at the door, Kirk thought he heard agitated breathing, and then, a distinct creak. He gestured, and Spock and the security men covered him.

"Come out," he called. "We mean no harm. Come on out."

There was no answer, but the breathing was definite now. With a sudden jerk, he opened the door.

Huddled on the floor of the closet, amid heaps of moldering clothing, old shoes, a dusty umbrella, was a dark-haired young girl, no more than fourteen—probably younger. She was obviously in abject terror.

"Please," she said. "No, don't hurt me. Why did you come back?"

"We won't hurt you," Kirk said. "We want to help." He held out his hand to her, but she only tried to shrink farther back into the closet. He looked helplessly at Yeoman Rand, who came forward and knelt at the open door.

"It's all right," she said. "Nobody's going to hurt you. We promise."

"I remember the things you did," the girl said, without stirring. "Yelling, burning, hurting people."

"It wasn't us," Janice Rand said. "Come out and tell us about it."

The girl looked dubious, but allowed Janice to lead her to a chair. Clouds of dust came out of it as she sat down, still half poised to spring up and run.

"You've got a foolie," she said. "But I can't play. I don't know the rules."

"We don't either," Kirk said. "What happened to all the people? Was there a war? A plague? Did they just go someplace else and accidentally leave you here?"

"You ought to know. You did it—you and all the other grups."

"Grups? What are grups?"

The girl looked at Kirk, astonished. "You're grups. All the old ones."

"Grown-ups," Janice said. "That's what she means, Captain."

Spock, who had been moving quietly around the room with a tricorder, came back to Kirk, looking puzzled. "She can't have lived here, Captain," he said. "The dust here hasn't been disturbed for at least three hundred years, possibly longer. No radioactivity, no chemical contamination—just very old dust."

Kirk turned back to the girl. "Young lady—by the way, what's your name?"

"Miri."

"All right, Miri, you said the grups did something. Burning, hurting people. Why?"

"They did it when they started to get sick. We had to hide." She looked up hopefully at Kirk. "Am I doing it right? Is it the right foolie?"

"You're doing fine. You said the grown-ups got sick. Did they die?"

"Grups always die." Put that way, it was of course self-evident, but it didn't seem to advance the questioning much.

"How about the children?"

"The onlies? Of course not. We're here, aren't we?"

"More of them?" McCoy put in. "How many?"

"All there are."

"Mr. Spock," Kirk said, "take the security guards and see if you can find any more survivors . . . So all the grups are gone?"

"Well, until it happens—you know—when *it* happens to an only. Then you get to be like them. You want to hurt people, like they did."

"Miri," McCoy said, "somebody attacked us, outside. You saw that? Was that a grup?"

"That was Floyd," she said, shivering a little. "It happened to him. He turned into one. It's happening to me, too. That's why I can't hang around with my friends any more. The minute one of us starts changing, the rest get afraid . . . I don't like your foolie. It's no fun."

"What do they get afraid of?" Kirk persisted.

"You saw Floyd. They try to hurt everything. First you get those awful marks on your skin. Then you turn into a grup, and you want to hurt people, kill people."

"We're not like that," Kirk said. "We've come a long way, all the way from the stars. We know a good many things. Maybe we can help you, if you'll help us."

"Grups don't help," Miri said. "They're the ones that did this."

"We didn't do it, and we want to change it. Maybe we can, if you'll trust us."

Janice touched her on the side of the face and said, "Please?" After a long moment, Miri managed her first timid smile.

Before she could speak, however, there was a prolonged rattling and clanking sound from outside, as though someone had emptied a garbage can off a rooftop. It was followed by the wasplike snarl of a phaser bolt.

Far away, and seemingly high up a child's voice called: "Nyah nyah nyah nyah. NYAH, Nyah!"

"Guards!" Spock's voice shouted.

Many voices answered, as if from all sides: "Nyah nyah nyah nyah NYAH, nyah!"

Then there was silence, except for the echoes.

"It seems," Kirk said, "that your friends don't want to be found."

"Maybe that's not the first step anyhow, Jim," McCoy said. "Whatever happened here, somewhere there must be records about it. If we're to do anything, we have to put our fingers on the cause. The best place would probably be the local public health center. What about that, Miri? Is there a place where the doctors used to work? Maybe a government building?"

"I know that place," she said distastefully. "Them and their needles. That's a bad place. None of us go there."

"But that's where we have to go," Kirk said. "It's important if we're to help you. Please take us."

He held out his hand, and, very hesitantly, she took it. She looked up at him with something like the beginnings of wonder.

"Jim is a nice name," she said. "I like it."

"I like yours, too. And I like you."

"I know you do. You can't really be a grup. You're—something different." She smiled and stood up, gracefully. As she did so, she looked down, and he felt her grip stiffen. Then, carefully, she disengaged it.

"Oh!" she said in a choked voice. "Already!"

He looked down too, already more than half aware of what he would see. Across the back of his hand was a sprawling blue blotch, about the size of a robin's egg.

The laboratory proved to be well-equipped, and since it had been sealed and was windowless, there was less than the expected coating of dust on the tables and equipment. Its size and lack of windows also made it seem unpleasantly like the inside of a tomb, but nobody was prepared to complain about that; Kirk was only grateful that its contents had proved unattractive to any looters who might have broken into it.

The blue blotches had appeared upon all of them now, although those on Mr. Spock were the smallest and appeared to spread more slowly; that was to have been expected, since he came from far different stock than did the rest of the crew, or the colonists for that matter. Just as clearly, his nonterrestrial origin conferred no immunity on him, only a slight added resistance.

McCoy had taken biopsies from the lesions; some of the samples he stained, others he cultured on a variety of media. The blood-agar plate had produced a glistening, wrinkled blue colony which turned out to consist of active, fecund bacteria strongly resembling spirochetes. McCoy, however, was convinced that these were not the cause of the disease, but only secondary invaders.

"For one thing, they won't take on any of the lab animals I've had sent down from the ship," he said, "which means I can't satisfy Koch's Postulates. Second, there's an abnormally high number of mitotic figures in the stained tissues, and the whole appearance is about halfway between squamous metaplasia and frank neoplasm. Third, the chromosome table shows so many displacements—"

"Whoa, I'm convinced," Kirk protested. "What does it add up to?"

"I think the disease proper is caused by a virus," McCoy said. "The spirochetes may help, of course; there's an Earthly disease called Vincent's angina that's produced by two micro-organisms working in concert."

"Is the spirochete communicable?"

"Highly, by contact. You and Yeoman Rand got yours from Miri; we got them from you two."

"Then I'd better see that no one else does," Kirk said. He told his communicator: "Kirk to *Enterprise*. No one, repeat, no one, under any circumstances, is to transport down here until further notice. The planet is heavily infected. Set up complete decontamination procedures for any of us who return."

"Computer?" McCoy nudged.

"Oh yes. Also, ship us down the biggest portable biocomputer—the cat-brain job. That's to get the live-steam treatment too when it goes back up."

"Captain," Spock called. He had been going through a massed rank of file cabinets which occupied almost all of one wall. Now he was beckoning, a folder in one hand. "I think we've got something here."

They all went over except McCoy, who remained at the microscope. Spock handed the folder to Kirk and began pulling others. "There's a drawer-full of these. Must have been hundreds of people working on it. No portable bio-comp is going to process this mass of data in anything under a year."

"Then we'll feed the stuff to the ship's computer by communicator," Kirk said. He looked down at the folder.

It was headed:

Progress Report
LIFE PROLONGATION PROJECT
Genetics Section

"So *that's* what it was," Janice Rand said.

"We don't know yet," Kirk said. "But if it was, it must have been the galaxy's biggest backfire. All right, let's get to work. Miri, you can help too: lay out these folders on the long table there by categories—one for genetics, one for virology, one for immunology, or whatever. Never mind what the words mean, just match 'em up."

The picture merged with maddening slowness. The general principle was clear almost from the start: an attempt to counter the aging process by selectively repairing mutated body cells. Aging is primarily the accumulation in the body of cells whose normal functions have been partly damaged by mutations, these in turn being caused by the entrance of free radicals into the cell nucleus, thus deranging the genetic code. The colony's scientists had known very well that there was no blocking out the free radicals, which are created everywhere in the environment, by background radiation, by sunlight, by combustion, and even by digestion. Instead, they proposed to create a self-replicating, viruslike substance which would remain passive in the bloodstream until actual cell damage occurred; the virus would then penetrate the cell and replace the damaged element. The injection would be given at birth, before the baby's immunity mechanism was fully in action, so that it would be "selfed"—that is, marked as a substance normal to the body rather than an invader to be battled; but it would remain inactive until triggered by the hormones of puberty, so as not to interfere with normal growth processes.

"As bold a project as I've heard of in all my life," McCoy declared. "Just incidentally, had this thing worked, it would have been the perfect cancer preventive. Cancer is essentially just a local explosion of the aging process, in an especially virulent form."

"But it didn't work," Spock said. "Their substance was entirely *too* much like a virus—and it got away from them. Oh, it prolongs life, all right—but only in children. When puberty finally sets in, it kills them."

"How much?" Janice Rand asked.

"You mean, how long does it prolong life? We don't know because the experiment hasn't gone on that long. All we know is the rate: the injected person ages about a month, physiological time, for every hundred years, objective time. For the children, it obviously does work that way."

Janice stared at Miri. "A month in a hundred years!" she said. "And the experiment was three centuries ago! Eternal childhood . . . It's like a dream."

"A very bad dream, Yeoman," Kirk said. "We learn through example and responsibilities. Miri and her friends were deprived of both. It's a dead end street."

"With a particularly ugly death at the end," McCoy agreed. "It's amazing that so many children did survive. Miri, how did you get along after all the grups died?"

"We had foolies," Miri said. "We had fun. There wasn't anybody to tell us not to. And when we got hungry, we just took something. There were lots of things in cans, and lots of mommies."

"Mommies?"

"You know." Miri wound her hand vigorously in mid-air, imitating the motion of a rotary can-opener. Janice Rand choked and turned away. "Jim . . . now that you found what you were looking for . . . are you going away?"

"Oh no," Kirk said. "We've still got a great deal more to learn. Your grups seemed to have done their experiments in a certain definite sequence, a sort of timetable. Any sign of that yet, Mr. Spock?"

"No, sir. Very likely it's kept somewhere else. If this were my project, I'd keep it in a vault; it's the key to the whole business."

"I'm afraid I agree. And unless we can figure it out, Miri, we won't be able to identify the virus, synthesize it, and make a vaccine."

"That's good," Miri said. "Your not going, I mean. We could have fun—until *it* happens."

"We still may be able to stop it. Mr. Spock, I gather you couldn't get close to any of the other children?"

"No chance. They know the area too well. Like mice."

"All right, let's try another approach. Miri, will you help us find some of them?"

"You won't find any," Miri said positively. "They're afraid. They won't like you. And they're afraid of me, too, now, ever since . . ." she stopped.

"We'll try to make them understand."

"Onlies?" the girl said. "You couldn't do it. That's the best thing about being an only. Nobody expects you to understand."

"*You* understand."

Abruptly Miri's eyes filled with tears. "I'm not an only any more," she said. She ran out of the room. Janice looked after her compassionately.

Janice said: "That little girl—"

"—is three hundred years older than you are, Yeoman," Kirk finished for her. "Don't leap to any conclusions. It's got to make some sort of a difference in her—whether we can see it yet or not."

But in a minute Miri was back, the cloudburst passed as if it had never been, looking for something to do. Mr. Spock set her to sharpening pencils, of which the ancient laboratory seemed to have scores. She set to it cheerfully—but throughout, her eyes never left Kirk. He tried not to show that he was aware of it.

"Captain? This is Farrell on the *Enterprise*. We're ready to compute."

"All right, stand by. Mr. Spock, what do you need?"

Miri held up a fistful of pencils. "Are these enough?"

"Uh? Oh—we could use more, if you don't mind."

"Oh no, Jim," she said. "Why should I mind?"

"This fellow," Spock said, fanning out a sheaf of papers on the table, "left these notes in the last weeks—after the disaster began. I disregarded these last entries; he said he was too far gone himself, too sick, to be sure he wasn't delirious, and I agree. But these earlier tables ought to show us how much time we have left. By the way, it's clear that the final stages we've seen here are typical. Homicidal mania."

"And nothing to identify the virus strain—or its chemistry?" McCoy said.

"Not a thing," Spock said. "He believed somebody else was writing that report. Maybe somebody was and we just haven't found it yet—or maybe that was the first of his hallucinations. Anyhow, the first overt stage is intense fever . . . pain in the joints . . . fuzziness of vision. Then, gradually, the mania takes over. By the way, Dr. McCoy, you were right about the spirochetes—they do contribute. They create the mania, not the virus. It'll be faster in us because we haven't carried the disease in latent form as long as Miri."

"What about her?" Kirk said in a low voice.

"Again, we'll have to see what the computer says. Roughly, I'd guess that she could survive us by five or six weeks—if one of us doesn't kill her first—"

"Enough now?" Miri said simultaneously, holding up more pencils.

"No!" Kirk burst out angrily.

The corners of her mouth turned down and her lower lip protruded. "Well, all right, Jim," she said in a small voice. "I didn't mean to make you mad."

"I'm sorry, Miri. I wasn't talking to you. I'm not mad." He turned back to Spock. "All right, so we still don't know what we're fighting. Feed your figures to Farrell and then at least we'll know what the time factor is. Damnation! If we could just put our hands on that virus, the ship could develop a vaccine for us in twenty-four hours. But there's just no starting point."

"Maybe there is," McCoy said slowly. "Again, it'd be a massive computational project, but I think it might work. Jim, you know how the desk-bound mind works. If this lab was like every other government project I've run across, it had to have order forms in quintuplicate for everything it used. Somewhere here there ought to be an accounting file containing copies of those orders. They'd show us what the consumption of given reagents was at different times. I'll be able to spot the obvious routine items—culture media and shelf items, things like that—but we'll need to analyze for what is significant. There's at least a chance that such an analysis would reconstruct the missing timetable."

"A truly elegant idea," Mr. Spock said. "The question is—"

He was interrupted by the buzzing of Kirk's communicator.

"Kirk here."

"Farrell to landing party. Mr. Spock's table yields a cut-off point at seven days."

For a long moment there was no sound but the jerky whirring of the pencil sharpener. Then Spock said evenly:

"That was the question I was about to raise. As much as I admire Dr. McCoy's scheme, it will almost surely require more time than we have left."

"Not necessarily," McCoy said. "If it's true that the spirochete creates the mania, we can possibly knock it out with antibiotics and keep our minds clear for at least a while longer—"

Something hit the floor with a smash. Kirk whirled. Janice Rand had been cleaning some of McCoy's slides in a beaker of chromic acid. The corrosive yellow stuff was now all over the floor. Some of it had spattered Janice's legs. Grabbing a wad of cotton, Kirk dropped to his knees to mop them.

"No, no," Janice sobbed. "You can't help me—you can't help me!"

Stumbling past McCoy and Spock, she ran out of the laboratory, sobbing. Kirk started after her.

"Stay here," he said. "Keep working. Don't lose a minute."

Janice was standing in the hallway, her back turned, weeping convulsively. Kirk resumed swabbing her legs, trying not to notice the ugly blue blotches marring them. As he worked, her tears gradually died back. After a while she said in a small voice:

"Back on the ship you never noticed my legs."

Kirk forced a chuckle. "The burden of command, Yeoman: to see only what regs say is pertinent . . . That's better, but soap and water will have to be next."

He stood up. She looked worn, but no longer hysterical. She said:

"Captain, I didn't really want to do that."

"I know," Kirk said. "Forget it."

"It's so stupid, such a waste . . . Sir, do you know all I can think about? I should know better, but I keep thinking, I'm only twenty-four—and I'm scared."

"I'm a little older, Yeoman. But I'm scared too."

"You are?"

"Of course. I don't want to become one of those things, any more than you do. I'm more than scared. You're my people. I brought you here. I'm scared for all of us."

"You don't show it," she whispered. "You never show it. You always seem to be braver than any ten of us."

"Baloney," he said roughly. "Only an idiot isn't afraid when there's something to be afraid of. The man who feels no fear isn't brave, he's just stupid. Where courage comes in is in going ahead and coping with danger, not being paralyzed by fright. And especially, not letting yourself be panicked by the other guy."

"I draw the moral," Janice said, trying to pull herself erect. But at the same time, the tears started coming quietly again. "I'm sorry," she repeated in a strained voice. "When we get back, sir, you'd better put in for a dry-eyed Yeoman."

"Your application for a transfer is refused." He put his arm around her gently, and she tried to smile up at him. The movement turned them both around toward the entrance to the lab.

Standing in it was Miri, staring at them with her fists crammed into her mouth, her eyes wide with an unfathomable mixture of emotions—

amazement, protest, hatred even? Kirk could not tell. As he started to speak, Miri whirled about and was gone. He could hear her running footsteps receding; then silence.

"Troubles never come alone," Kirk said resignedly. "We'd better go back."

"Where was Miri going?" McCoy asked interestedly, the moment they re-entered. "She seemed to be in a hurry."

"I don't know. Maybe to try and look for more onlies. Or maybe she just got bored with us. We haven't time to worry about her. What's next?"

"Next is accident prevention time," McCoy said. "I should have thought of it before, but Janice's accident reminded me of it. There are a lot of corrosive reagents around here, and if we have any luck, we'll soon be playing with infectious material too. I want everyone out of their regular clothes and into lab uniforms we can shuck the minute they get something spilled on them. There's a whole locker full of them over on that side. All our own clothes go out of the lab proper into the anteroom, or else we'll just have to burn 'em when we get back to the ship."

"Good; so ordered. How about equipment—phasers and so on?"

"Keep one phaser here for emergencies if you're prepared to jettison it before we go back," McCoy said. "Everything else, out."

"Right. Next?"

"Medical analysis has got as far as I can take it," McCoy said. "From here on out, it's going to be strictly statistical—and though the idea was mine, I'm afraid Mr. Spock is going to have to direct it. Statistics make me gibber."

Kirk grinned. "Very well, Mr. Spock, take over."

"Yes sir. First of all, we've got to find those purchase orders. Which means another search of the file cabinets."

The problem was simple to pose: Invent a disease.

The accounting records turned up, relatively promptly, and in great detail. McCoy's assumption had been right that far: the bureaucratic mind evidently underwent no substantial change simply by having been removed more than a dozen light-years from the planet where it had evolved. Everything the laboratory had ever had to call for had at least three pieces of paper that went along with it.

McCoy was able to sort these into rough categories of significance, on a scale of ten (from 0 = obvious nonsense to 10 = obviously crucial), and the bio-comp coded everything graded "five" or above so that it could be fed to the orbiting *Enterprise's* computer with the least possible loss of time. The coding was very fast; but assigning relative weights to the items to be coded was a matter for human judgment, and despite his disclaimers, McCoy was the only man present who could do it with any confidence in well more than half of the instances. Spock could tell, within a given run of samples, what appeared to be statistically significant, but only McCoy could then guess whether the associations were medical, financial, or just make-work.

It took two days, working around the clock. By the morning of the third day, however, Spock was able to say:

"These cards now hold everything the bio-comp can do for us." He turned to Miri, who had returned the day before, with no explanations, but without the slightest change in her manner, and as willing to work as ever. "Miri, if you'll just stack them and put them back in that hopper, we'll rank them for the *Enterprise,* and then we can read-and-feed to Farrell. I must confess, I still don't see the faintest trace of a pattern in them."

"I do," McCoy said surprisingly. "Clearly the active agent can't be a pure virus, because it'd be cleaned out of the body between injection and puberty if it didn't reproduce; and true viruses can't reproduce without invading a body cell, which this thing is forbidden to do for some ten or twelve years, depending on the sex of the host. This has to be something more like some of the rickettsiae, with some enzymatic mechanisms intact so it can feed and reproduce from material it can absorb from the body fluids, *outside* the cells. When the hormones of puberty hit it, it sheds that part of its organization and becomes a true virus. Ergo, the jettisoned mechanism has to be steroid-soluble. And only the sexual steroids can be involved. All these conditions close in on it pretty implacably, step by step."

"Close enough to put a name to it?" Kirk demanded tensely.

"By no means," McCoy said. "I don't even know if I'm on the right track; this whole scholium is intuitive on my part. But it makes sense. I think something very like that will emerge when the ship's computer processes all these codes. Anybody care to bet?"

"We've already bet our lives, like it or not," Kirk said. "But we ought to have the answer in an hour now. Mr. Spock, call Farrell."

Spock nodded and went out into the anteroom, now kept sealed off from the rest of the lab. He was back in a moment. Though his face was almost incapable of showing emotion, something in his look brought Kirk to his feet in a rush.

"What's the matter?"

"The communicators are gone, Captain. There's nothing in those uniforms but empty pockets."

Janice gasped. Kirk turned to Miri, feeling his brows knotting together. The girl shrank a little from him, but returned his look defiantly all the same.

"What do you know about this, Miri?"

"The onlies took them, I guess," she said. "They like to steal things. It's a foolie."

"Where did they take them?"

She shrugged. "I don't know. That's a foolie, too. When you take something, you go someplace else."

He was on her in two strides, grasping her by the shoulders. "This is not a foolie. It's a disaster. We have to have those communicators—otherwise we'll never lick this disease."

She giggled suddenly. "Then you won't have to go," she said.

"No, we'll die. Now cut it out. Tell us where they are."

The girl drew herself up in an imitation of adult dignity. Considering that she had never seen an adult after the disaster until less than a week ago, it was a rather creditable imitation.

"Please, Captain, you're hurting me," she said haughtily. "What's the matter with you? How could *I* possibly know?"

Unfortunately, the impersonation broke at the end into another giggle —which, however, did Kirk no good as far as the issue at hand was concerned. "What is this, blackmail?" Kirk said, beyond anger now. He could feel nothing but the total urgency of the loss. "It's your life that's at stake too, Miri."

"Oh no," Miri said sweetly. "Mr. Spock said that I'd live five or six weeks longer than you will. Maybe some of you'll die ahead of some others. I'll still be here." She flounced in her rags toward the door. Under any other circumstances she might have been funny, perhaps even charming. At the last moment she turned, trailing a languid hand through the air. "Of course I don't know what makes you think I know anything about this. But maybe if you're very nice to me, I could ask my friends some questions. In the meantime, Captain, farewell."

There was an explosion of pent breaths as her footsteps dwindled.

"Well," McCoy said, "one can tell that they had television on this planet during part of Miri's lifetime, at least."

The grim joke broke part of the tension.

"What can we do without the ship?" Kirk demanded. "Mr. Spock?"

"Very little, Captain. The bio-comp's totally inadequate for this kind of job. It takes hours, where the ship's computer takes seconds, and it hasn't the analytical capacity."

"The human brain was around long before there were computers. Bones, what about your hunch?"

"I'll ride it, of course," McCoy said wearily. "But time is the one commodity the computer could have saved us, and the one thing we haven't got. When I think of that big lumbering ship up there, with everything we need on board it, orbiting around and around like so much inert metal—"

"And complaining just wastes more time," Kirk snarled. McCoy stared at him in surprise. "I'm sorry, Bones. I guess it's starting to get me, too."

"I *was* complaining," McCoy said. "The apology is mine. Well then, the human brain it will have to be. It worked for Pasteur . . . but he was a good bit smarter than me. Mr. Spock, take those cards away from that dumb cat and let's restack them. I'll want to try a DNA analysis first. If that makes any sort of reasonable pattern, enough to set up a plausible species, we'll chew through them again and see if we can select out a clone."

"I'm not following you," Spock admitted.

"I'll feed you the codes, there's no time for explanations. Pull everything coded LTS-426 first. Then we'll ask the cat to sort those for uncoded common factors. There probably won't be any, but it's the most promising beginning I can think of."

"Right."

Kirk felt even more out of it than Mr. Spock; he had neither the medical nor the statistical background to understand what was going on. He simply stood by, and did what little donkey-work there was to do.

The hours wore away into another day. Despite the stim-pills McCoy doled out, everyone seemed to be moving very slowly, as if underwater. It was like a nightmare of flight.

Somewhere during that day, Miri turned up, to watch with what she probably imagined was an expression of aloof amusement. Everyone ignored her. The expression gradually faded into a frown; finally, she began to tap her foot.

"Stop that," Kirk said without even turning to look at her, "or I'll break your infant neck."

The tapping stopped. McCoy said: "Once more into the cat, Mr. Spock. We are now pulling all T's that are functions of D-2. If there are more than three, we're sunk."

The bio-comp hummed and chuttered over the twenty-two cards

Spock had fed it. It threw out just one. McCoy leaned back in his hard-backed straight chair with a whoosh of satisfaction.

"Is that it?" Kirk asked.

"By no means, Jim. That's *probably* the virus involved. Just probably, no more."

"It's only barely significant," Spock said. "If this were a test on a new product survey or something of that sort, I'd throw it out without a second thought. But as matters stand—"

"As matters stand, we next have to synthesize the virus," McCoy said, "and then make a killed-virus vaccine from it. No, no, that won't work at all, what's the matter with me? Not a vaccine. An antitoxoid. Much harder. Jim, wake those security guards—a lot of good they did us in the pinch! We are going to need a lot of bottles washed in the next forty-eight hours."

Kirk wiped his forehead. "Bones, I'm feeling outright lousy, and I'm sure you are too. Officially we've got the forty-eight hours left—but are we going to be functioning sensibly after the next twenty-four?"

"We either fish or cut bait," McCoy said calmly. "All hands on their feet. The cookery class is hereby called to order."

"It's a shame," Spock said, "that viruses aren't as easy to mix as metaphors."

At this point Kirk knew that he was on the thin edge of hysteria. Somehow he had the firm impression that Mr. Spock had just made a joke. Next he would be beginning to believe that there really was such a thing as a portable computer with a cat's brain in it. "Somebody hand me a bottle to wash," he said, "before I go to sleep on my feet."

By the end of twenty hours, Janice Rand was raving and had to be strapped down and given a colossal tranquilizer dose before she would stop fighting. One of the guards followed her down an hour later. Both were nearly solid masses of blue marks; evidently, the madness grew as the individual splotches coalesced into larger masses and proceeded toward covering the whole skin surface.

Miri disappeared at intervals, but she managed to be on the scene for both these collapses. Perhaps she was trying to look knowing, or superior, or amused; Kirk could not tell. The fact of the matter was that he no longer had to work to ignore Miri, he was so exhausted that the small chores allotted him by his First Officer and his ship's surgeon took up the whole foreground of his attention, and left room for no background at all.

Somewhere in there, McCoy's voice said: "Everything under the SPF hood now. At the next stage we've got a live one. Kirk, when I take the lid off the Petri dish, in goes the two cc's of formalin. Don't miss."

"I won't."

Somehow, he didn't. Next, after a long blank, he was looking at a rubber-capped ampule filled with clear liquid, into which McCoy's hands were inserting the needle of a spray hypo. Tunnel vision; nothing more than that: the ampule, the hypo, the hands.

"That's either the antitoxoid," McCoy's voice was saying from an infinite distance, "or it isn't. For all I know it may be pure poison. Only the computer could tell us which for sure."

"Janice first," Kirk heard himself rasp. "Then the guard. They're the closest to terminal."

"I override you, Captain," McCoy's voice said. "I am the only experimental animal in this party."

The needle jerked out of the rubber cap. Somehow, Kirk managed to reach out and grasp McCoy's only visible wrist. The movement hurt; his joints ached abominably, and so did his head.

"Wait a minute," he said. "One minute more won't make any difference."

He swivelled his ringing skull until Miri came into view down the optical tunnel. She seemed to be all fuzzed out at the edges. Kirk walked toward her, planting his feet with extraordinary care on the slowly tilting floor.

"Miri," he said. "Listen to me. You've got to listen to me."

She turned her head away. He reached out and grabbed her by the chin, much more roughly than he had wanted to, and forced her to look at him. He was dimly aware that he was anything but pretty—bearded, covered with sweat and dirt, eyes rimmed and netted with red, mouth working with the effort to say words that would not come out straight.

"We've . . . only got a few hours left. Us, and all of you . . . you, and your friends. And . . . we may be wrong. After that, no grups, and no onlies . . . no one . . . forever and ever. Give me back just one of those . . . machines, those communicators. Do you want the blood of a whole world on your hands? Think, Miri—think for once in your life!"

Her eyes darted away. She was looking toward Janice. He forced her to look back at him. "Now, Miri. Now. *Now.*"

She drew a long, shuddering breath. "I'll—try to get you one," she said. Then she twisted out of his grasp and vanished.

"We can't wait any longer," McCoy's voice said calmly. "Even if we had the computer's verdict, we couldn't do anything with it. We have to go ahead."

"I will bet you a year's pay," Spock said, "that the antitoxoid is fatal in itself."

In a haze of pain, Kirk could see McCoy grinning tightly, like a skull. "You're on," he said. "The disease certainly is. But if I lose, Mr. Spock, how will you collect?"

He raised his hand.

"Stop!" Kirk croaked. He was too late—even supposing that McCoy in this last extremity would have obeyed his captain. This was McCoy's world, his universe of discourse. The hypo hissed against the surgeon's bared, blue-suffused arm.

Calmly, McCoy laid the injector down on the table, and sat down. "Done," he said. "I don't feel a thing." His eyes rolled upward in their sockets, and he took a firm hold on the edge of the table. "You see . . . gentlemen . . . it's all perfectly . . ."

His head fell forward.

"Help me carry him," Kirk said, in a dead voice. Together, he and Spock carried the surgeon to the nearest cot. McCoy's face, except for the blotches, was waxlike; he looked peaceful for the first time in days. Kirk sat down on the edge of the cot beside him and tried his pulse. It was wild and erratic, but still there.

"I . . . don't see how the antitoxoid could have hit him that fast," Spock said. His own voice sounded like a whisper from beyond the grave.

"He could only have passed out. I'm about ready, myself. Damn the man's stubbornness."

"Knowledge," Spock said remotely, "has its privileges."

This meant nothing to Kirk. Spock was full of these gnomic utterances; presumably they were Vulcanian. There was a peculiar hubbub in Kirk's ears, as though the visual fuzziness was about to be counterpointed by an aural one.

Spock said, "I seem to be on the verge myself—closer than I thought. The hallucinations have begun."

Wearily, Kirk looked around. Then he goggled. If Spock was having a hallucination, so was Kirk. He wondered if it was the same one.

A procession of children was coming into the room, led by Miri. They were of all sizes and shapes, from toddlers up to about the age of twelve. They looked as though they had been living in a department store. Some of the older boys wore tuxedos; some were in military uniforms; some in scaled-down starmen's clothes; some in very loud and mismatched sports clothes. The girls were a somewhat better matched lot, since almost all of them were wearing some form of party dress, several of them trailing opera cloaks and loaded with jewelry. Dominating them all was a tall, red-headed boy—or no, that wasn't his own hair, it was a wig, long at the back and sides and with bangs, from which the price-tag still dangled. Behind him hopped a fat little boy who was carrying, on a velvet throw-pillow, what appeared to be a crown.

It was like some mad vision of the Children's Crusade. But what was maddest about it was that the children were loaded with equipment—the landing party's equipment. There were the three communicators—Janice and the security guards hadn't carried any; there were the two missing tricorders—McCoy had kept his in the lab; and the red-wigged boy even had a phaser slung at his hip. It was a measure of how exhausted they had all been, even back then, that they hadn't realized one of the deadly objects was missing. Kirk wondered whether the boy had tried it, and if so, whether he had hurt anybody with it.

The boy saw him looking at it, and somehow divined his thought.

"I used it on Louise," he said gravely. "I had to. She went grup all at once, while we were playing school. She was—only a little older than me."

He unbuckled the weapon and held it out. Numbly, Kirk took it. The other children moved to the long table and solemnly began to pile the rest of the equipment on it. Miri came tentatively to Kirk.

"I'm sorry," she said. "It was wrong and I shouldn't have. I had a hard time, trying to make Jahn understand that it wasn't a foolie any more." She looked sideways at the waxy figure of McCoy. "Is it too late?"

"It may be," Kirk whispered; that was all the voice he could muster. "Mr. Spock, do you think you can still read the data to Farrell?"

"I'll try, sir."

Farrell was astonished and relieved, and demanded explanations. Spock cut him short and read him the figures. Then there was nothing to do but wait while the material was processed. Kirk went back to looking at McCoy, and Miri joined him. He realized dimly that, for all the trouble she had caused, her decision to bring the communicators back had been a giant step toward growing up. It would be a shame to lose her now, Miri most of all in the springtime of her promise—a springtime for which she had waited three sordid centuries. He put his arm around her, and she looked up at him gratefully.

Was it another failure of vision, or were the blotches on McCoy fading a little? No, some of them were definitely smaller and had lost color. "Mr. Spock," he said, "come here and check me on something."

Spock looked and nodded. "Retreating," he said. "Now if there are no serious side-effects—" The buzz of his communicator interrupted him. "Spock here."

"Farrell to landing party. The identification is correct, repeat, correct. Congratulations. Do you mean to tell me you boiled down all that mass of bits and pieces with nothing but a bio-comp?"

Kirk and Spock exchanged tired grins. "No," Spock said, "we did it all in Doctor McCoy's head. Over and out."

"The bio-comp did help," Kirk said. He reached out and patted the squat machine. "Nice kitty."

McCoy stirred. He was trying to sit up, his expression dazed.

"Begging your pardon, Doctor," Kirk said. "If you've rested sufficiently, I believe the administration of injections *is* your department."

"It worked?" McCoy said huskily.

"It worked fine, the ship's computer says it's the right stuff, and you are the hero of the hour, you pig-headed idiot."

They left the system a week later, having given all the antitoxoid the ship's resources could produce. Together with Farrell, the erstwhile landing party stood on the bridge of the *Enterprise,* watching the planet retreat.

"I'm still a little uneasy about it," Janice Rand said. "No matter how old they are chronologically, they're still just children. And to leave them there with just a medical team to help them—"

"They haven't lived all those years for nothing," Kirk said. "Look at the difficult thing Miri did. They'll catch on fast, with only a minimum of guidance. Besides, I've already had Lieutenant Uhura get the word back to Earth . . . If that planet had had subspace radio, they would have been saved a lot of their agony. But it hadn't been invented when the original colonists left . . . Space Central will send teachers, technicians, administrators—"

"—And truant officers, I presume," McCoy said.

"No doubt. The kids will be all right."

Janice Rand said slowly: "Miri . . . she . . . really loved you, you know, Captain. That was why she played that trick on you."

"I know," Kirk said. "And I'm duly flattered. But I'll tell you a secret, Yeoman Rand. I make it a policy never to get involved with women older than I am."

THE CONSCIENCE OF THE KING
(Barry Trivers)

"A curious experience," Kirk said. "I've seen *Macbeth* in everything from bearskins to uniforms, but never before in Arcturian dress. I suppose an actor has to adapt to all kinds of audiences."

"This one has," Dr. Leighton said. He exchanged a glance with Martha Leighton; there was an undertone in his voice which Kirk could not fathom. There seemed to be no reason for it. The Leightons' garden, under the bright sun of the Arcturian system, was warm and pleasant; their hospitality, including last night's play, had been unexceptionable. But time was passing, and old friends or no, Kirk had to be back on duty shortly.

"Karidian has an enormous reputation," he said, "and obviously he's earned it. But now, Tom, we'd better get down to business. I've been told this new synthetic of yours is something we badly need."

"There is no synthetic," Leighton said heavily. "I want you to think about Karidian. About his voice in particular. You should remember it; you were there."

"I was where?" Kirk said, annoyed. "At the play?"

"No," Leighton said, his crippled, hunched body stirring restlessly in its lounger. "On Tarsus IV, during the Rebellion. Of course it was twenty years ago, but you couldn't have forgotten. My family murdered —and your friends. And you saw Kodos—and heard him, too."

"Do you mean to tell me," Kirk said slowly, "that you called me three light-years off my course just to accuse an actor of being Kodos the Executioner? What am I supposed to put in my log? That you lied? That you diverted a starship with false information?"

"It's not false. Karidian is Kodos."

"That's not what I'm talking about. I'm talking about your invented story about the synthetic food process. Anyhow, Kodos is dead."

"Is he?" Leighton said. "A body burned beyond recognition—what kind of evidence is that? And there are so few witnesses left, Jim: you, and I, and perhaps six or seven others, people who actually saw Kodos and heard his voice. You may have forgotten, but I never will."

Kirk turned to Martha, but she said gently: "I can't tell him anything, Jim. Once he heard Karidian's voice, it all came back. I can hardly blame him. From all accounts, that was a bloody business . . . and Tom wasn't just a witness. He was a victim."

"No, I know that," Kirk said. "But vengeance won't help, either—and I can't allow the whole *Enterprise* to be sidetracked on a personal vendetta, no matter how I feel about it."

"And what about justice?" Leighton said. "If Kodos is still alive, oughtn't he to pay? Or at least be taken out of circulation—before he contrives another massacre? Four thousand people, Jim!"

"You have a point," Kirk admitted reluctantly. "All right, I'll go this far: Let me check the ship's library computer and see what we have on *both* men. If your notion's just a wild hare, that's probably the quickest way to find out. If it isn't—well, I'll listen further."

"Fair enough," Leighton said.

Kirk pulled out his communicator and called the *Enterprise*. "Library computer . . . Give me everything you have on a man named or known as Kodos the Executioner. After that, a check on an actor named Anton Karidian."

"Working," the computer's voice said. Then: "Kodos the Executioner. Deputy Commander, forces of Rebellion, Tarsus IV, twenty terrestrial years ago. Population of eight thousand Earth colonists struck by famine after fungus blight largely destroyed food supply. Kodos used situation to implement private theories of eugenics, slaughtered fifty per cent of colony population. Sought by Earth forces when rebellion overcome. Burned body found and case closed. Biographical data—"

"Skip that," Kirk said. "Go on."

"Karidian, Anton. Director and leading man of traveling company of actors, sponsored by Interstellar Cultural Exchange project. Touring official installations for past nine years. Daughter, Lenore, nineteen years old, now leading lady of troupe. Karidian a recluse, has given notice current tour is to be his last. Credits—"

"Skip that too. Data on his pre-acting years?"

"None available. That is total information."

Kirk put the communicator away slowly. "Well, well," he said. "I still think it's probably a wild hare, Tom . . . but I think I'd better go to tonight's performance, too."

After the performance, Kirk went backstage, which was dingy and traditional, and knocked on the door with the star on it. In a moment, Lenore Karidian opened it, still beautiful, though not as bizarre as she had looked as an Arcturian Lady Macbeth. She raised her eyebrows.

"I saw your performance tonight," Kirk said. "And last night, too. I just want to . . . extend my appreciation to you and to Karidian."

"Thank you," she said, politely. "My father will be delighted, Mr. . . . ?"

"Capt. James Kirk, the starship *Enterprise*."

That told, he could tell; that and the fact that he had seen the show two nights running. She said: "We're honored. I'll carry your message to father."

"Can't I see him personally?"

"I'm sorry, Captain Kirk. He sees no one personally."

"An actor turning away his admirers? That's very unusual."

"Karidian is an unusual man."

"Then I'll talk with Lady Macbeth," Kirk said. "If you've no objections. May I come in?"

"Why . . . of course." She moved out of the way. Inside, the dressing room was a clutter of theatrical trunks, all packed and ready to be moved. "I'm sorry I have nothing to offer you."

Kirk stared directly at her, smiling. "You're being unnecessarily modest."

She smiled back. "As you see, everything is packed. Next we play two performances on Benecia, if the *Astral Queen* can get us there; we leave tonight."

"She's a good ship," Kirk said. "Do you enjoy your work?"

"Mostly. But, to play the classics, in these times, when most people prefer absurd three-V serials . . . it isn't always as rewarding as it could be."

"But you continue," Kirk said.

"Oh yes," she said, with what seemed to be a trace of bitterness. "My father feels that we owe it to the public. Not that the public cares."

"They cared tonight. You were very convincing as Lady Macbeth."

"Thank you. And as Lenore Karidian?"

"I'm impressed." He paused an instant. "I think I'd like to see you again."

"Professionally?"

"Not necessarily."

"I . . . think I'd like that. Unfortunately, we must keep to our schedule."

"Schedules aren't always as rigid as they seem," Kirk said. "Shall we see what happens?"

"Very well. And hope for the best."

The response was promising, if ambiguous, but Kirk had no chance to explore it further. Suddenly his communicator was beeping insistently.

"Excuse me," he said. "That's my ship calling . . . Kirk here."

"Spock calling, Captain. Something I felt you should know immediately. Dr. Leighton is dead."

"Dead? Are you sure?"

"Absolutely," Spock's voice said. "We just had word from Q Central. He was murdered—stabbed to death."

Slowly, Kirk put the device back in his hip pocket. Lenore was watching him. Her face showed nothing but grave sympathy.

"I'll have to go," he said. "Perhaps you'll hear from me later."

"I quite understand. I hope so."

Kirk went directly to the Leightons' apartment. The body was still there, unattended except by Martha, but it told him nothing; he was not an expert in such matters. He took Martha's hand gently.

"He really died the first day those players arrived," she said, very quietly. "Memory killed him. Jim . . . do you suppose survivors ever really recover from a tragedy?"

"I'm deeply sorry, Martha."

"He was convinced the moment we saw that man arrive," she said. "Twenty years since the terror, but he was sure Karidian was the man. Is that possible, Jim? Is he Kodos, after all?"

"I don't know. But I'm trying to find out."

"Twenty years and he still had nightmares. I'd wake him and he'd tell me he still heard the screams of the innocent—the silence of the executed. They never told him what happened to the rest of his family."

"I'm afraid there's not much doubt about that," Kirk said.

"It's the not knowing, Jim—whether the people you love are dead or alive. When you know, you mourn, but the wound heals and you go on. When you don't—every dawn is a funeral. That's what killed my husband, Jim, not the knife . . . . But with him, I know."

She managed a small smile and Kirk squeezed her hand convulsively. "It's all right," she said, as if she were the one who had to do the comforting. "At least he has peace now. He never really had it before. I suppose we'll never know who killed him."

"I," Kirk said, "am damn well going to find out."

"It doesn't matter. I've had enough of all this passion for vengeance. It's time to let it all rest. More than time."

Suddenly the tears welled up. "But I shan't forget him. Never."

Kirk stomped aboard ship in so obvious a white fury that nobody dared even to speak to him. Going directly to his quarters, he barked into the intercom: "Uhura!"

"Yes, Captain," the Communications Officer responded, her normally firm voice softened almost to a squeak.

"Put me through to Captain Daly, the *Astral Queen,* on orbit station. And put it on scramble."

"Yes, *sir* . . . He's on, sir."

"John, this is Jim Kirk. Can you do me a little favor?"

"I owe you a dozen," Daly's voice said. "And two dozen drinks, too. Name your poison."

"Thanks. I want you to pass up your pickup here."

"You mean strand all them actors?"

"Just that," Kirk said. "I'll take them on. And if there's any trouble, the responsibility is mine."

"Will do."

"I appreciate it. I'll explain later—I hope. Over and out . . . Lieutenant Uhura, now I want the library computer."

"Library."

"Reference the Kodos file. I'm told there were eight or nine survivors of the massacre who were actual eyewitnesses. I want their names and status."

"Working . . . In order of age: Leighton, T., deceased. Molson, E., deceased—"

"Wait a minute, I want survivors."

"These were survivors of the massacre," the computer said primly. "The deceased are all recent murder victims, all cases open. Instructions."

Kirk swallowed. "Continue."

"Kirk, J., Captain, S.S. *Enterprise.* Wiegand, R., deceased. Eames, S., deceased. Daiken, R. Communications, S.S. *Enterprise*—"

"What!"

"Daiken, R., Communications, *Enterprise,* five years old at time of Kodos incident."

"All right, cut," Kirk said. "Uhura, get me Mr. Spock . . . Mr. Spock, arrange for a pickup for the Karidian troupe, to be recorded in the log as stranded, for transfer to their destination; company to present special performance for officers and crew. Next destination to be Eta Benecia; give me arrival time as soon as it's processed."

"Aye, aye, sir. What about the synthetic food samples we were supposed to pick up from Dr. Leighton?"

"There aren't any, Mr. Spock," Kirk said shortly.

"That fact will have to be noted, too. Diverting a starship—"

"Is a serious business. Well, a black mark against Dr. Leighton isn't going to hurt him now. One more thing, Mr. Spock. I want the privacy of the Karidian company totally respected. They can have the freedom of the ship within the limits of regulations, but their quarters are off limits. Pass it on to all hands."

"Yes, sir." There was no emotion in Spock's voice; but then, there never was.

"Finally, Mr. Spock, reference Lt. Robert Daiken, in Communications. Please have him transferred to Engineering."

"Sir," Spock said, "he came up from Engineering."

"I'm aware of that. I'm sending him back. He needs more experience."

"Sir, may I suggest a further explanation? He's bound to consider this transfer a disciplinary action."

"I can't help that," Kirk said curtly. "Execute. And notify me when the Karidians come aboard."

He paused and looked up at the ceiling, at last unable to resist a rather grim smile. "I think," he said, "I shall be taking the young lady on a guided tour of the ship."

There was quite a long silence. Then Spock said neutrally:

"As you wish, sir."

At this hour, the engine room was empty, and silent except for the low throbbing of the great thrust units; the *Enterprise* was driving. Lenore looked around, and then smiled at Kirk.

"Did you order the soft lights especially for the occasion?" she said.

"I'd like to be able to say yes," Kirk said. "However, we try to duplicate conditions of night and day as much as possible. Human beings have a built-in diurnal rhythm; we try to adjust to it." He gestured at the hulking drivers. "You find this interesting?"

"Oh yes . . . All that power, and all under such complete control. Are you like that, Captain?"

"I hope I'm more of a man than a machine," he said.

"An intriguing combination of both. The power's at your command; but the decisions—"

"—come from a very human source."

"Are you sure?" she said. "Exceptional, yes; but human?"

Kirk said softly, "You can count on it."

There was a sound of footsteps behind them. Kirk turned reluctantly. It was Yeoman Rand, looking in this light peculiarly soft and blonde despite her uniform—and despite a rather severe expression. She held out an envelope.

"Excuse me, sir," she said. "Mr. Spock thought you ought to have this at once."

"Quite so. Thank you." Kirk pocketed the envelope. "That will be all."

"Very good, sir." The girl left without batting an eyelash. Lenore watched her go, seemingly somewhat amused.

"A lovely girl," she said.

"And very efficient."

"Now *there's* a subject, Captain. Tell me about the women in your world. Has the machine changed them? Made them, well, just people, instead of women?"

"Not at all," Kirk said. "On this ship they have the same duties and functions as the men. They compete equally, and get no special privileges. But they're still women."

"I can see that. Especially the one who just left. So pretty. I'm afraid she didn't like me."

"Nonsense," Kirk said, rather more bluffly than he had intended. "You're imagining things. Yeoman Rand is all business."

Lenore looked down. "You are human, after all. Captain of a starship, and yet you know so little about women. Still I can hardly blame her."

"Human nature hasn't changed," Kirk said. "Grown, perhaps, expanded . . . but not changed."

"That's a comfort. To know that people can still feel, build a private dream, fall in love . . . all that, and power too! Like Caesar—and Cleopatra."

She was moving steadily closer, by very small degrees. Kirk waited a moment, and then took her in his arms.

The kiss was warm and lingering. She was the first to draw out of it, looking up into his eyes, her expression half sultry, half mocking.

"I had to know," she whispered against the power hum. "I never kissed a Caesar before."

"A rehearsal, Miss Karidian?"

"A performance, Captain."

They kissed again, hard. Something crackled against Kirk's breast. After what seemed to be all too short a while, he took her by the shoulders and pushed her gently away—not very far.

"Don't stop."

"I'm not stopping, Lenore. But I'd better see what it was that Spock thought was so important. He had orders not to know where I was."

"I see," she said, her voice taking on a slight edge. "Starship captains tell *before* they kiss. Well, go ahead and look at your note."

Kirk pulled out the envelope and ripped it open. The message was brief, pointed, very Spock-like. It said:

SHIP'S OFFICER DAIKEN POISONED, CONDITION SERIOUS. DR. McCOY ANALYZING FOR CAUSE AND ANTIDOTE, RE-QUESTS YOUR PRESENCE.

                                                     SPOCK

Lenore watched his face change. At last she said, "I see I've lost you. I hope not permanently."

"No, hardly permanently," Kirk said, trying to smile and failing. "But I should have looked at this sooner. Excuse me, please; and goodnight, Lady Macbeth."

Spock and McCoy were in the sick bay when Kirk arrived. Daiken was on the table, leads running from his still, sweating form to the body function panel, which seemed to be quietly going crazy. Kirk flashed a glance over the panel, but it meant very little to him. He said: "Will he make it? What happened?"

"Somebody put tetralubisol in his milk," McCoy said. "A clumsy job; the stuff is poisonous, but almost insoluble, so it was easy to pump out. He's sick, but he has a good chance. More than I can say for you, Jim."

Kirk looked sharply at the surgeon, and then at Spock. They were both watching him like cats.

"Very well," he said. "I can see that I'm on the spot. Mr. Spock, why don't you begin the lecture?"

"Daiken was the next to last witness of the Kodos affair," Spock said evenly. "You are the last. Dr. McCoy and I checked the library, just as you did, and got the same information. We suppose you are courting Miss Karidian for more information—but the next attempt will be on you. Clearly, you and Daiken are the only survivors because you are both aboard the *Enterprise;* but if Dr. Leighton was right, you no longer have that immunity, and the attempt on Daiken tends to confirm that. In short, you're inviting death."

"I've done that before," Kirk said tiredly. "If Karidian is Kodos, I mean to nail him down, that's all. Administering justice is part of my job."

"Are you certain that's all?" McCoy said.

"No, Bones, I'm not at all certain. Remember that I was there on Tarsus—a midshipman, caught up in a revolution. I saw women and children forced into a chamber with no exit . . . and a half-mad self-appointed messiah named Kodos throw a switch. And then there wasn't anyone inside any more. Four thousand people, dead, vanished—and I had to stand by, just waiting for my own turn . . . I can't forget it, any more than Leighton could. I thought I had, but I was wrong."

"And what if you decide Karidian is Kodos?" McCoy demanded. "What then? Do you carry his head through the corridors in triumph? That won't bring back the dead."

"Of course it won't," Kirk said. "But they may rest easier."

"Vengeance is mine, saith the Lord," Spock said, almost in a whisper. Both men turned to look at him in astonishment.

At last Kirk said, "That's true, Mr. Spock, whatever it may mean to an outworlder like you. Vengeance is not what I'm after. I am after justice—and prevention. Kodos killed four thousand; if he is still at large, he may massacre again. But consider this, too: Karidian is a human being, with rights like all of us. He deserves the same justice. If it's at all possible, he also deserves to be cleared."

"I don't know who's worse," McCoy said, looking from Spock to Kirk, "the human calculator or the captain-cum-mystic. Both of you go the hell away and leave me with my patient."

"Gladly," Kirk said. "I'm going to talk to Karidian, and never mind his rule against personal interviews. He can try to kill me if he likes, but he'll have to lay off my officers."

"In short," Spock said, "you *do* think Karidian is Kodos."

Kirk threw up his hands. "Of course I do, Mr. Spock," he said. "Would I be making such an idiot of myself if I didn't? But I am going to make sure. That's the only definition of justice that I know."

"I," Spock said, "would have called it logic."

Karidian and his daughter were not only awake when they answered Kirk's knock, but already half in costume for the next night's command performance which was part of the official excuse for their being on board the *Enterprise* at all. Karidian was wearing a dressing-gown which might have been the robe of Hamlet, the ghost, or the murderer king; whichever it was, he looked kingly, an impression which he promptly reinforced by crossing to a tall-backed chair and sitting down in it as if it were a throne. In his lap he held a much-worn prompter's copy of the play, with his name scrawled across it by a felt pen.

Lenore was easier to tape: she was the mad Ophelia . . . or else, simply a nineteen-year-old girl in a nightgown. Karidian waved her into the background. She withdrew, her expression guarded, but remained standing by the cabin door.

Karidian turned steady, luminous eyes on Kirk. He said, "What is it you want, Captain?"

"I want a straight answer to a straight question," Kirk said. "And I promise you this: You won't be harmed aboard this ship, and you'll be dealt with fairly when you leave it."

Karidian only nodded, as if he had expected nothing else. He was certainly intimidating. Finally Kirk said:

"I suspect you, Mr. Karidian. You know that. I believe the greatest performance of your life is the part you're acting out offstage."

Karidian smiled, a little sourly. "Each man in his time plays many parts."

"I'm concerned with only one. Tell me this: Are you Kodos the Executioner?"

Karidian looked toward his daughter, but he did not really seem to see her; his eyes were open, but shuttered, like a cat's.

"That was a long time ago," he said. "Back then I was a young character actor, touring the Earth colonies . . . As you see, I'm still doing it."

"That's not an answer," Kirk said.

"What did you expect? Were I Kodos, I would have the blood of thousands on my hands. Should I confess to a stranger, after twenty years of fleeing much more organized justice? Whatever Kodos was in those days, I have never heard it said that he was a fool."

"I have done you a favor," Kirk said. "And I have promised to treat you fairly. That's not an ordinary promise. I am the captain of this ship, and whatever justice there is aboard it is in my hands."

"I see you differently. You stand before me as the perfect symbol of our technological society: mechanized, electronicized, uniformed . . . and not precisely human. I hate machinery, Captain. It has done away with humanity—the striving of men to achieve greatness through their own resources. That's why I am a live actor, still, instead of a shadow on a three-V film."

"The lever is a tool," Kirk said. "We have new tools, but great men still strive, and don't feel outclassed. Wicked men use the tools to murder, like Kodos; but that doesn't make the tools wicked. Guns don't shoot people. Only men do."

"Kodos," Karidian said, "whoever he was, made decisions of life and death. Some had to die that others could live. That is the lot of kings, and the cross of kings. And probably of commanders, too—otherwise why should you be here now?"

"I don't remember ever having killed four thousand innocent people."

"I don't remember it either. But I do remember that another four thousand were saved because of it. Were I to direct a play about Kodos, that is the first thing I would bear in mind."

"It wasn't a play," Kirk said. "I was there. I saw it happen. And since then, all the surviving witnesses have been systematically murdered, except two . . . or possibly, three. One of my officers has been poisoned. I may be next. And here you are, a man of whom we have no record until some nine years ago—and positively identified, positively, no matter how mistakenly, by the late Dr. Leighton. Do you think I can ignore all that?"

"No, certainly not," Karidian said. "But that is your role. I have mine. I have played many." He looked down at his worn hands. "Sooner or later, the blood thins, the body ages, and finally one is grateful for a failing memory. I no longer treasure life—not even my own. Death for me will be a release from ritual. I am old and tired, and the past is blank."

"And that's your only answer?"

"I'm afraid so, Captain. Did you ever get everything you wanted? No, nobody does. And if you did, you might be sorry."

Kirk shrugged and turned away. He found Lenore staring at him, but there was nothing he could do for her, either. He went out.

She followed him. In the corridor on the other side of the door, she said in a cold whisper: "You are a machine. And with a big bloody stain of cruelty on your metal hide. You could have spared him."

"If he's Kodos," Kirk said, equally quietly, "then I've already shown him more mercy than he deserves. If he isn't, then we'll put you ashore at Eta Benecia, with no harm done."

"Who are you," Lenore said in a dangerous voice, "to say what harm is done?"

"Who do I have to be?"

She seemed to be about to answer; cold fire raged in her eyes. But at the same moment, the door slid open behind her and Karidian stood there, no longer so tall or so impressive as he had been before. Tears began to run down over her cheeks; she reached for his shoulders, her head drooping.

"Father . . . father . . ."

"Never mind," Karidian said gently, regaining a little of his stature. "It's already all over. I am thy father's spirit, doomed for a certain time to walk the night—"

"Hush!"

Feeling like six different varieties of monster, Kirk left them alone together.

For the performance, the briefing room had been redressed into a small theater, and cameras were spotted here and there so that the play could be seen on intercom screens elsewhere in the ship for the part of the crew that had to remain on duty. The lights were already down. Kirk was late, as usual; he was just settling into his seat—as captain he was entitled to a front row chair and had had no hesitation about claiming it—when the curtains parted and Lenore came through them, in the flowing costume of Ophelia, white with make-up.

She said in a clear, almost gay voice: "Tonight the Karidian Players present *Hamlet*—another in a series of living plays in space—dedicated to the tradition of the classic theater, which we believe will never die. *Hamlet* is a violent play about a violent time, when life was cheap and ambition was God. It is also a timeless play, about personal guilt, doubt, indecision, and the thin line between Justice and Vengeance."

She vanished, leaving Kirk brooding. Nobody needed to be introduced to *Hamlet;* that speech had been aimed directly at him. He did not need the reminder, either, but he had got it nonetheless.

The curtains parted and the great, chilling opening began. Kirk lost most of it, since McCoy chose that moment to arrive and seat himself next to Kirk with a great bustle.

"Here we are, here we are," McCoy muttered. "In the long history of medicine no doctor has ever caught the curtain of a play."

"Shut up," Kirk said, *sotto voce.* "You had plenty of notice."

"Yes, but nobody told me I'd lose a patient at the last minute."

"Somebody dead?"

"No, no. Lieutenant Daiken absconded out of sick bay, that's all. I suppose he wanted to see the play too."

"It's being piped into sick bay!"

"I know that. Pipe down, will you? How can I hear if you keep mumbling?"

Swearing silently, Kirk got up and went out. Once he was in the corridor, he went to the nearest open line and ordered a search; but it turned out that McCoy already had one going.

Routine, Kirk decided, was not enough. Daiken's entire family had been destroyed on Tarsus . . . and somebody had tried to kill him. This was no time to take even the slightest chance; with the play going on, not only Karidian, but the whole ship was vulnerable to any access of passion . . . or vengeance.

"Red security alert," Kirk said. "Search every inch, including cargo."

Getting confirmation, he went back into the converted briefing room. He was still not satisfied, but there was nothing more he could do now.

His ears were struck by a drum beat. The stage was dim, lit only by a wash of red, and the characters playing Marcellus and Horatio were just going off. Evidently the play had already reached Act One, Scene 5. The figure of the ghost materialized in the red beam and raised its arm, beckoning to Hamlet, but Hamlet refused to follow. The ghost—Karidian—beckoned again, and the drum beat heightened in intensity.

Kirk could think of nothing but that Karidian was now an open target. He circled the rapt audience quickly and silently, making for the rear of the stage.

"Speak," Hamlet said. "I'll go no further."

"Mark me," said Karidian hollowly.

"I will."

"My hour is almost come, when I to sulphurous and tormenting flames must render up myself—"

There was Daiken, crouching in the wings. He was already leveling a phaser at Karidian.

"—and you must seek revenge—"

"Daiken!" Kirk said. There was no help for it; he had to call across the stage. The dialogues intercut.

"I am thy father's spirit, doomed for a certain term to walk the night—"

"He murdered my father," Daiken said. "And my mother."

"—And for the day confined to fast in fires, Till the foul crimes done in my days—"

"Get back to sick bay!"

"I know. I saw. He murdered them."

"—are burnt and purged away."

The audience had begun to murmur; they could hear every word. So could Karidian. He looked off toward Daiken, but the light was too bad for him to see anything. In a shaken voice, he tried to go on.

"I . . . I could a tale unfold whose lightest word—"

"You could be wrong. Don't throw your life away on a mistake."

"—would t-tear up thy soul, freeze thy young blood—"

"Daiken, give me that weapon."

"No."

Several people in the audience were standing now, and Kirk could see a few security guards moving cautiously down the sidelines. They would be too late; Daiken had a dead bead on Karidian.

Then the scenery at the back tore, and Lenore came out. Her eyes were bright and feverish, and in her hand she carried an absurdly long dagger.

"It's over!" she said in a great, theatrical voice. "Never mind, father, I'm strong! Come, ye spirits of the air, unsex me now! Hie thee hither, that in the porches of thine ear—"

"Child, child!"

She could not hear him. She was the mad Ophelia; but the lines were Lady MacBeth's.

"All the ghosts are dead. Who would have thought they had so much blood in 'em? I've freed you, father. I've taken the blood away from you. Had he not so much resembled my father as he slept, I'd have done it—"

"No!" Karidian said, his voice choked with horror. "You've left me nothing! You were untouched by what I did, you weren't even born! I wanted to leave you something clean—"

"Balsam! I've given you everything! You're safe, no one can touch you! See Banquo there, the Caesar, even he can't touch you! This castle hath a pleasant seat."

Kirk went out onto the stage, watching the security guards out of the corner of his eyes. Daiken seemed to be frozen by the action under the lights, but his gun still had not wavered.

"That's enough," Kirk said. "Come with me, both of you."

Karidian turned to him, spreading his hands wide. "Captain," he said. "Try to understand. I was a soldier in a great cause. There were things that had to be done—hard things, terrible things. You know the price of that; you too are a captain."

"Stop it, father," Lenore said, in a spuriously rational voice. "There is nothing to explain."

"There is. Murder. Flight. Suicide. Madness. And still the price is not enough; my daughter has killed too."

"For you! For you! I saved you!"

"For the price of seven innocent men," Kirk said.

"Innocent?" Lenore gave a great theatrical laugh, like a coloratura playing Medea. "Innocent! They saw! They were guilty!"

"That's enough, Lenore," Kirk said. "The play is over. It was over twenty years ago. Are you coming with me, or do I have to drag you?"

"Better go," Daiken's voice said from the wings. He stood up and came forward into the light, the gun still leveled. "I wasn't going to be so merciful, but we've had enough madness. Thanks, Captain."

Lenore spun on him. With a movement like a flash of lightning, she snatched the gun away from him.

"Stand back!" she screamed. "Stand back, everyone! The play goes on!"

"No!" Karidian cried out hoarsely. "In the name of God, child—"

"Captain Caesar! You could have had Egypt! Beware the Ides of March!"

She pointed the gun at Kirk and pulled the trigger. But fast as she was in her madness, Karidian was even quicker. The beam struck him squarely on the chest. He fell silently.

Lenore wailed like a lost kitten and dropped to her knees beside him. The security guards stampeded onto the stage, but Kirk waved them back.

"Father!" Lenore crooned. "Father! Oh proud death, what feast is toward in thine eternal cell, that thou such a prince at a shot so bloodily has struck!" She began to laugh again. "The cue, father, the cue! No time to sleep! The play! The play's the thing, wherein we'll catch the conscience of the king . . ."

Gentle hands drew her away. In Kirk's ear, McCoy's voice said: "And in the long run, she didn't even get the lines right."

"Take care of her," Kirk said tonelessly. "Kodos is dead . . . but I think she may walk in her sleep."

Book II
Star Trek 4

ALL OUR YESTERDAYS

(Jean Lisette Aroeste)

The star Beta Niobe, the computer reported, was going to go nova in approximately three and a half hours from now. Its only satellite, Sarpeidon, was a Class M world which at last report had been inhabited by a humanoid species, civilized, but incapable of space flight. Nevertheless, the sensors of the *Enterprise* showed that no intelligent life remained on the planet.

But they did show that a large power generator was still functioning down there. That meant, possibly, that there were still some few survivors after all, in which case they had to be located and taken off before the planet was destroyed.

Homing the Transporter on the power signal, Kirk, Spock and McCoy materialized in the center of a fairly large room, subdivided by shelving and storage cabinets into several areas. One alcove contained a consultation desk, with shelves of books behind it. Another held several elaborate machines which were obviously in operation, humming and spinning and blinking. Kirk stared at these with bafflement, and then turned to Spock, who scanned them with his tricorder and raised his hands in a slight gesture.

"The power pulse source, obviously," the First Officer said. "But what it all *does* is another question."

Along one side was a less puzzling installation: an audiovisual facility containing several carrels (individual study desks) with headsets, projectors and small screens. The nearby wall was pierced by a door and a window. A tape storage area at the end of the room had been caged in, but its door stood ajar.

"May I help you?"

The three officers spun around. Facing them was a dignified, almost imposing man of early middle age. "I am the librarian," he added cordially.

Spock said, "Perhaps you can, Mr. . . . ?"

"Mr. Atoz. I confess that I am a little surprised to see you; I had thought that everyone had long since gone. But the surprise is a pleasant one. After all, a library serves no purpose unless someone is using it."

"You say that everyone has gone," Kirk said. "Where?"

"It depended upon the individual, of course. If you wish to trace a specific person, I'm sorry, but that information is confidential."

"No, no particular person," McCoy said. "Just—in general—where did they go?"

"Ah, you find it difficult to choose, is that it? Yes, a wide range of alternatives is a mixed blessing, but perhaps I can help. Would you come this way, please?" With a little bow, Atoz invited them to precede him to the audiovisual area. Apparently, Kirk thought, Atoz thought the three officers were natives, and that they wanted to go where the others had gone. Well, what better way to find out?

It was impossible not to be surprised, however, when Atoz, whom he would have sworn had been behind them, emerged smiling from the tape storage cage.

"How the devil did he get over there?" McCoy said in a penetrating stage whisper.

"Each viewing station in this facility is independently operated," Atoz said, as if that explained everything. "You may select from more than twenty thousand Verisim tapes, several hundred of which have only recently been added to the collection. I'm sure that you will find something here that pleases you." He turned toward Kirk. "You, sir, what is your particular field of interest?"

"How about recent history?" Kirk suggested.

"Really? That is too bad. We have so little on recent history; there was no demand for it."

"It doesn't have to be extensive," Kirk said. "Just the answers to a few questions."

"Ah, of course. In that case, Reference Service is available in the second alcove to your right."

It was not quite so surprising, this time, to find the incredible Mr. Atoz already waiting for them at the reference desk. But there was something else: Kirk had the instant impression that Atoz had somehow never seen them before; a guess which was promptly confirmed by the man's first words.

"You're very late," he said angrily. "Where have you been?"

"We came as soon as we knew what was happening."

"It is my fault, sir," Spock said. "I must have miscalculated. Remember, the ship's sensors indicated there was no one here at all."

"In a very few hours, you would have been absolutely correct," Atoz said. "You three would have perished—vaporized. You arrived just in time."

"Then you know what's going to happen?" McCoy queried.

"You idiot! Of course I know. Everyone was warned of the coming nova long ago. They followed instructions and are now safe. And you had better do the same."

"Did you say they were *safe?*" asked Kirk.

"Absolutely," Atoz said with pride. "Every single one."

"Safe where? Where did they go?"

"Wherever they wanted to go, of course. It is strictly up to the individual's choice."

"And did you alone send all the people of this planet to safety?"

"Yes," Atoz said. "I am proud to say I did. Of course, I had to delegate the simple tasks to my replicas; but the responsibility was mine alone."

"I believe we've met two of them," Kirk said, a little grimly. "You're the real thing, I take it."

"Of course."

McCoy was already scanning Atoz with his tricorder. "As a matter of fact, he is quite real, Jim. And that may explain the report of the ship's sensors; just one remaining man is a difficult object for detection. Sir, are you aware that you will die if you remain here?"

"Of course, but I plan to join my wife and family when the time comes. Do not be concerned about me. Think of yourselves."

Kirk sighed. The man was single-minded almost to the point of mania. But then, that was just the kind of man who'd be given a job like this. Or the kind of man such a job would soon make him. "All right," he said resignedly. "How? What shall we do?"

"The history of the planet is available in every detail," Atoz said, rising and leading them toward the tape carrels. "Just choose what interests you the most—the century, the date, the moment. But, remember, you are very late."

Kirk and McCoy donned headsets, and Atoz selected tapes from the shelves, inserting one in each viewer.

"Thank you, sir," Kirk said. "We will be as quick as we can." He offered a headset to Spock, but the First Officer shook his head and walked off toward the big machine that had mystified him earlier, and which Atoz now appeared to be activating. At the same time, Kirk's screen lighted and he found himself looking at an empty street—it was little more than an alley—which on Earth he would have guessed to be seventeenth-century English. A quick glance to his left revealed that McCoy's screen showed something even less interesting: an Arctic waste. Atoz certainly had peculiar ideas of . . .

A woman screamed, piercingly.

Kirk jumped to his feet, tearing off the headset. The scream came again—not from the headset, obviously, but from the entrance to the observatory-library.

"Help! They're murdering me!"

"Spock! Bones!" Kirk shouted, charging for the door. "Over here, quick!"

Behind him, Atoz' voice cried out: "Stop! I have not prepared you! Wait, you must be . . ."

As Kirk shot out the door, the voice was cut off as if someone had thrown a switch . . .

. . . and he skidded to a halt in the alley he had seen on the screen!

There was no time for puzzlement. The alley was chill and misty, but real enough and the screams came from around the next corner, followed this time by a man's voice.

"Be sweet, love, and I might have a mind to be generous."

Kirk rounded the corner cautiously. A young man wearing velvet, lace and a sword was struggling with a woman dressed like a gypsy. She seemed to be giving him little trouble; though she was kicking and scratching, his handling was as much amorous as it was brutal. A second, even more foppish young man was lounging against the nearby wall, watching with amusement. Then the woman managed to bite the first one on the hand.

"Ow! Vixen!" He aimed a savage cuff at her cheek. The blow never fell; Kirk's hand closed around his upraised arm.

"Let her go," Kirk said.

The woman wiggled free, and the fop's face hardened. "Come when you are bidden, slave," he said, and aimed a roundhouse blow at Kirk's head. Kirk checked the swing and followed through, and a moment later his opponent was sprawling in the dirt.

The second fop shoved the woman aside and moved threateningly toward Kirk, his hand hovering over his rapier hilt. "You need a lesson in how to use your betters," he said. "Who's your master, fellow?"

"I am a freeman."

This seemed to put the fop almost into good humor again. He smiled nastily and drew his rapier.

"Freedom dresses you in poor livery, like a mountebank—and you want better manners, too, freeman." The rapier point slashed Kirk's sleeve.

"The other's behind you, friend!" the woman's voice called, but too late; Kirk was seized from behind. He elbowed his captor in the midriff and, when he broke away, he had the man's sword in his left hand. These creatures really seemed to know nothing at all about unarmed combat, but it would be as well to put an end to this right now. He drew his phaser and fired point-blank.

It didn't go off.

Dropping it, Kirk shifted sword hands and closed on the second fop. He was only fair as a swordsman, too; his lunges were clumsy enough to allow Kirk plenty of freedom to keep the weaponless first fop on the ropes with left-handed karate chops. The swordsman's eyes bulged when his companion went down for the third time and began to back away.

"Sladykins! He's a devil! I'll have no more of this."

He disengaged and ran, his friend not far behind. Kirk picked up and holstered the ineffective phaser and turned to the woman, who was patting her hair and checking her clothes for damage. The clothes were none too clean, and neither was she, although she was pretty enough.

"Thankee, man," she said. "I thought to be limbered sure when the gull caught me drawing his boung."

"I don't follow you. Are you all right?"

The woman looked him over calculatingly. "Ah, I took you for an angler, but you're none of us. Well, you're a bully fine cope for all that. What a handsome dish you served them, the coxcombs!"

She seemed to be becoming more incomprehensible by the minute. "I'm afraid you may be hurt," Kirk said. "You'd better come back into the library with me. You'll be safe there, and Dr. McCoy can see to those bruises."

"I'm game, luv. Lead and I'll follow. Where's library?"

"Just back there . . ."

But when they got to the alley wall, it was blank. The door through which Kirk had come had vanished.

He prowled back and forth, then turned to the woman, who said, puzzled, "What's wi' you, man? Let's make off before coxcombs come wi' shoulder-clappers."

"Do you happen to remember when you first saw me? Do you remember whether I came through some kind of door?"

"I think that rum gull knocked you in the head. Come, luv. I know a leech who'll ask no questions."

"Wait. It must be here somewhere. Bones! Spock!"

"Here, Captain," the First Officer's voice said at once, to the woman's obvious alarm. "We hear you, but we cannot see you. Are you all right?"

"We followed you," McCoy's voice added, "but you'd disappeared."

"We must have missed each other in the fog."

"Fog, Captain?" Spock's voice said. "We have encountered no fog."

"Mercy on us," said the woman. "It's a spirit!"

"No, don't be frightened," Kirk said hastily. "These are friends of mine. They're—on the other side of the wall. Spock! Are you still in the library?"

"Indeed not," Spock's voice said. "We are in a wilderness of arctic characteristics . . ."

"He means that it's cold," McCoy's voice broke in drily.

"Approximately minus twenty-five centigrade. There is no library that we can see. We are at the foot of an ice cliff, and apparently we came *through* the cliff, since there is no visible aperture."

"There's no sign of a door here either," Kirk said. "Only the wall. It's foggy here, and I can smell the ocean."

"Yes. That is the period you were looking at in the viewer. Dr. McCoy, on the other hand, was watching a tape of Sarpeidon's last ice age—and here he is, and I with him because we left the library at the same instant."

"Which explains the disappearance of the inhabitants," Kirk concluded. "We certainly underestimated Mr. Atoz."

The woman, clearly terrified by the disembodied voices, was edging away from him. Well, that wasn't important now.

"Yes," Spock was saying. "Apparently they have all escaped from the destruction of their world by retreating into the past."

"Well, we know how we got here. Can we get back? The portal's invisible, but we can still hear each other. There must be a portion of this wall that only *looks* solid . . ."

He was interrupted by still another scream from the woman, with whom he was beginning to feel definitely annoyed. He turned to find that her attempt to run out of the alley had been blocked by the two fops, who had returned with a pair of obvious constables.

"My friends are back—a couple of, uh, coxcombs I had a run-in with a little earlier. And they've brought reinforcements."

"Keep looking, Jim," McCoy's voice urged. "You *must* be close to the portal. We're looking too."

"There's the mort's accomplice," one of the fops said, pointing at Kirk. "Arrest him."

"We are the law," one of the constables told Kirk, "and do require that you yield to us."

"On what charge?"

"Thievery and purse-cutting."

"Nonsense. I'm no thief."

"Jim," McCoy's voice said. "What's happening?"

"Lord help us, what's that?" exclaimed the other constable.

"It's spirits!" the woman cried.

The second constable crossed his sword and dagger and held them before him gingerly. He looked frightened, but he resumed advancing. "Depart, spirits, and let honest men approach."

Kirk seized his advantage. "Keep talking, Bones," he said, edging away.

"They speak at *his* bidding," one of the fops said excitedly. "Stop his mouth and they'll quiet!"

"You must be close to the portal now," Spock's voice said.

"Just keep talk . . ."

But the other constable had crept around to the other side. A heavy blow exploded against Kirk's head, and that was the end of that.

The landscape was barren, consisting entirely of ice and rocks, over which the wind howled mercilessly. The ruined buildings surrounding the library had vanished, and so had the library itself. There was nothing but the ice cliff and, on the other side, the rocky glacial plain stretching endlessly into the distance.

Spock continued to feel carefully along the cliff, trying not to maintain contact for more than a few seconds each time. Beside him, McCoy shivered and blew on his hands, then chafed his ears and face.

"Jim's gone!" the surgeon said. "Why can't we hear him?"

"I am afraid that Mr. Atoz may have closed the portal; I doubt that I shall find it now, in any event. We had best move along."

"Jim sounded as if he might be in trouble."

"He doubtless was in trouble, but so are we. We must find shelter, or we will very quickly perish in this cold."

McCoy stumbled. Spock caught him and helped him to a seat on a large boulder, noting that his chin, nose and ears had become whitened and bloodless. The First Officer knew well enough what that meant. He also knew, geologically, where they were; in a terminal moraine, the rock-tumble pushed ahead of itself by an advancing glacier. The chances of finding shelter here were nil. It seemed a curious sort of refuge for a time-traveling people to pick, with so many milder environments available at will.

"Spock," McCoy said. "Leave me here."

"We go together or not at all."

"Don't be a fool. My face and hands are getting frost-bitten. I can hardly feel my feet. Alone, you'll have a chance—at least to try to get back to Jim!"

"We stay together," Spock said.

"Stubborn, thickheaded . . ."

His voice faded. Spock looked about grimly. To his astonishment, he saw that they were being watched.

In the near distance was a cryptic figure clad in fur coveralls and a parka, its face concealed by a snow mask out of which two eyes stared intently. After a moment the figure beckoned, unmistakably.

Spock turned to McCoy, to find that he had fallen. He shook the medical officer, but there was no response. Spock put his ear to McCoy's chest; yes, heart still beating, but feebly.

A shadow fell across them both. The figure was standing over them; and again it gestured, *Follow me.*

"My companion is ill."

Follow me.

Logic dictated no better course. Slinging McCoy over his shoulder, Spock stood. The weight was not intolerable, though it threw him out of balance. The figure moved off among the rocks. Spock followed.

The way eventually took them underground, as Spock had already deduced that it would; where else, after all, could there be shelter in this wilderness? There were two rooms—caves, really—and one was a sleeping room, fairly small, windowless of necessity, furnished most simply. Near the door was a rude bed on which Spock placed McCoy.

"Blankets," Spock said.

The figure pointed, then helped him cover the sick man. Spock looked through McCoy's medical pouch, found his tricorder, and began checking. The figure sat at the foot of the bed, watching Spock, still silent, utterly enigmatic.

"He cannot stand your weather. Unfortunately, he is the physician, not I. I'll not risk giving him medication at this point. If he is kept quiet and warm, he may recover naturally." He scrutinized the mysterious watcher. "It is quite agreeably warm in here. Have you a reason for continuing to wear that mask? Is there a taboo that prohibits my seeing your face?"

From behind the mask there came a musical feminine laugh, and then a feminine voice. "I had forgotten I still had these things on."

She took off the mask and parka, but her laughter died as she inspected Spock more closely. "Who are you?"

"I am called Spock."

"Even your name is strange. Forgive me—you are so unlike anyone I have ever seen."

"That is not surprising. Please do not be alarmed."

"Why are you here?" the woman asked hesitantly. "Are you prisoners too?"

"Prisoners?"

"This is one of the places—or rather, times—Zor Khan sends people when he wishes them to disappear. Didn't you come back through the time-portal?"

"Yes, but not as prisoners. We were sent here by mistake; or such is my hypothesis."

She considered this. "The Atavachron is far away," she said at last, "but I think you come from somewhere farther than that."

"That is true," Spock said. He looked at her more closely. This face out of the past, eager yet reposeful, without trace of artifice, was—could it be what Earthmen called *touching?* "Yes—I am not from the world you know at all. My home is a planet many light-years away."

"How wonderful! I've always loved the books about such possibilities." Her expression, though, darkened suddenly. "But they're only stories. This isn't real. I'm imagining all this. I'm going mad. I always thought I would."

As she shrank from him, Spock reached out and took her hand. "I am firmly convinced that I do in fact exist. I am substantial. You are not imagining this."

"I've been alone here for so long, longer than I want to remember," she said, with a weak smile. She was beginning to relax again. "When I saw you out there, I couldn't believe it."

Spock was beginning to feel something very like compassion for her, which was so unusual that it confused him—which was more unusual still. He turned back to McCoy and checked the unconscious man with the tricorder; this added alarm to the complex.

"I was wrong not to give him the coradrenaline," he said, taking the hypo out of the medical pouch and using it.

"What's happening? Is he dying? I have a few medicines . . ."

"Contra-indicated. Your physiology may be radically different. But I may have given him too much. Well, it's done now."

The woman watched him. "You seem so very calm," she said, "but I sense that he is someone close to you."

"We have gotten used to each other over the years. Aha . . ."

McCoy groaned, stirred and his breathing harshened, as though he were fighting for air. Spock leaned over him.

"Dr. Leonard McCoy, wake up," he said formally but urgently. Then, *"Bones!"*

McCoy's breathing quieted gradually and Spock stepped back. The surgeon's eyes opened, and slowly came to focus on the woman.

"Who are you?" he asked fuzzily.

"My name is Zarabeth."

Somehow, Spock had never thought to ask that.

"Where's Spock?"

"I'm here, Doctor."

"Are we back in the library?"

"We are still in the ice age," Spock said. "But safe, for the moment."

McCoy tried to sit up, though it was obvious that he was still groggy. "Jim! Where's Jim? We've got to find Jim!"

"You are in no condition to get up. Rest now, and I will attempt to find the Captain."

McCoy allowed Spock to settle him back in bed. "Find him, Spock. Don't worry about me. Find him!"

He closed his eyes, and after a moment, Spock nodded silently toward the door. Zarabeth led the way back into the underground living room, then asked, "Who is this Jim?"

"Our Commanding Officer. Our friend."

"I saw only the two of you. I did not know that there was another."

"There—is not. He did not come with us. The time-portal sent him to another historical period, much later than this one. If I am to find him, there is only one avenue. Will you show me where the time-portal is?"

"But your friend—in the other room," Zarabeth said. "He is ill."

"It is true that if I leave him, there is the danger that he may never regain the ship." Spock thought it over. It proved to be peculiarly difficult. "He would then be marooned in this time-period. But he is no longer in danger of death, so my primary duty to him has been discharged . . . If I remain here, no one of our party can aid Captain Kirk . . ."

"You make it sound like an equation."

"It should be an equation," Spock said, frowning. "I should be able to resolve the problem logically. My impulse is to try to find the Captain, and yet—" he found that he was pacing, although it didn't seem to help much. "I have already made one error of judgment that nearly cost McCoy's life. I must not make another now. Perhaps it has to do with the Atavachron. If I knew more about how it works . . . Zarabeth, you say that you are a prisoner here. May I ask . . ."

". . . why? My crime was in choosing my kinsmen unwisely. Two of them were involved in a conspiracy to kill Zor Khan. It wasn't enough to execute my kinsmen. Zor Khan determined to destroy our entire family. He used the Atavachron to send us to places where no one could ever find us."

"Ah. Then the solution is simple. Zor Khan exists no more. You and I can carry McCoy back to the library. I'll send you and McCoy to the ship, and have Mr. Atoz send me to wherever Jim . . ."

"No!" Zarabeth cried, in obvious terror. "I can't go back through the portal now! I will be dead!"

"You cannot go back?"

"None of us can go back," she said, a little more calmly. "When we come through the portal, we are changed by the Atavachron. That is its function. Our basic metabolic structure is adjusted to the time we enter. You can't go back; if you pass through the portal again, you will be dead when you reach the other side."

And there it was. He and McCoy were trapped here, for the rest of their lives. And so was Jim, wherever *he* was.

When Kirk came to, he found himself all too obviously in jail, and a pretty primitive jail at that, lying on a rough pallet which squeaked of straw. Fingering his head and wincing, he got up and went to the barred door. There was nothing to be seen but a gloomy corridor and the cell opposite his. The gypsy was in it.

She seemed to be about to speak to him, but at that moment there were voices in the near distance and, instead, she shrank into a far corner of her cell. In another moment the constable hove into view, leading a man whose demeanor was all too obviously that of a public prosecutor.

"That's the man," the constable said, pointing to Kirk. "That's the mort's henchman."

He let the prosecutor into the cell. The man regarded Kirk curiously. "You are the thief who talks to spirits?"

"Your honor. I am a stranger here."

"Where are you from?"

Kirk hesitated. "An island."

"What is this island?"

"We call it Earth."

"I know of no island Earth. No matter. Continue."

"I'd never seen the lady across the way before tonight when I heard her scream. As far as I could tell, she was being attacked."

"Then you deny that you're the wench's accomplice?"

"Yes. I was reading in the library when I heard her scream." The prosecutor started visibly at the word "library," and Kirk pursued the advantage, whatever it might be. "Perhaps you remember where the library is?"

"Well, well, perhaps your part in this is innocent," the prosecutor said, with some agitation. "I believe you to be an honest man."

"He's a witch!" screamed the woman from her cell.

"Now, wait a minute . . ."

"Take care, woman," the prosecutor said heavily. "I am convinced you're guilty. Do not compound it with false accusation."

"He speaks to unclean spirits! He's a witch. Constable, you heard the voices!"

"It's truth, my lord," the constable said. "I heard the spirit call him. He answered and did call it 'Bones.' "

"He's a witch," the woman insisted. "He cast a spell and made me steal against my wish."

Aghast, Kirk looked into each face in turn. There was no doubt about it; they believed in witches, all of them. The prosecutor, looking even graver than before, asked the constable, with some reluctance, "You heard these—spirits?"

"Aye, my lord. I'll witness to it."

"The 'voices' they heard were only friends of mine," Kirk said desperately. "They were still on the other side of the wall, in the library, my lord."

"I know nothing of this," the prosecutor said agitatedly. "*I* cannot judge so grave a matter. Let someone learned in witchcraft examine him. I will have no more to do with this."

"Look, sir. Couldn't you at least arrange for me to see Mr. Atoz? You do remember Mr. Atoz, don't you?"

"I know of no Atoz. I know nothing of this, nothing of these matters. Take him. I will not hear him."

The constable let the prosecutor out, and together they hurried down the corridor.

Kirk called after them, "Only let me speak to you, my lord!"

They vanished without looking back. Kirk shook the bars, frustrated, angry, hopelessly aware that he was alone and friendless here. Across the corridor, the woman's face was contorted with fear and hatred.

"Witch! Witch!" she shrilled. "They'll burn you!"

They took her away later the next day. Kirk scarcely noticed. He was trying to work out a course of action. He had never seen a jail that looked easier to break, but all attempts to think beyond that point were impeded by a growing headache; and when he got up from the pallet to make sure his hands would fit freely through the bars, he had a sudden spell of faintness. Had he caught some kind of bug?

Down the corridor there was a jingling of keys. The jailer was coming with food. It was now or never.

He was sitting on the pallet again when the jailer arrived; but when the jailer straightened from setting down the bowl of food, Kirk's arm was around his throat, his other hand lifting the ring of keys from his belt. Opening the door from the outside, Kirk pulled the terrified man into the cell and shut the door again.

Releasing his grip, Kirk allowed the jailer a single cry, then knocked him out with a quick chop and rolled him under the pallet. End of Standard Escape Maneuver One. With any luck, that cry should bring the constable, and safe-conduct. Curious how dizzy he felt. On an impulse, he lay down and closed his eyes.

He heard hurrying feet, then the creak of the hinges as the newcomer tried the door. The subsequent muffled exclamation told him that he had been luckier than he knew; the man outside was the prosecutor. Kirk emitted a muffled groan.

Shuffling noises, and then the sound of breathing told him that the prosecutor was bending over him. A quick glance through half-closed lids told him where the nearest wrist was. He grabbed it.

"If you yell, I'll kill you," he whispered with fierce intensity.

The prosecutor neither yelled nor struggled. He merely said, "It will go harder with you if you persist."

"I am being falsely accused. You know it."

"You are to come with me to the Inquisitional Tribunal. There the matter of your witchcraft will be decided."

"There are no such things as witches."

"I shan't say you said so," the prosecutor said. "That is heresy. If they hear you, they will burn you for such beliefs."

"You are the only one who can hear me. Before the Inquisitor, it will be different. I'll denounce you as a man who came from the future, just as I did. Therefore, you too are a witch."

"They would surely burn me as well," the prosecutor agreed. "But what good would that do you?"

"Use your head, man," Kirk said. "I need your help."

"How can I help you? I will do my utmost to plead your innocence. I may be able to get you off—providing you say nothing of the comrades you left behind."

"Not good enough. I want you to help me to return to the library."

"You cannot go back."

"I tell you, I must. My comrades are lost in another time-period. I have to find them. Why don't you go back too?"

"We can never go back," the prosecutor said. "We must live out our lives here in the past. The Atavachron has prepared our cell structure and brain pattern to make life here natural. To return to the future would mean instant death."

"Prepared?" Kirk said. "I am here by accident. Your Mr. Atoz did not prepare me in any way." As he spoke, his temples began to throb again.

"Then you must get back at once. If you were not transformed, you cannot survive more than a few days here."

"Then you'll show me where the portal is?"

"Yes—approximately. But you must find the exact spot yourself. You understand I dare not wait with you . . ."

"Of course. Let's go."

Five minutes later, Kirk was back in the library. It looked as empty as it had when he had first seen it. He checked the contemporary time with the *Enterprise,* shunting aside a barrage of frantic questions. It was seventeen minutes to nova. Evidently, no matter how much time he spent in the past, the gate at its present setting would always return him to this day. It had to; for the gate, there would be no tomorrow.

He drew his phaser. It had not worked in the past, but he was quite certain it would work here. And this time, Mr. Atoz, he thought grimly, you are going to be *helpful.*

McCoy was still abed, but he was feeling distinctly better, as his appetite proved. Zarabeth, who had adopted a flowing gown which made her look positively beautiful, was out in her work area, making something she had promised would be a delicacy.

"I hope the *Enterprise* got away in time," McCoy said.

"I hope it will get away. The event is a hundred thousand years in the future."

"Yes, I know. I wonder where Jim is?"

"Who knows?" Spock said. "We can only hope he is well, wherever he is."

"What do you mean, we can only hope? Haven't you done anything about it?"

"What was there to do?"

"Locate the portal," McCoy said impatiently. "We certainly didn't come very far from it."

"We've been through all that already, Doctor. What's the point of rehashing the subject? We can't get back. Wasn't that clear to you?"

"Perfectly. I just don't believe it. I refuse to give up trying."

"It would be suicide if you succeeded."

McCoy sighed. "I never thought I'd see it. But I understand. You want to stay here. I might say, you are highly motivated to remain in this forsaken waste."

And not ten minutes ago, Spock thought, it had been McCoy who had been praising Zarabeth's cooking, and offering other small gallantries. "The prospect seemed quite attractive to you a few moments ago."

"Listen to me," McCoy said, "you point-eared Vulcan . . ."

Before Spock fully realized what he was doing, he found himself leaning forward and lifting McCoy off the bed.

"I don't like that," he said. "I don't believe I ever did. Now I'm sure."

McCoy did not look in the least alarmed. He simply seemed to be studying Spock intently. "What is it, Spock?" he asked. "What's happening?"

Spock let him drop. "Nothing that shouldn't have happened long ago."

"Long ago," McCoy said softly. The intent scrutiny did not waver. "Yes, I guess so . . . Long ago."

The stare disturbed the First Officer, for reasons he did not understand. Wheeling, he went into the underground living room, where Zarabeth was setting a table. She looked up and smiled.

"Ready soon. Would you like a sample?"

"Thank you, but I am not hungry."

She came over and sat down near him. "I can imagine how you must feel. I know what it's like to be sent here against your will."

"My feelings, as you call them, are of no concern," Spock said. "I have accepted the situation."

"I cannot pretend that I am sorry you are here, though I realize that it is a misfortune for you. I am here against my will, too, just as you are."

"I'm sorry I know of no way to return you to your own time."

"I don't mean that I wish to return," Zarabeth said. "This is my time now. I've had to face that. But it has been lonely here. Do you know what it is like to be alone, really alone?"

"Yes. I know what it is like."

"I believe you do. Won't you eat something? Please?"

"If it pleases you." He walked to the table and surveyed it. He felt a faint shock, but it seemed far away. "This is animal flesh."

"There isn't much else to eat here, I'm afraid."

"Naturally, because of the climate. What is the source of heat in this shelter?"

"There is an underground hot spring that furnishes natural steam heat and power."

"And there is sunlight available outside. Excellent. It should be possible to build a greenhouse of sorts. Until then, this will have to do as a source of nourishment." He picked up the most innocuous-looking morsel, surveyed it with distaste, and bit into it. It was quite good; he took another.

"There aren't many luxuries here," Zarabeth said, watching him with evident approval. "Zor Khan left me only what was necessary to survive."

"But he evidently intended you to continue living," Spock said, sampling another dish.

"Yes. He gave me weapons, a shelter, food—everything I needed to live—except companionship. He did not want it said that he had had me killed. But to send me here alone—if that is not death, what is? A very inventive mind, that man."

"But insensitive, to send such a beautiful woman into exile." Instantly, he was badly startled. "Forgive me! I am not usually given to personal remarks."

"How could I possibly take offense?" Zarabeth said.

Spock scarcely heard her. "The cold must have affected me more than I realized. Please—pay no attention. I am not myself."

And that, he thought, was an understatement. He was behaving disgracefully. He had eaten animal flesh—and had enjoyed it! What was wrong with him? He put his hands to his temples.

"I say you are beautiful," he said, feeling a dawning wonder. "But you *are* beautiful. Is it so wrong to tell you so?"

Zarabeth came to him. "I have longed to hear you say it," she said softly.

Then she was in his arms. When the kiss ended, he felt as though a man who had always been locked up inside him had been set free.

"You are beautiful," he said, "beautiful beyond any dream of beauty I have ever had. I shall never stop telling you of it."

"Stay," she whispered. "I shall make you happy."

"My life is here."

"*You lie,*" said a voice from the doorway. Spock spun, furious with McCoy and enjoying it.

"I speak the present truth," he said. "We are here, for good. I have given you the facts."

"The facts as *you* know them. But you are also being dishonest with yourself, and that's also something new for you. You accepted Zarabeth's word because it was what you wanted to believe. But Zarabeth is a woman condemned to a terrible life of loneliness. She will do anything to anybody to change that, won't you, Zarabeth?"

"I told you what I know," Zarabeth said.

"Not quite, I believe. You said *we* can't get back. The truth is that *you* can't get back. Isn't it?"

"She would not jeopardize other lives . . ."

"To save herself from this life alone," McCoy said, "she would lie—and even murder me, the Captain, the whole crew of the *Enterprise,* to keep you here with her." His hand lashed out and caught her by the wrist. "Tell Spock the truth—you would kill to keep him here!"

Zarabeth cried out in terror, and in the next instant Spock found his hands closing around the physician's throat. McCoy did not resist.

"Spock!" he said intensely. "Think! Are you trying to kill me? Is that what you want? What are you feeling? Rage? Jealousy? Have you ever felt them before?"

Spock's hands dropped. His head was whirling. "Impossible," he said. "This is impossible. I am a Vulcan."

"The Vulcan you knew will not exist for another hundred thousand years! Think, Spock—what is it like on your planet now, at this moment?"

"My ancestors are barbarians. Irrational, warlike barbarians . . ."

"Who nearly killed themselves off with their passions! And now you are regressing to what they were!"

"I have lost myself," Spock said dully. "I do not know who I am. Zarabeth—can we go back?"

"I do not know. I do not know. It is impossible for me to go back. I thought it was true for you."

"I am going to try, Spock," McCoy said. "My life is there, and I want the life that belongs to me. I must go *now*. There isn't much time—I too am changing. Zarabeth, will you help me find my way to the portal?"

"I—Yes. If I must."

"Let's get dressed, then."

The cold seemed more intense than ever, and McCoy, wrapped in a blanket, still had little resistance to it. He leaned against the ice cliff, partially supported by Zarabeth, who once more was almost anonymous in her furs. Spock tapped the cliff, without success.

"There is no portal here," he said. "It's hopeless, McCoy."

"I suppose you're right."

"You're too ill to stay out here in the cold any longer. Give it up."

And then, faintly, they heard Kirk's voice. "Spock! Can you hear me?"

"It's Jim!" McCoy shouted. "Here we are!"

"Stop, we've found them," Kirk's voice said. "Hold it steady, Atoz. Can you hear me any better?"

"Yes," Spock said. "We hear you perfectly now."

"Follow my voice."

McCoy reached out. His hand disappeared into the cliff. "Here it is! Come on, Spock!"

"Start ahead." He turned to Zarabeth. "I do not wish to part from you."

"I can't come with you. You know that."

"What are you waiting for?" Kirk's voice said. "Hurry! Scotty says we've got to get back on board right now!"

"They will have to come through together," the voice of Atoz added, "as they went out together. Singly, the portal will reject them."

Spock and Zarabeth looked at each other with despair. He touched her face with his fingertips.

"I did lie," she said. "I knew the truth. I will pay. Goodbye."

Then they were in the library, Kirk pulling them through. Atoz was spinning the dials of the Atavachron frantically, and then, dashing past them, dived into the portal and vanished.

"Atoz!" McCoy called.

"He had his escape planned," Kirk said. "I'm glad he made it." He raised his communicator. "Are you there, Scotty?"

"Aye. It's now or never."

Spock turned toward the portal and raised his fist as if to strike it, but he did not complete the gesture.

"Beam us up. Maximum warp as soon as we are on board."

The library shimmered out of existence, and they were standing in the Transporter Room of the *Enterprise*. McCoy, still wrapped in his blanket, was once more regarding Spock with his intent clinical stare.

"There is no further need for you to observe me, Doctor," Spock said. "As you see, I have returned to the present. In every sense."

"Are you sure? It did happen, Spock."

"Yes, it happened," the First Officer said. "But that was a hundred thousand years ago. They are all dead. Dead and buried long ago."

The ship fled outward. Behind it, the nova began to erupt, in all its terrifying, inhuman glory.

THE DEVIL IN THE DARK

(Gene L. Coon)

Janus was an ugly planet, reddish-brown, slowly rotating, with a thick layer of clouds so turbulent that it appeared to be boiling. Not a hospitable place, but a major source of pergium—an energy metal-like plutonium, meta-stable, atomic number 358; the underground colony there was long-established, highly modern, almost completely automated. It had never given any trouble.

"Almost fifty people butchered," Chief Engineer Vanderberg said bitterly. He was standing beside his desk, nervous and urgent; facing him were Kirk, Spock, Lt. Commander Giotto, Doc McCoy and a security officer named Kelly. "Production's at an absolute stop."

"I can see that," Kirk said, gesturing toward the chart on the office wall, which showed a precipitous dip. "But please slow down, Mr. Vanderberg. What's the cause?"

"A monster." Vanderberg stared at the *Enterprise* delegation with belligerent defensiveness, as though daring them to deny it. He was clearly highly overwrought.

"All right," Kirk said. "Let's assume there's a monster. What has it done? When did it start?"

Vanderberg made an obvious effort to control himself. He pushed a button on his desk communicator, which sat near a globe some ten inches in diameter of what appeared to be some dark-gray crystalline solid. "Send Ed Appel in here," he told it, and then added to Kirk, "My production engineer. About three months ago, we opened a new level. It was unusually rich in pergium, platinum, uranium, even gold. The whole planet's a treasure house, but I've never seen anything like this before, even here. We were just setting up to mine it when things began to happen. First the automatic machinery began to disintegrate, piece by piece. The metal just seemed to dissolve away. No mystery about the agent; it was aqua regia, possibly with a little hydrofluoric acid mixed in—vicious stuff. We don't store vast quantities of such stuff here, I can tell you that. Offhand I don't even know what we'd keep it *in*."

"Telfon," Spock suggested.

"Yes, but my point is, we *don't*."

"You said people were butchered," Kirk reminded him gently.

"Yes. First our maintenance engineers. Sent them down into the halls to repair the corroded machinery. We found them—burned to a crisp."

"Not lava, I suppose," Kirk said.

"There is no current volcanic activity on this planet, Captain," Spock said.

"He's right. None. It was that same damn acid mixture. At first the deaths were down deep, but they've been moving up toward our levels. The last man who died, three days ago, was only three levels below this one."

"I'd like to examine his body," McCoy said.

"We kept it for you—what was left. It isn't pretty."

The office door opened to admit a tough-looking, squat, businesslike man of middle age, wearing a number one phaser at his belt.

"You posted guards? Sentries?" Kirk asked.

"Of course. And five of them have died."

"Has anyone seen this—this monster of yours?"

"I did," said the newcomer.

"This is Ed Appel. Describe it, Ed."

"I can't. I only got a glimpse of it. It was big, and kind of shaggy. I shot at it, and I hit it square, too, a good clean shot. It didn't even slow it down."

"Anything a phaser will not affect," Spock said, "has to be an illusion. Any life-form, that is."

"Tell that to Billy Anderson," Appel said grimly. "He never had a chance. I only got away by the skin of my teeth."

"That's the story," Vanderberg said. "Nobody'll go down into the lower levels now, and I don't blame them. If the Federation wants pergium from us, they'll have to do something about it."

"That's what we're here for, Mr. Vanderberg," Kirk said.

"Pretty tough, aren't you?" said Appel. "Starship, phaser banks, energy from anti-matter, the whole bit. Well, you can't get your starship down into the tunnels."

"I don't think we'll need to, Mr. Appel. Mr. Spock, I'll want a complete computer evaluation, with interviews from everyone who knows anything about the events here. Mr. Vanderberg, have you a complete subsurface chart of all drifts, tunnels, galleries and so on?"

"Of course."

Spock had been inspecting the dark-gray sphere on the desk. He stepped forward and touched it. "This, Mr. Vanderberg. What is it?"

"It's a silicon nodule. There's a million of them down there. No commercial value."

"But a geological oddity, to say the least, especially in igneous rocks. Pure silicon?"

"A light oxide layer on the outside, a few trace elements below. Look, we didn't call you here so you could collect rocks."

"Mr. Spock collects information, and it's often useful," Kirk said. "We'll need your complete cooperation."

"You'll get it. Just find this creature, whatever it is. I'm dead sick of losing my men—and I've got a quota to meet, too."

"Your order of priorities," Kirk said, "is the same as mine."

They worked in a room just off Vanderberg's office, feeding data to the *Enterprise's* computer and getting evaluations back by communicator. The charts with which Vanderberg supplied them turned out to be immensely involved—thousands of serpentine lines crossing and recrossing. Their number was incredible, even after allowing for fifty years of tunneling with completely automated equipment. The network extended throughout the entire crust of the planet, and perhaps even deeper.

"Not man-made," Spock agreed. "They may be lava tubes, but if so, they are unique in my experience."

"They won't make hunting any easier," Kirk said. "Bones, what's the word on the autopsy?"

"The plant's physician and the chemists were right, Jim. Schmitter wasn't burned to death. He was flooded or sprayed with that acid mixture."

"Could it eat away machinery, too?"

"Aqua regia will dissolve even gold. What puzzles me is the trace of hydrofluoric acid. It's a very *weak* acid, but there are two things it attacks strongly. One of them is glass—you have to keep it in wax bottles, or, as Spock suggested, telfon."

"And the other thing?"

"Human flesh."

"Hmm. It sounds like a mixture somebody calculated very carefully.

Mr. Spock, do you think this monster story could be a blind for some kind of sabotage?"

"Possibly, Captain. For example, Mr. Vanderberg thinks that the creature uses the network of tubes to move through. But if you plot the deaths and the acts of destruction, and their times, you find that the creature cannot possibly have appeared at all these points as rapidly as indicated."

"How recent are those tunnel charts?"

"They were made last year—before the first appearance of the alleged monster, but not long before. Moreover, Captain, a sensor check indicates *no* life under the surface of Janus but the accountable human residents of the colony. We are confronted with two alternatives: either to patrol thousands of miles of tunnels, on foot, in the faint hope of encountering the alleged monster; or to find a plausible human suspect who has managed to manufacture and hide an almost inexhaustible supply of this intractable corrosive, and who has a portable, innocuous-looking carrier for it with a capacity of at least thirty liters."

"I rather prefer the monster theory," McCoy said. "If we catch a man behind these murders, I think we ought to lower him into his own acid vat a quarter of an inch at a time."

"If," Spock said, "is the operative word in either case . . ."

He was interrupted by a distant, heavy boom. The room shuddered, the lights flickered, and then an alarm bell was clanging. A moment later, Vanderberg burst in from his office.

"Something's happened in the main reactor room!" he shouted.

They left at a dead run, Vanderberg leading the way, McCoy bringing up the rear. The trail wound up in a tunnel elaborately posted with signs reading CAUTION: RADIATION—MAIN REACTOR CHAMBER—ONLY AUTHORISED PERSONS BEYOND THIS POINT. The floor of the tunnel looked as though something very heavy had been dragged along it. At the far end was what had once been a large metal door, but which now consisted chiefly of curled strips around a huge hole. Before it was a small, blackened lump which might once have been a man.

Vanderberg recoiled. "Look at that!" Then he hurried toward the ruined door. McCoy knelt quickly beside the charred lump, tricorder out; Kirk and Spock followed Vanderberg.

Inside, the bulk of the reactor was buried in the walls, showing only a large faceplate and a control panel. Pipes crisscrossed the chamber; and an appalled Vanderberg was standing looking down at a sort of nexus of these—a junction that ended in nothing.

Kirk scanned the control panel. "I didn't know anyone still used fission for power."

"I don't suppose anybody does but us. But pergium is money—we ship it all out—and since we have so much uranium nobody wants, we use it here. Or we did until now."

"Explain."

"The main moderator pump's gone. Lucky the cutouts worked, or this whole place would be a flaming mass of sodium."

Spock knelt and inspected the aborted junctions. "Acid again. Like the door. Mr. Vanderberg, do you have a replacement for the missing pump?"

"I doubt it. It was platinum, corrosion-proof, never gave us any trouble; should have lasted forever." Suddenly, visibly, Vanderberg began to panic. "Look, the reactor's shut down now—and it provides heat and electricity and life support for the whole colony! And if we override, we'll have a maximum accident that will poison half the planet!"

"Steady," Kirk said. "Mr. Spock, might we have a replacement on shipboard?"

"No, Captain. To find one, you would need a museum."

Kirk took out his communicator. "Kirk to *Enterprise* . . . Lt. Uhura, get me Mr. Scott . . . Scotty, this is the Captain. Could you contrive a perfusion pump for a PXK fission reactor?"

"Hoo, Captain, you must be haverin'."

"I'm dead serious; it's vital."

"Well, sir—I could put together some odds and ends. But they wouldn't hold for long."

"How long?"

"Forty-eight hours, maybe, with a bit of luck. It all ought to be platinum, ye see, and I've not got enough, so I'll have to patch in with gold, which won't bear the pressure long . . ."

"Get together what you need and beam down here with it."

Kirk put away the communicator and bent upon Vanderberg a look of deep suspicion. "Mr. Vanderberg, I have to tell you that I don't like the way these coincidences are mounting up. How could some hypothetical monster attack precisely the one mechanism in an almost ancient reactor which would create a double crisis like this? And how would it happen to be carrying around with it a mixture of acids precisely calculated to dissolve even platinum—and also human flesh?"

"I don't know," Vanderberg said helplessly. "You suspect sabotage? Impossible. Besides, Ed Appel *saw* the monster."

"He says."

"Ed's been my production chief almost throughout my entire career. I'd trust him with my life. And besides, what would be his motive? Look, dammit, Kirk, my people are being murdered! This is no time for fantasies about spies! The thing is there, it's free, it's just shut us down right under your nose! Why in God's name don't you *do* something?"

"Captain," Spock's voice said from behind them. "Will you come out and look at this, please?"

Kirk went out into the main tunnel to find the First Officer contemplating a side branch. "This is most curious," he said. "This tunnel is not indicated on any of the charts we were provided. It simply was not there before."

"Too recent to be on the maps, maybe?"

"Yes, but how did it get here, Captain? It shows no signs of having been drilled."

Kirk looked closer. "That's so. And the edges are fused. Could it be a lava tube?"

"That seems most unlikely," Spock said. "Had there been any vulcanism on this level since we arrived, everybody would be aware of it. And it joins a charted tunnel back there about fifty yards."

"Hmm. Let's go back to the ship. I feel the need for a conference."

Spock brought with him into the briefing room of the *Enterprise* one of the strange spherical objects Vanderberg had called silicon nodules, and set it on the table. Then he sat down and stared into it, looking incongruously like a fortune-teller in uniform.

"I think it's mass hysteria," McCoy said.

"Hysteria?" Kirk said. "Dozens of people have been killed."

"Some—natural cause. A phenomenon—and people have dreamed up a mysterious monster to account for it."

Spock stirred. "Surely, Doctor. A natural cause. But not hysteria."

"All right. You asked my opinion. I gave it to you. How do I know? Maybe there is some kind of a monster . . ."

"No creature is monstrous in its own environment, Doctor. And this one appears to be intelligent, as well."

"What makes you think so?"

"The missing pump was not taken by accident," Spock said. "It was the one piece of equipment absolutely essential to the operation of the reactor."

Kirk looked at his First Officer. "You think this creature is trying to drive the colonists off the planet?"

"It seems logical."

"Why just now, Mr. Spock? This production facility was established here fifty years ago."

"I do not know, sir." Spock resumed staring at the round object. "But it is perhaps indicative that Mr. Appel claimed to have hit it with his phaser. He strikes me as a capable but unimaginative man. If he said he hit it, I tend to believe he did. Why was the creature not affected? I have a suggestion, though Dr. McCoy will accuse me of creating fantasies."

"You?" McCoy said. "I doubt it."

"Very well. To begin with, the colonists are equipped only with phaser number one, no need for the more powerful model having been encountered. This instrument, when set to kill, coagulates proteins, which are carbon-based compounds. Suppose this creature's 'organic' compounds are based on silicon instead?"

"Now surely that *is* a fantasy," Kirk said.

"No, it's possible," McCoy said. "Silicon has the same valence as carbon, and a number of simple silicoid 'organics' have been known for a long time. And by the stars, it explains the acids, too. We have hydrochloric acid in our own stomachs, after all. But we're mostly water. Silicon isn't water-soluble, so the aqua regia may be the substrate of the creature's bloodstream. And the hydrofluoric—well, fluorine has an especial affinity for silicon; the result is telfon, which may be what the creature's internal tubing is made of."

"Do you mean to imply," Kirk said slowly, "that this being goes about killing men with its own blood?"

"Not necessarily, Jim. It may spit the stuff—and sweat it, too, for all I know. Its tunneling suggests that it does."

"Hmm. It also suggests that it would have to have a form of natural armor plating. But our people have phasers number two, and I defy anything to stand up against that at high power, no matter what it's made of. The question is, how do we locate it?"

"I would suggest," Spock said, "that we start at whatever level these silicon nodules were found."

"Why? How do they tie in?"

"Pure speculation, Captain. But it would be helpful if it were confirmed."

"Very well, assemble security forces. I assume that Mr. Scott is already at work on the reactor? Very good, we'll assemble in Vanderberg's office."

"You will each be given a complete chart of all tunnels and diggings under this installation," Kirk told his forces. "You will proceed from level to level, checking out every foot of opening. You will be searching for some variety of creature which apparently is highly resistant to phaser fire, so have your phasers set on maximum. And remember this—fifty people have already been killed. I want no more deaths . . ."

"Except the bloody thing!" Vanderberg exploded.

Kirk nodded. "The creature may or may not attack on sight. However, you must. A great deal depends on getting this installation back into production."

"Mr. Vanderberg," Spock said, "may I ask at which level you discovered the nodules of silicon?"

"The twenty-third. Why?"

"Commander Giotto," Kirk said, "you will take your detail directly to the twenty-third level and start your search from there. Mr. Vanderberg, I want all of your people to stay on the top level. Together. In a safe place."

"I don't know any safe place, Captain. The way this thing comes and goes . . ."

"We'll see what we can do about that. All right, gentlemen. You have your instructions. Let's get at it."

Spock, Kirk, Giotto and two security guards paused on the twenty-third level while Spock adjusted his tricorder. Most of Giotto's men had already fanned out through the tunnels. Kirk pointed to a spot on Giotto's map.

"We are here. You and your guards take this tunnel, which is the only one of this complex that doesn't already have men in it. As you see, they converge up ahead. We'll rendezvous at that point."

"Aye aye, sir." The three disappeared into the darkness. Spock continued to scan.

"A strange sensation," the First Officer said. "There are men all about us, and yet because the tricorder is now set for silicon life, it says we are alone down here. No, not quite."

"Traces?"

"A great many—but they are all extremely old. Many thousands of years old. Yet, again, there are many brand new tunnels down here. It does not relate."

"Perhaps it does," Kirk said thoughtfully. "Not tunnels. Not lava tubes. Highways. Roads. Thoroughfares. Mr. Spock, give me an environmental reading, for a thousand yards in any direction."

"Yes, sir—ah. A life-form. Bearing, one hundred eleven degrees, angle of elevation four degrees."

"Not one of our people?"

"No, sir, they would not register."

"Come on!"

They set off quickly, keeping as close on the bearing as the convolutions of the tunnels would allow. Then, ahead, someone screamed—or tried to, for the sound was suddenly cut off. They ran.

A moment later they were looking at a small, blackened lump on the tunnel floor, with a phaser beside it. Grimly, Spock picked up the weapon and checked it.

"One of the guards," he said. "He did not have a chance to fire, Captain."

"And it's only been seconds since we heard him scream . . ."

There was a slithering sound behind them. They whirled together.

In the darkness it was difficult to make out details, except for movement, an undulating crawl forward. The creature was large, low to the ground, somehow wormlike. It was now making another noise, a menacing rattle, like pebbles being shaken in a tin can.

"Look out!" Kirk shouted. "It's charging!"

Both men fired. The monster swung around as the two phaser beams struck its side. With an agonized roar, it leapt backward and vanished.

"After it!"

But the tunnel was empty. It was astonishing that anything of that bulk could move so rapidly. Kirk reached out to touch the wall of the tunnel, then snatched his hand back.

"Mr. Spock! These walls are hot."

"Indeed, Captain. The tricorder says it was cut within the last two minutes."

Kirk heard running footsteps, and then Giotto and a guard, phasers at the ready, appeared behind them.

"Are you all right, Captain? That scream . . ."

"Perfectly, Commander. But one of your men . . ."

"Yes, I saw. Poor Kelly. Did you see the thing, sir?"

"We saw it. In fact, we took a bite out of it."

Spock bent over, then straightened with a large chunk of something in his hand. "And here it is, Captain."

He handed the stuff to Kirk, who examined it closely. Clearly, it was not animal tissue; it looked more like fibrous asbestos. Obviously, Spock's guess had been right.

"Commander Giotto, it looks as though killing this thing will require massed phasers—or a single phaser with much longer contact. Pass the word to your men. And another thing. We already knew it was a killer. Now it's wounded—probably in pain—back in there somewhere. There's nothing more dangerous than a wounded animal. Keep that in mind."

"The creature is moving rapidly through native rock at bearing two hundred one, eleven hundred yards, elevation angle five degrees," Spock said.

"Right." Giotto and the guard went out, and Kirk started to follow them, but Spock remained standing where he was, looking pensive. Kirk said, "What's troubling you, Mr. Spock?"

"Captain, there are literally hundreds of these tunnels in this general area alone. Far too many to be cut by the one creature in an ordinary lifetime."

"We don't know how long it lives."

"No, sir, but its speed of movement indicates a high metabolic rate. That is not compatible with a lifetime much longer than ours."

"Perhaps not," Kirk said. "I fail to see what bearing that has on our problem."

"I mention it, Captain, because if this is the only survivor of a dead race, to kill it would be a crime against science."

"Our concern is the protection of this colony, Mr. Spock. And to get pergium production moving again. This is not a zoological expedition."

"Quite so, Captain. Still . . ."

"Keep your tricorder active. Maintain a constant reading on the creature. We'll try to use the existing tunnels to cut it off. If we have to, we'll use our phasers to cut our own tunnels." Kirk paused, then added more gently, "I'm sorry, Mr. Spock, I'm afraid it must die."

"Sir, if the opportunity arose to capture it instead . . ."

"I will lose no more men, Mr. Spock. The creature will be killed on sight. That's the end of it."

"Very well, sir."

But Kirk was not satisfied. Killing came hard to them all, but Spock in particular was sometimes inclined to hold his fire when his conservation instincts, or his scientific curiosity, were aroused. After a moment, Kirk added, "Mr. Spock, I want you to return to the surface, to assist Mr. Scott in the maintenance of his makeshift circulating pump."

Spock's eyebrows went up. "I beg your pardon, Captain?"

"You heard me. It's vital that we keep that reactor in operation. Your scientific knowledge . . ."

". . . is not needed there. Mr. Scott knows far more about reactors than I do. You are aware of that."

After another pause, Kirk said: "Very well. I am in command of the *Enterprise*. You are second in command. This hunt will be dangerous. Either one of us, by himself, is expendable. Both of us are not."

"I will, of course, follow your orders, Captain," Spock said. "But we are dealing with a grave scientific problem right here, so on those grounds, this is where I should be, not with Mr. Scott. Besides, sir, there are approximately one hundred of us engaged in this search, against one creature. The odds against both you and me being killed are—" there was a very slight pause, "two hundred twenty-six point eight to one."

Not for the first time, Kirk found himself outgunned. "Those are good odds. Very well, you may stay. But keep out of trouble, Mr. Spock."

"That is always my intention, Captain."

Kirk's communicator beeped, and he flipped it open. "Kirk here."

"Scotty, Captain. My brilliant improvisation just gave up the ghost. It couldn't take the strain."

"Can you fix it again?"

"Nay, Captain. It's gone for good."

"Very well. Start immediate evacuation of all colonists to the *Enterprise*."

Vanderberg's voice came through. "Not all of them, Captain. Me and some of my key personnel are staying. We'll be down to join you."

"We don't have phasers enough for all of you."

"Then we'll use clubs," Vanderberg's voice said. "But we won't be chased away from here. My people take orders from me, not from you."

Kirk thought fast. "Very well. Get everybody else on board the ship. The fewer people we have breathing the air, the longer the rest of us can hold out. How long is that, Scotty?"

"It's got naught to do with the air, Captain. The reactor will go supercritical in about ten hours. You'll have to find your beastie well before then."

"Right. Feed us constant status reports, Scotty. Mr. Vanderberg, you and your men assemble on level twenty-three, checkpoint Tiger. There you'll team up with *Enterprise* security personnel. They're better armed than you are, so stay in sight of one of them at all times—buddy system. Mr. Spock and I will control all operations by communicator. Understood—and agreed?"

"Both," Vanderberg's voice said grimly. "Suicide is no part of my plans."

"Good. Kirk out . . . Mr. Spock, you seem to have picked up something."

"Yes, Captain. The creature is now quiescent a few thousand yards from here, in that direction."

Kirk took a quick look at his chart. "The map says these two tunnels converge there. Take the left one, Mr. Spock. I'll go to the right."

"Should we separate?"

"Two tunnels," Kirk said. "Two of us. We separate."

"Very well, Captain," Spock said, but his voice was more than a little dubious. But it couldn't be helped. Kirk moved down the right-hand tunnel, slowly and tensely.

The tunnel turned, and Kirk found himself in a small chamber, streaked with bright strata quite unlike the rest of the rock around him. Imbedded in there were dozens of round objects like the one Vanderberg had on his desk, or the one which had so fascinated Spock. He lifted his communicator again. "Mr. Spock."

"Yes, Captain."

"I've found a whole layer of those silicon nodules of yours."

"Indeed, Captain. Most illuminating. Captain—be absolutely certain you do not damage any of them."

"Explain."

"It is only a theory, Captain, but . . ."

His voice was drowned out by the roar of hundreds of tons of collapsing rock and debris. Kirk threw himself against the wall, choking clouds of dust rising around him. When he could see again, it was evident that the roof of the tunnel had fallen across the way he had just come.

"Captain! Are you all right? Captain!"

"Yes, Mr. Spock. Quite all right. But we seem to have had a cave-in."

"I can phaser you out," Spock's voice said.

"No, any disturbance would bring the rest of the wall down. Anyway, it isn't necessary. The chart said our tunnels meet further on. I can just walk out."

"Very well. But I find it disquieting that your roof chose to collapse at that moment. Please proceed with extreme caution. I shall double my pace."

"Very well, Mr. Spock. I'll meet you at the end of the tunnel. Kirk out."

As he tucked the communicator away, there came from behind him a sound as of pebbles being shaken in a can. He spun instantly, but it was too late. The way was blocked.

It was his first clear sight of the creature, which was reared in the center of the tunnel. It was huge, shaggy, multicolored, and knobby with objects which might have been heads, sense organs, hands—Kirk could not tell. It was quivering gently, still making that strange noise.

Kirk whipped up his phaser. At once the creature shuffled backward. Was it now afraid of just one gun? He raised the weapon again, but this time the creature retreated no further. Neither did it advance.

Phaser at the ready, Kirk moved toward the animal, trying to get around it. At once, it moved to block him—not threateningly, as far as Kirk could tell, but just getting in his way.

Spock chose this moment to call him again. "Captain, a new reading shows the creature . . ."

"I know exactly where the creature is," Kirk said, his phaser steadily on it. "Standing about ten feet away from me."

"Kill it, Captain! Quickly!"

"It's—not making any threatening moves, Mr. Spock."

"You don't dare take the chance! Kill it!"

"I thought you were the one who wanted it kept alive," Kirk said, with grim amusement. "Captured, if possible."

"Your life is in danger, Captain. You can't take the risk."

"It seems to be waiting for something. I want to find out what. I'll shoot if I have to."

"Very well, Captain. I will hurry through my tunnel and approach it from the rear. I remind you that it is a proven killer. Spock out."

The creature was silent now. Kirk lowered his phaser a trifle, but there was no reaction.

"All right," Kirk said. "What do we do now? Talk it over?"

He really had not expected an answer, nor did he get one. He took a step forward and to one side. Again the creature moved to block him; and as it did, Kirk saw along one of its flanks a deep, ragged gouge, leaving a glistening, rocklike surface exposed. It was obviously a wound.

"Well, you can be hurt, can't you?"

He lifted the phaser again. The creature rattled, and shrank back, but held its ground. Obviously it was afraid of the weapon, but it would not flee.

Kirk lowered the phaser, and the rattling stopped. Then he moved deliberately back against the nearest wall and dropped slowly into a squatting position, the phaser held loosely between his knees.

"All right. Your move. Or do we just sit and wait for something to happen?"

It was not a long wait. Almost at once, Spock burst into the area from the open end of the tunnel. He took in the situation instantly and his own phaser jerked up.

"Don't shoot!" Kirk shouted. Echoes went bounding away through the galleries and tunnels.

Spock looked from one to the other. As he did so, the creature moved slowly to the other side of the tunnel. Kirk guessed that he could get past it now before it could block him again. Instead, he said, "Come on over, Mr. Spock."

With the utmost caution, his highly interested eyes fastened on the creature, Spock moved to Kirk's side. He looked up at the walls in which the silicon nodules were imbedded. "Logical," he said.

"But what do they mean?"

"I'd rather not say just yet. If I could possibly get into Vulcan mind-lock with that creature—it would be easier if I could touch it . . ."

Before Kirk could even decide whether to veto this notion, Spock stepped toward the animal, his hand extended. It lurched back at once, its rattling loud and angry-sounding.

"Too bad," Spock said. "But obviously it will permit no contact. Well, then, I must do it the hard way. If you will be patient, Captain . . ."

Spock's eyes closed as he began to concentrate. The intense mental power he was summoning was almost physically visible. Kirk held his breath. The creature twitched nervously, uneasily.

Suddenly Spock's face contorted in agony, and he screamed. "The pain! The pain!" With a great shudder, his face ashen, he began to fall; Kirk got to him just in time.

"Thank—you, Captain," Spock said, gasping and steadying himself. "I am sorry—but that is all I got. Just waves and waves of searing pain. Oh, and a name. It calls itself a Horta. It is in great agony because of the wound—but not reacting at all like a wounded animal."

Abruptly, the creature slithered forward to a smooth expanse of floor, and clung there for a moment. Then it moved away. Where it had been, etched into the floor in still smoking letters, were the words: NO KILL I. Both men stared at the sentence in astonishment.

" 'No kill I'?" Kirk said. "What's that? It could be a plea to us not to kill it—or a promise that it won't kill us."

"I don't know. It appears it learned more from me during our empathy than I did from it. But observe, Captain, that it thinks in vocables. That means it can hear, too."

"Horta!" Kirk said loudly. The creature rattled at once and then returned to silence.

"Mr. Spock, I hate to do this to you, but—it suddenly occurs to me that the Horta couldn't have destroyed that perfusion pump. It was platinum, and immune to the acid mix. It must have hidden it somewhere—and we have to get it back. You'll have to re-establish communications, no matter how painful it is."

"Certainly, Captain," Spock said promptly. "But it has no reason to give us the device—and apparently every reason to wish us off the planet."

"I'm aware of that. If we can win its confidence . . ."

Kirk took out his communicator. "Dr. McCoy. This is the Captain."

"Yes, Captain," McCoy's voice answered.

"Get your medical kit and get down here on the double. We've got a patient for you."

"Somebody injured? How?"

"I can't specify, it's beyond my competence. Just come. Twenty-third level; find us by tricorder. And hurry. Kirk out."

"I remind you, Captain," Spock said. "This is a silicon-based form of life. Dr. McCoy's medical knowledge may be totally useless."

"He's a healer. Let him heal. All right, go ahead, Mr. Spock. Try to contact it again. And try to find out why it suddenly took to murder."

The creature moved nervously as Spock approached it, but did not shy off; it merely quivered, and made its warning pebble-sound. Spock's eyes closed, and the rattling slowly died back.

Kirk's communicator beeped again. "Kirk here."

"Giotto, Captain. Are you all right?"

"Perfectly all right. Where are you?"

"We're at the end of the tunnel. Mr. Vanderberg and his men are here. They're pretty ugly. I thought I'd check with you first . . ."

"Hold them there, Commander. Under no circumstances allow them in here yet. The minute Dr. McCoy gets there, send him through."

"Aye aye, sir. Giotto out."

Spock was now deep in trance. He began to murmur.

"Pain . . . pain . . . Murder . . . the thousands . . . devils . . . Eternity ends . . . horrible . . . horrible . . . in the Chamber of the Ages . . . the Altar of Tomorrow . . . horrible . . . Murderers . . . Murderers . . ."

"Mr. Spock! The pump . . ."

"Stop them . . . kill . . . strike back . . . monsters . . ."

There was the sound of rapidly approaching footsteps and Dr. McCoy, medical bag in hand, broke through into the area. Then he stopped, obviously stunned at what he saw. Kirk silently signaled him to join them, and McCoy, giving the quiescent creature a wide berth, moved to Kirk's side. He said in a low whisper, "What in the name of . . ."

"It's wounded—badly," Kirk whispered back. "You've got to help it."

"Help—*this?*"

"Take a look at it."

McCoy cautiously approached the creature, which was now as immobile as a statue; nor did Spock take any notice.

"The end of life . . . the murderers . . . killing . . . the dead children . . ."

McCoy stared at the gaping wound, and then touched it tentatively here and there. Producing his tricorder, he took a reading, at which he stared in disbelief. Then he came back to Kirk, his face indignant.

"You can't be serious. That thing is virtually made out of stone on the outside, and its guts are plastics."

"Help it. Treat it."

"I'm a doctor, not a bricklayer!"

"You're a healer," Kirk said. "That's your patient. That's an order, Doctor."

McCoy shook his head in wonder, but moved back toward the animal. Spock's eyes were still closed, his face sweating with effort. Kirk went to him.

"Spock. Tell it we're trying to help. A doctor."

"Understood. Understood. It is the end of Life. Eternity stops. Go out. Into the tunnel. To the Passage of Immortality. To the Chamber of the Ages. Cry for the children. Walk carefully in the Vault of Tomorrow. Sorrow for the murdered children. Weep for the crushed ones. Tears for the stolen ones. The thing you search for is there. Go. Go. Sadness for the end of things."

Kirk could not tell whether he was being given directions, or only eavesdropping upon a meditation. He looked hesitantly toward the tunnel entrance.

"Go!" Spock said. "Into the tunnel. There is a small passage. Quickly. Quickly. Sorrow . . . such sorrow. Sadness. Pain." There were tears running down his cheeks now. "Sorrow . . . the dead . . . the children . . ."

Kirk felt a thrill of sympathy. He did not in the least understand this litany, but no one could hear so many emotionally loaded words chanted in circumstances of such tension without reacting.

But the directions turned out to be clear enough. Within a minute he was able to return, the pump in one hand, a silicon nodule in the other.

McCoy was kneeling by the flank of the animal, and speaking into his communicator. "That's right, Lieutenant. Beam it down to me immediately. Never mind what I want it for, I just want it. Move!"

"The ages die," Spock said. "It is time to sleep. It is over. Failure. The murderers have won. Death is welcome. Let it end here, with the murdered children . . ."

"Mr. Spock!" Kirk called. "Come back! Spock!"

Spock shuddered with the effort to disengage himself. Kirk carefully put the pump on the floor of the tunnel, then waited until Spock's eyes were no longer glazed.

"I found the unit," Kirk said. "It's in good shape. I also found about a thousand of these silicon balls. They're—eggs, aren't they, Mr. Spock?"

"Yes, Captain. Eggs. And about to hatch."

"The miners must have broken into the hatchery. Their operations destroyed hundreds of them. No wonder . . ."

There was a roar of sound, and Vanderberg, Appel and what seemed to be an army of armed civilians were trying to jam themselves into the tunnel. They shouted in alarm as they saw the creature. Phasers were raised. Kirk jumped forward.

"No!" he shouted. "Don't shoot!"

"Kill it, kill it!" Appel yelled.

Kirk raised his own weapon. "The first man who shoots, dies."

"You can't mean it," Vanderberg said, pointing at the Horta with a finger quivering with hatred. "That thing has killed fifty of my men!"

"And you've killed hundreds of her children," Kirk said quietly.

"What?"

"Those 'silicon nodules' you've been collecting and destroying are eggs. Tell them, Mr. Spock."

"There have been many generations of Horta on this planet," Spock said. "Every fifty thousand years the entire race dies—all but one, like this one. But the eggs live. She protects them, cares for them, and when they hatch, she is the mother to them—thousands of them. This creature here is the mother of her race."

"She's intelligent, peaceful and mild," Kirk added. "She had no objection to sharing the planet with you people—until you broke into the nursery and started destroying her eggs. Then she fought back, in the only way she could—as any mother would—when her children were endangered."

"How were we to know?" Vanderberg said, chastened and stunned. "But—you mean if those eggs hatch, there'll be thousands of them crawling around down here? We've got pergium to deliver!"

"And now you've got your reactor pump back," Kirk said. "She gave it back. You've complained that this planet is a minerological treasure house, if only you had the equipment to get at everything. Well, the Horta moves through rock the way we move through air—and leaves a tunnel. The greatest natural miners in the universe.

"I don't see why we can't make an agreement—reach a *modus vivendi*. They tunnel, you collect and process. You get along together. Your processing operation would be a thousand times more profitable than it is now."

"Sounds all right," Vanderberg said, still a little dubiously. "But how do you know the thing will go for it?"

"Why should it not?" Spock said. "It is logical. But there is one problem. It is badly wounded. It may die."

McCoy rose to his feet, a broad smile on his face. "It won't die. By golly, I'm beginning to think I can cure a rainy day."

"You cured it?" Kirk said in amazement. "How?"

"I had the ship beam down ten pounds of thermoconcrete, the kind we build emergency shelters out of. It's mostly silicon. I just troweled it over the wound. It'll act as a 'bandage' until it heals of itself. Take a look. Good as new."

"Bones, my humblest congratulations. Mr. Spock, I'll have to ask you to get in contact with the Horta again. Tell it our proposition. She and her children make all the tunnels they want. Our people will remove the minerals, and each side will leave the other alone. Think she'll go for it?"

"As I said, Captain, it seems logical. The Horta has a very logical mind." He paused a moment. "And after years of close association with humans, I find it curiously refreshing."

JOURNEY TO BABEL
(D. C. Fontana)

The honor guard of eight security men was lined up before the airlock, four men to a side, with Kirk, Spock and McCoy, all three in formal dress blue uniforms, at the end of this human tube. McCoy tugged at his collar, which he had previously described as "like having my neck in a sling." He asked Spock, "How does that Vulcan salute go?"

Spock demonstrated. The gesture was complex and McCoy's attempt to copy it was not very convincing.

The surgeon shook his head. "That hurts worse than the uniform."

The uniforms were the least of their discomforts, Kirk thought a little grimly. They'd soon be out of those, after the formal reception tonight, and the Vulcans were the last group of delegates the *Enterprise* had to pick up. Then would come the trip to the neutral planetoid code-named "Babel"—a two-week journey with a hundred and fourteen Federation delegates aboard, thirty-two of them ambassadors, half of them mad at the other half, and the whole lot touchier than a raw anti-matter pile over the Coridian question. Now *that* was going to be uncomfortable.

The airlock opened, and the Vulcan Ambassador, Sarek, stepped through. Because of Vulcan longevity, it would have been impossible to guess his age—he looked to be no more than in his late forties—but Kirk knew it to be in fact a hundred and two, which was middle age by Vulcan standards. He was followed, several paces behind, by a woman wearing a traveling outfit with a colorful hooded cloak; she in turn was followed by two Vulcan aides.

Kirk, Spock and McCoy stood at attention as the party walked past the honor guard to the Captain. Spock stepped formally in front of Sarek and gave the complex salute.

"Vulcan honors us with your presence," he said. "We come to serve."

Sarek pointedly ignored him and saluted Kirk instead. When he spoke, his voice was almost without inflection.

"Captain, your service honors us."

"Thank you, Ambassador," Kirk said with a slight bow. "Captain James Kirk. My First Officer, Commander Spock. Dr. McCoy, Chief Medical Officer."

Sarek nodded briefly in turn and indicated the rest of his party. "My aides." He held up his hand, first and second fingers extended. The woman stepped forward and touched her first and second fingers to his. "And Amanda, she who is my wife."

"Captain Kirk," the woman said.

"My pleasure, madam. Ambassador, as soon as you're settled, I'll arrange a tour of the ship. My First Officer will conduct you."

"I prefer another guide, Captain," Sarek said.

He was absolutely expressionless, and so was Spock. This snub was just as baffling and even more pointed than before, but it would not be a good idea to offend a ranking ambassador.

"Of course—if you wish. Mr. Spock, we have two hours until we leave orbit. Would you like to beam down and visit your parents?"

There was a slight but noticeable silence. Then Spock said, "Captain —Ambassador Sarek and his wife *are* my parents."

Was I just telling myself, Kirk thought glumly after the first shock, that this trip was going to be just "uncomfortable"?

Upon reflection, Kirk gave himself the job of guiding the tour. He found Spock's mother especially interesting—remarkable, even—though she was hard to study because she habitually walked behind and to the side of any man, her husband most notably. This was a Vulcan ritual to which she had adapted, for Amanda was an Earthwoman; almost everyone in the crew knew that much about Spock.

Though in her late fifties, she was still straight, slim and resilient. She had married a Vulcan and come to live on his world where her human-woman emotions had no place. Kirk strongly suspected that she had not lost any of her human humor and warmth, but that it was buried inside, in deference to her husband's customs and society.

He led them into the Engineering Room. Spock, by now in regular uniform, was working at the computer banks behind the grilled partition.

"This is the engineering section," Kirk told his guests. "There are emergency backup systems for the main controls. We also have a number of control computers here."

Amanda was still behind them and, without Sarek appearing to notice, she moved over to Spock. Out of the corner of his eye, Kirk saw each of them cross hands and touch them, palms out, in a ritual embrace. Then they began to murmur. Spock's face was expressionless, as usual. Once, Amanda shook her head ruefully.

Kirk continued his lecture, hoping to avoid trouble, but Sarek's eyes were as alert as his own. "My wife, attend," the Ambassador said. He held up his first and second fingers. Without a word, Amanda nodded to Spock to excuse herself and obediently moved to Sarek, joining her fingers with his, though Kirk guessed that she was really not much interested in the console and its instruments.

Spock, gathering up a handful of tapes, rose and headed for the door. Kirk had a sudden idea.

"Mr. Spock—a moment, please."

The First Officer turned reluctantly. "Yes, Captain?"

"Ambassador, I'm not competent to explain our computer setup. Mr. Spock, will you do so, please?"

"I gave Spock his first instruction in computers," Sarek said woodenly. "He chose to devote his knowledge to Starfleet rather than the Vulcan Science Academy."

That tore it. In trying to be helpful, Kirk had unwittingly put his foot right into the heart of the family quarrel. Apologetically, he nodded dismissal to Spock, and turned to Sarek.

"I'm sorry, Ambassador. I didn't mean to offend you in . . ."

"Offense is a human emotion, Captain. For other reasons, I am returning to my quarters. Continue, my wife."

Amanda bowed her head in characteristic acceptance, and Sarek left. Kirk, puzzled and confused as never before by his First Officer and his relatives, turned to her, shaking his head.

"I'm afraid I don't understand, Mrs. Sarek."

"Amanda," she said quickly. "I'm afraid you couldn't pronounce the Vulcan family name."

"Can you?"

A smile fluttered on her lips, then vanished as habit overtook her. "After a fashion, and after many years of practice . . . Shall we continue the tour? My husband did request it."

"It sounded more like a command."

"Of course. He's a Vulcan. I'm his wife."

"Spock is his son."

Amanda glanced at him sharply, as though surprised, but recovered quickly. "You don't understand the Vulcan way, Captain. It's logical. It's a better way than ours—but it's not easy. It has kept Spock and Sarek from speaking as father and son for eighteen years."

"Spock is my best officer," Kirk said. "And my best friend."

"I'm glad he has such a friend. It hasn't been easy for Spock—neither Vulcan nor human; at home nowhere, except Starfleet."

"I gather Spock disagreed with his father over his choice of a career."

"My husband has nothing against Starfleet. But Vulcans believe peace should not depend on force. Sarek wanted Spock to follow his teaching as Sarek followed the teaching of *his* father."

"And they're both stubborn."

Amanda smiled. "Also a human trait, Captain."

Abruptly, Uhura's voice interrupted from a console speaker. "Bridge to Captain Kirk."

Kirk snapped a toggle. "Kirk here."

"Captain, I've picked up some sort of signal; just a few symbols, nothing intelligible."

"Source?"

"That's what bothers me, sir. Impossible to locate. There wasn't enough of it. Sensors show nothing in the area. But it was a strong signal, as though it was very close."

"Go to alert status four. Begin long-range scanning. Kirk out." Kirk frowned thoughtfully and flicked off the switch. "Madame—Amanda—I'll have to ask you to excuse me. I shall hope to see you again at the reception this evening."

"Certainly, Captain. Both Vulcans and humans know what duty is."

The reception was already going full blast when Kirk arrived. Amid a murmur of conversation, delegates circulated, or sampled the table of exotic drinks, *hors d'oeuvre*. There was a fantastic array of them from many cultures.

Over it all was a faint aura of edgy politeness verging on hostility. The Interplanetary Conference had been called to consider the petition of the Coridian planets to be admitted to the Federation. The Coridian system had already been claimed by some of the races who now had delegates aboard the *Enterprise,* races who therefore had strong personal reasons for keeping Coridan *out* of the Federation. Keeping open warfare from breaking out among the delegates before the Conference even began was going to be a tough problem; many of them were not even trained diplomats, but minor officials who had been handed a hot potato by bosses who did not want to be saddled with the responsibility for whatever happened on Babel.

Kirk spotted Spock and McCoy in a group which included a Tellarite named Gav, two Andorians called Shras and Thelev, and Sarek and Amanda. Well, at least Spock was—er—associating with his family, however distantly.

As Kirk joined the group, McCoy was saying, "Mr. Ambassador, I understood that you had retired from public service before this conference was called. Forgive my curiosity, but, as a doctor, I'm interested in Vulcan physiology. Isn't it unusual for a Vulcan to retire at your age? You're only a hundred or so."

As was characteristic of Andorians because of their sensitive antennae, Shras was listening with his head down and slightly tilted, while Gav, sipping a snifter of brandy, was staring directly into Sarek's face. For an Earthman unaccustomed to either race, it would have been hard to say which of them, if either, was being rude.

Sarek said, "One hundred and two point four three seven, measured in your years. I had other—concerns."

Gav put his snifter down and leaned still farther forward. When he spoke, his voice was rough, grating and clumsy; English was very difficult for all his people, if he spoke it better than most. "Sarek of Vulcan, do you vote to admit Coridan to the Federation?"

"The vote will not be taken here, Ambassador Gav. My government's instructions will be heard in the Council Chamber on Babel."

"No—*you*. How do *you* vote, Sarek of Vulcan?"

Shras lifted his head. "Why must you know, Tellarite?" His voice was whispery, almost silken.

"In Council, his vote carries others," Gav said, stabbing a finger toward Sarek. "I will know where he stands, and why."

"Tellarites do not argue for reasons," Sarek said. "They simply argue."

"That is a . . ."

"Gentlemen," Kirk interrupted firmly. "As Ambassador Sarek pointed out, this is not the Council Chamber on Babel. I'm aware the admission of Coridan is a highly debatable issue, but you can't solve it here."

For a moment the three Ambassadors stared defensively at each other. Then Sarek nodded to Kirk. "You are correct, Captain. Quite logical."

"Apologies, Captain," Shras whispered.

Gav remained rigid for a moment, then nodded and said in an angry voice, "You will excuse me," and left the group.

"You have met Gav before, Ambassador," Shras said softly to Sarek.

"We debated at my last Council session."

"Ambassador Gav lost," Amanda added with a straight face. If Shras was amused, his face was incapable of showing it. He nodded solemnly and moved off.

"Spock, I've always suspected you were more human," McCoy said, in an obvious attempt to lighten the atmosphere. "Mrs. Sarek, I know about the rigorous training of Vulcan boys, but didn't he ever run and play like human youngsters? Even in secret?"

"Well," said Amanda, "he did have a sehlat he was very fond of."

"Sehlat?"

"It's rather like a fat teddy bear."

McCoy's eyes went wide. "A teddy bear?"

Several other crew personnel had overheard this and there was a general snicker. Quickly, Sarek turned to his wife and took her arm firmly.

"Excuse us, Doctor," he said. "It has been a long day for my wife." He propelled her toward the door amid a barrage of "good nights."

McCoy turned back to Spock, who did not appear the least bit discomforted. "A teddy bear!"

"Not precisely, Doctor," Spock said. "On Vulcan, the 'teddy bears' are alive and have six-inch fangs."

McCoy, no Vulcan, was obviously rocked. He was bailed out by a nearby wall communicator, which said in Chekov's voice, "Bridge to Captain Kirk."

"Kirk here."

"Captain, sensors are registering an unidentified vessel pacing us."

"On my way. Duty personnel on yellow alert. Passengers are not to be alarmed . . . Mr. Spock!"

The intruder turned out to be a small ship, about the size of a scout, of no known configuration, and unauthorized in this quadrant. It had been paralleling the course of the *Enterprise* for five minutes, outside phaser range and indeed at the extreme limit of the starship's sensors, and would not answer hails on any frequency or in any language. An attempt to intercept showed the intruder not only more maneuverable than the *Enterprise,* but faster, by a nearly incredible two warps. Kirk ordered full analysis of all sensor readings made during the brief approach, and went back to the reception, leaving Spock in command.

It seemed to be petering out. Gav was still there, sitting isolated, still working on the brandy. If he was trying to get drunk, he was due for a disappointment, Kirk knew; alcohol had no effect on Tellarites except to shorten their already short tempers. Shras and Thelev were also still present, heads down, plus a few other delegates.

Most interestingly, Sarek had returned, by himself. Now why? Had his intent been only to get Amanda off the scene before she could further embarrass their son? There could be no emotional motive behind such a move. What would the logical one be? That whether Sarek approved of Starfleet or not, Spock was an officer in it, and could not function properly if he did not command respect? It seemed as good a guess as any; but Kirk knew that his understanding of Vulcan psychology was, to say the least, insecure.

While he was ruminating, Sarek had gone to a drink dispenser, with the aid of which he seemed to have downed a pill of some kind, and Gav had risen and come up behind him. Sensing trouble, Kirk moved unobtrusively closer. Sure enough, Gav had brought up the Coridan question again.

Sarek was saying: "You seem unable to wait for the Council meeting, Ambassador. No matter. We favor admission."

"You favor? *Why?*"

"Under Federation law, Coridan can be protected—its wealth administered for the benefit of its people."

"It's well for you," Gav said. "Vulcan has no mining interest."

"The Coridians have a nearly unlimited wealth of dilithium crystals, but are underpopulated and unprotected. This invites illegal mining operations."

"Illegal! You accuse us . . . ?"

"Of nothing," Sarek said. "But reports indicate your ships have been carrying Coridian dilithium crystals."

"You call us thieves?" Without an instant's warning, Gav leaped furiously forward, grasping for Sarek's throat. Sarek blocked the Tellarite's hands and effortlessly slammed him away, against a table. As Gav started to lunge at Sarek again, Kirk caught him and forced him back. "Lies!" Gav shouted over his shoulder. "You slander my people!"

"*Gentlemen!*" Kirk said.

Gav stopped struggling and Kirk stepped back, glaring coldly at both Ambassadors. "Whatever arguments you have among yourselves are your business," Kirk said. "*My* business is running this ship—and as long as I command it, *there will be order.*"

"Of course, Captain," Sarek said.

"Understood," Gav said sullenly after a moment. "But Sarek, there will be payment for your slander."

"Threats are illogical," Sarek said. "And such 'payment' is usually expensive."

However, the fight seemed to be over—and the reception as well. Kirk went to his quarters, almost too tired to worry. It had been a day full of tensions, not one of which was yet resolved. Most of the ship was on night status now, and it was a weary pleasure to go through the silent, empty corridors.

But it was not over yet. In his quarters, he had just gotten out of the dress uniform with relief when his intercom said: "Security to Captain Kirk."

What now? "Kirk here."

"Lt. Josephs, sir. I'm on Deck 11, Section A-3. I just found one of the Tellarites, murdered and stuffed into the Jefferies tube. I think it's the Ambassador himself, sir."

So a part of his mission—to keep the peace on board—had failed already.

McCoy knelt in the corridor next to the Jefferies tube and probed Gav's body, using no instruments but his surgeon's fingers. Kirk and Spock watched; Lt. Josephs and two security guards waited for orders to remove the body. At last McCoy rose.

"How was he killed?" Kirk asked.

"His neck was broken. By an expert."

Spock glanced sharply at McCoy and then bent to examine the body himself. Kirk said, "Explain."

"From the location and nature of the break, I'd say the killer knew exactly where to apply pressure to snap the spine instantly. Not even a blow was used—no bruise."

"Who aboard would have that knowledge besides yourself?"

"Vulcans," Spock said, straightening again. "On Vulcan, the method is called *tal-shaya*—considered a merciful method of execution in ancient times."

"Mr. Spock," Kirk said, "a short time ago I broke up an argument between your father and Gav."

"Indeed, Captain? Interesting."

"Interesting? Spock, do you realize that makes your father the most likely suspect?"

"Vulcans do not approve of violence."

"Are you saying your father couldn't have done this?"

"No," Spock said. "But it would be illogical to kill without reason."

"But if he had such a reason?"

"If there were a reason," Spock said, "my father is quite capable of killing—logically and efficiently. He has the skill, and is still only in middle age."

Kirk stared at his First Officer for a moment, appalled. Then he said, "Come with me. You too, Bones."

He led the way to Sarek's quarters which, he was surprised to see when they were admitted by a smiling Amanda, had not been made up to suit Vulcan taste. He would have thought that Spock would have seen to that. He said, "I'm sorry to disturb you. But I must speak with your husband."

"He's been gone for some time. It's his habit to meditate in private before retiring. What's wrong? Spock?"

At that moment the door opened again and Sarek entered. "You want something of me, Captain?"

Kirk observed that he looked somewhat tense, not exactly with anxiety, but as though he were fighting something back. "Ambassador, the Tellarite Gav has been found murdered. His neck was broken—in what Spock describes as *tal-shaya*."

Sarek glanced at his son, lifting an eyebrow in the same familiar manner. "Indeed? Interesting."

"Ambassador, where were you in the past hour?"

"This is ridiculous, Captain," Amanda said. "You aren't accusing him . . . ?"

Spock said, "If only on circumstantial evidence, he is a logical suspect, Mother."

"I quite agree," Sarek said, but he seemed more tense than before. "I was in private meditation. Spock will tell you that such meditation is a personal experience, not to be discussed. Certainly not with Earthmen."

"That's a convenient excuse, Ambassador, but . . ."

He broke off as Sarek gasped and started to crumple. He went to his knees before Kirk and Spock could catch him, clutching at his rib cage. A moan escaped him; any pain that could force such a sound from a Vulcan must have been agonizing indeed.

McCoy took a quick reading, then took out a pressure hypo, set it, and gave Sarek a quick injection. Then he went back to the instruments, taking more time with them now.

"What's wrong?" Amanda asked him.

"I don't know—I can't be sure with Vulcan physiology. It looks like something to do with his cardiovascular system, but . . ."

"Can you help him, Bones?"

"I don't know *that* yet, either."

Kirk looked at mother and son in turn. Spock was as expressionless as always, but Amanda's eyes were haunted; not even years of adaptation to Vulcan tradition could cover a worry of this kind.

"I must go off duty," he told her apologetically. "Still another problem confronts me in the morning, for which I'll need a fresh mind. Should I be needed here before then, Dr. McCoy will of course call me."

"I quite understand, Captain," she said gently. "Good night, and thank you."

A truly remarkable woman.

Not much progress, it turned out on the next trip, had been made on the problem of the ship shadowing the *Enterprise*. Readings taken during the brief attempt at interception showed only that it either had a high-density hull or was otherwise cloaked against sensor probes. It was definitely manned, but by what? The Romulans had nothing like it, nor did the Federation or neutral planets, and that it was Klingon seemed even more unlikely.

Two fragmentary transmissions had been picked up, in an unknown code—with a reception point somewhere inside the *Enterprise* herself. Kirk ordered the locator field tightened to include only the interior of his own ship; if somebody aboard had a personal receiver—as seemed all too likely now—it might be pinned down, *if* the shadow sent another such message.

There seemed to be nothing further to be done on that for the moment. With Spock, whose only concern over his father's illness seemed to be over its possible adverse effect upon the mission, Kirk paid a visit to Sickbay. Sarek was bedded down there, with McCoy and Nurse Christine Chapel trying to make sense of the strange reports the body function panel was giving them; Amanda hovered in the door, trying to keep out of the way. As for Sarek himself, he looked as though he felt inconvenienced, but no longer in uncontrollable pain.

"How is he, Bones?"

"As far as I can tell, our prime suspect has a malfunction in one of the heart valves. I couldn't make a closer diagnosis on a Vulcan without an exploratory. Mrs. Sarek, has he had any previous attacks of this sort?"

"No," Amanda said.

"Yes," Sarek said almost simultaneously. "There were three others. My physician prescribed benjasidrine for the condition."

"Why didn't you tell me?" Amanda asked.

"There was nothing you could have done. The prognosis was not serious, providing I retired, which, of course, I did."

"When did you have these attacks, Ambassador?" McCoy said.

"Two before my retirement. The third, while I was meditating on the Observation Deck when the Tellarite was murdered. I was quite incapacitated."

"I saw you taking a pill not long before that," Kirk said. "If you'll give one to Dr. McCoy for analysis, it should provide circumstantial evidence in your favor. Were there any witnesses to the Observation Deck attack?"

"None. I do not meditate among witnesses."

"Too bad. Mr. Spock, you're a scientist and you know Vulcan. Is there a standard procedure for this condition?"

"In view of its reactivation by Sarek's undertaking this mission," Spock said, "the logical approach would be a cryogenic open-heart operation."

"Unquestionably," Sarek said.

"For that, the patient will need tremendous amounts of blood," McCoy said. "Christine, check the blood bank and see if we've got enough Vulcan blood and plasma. I strongly suspect that we don't have enough even to begin such an operation."

"There are other Vulcans aboard."

"You will find," Sarek said, "that my blood type is T-negative. It is rare. That my two aides should be lacking this factor is highly unlikely."

"I, of course," Spock said, "also have T-negative blood."

"There are human factors in your blood that would have to be filtered out, Mr. Spock," Christine said. "You just couldn't give enough to compensate for that."

"Not necessarily," Spock said. "There is a drug which speeds up replacement of blood in physiologies like ours . . ."

"I know the one you mean," McCoy said. "But it's still experimental and has worked only on a Rigellian. The two physiologies are similar, but not identical. Even with the Rigellian, it put a tremendous strain on the liver and the spleen, to say nothing of the bone marrow—and I'd have to give it to *both* of you. Plus which, I've never operated on a Vulcan. I've studied Vulcan anatomy, but that's a lot different from having actual surgical experience. If I don't kill Sarek with the operation, the drug probably will; it might kill both of them."

Sarek said, "I consider the safety factor to be low, but acceptable."

"Well, I don't," McCoy said, "and in this Sickbay, what I think is law. I can't sanction it."

"And *I* refuse to permit it," Amanda said. "I won't risk both of you . . ."

"You must understand, Mother," Spock said. "The chances of finding sufficient T-negative blood otherwise are vanishingly small. I would estimate them at . . ."

"Please don't," Amanda said.

"Then you automatically condemn Sarek to death," Spock said evenly. "And Doctor, you have no choice either. You must operate, and you have both the drug and a donor."

"It seems the only answer," Sarek said.

Reluctantly, McCoy nodded. Amanda turned a stricken face to Kirk, but he could offer her no help; he could not even help himself in this dilemma.

"I don't like it either, Amanda, believe me," he said. "But we must save your husband. You know very well, too, how much I value your son; but if we must risk him too, then we must. Dr. McCoy has agreed—and I learned long ago never to overrule him in such matters. In fact, I have made him the only officer on the *Enterprise* who has the power to give *me* orders. Please try to trust him as I do."

"And as I do also," Spock said, to McCoy's obvious startlement.

"I'll—try," Amanda said.

"You can do no more. Should you need me, I'll be at my station."

With a great deal more distress than he hoped he had shown, Kirk bowed formally and left.

And halfway to the bridge, deep in thought, he was jumped from behind.

A heavy blow to the head with some sort of club staggered him, but he nevertheless managed to throw his assailant from him against the wall. He got a quick impression of a figure taller but slighter than his own, and the flash of a bladed weapon. In the melee that followed, the other man proved himself to be an experienced infighter, and Kirk was already dazed by the first blow. He managed at last to drop his opponent, perhaps permanently—but not before getting the knife in his own back.

He barely made it to an intercom before losing consciousness.

He came to semiconsciousness to the sound of McCoy's voice.

"It's a bad wound—punctured the left lung. A centimeter or so lower and it would have gone through the heart. Thank goodness he had sense enough not to try to pull the knife out, if he had time to think of it at all."

"The attacker was Thelev. Unconscious, but not seriously injured; just knocked about quite a lot." That was Spock. "He must have caught the Captain by surprise. I'll be in the brig, questioning him, and Shras as well."

"Doctor." This time it was Christine Chapel's voice. "The K-two factor is dropping."

"Spock," McCoy said, "your father is much worse. There's no longer a choice. I'll have to operate immediately. We can begin as soon as you're prepared."

"No," Spock said.

"What?"

Then came Amanda's voice. "Spock, the little chance your father has depends entirely on you. You volunteered."

"My immediate responsibility is to the ship," Spock said. "Our passengers' safety is, by Starfleet order, of first importance. We are being followed by an alien, possibly hostile ship. I cannot relinquish command under these circumstances."

"You can turn command over to Scott," McCoy said harshly.

"On what grounds, Doctor? Command requirements do not recognize personal privilege. I will be in the brig interrogating the Andorian."

Then the darkness closed down again. When he awoke once more, he felt much better. Opening his eyes, he saw Sarek in the bed beside him, apparently asleep, with McCoy and Christine bending over him.

Kirk tried to rise. The attempt provoked a wave of dizziness and nausea and he promptly lay down again—even before McCoy, who had turned instantly at the motion, had to order him to.

"Let that be a lesson to you," McCoy said. "Just lie there and be happy you're still alive."

"How's Sarek?"

"Not good. If I could only operate . . ."

"What's stopping you? Oh, I remember now. Well, Spock's right, Bones. I can't damn him for his loyalty, or for doing his duty. But I'm not going to let him commit patricide."

He sat up, swinging his feet off the bed. McCoy caught his shoulders, preventing him from rising. "Jim, you can't even stand up. You could start the internal bleeding again."

"Bones, Sarek will die without that operation." McCoy nodded. "And you can't operate without the transfusions from Spock." Again a nod. "I'll convince Spock I'm all right, and order him to report here. Once he's off the bridge, I'll turn command over to Scotty and go to my quarters. Will that fill your prescription?"

"Well, no—but it sounds like the best compromise. Let me give you a hand up."

"Gladly."

McCoy supported him all the way to the bridge, but released him just before the elevator doors snapped open. Spock turned, looking surprised and pleased, but masking it immediately.

"Captain."

Kirk stepped very carefully down to his command chair. He tried to appear as though he were casually surveying the bridge, though in fact he was keeping precarious hold of his balance as spasms of dizziness swept him. McCoy remained glued to his side, but ostentatiously offered him not so much as a hand.

Spock came down into the well of the bridge as Kirk reached his chair and eased himself into it. Kirk smiled and nodded approval.

"I'll take over, Spock. Report to Sickbay with Dr. McCoy."

Spock was studying him closely. Kirk was fighting off the dizziness, at least enough—he hoped—to keep it from showing, but he knew also that he was very pale, about which he could do nothing.

"Captain, are you quite all right?"

"I've certified him physically fit, Mr. Spock," McCoy said testily. "Now, I have an operation to perform. And since both of us are required . . ."

He gestured toward the elevator. Spock hesitated briefly, still studying Kirk, who said kindly, "Get out of here, Spock."

Spock nodded, and left with McCoy with something very like alacrity.

"Mr. Chekov," Kirk said, "what is the status of the intruder ship?"

"No change, sir. Maintaining its distance."

"Any further transmissions, Lt. Uhura?"

"None, sir."

Kirk nodded, relaxed a little—and found that he had to pull himself together sharply as the dizziness returned. "Call Mr. Scott to the bridge . . ."

"Captain," Chekov interrupted. "The alien vessel is moving closer!"

"Belay that last order, Lt. Uhura. I'm staying here." But the dizziness kept coming back. He raised a hand to wipe his brow and found that it was shaking.

"Captain," Uhura said. "I'm picking up the alien signal again. But it's coming from inside the *Enterprise*—from the brig."

"Call Security and order an immediate search of the prisoner. Tell them this time to look for implants."

Hours of weakness seemed to pass before the command communicator buzzed. Lt. Josephs' voice said, "Security, Captain. I had to stun the prisoner. He has some sort of transceiver imbedded in one of his antennae, sir; it broke off in my hand. I didn't know they were that delicate."

"They aren't. Thanks, Lieutenant. Neutralize it and send it to Mr. Scott for analysis. Kirk out."

"Captain," Chekov said. "The alien ship has changed course and speed. Moving directly toward us at Warp Eight."

"Lt. Uhura, tell Lt. Josephs to bring the prisoner to the bridge. Mr. Chekov, deflectors on. Red alert. Phasers stand by for fire on my signal."

"Aye, sir." The alarm began to sound. "Shields on. Phasers manned and ready."

"Take over Spock's scanners. Ensign, take the helm."

A blip appeared in the viewscreen and flashed by. It loomed large for an instant, but it was only a blur at this speed. Suddenly the bridge was slammed and rocked. The *Enterprise* had been hit.

"Damage, Mr. Chekov!"

"None, sir; deflected. Target moving away. Turning now. He's coming around again."

"Fire phasers as he passes, Ensign. Steady . . . Fire!"

Chekov studied the scanner. "Clean miss, sir."

At the same moment, there was another jolt. "Report on their weaponry."

"Sensors report standard phasers, sir."

Standard phasers. Good. The enemy had more speed, but they weren't giants.

Another wave of weakness passed through him. The *Enterprise* seemed to be standing up so far, but he was none too sure of himself.

"Captain, the intercom is jammed," Uhura said. "All the Ambassadors are asking what's going on."

"Tell them to—tell them to take a good guess, but *clear that board,* Lieutenant!"

The ship shook furiously again.

"Captain," Uhura said, "I've got an override from Dr. McCoy. He says that another shock like that and he may lose both patients."

"Tell him this is probably only the beginning. Mr. Chekov, lock fire control into the computers. Set photon torpedoes two, four and six for widest possible scatter at the three highest intercept probabilities . . ."

The enemy flashed by. The torpedoes bloomed harmlessly on the viewscreen. Another slam. Kirk's head reeled.

"Number four shield has buckled."

"Auxiliary power."

"Sir, Mr. Scott reports auxiliary power is being called upon by Sickbay."

"Divert."

"Switching over—shields firming up. Number four still weak, sir. If they hit us there again, it'll go altogether."

"Set computer to drop to number three and switch auxiliary back to Sickbay if it goes."

"Aye, sir."

Kirk heard the elevator doors open behind him, and then Lt. Josephs and another security guard were hustling Thelev before him, without ceremony. It took Kirk a moment to remember that he had ordered exactly this interruption. He stared harshly at the prisoner.

"Your friends out there are good," he said. "But they'll have to blast this ship to dust to win."

"That was intended from the beginning, Captain," Thelev said. He was, Kirk noted with a certain satisfaction, still rather lumpy from his attempt at killing, an impression heightened by the missing antenna. The small wound there had healed, but it looked more as though it had been a deep cut than the loss of a major organ.

"You're not an Andorian. What did it take to make you over?"

The *Enterprise* rocked again. Chekov said, "Shield four down."

"Damage control procedures, all decks," Kirk said. Then, to Thelev: "That ship out there carries phasers. It's faster than we are, but weapon for weapon, we have it outgunned."

Thelev only smiled. "Have you hit it yet, Captain?"

Another shock, and a heavier one. Chekov said, "Shield three weakening. Shall I redivert auxiliary power, sir?"

This was getting them nowhere; if it continued sheerly as a battle of attrition, the *Enterprise* would lose. And there was the operation to consider.

"Engineering, this is the Captain. Blank out all power on the port side of the ship except for phaser banks. On my signal, cut starboard power. Kirk out." He turned back to Thelev. "Who are you?"

"Find your own answers, Captain. You haven't long to live."

"You're a spy, surgically altered to pass as an Andorian. You were planted in the Ambassador's party to use terror and murder to disrupt us and prepare for this attack."

"Speculation, Captain."

The ship shook again. Chekov said, "Shield three is gone, sir."

"Engineering, blank out starboard power, all decks. Maintain until further orders."

The lights on the bridge went out, except for gleams from the telltales on the panels, and the glow of stars from the viewscreen. In the dimness, Thelev at last looked slightly alarmed. "What are you doing?" he said.

"*You* speculate."

"We're starting to drift, Captain," Chekov said. "Shall I hold her on course?"

"No. Stand by your phasers, Mr. Chekov."

"Aye, sir. Phasers standing by."

A blip of pulsing light again appeared in the screen, slowed down, held steady. Kirk leaned forward intently.

"He's just hovering out there, sir."

"Looking us over," Kirk said. "We're dead—as far as he knows. No starship commander would deliberately expose his ship like this, especially one stuffed with notables—or that's what I hope he thinks."

"Range decreasing. Sublight speed."

"Hold your fire."

"Still closing—range one hundred thousand kilometers—phasers locked on target . . ."

"Fire."

The blip flared brightly on the screen. A jubilant shout went up from Chekov. "Got him!"

"Lt. Uhura, open a hailing frequency. If they wish to surrender . . ."

He was interrupted by a glaring burst of light from the viewscreen. Everyone instinctively ducked; the light was blinding. When Kirk could see the screen again, there was nothing on it but stars.

"They could not surrender, Captain," Thelev said. "The ship had orders to self-destruct."

"Lt. Uhura, relay to Starfleet Command. Tell them we have a prisoner."

"Only temporarily, Captain," Thelev said. "You see, I had self-destruct orders, too. Slow poison—quite painless, actually, but there is no known antidote. I anticipate another ten minutes of life."

Kirk turned to the security guards. "Take him to Sickbay," he said harshly.

Josephs and the guard came down to flank Thelev, and began to shepherd him toward the elevator. As they reached the door, the spy crumpled, sagged, fell to his knees. He said tonelessly, "I seem to—have —miscalculated . . ."

He fell face down and was still. Kirk rose wearily.

"So did they," he said. "Put him in cold storage for an autopsy. Secure for General Quarters. Mr. Chekov, take over."

He went down to the operating room. It was empty, the operating table clear, the instruments mutely inactive. After a moment, McCoy came in from the Sickbay area. He looked as drawn and tired as Kirk felt.

"Bones?"

"Are you quite through shaking this ship around?" the surgeon asked.

"Sarek—Spock—how are they?"

"I don't mind telling you, you make things difficult for a surgeon conducting a delicate operation which . . ."

"*Bones.*"

The Sickbay doors opened again and Amanda appeared. "Captain, come in," she said. Kirk shoved past McCoy eagerly.

Inside, Sarek and Spock occupied two of the three beds, side by side. Both looked pale and exhausted, but reasonably chipper. Amanda sat down happily beside Sarek.

"That pigheaded Vulcan stamina," McCoy's voice said behind him. "I couldn't have pulled them through without it."

"Some doctors have all the luck."

"Captain," Spock said. "I believe the alien . . ."

"We damaged their ship," Kirk said. "They destroyed it to avoid capture. Bones, Thelev's body is being brought to your lab. I want an autopsy as soon as you feel up to it."

"I believe you'll find he's what's usually called an Orion, Doctor," Spock said. "There are intelligence reports that Orion smugglers have been raiding the Coridian system."

"But what could they gain by an attack on us?" Kirk asked.

"Mutual suspicion," Sarek suggested, "and perhaps interplanetary war."

Kirk nodded. "With Orion carefully neutral. She'd clean up by supplying dilithium to both sides—and continue to raid Coridan."

"It was the power utilization curve that confused me," Spock said. "I did not realize that until I was just going under the anesthetic. The curve made it appear more powerful than a starship—than anything known to us. That ship was constructed for a suicide mission. Since they never intended to return to base, they could utilize one hundred per cent power in their attacks. I cannot understand why I didn't realize that earlier."

Kirk looked at Sarek. "You might have had a few other things on your mind."

"That does not seem likely."

"No," Kirk said wryly. "But thank you anyway."

"And you, Sarek," Amanda said. "Would you also say thank you to your son?"

"I do not understand."

"For saving your life."

"Spock behaved in the only logical manner open to him," Sarek said. "One does not thank logic, Amanda."

Amanda stiffened and exploded. "Logic! Logic! I am sick to death of logic. Do you want to know how I feel about your logic?"

The two Vulcans studied the angry woman as though she were some sort of exhibit. Spock glanced at his father and said, quite conversationally, "Emotional, isn't she?"

"She has always been that way."

"Indeed? Why did you marry her?"

"At the time," Sarek said solemnly, "it seemed the logical thing to do."

Amanda stared at them, stunned. Kirk could not help grinning, and McCoy was grinning, too. Amanda, turning to them in appeal, was startled; and then, obviously, suddenly realized that her leg was being pulled. A smile broke over her face.

Equally suddenly, the room reeled. Kirk grabbed the edge of the table. Instantly, McCoy was beside him, guiding him toward the third bed.

"Bones—really—I'm all right."

"If you keep arguing with your kindly family doctor, you'll spend the next ten days right here. Cooperate and you'll get out in two."

Kirk subsided, but now Spock was sitting up. "If you don't mind, Doctor, I'll report to my own station now."

McCoy pointed firmly at the bed. "You're at your station, Spock."

The First Officer shrugged and settled back. McCoy surveyed his three restive patients with an implacable expression.

"Bones," Kirk said, "I think you're enjoying this."

"Indeed, Captain," Spock agreed. "I've never seen him look so happy."

"Shut up," McCoy commanded. There was a long silence. McCoy's expression gradually changed to one of incredulity.

"Well, what do you know?" he said to Amanda. "I finally got the last word!"

THE MENAGERIE*
(Gene Roddenberry)

When the distress signal from Talos IV came through, via old-fashioned radio, Captain Christopher Pike was of two minds about doing anything about it. The message said it was from survivors of the SS *Columbia,* and a library search by Spock showed that a survey ship of that name had indeed disappeared in that area—eighteen years ago. It had taken all of those years for the message, limited to the speed of light, to reach the *Enterprise,* which passed through its wave-front just slightly eighteen light-years from the Talos system. A long time ago, that had been.

In addition, Pike had his own crew to consider. Though the *Enterprise* had come out of the fighting around Rigel VIII—her maiden battle—unscarred, the ground skirmishing had not been as kind to her personnel. Spock, for example, was limping, though he was trying to minimize it, and Navigator Jose Tyler's left forearm was bandaged down to his palm. Pike himself was unhurt, but he felt desperately tired.

Nevertheless, the library also reported Talos IV to be habitable, so survivors from the *Columbia* might still be alive; and since the *Enter-*

---

* As originally produced, this story ran in two parts. The main story, which takes place so far back in the history of the *Enterprise* that the only familiar face aboard her then was Spock, appeared surrounded by and intercut with an elaborate "framing" story, in which Spock is up for court-martial on charges of mutiny and offers the main story as an explanation of his inarguably mutinous behavior. Dramatically, this was highly effective—indeed, as I've already noted, it won a "Hugo" award in this category for that year—but told as fiction, it involves so many changes of viewpoint, as well as so many switches from present to past, that it becomes impossibly confusing. (I know—I've tried!) Hence the present version adapts only the main story, incidentally restoring to it the ending it had—never shown on television—before the frame was grafted onto it. I think the producers also came to feel that the double-plotted version had been a mistake; at least, "The Menagerie" turned out to be the only two-part episode in the entire history of the series.
—J.B.

prise would be passing within visual scanning distance anyhow, it wouldn't hurt to take a look. The chances of finding anything at this late date . . .

But almost at once, Tyler picked up reflections from the planet's surface whose polarization and scatter pattern indicated large, rounded chunks of metal, which might easily have been parts of a spaceship's hull. Pike ordered the *Enterprise* into orbit.

"I'll want a landing party of six, counting myself. Mr. Tyler, you'll be second in command, and we'll need Mr. Spock too; both of you, see that there's a fresh dressing on your wounds. Also, Dr. Boyce, Chief Garrison and ship's geologist. Number One, you're in command of the *Enterprise* in our absence. Who seconds you now?"

"Yeoman Colt, sir."

Pike hesitated. That this left the bridge dominated by women didn't bother him; female competence to be in Starfleet had been tested and proven before he had been born. And Pike had the utmost confidence in Number One, ordinarily the ship's helmsman and, after the Rigel affair, the most experienced surviving officer. Slim and dark in a Nile Valley sort of way, she was one of those women who always look the same between the ages of twenty and fifty, but she had a mind like the proverbial steel trap and Pike had never seen her shaken in any situation. Yeoman Colt, however, was a recent replacement, and an unknown quantity. Well, the assignment was likely to prove a routine one, anyhow.

"Very well. We'll beam down to the spot where Mr. Tyler picked up those reflections."

This proved to be on a rocky plateau, not far from an obvious encampment—a rude collection of huts, constructed out of slabs of rock, debris from a spaceship hull, scraps of canvas and other odds and ends. Several fairly old men were visible, all bearded, all wearing stained and tattered garments. One was carrying water; the others were cultivating a plot of orange vegetation. The ingenuity and resolute will which had enabled them to exist for nearly two decades on this forbidding alien world were everywhere evident.

One of them looked up in the direction of the landing party and froze, clearly unable to believe his eyes. At last he called hoarsely, "Winter! *Look!*"

A second man looked up, and reacted almost as the first had. Then he shouted: "They're men! Human!"

The sound of their voices brought other survivors out of their huts and sheds. The youngest looked to be nearly fifty, but they were tanned, hardened, in extraordinarily good health. The two groups approached each other slowly, solemnly; Pike could almost feel the intensity of emotion. He stepped forward and extended a hand.

"Captain Christopher Pike, United Spaceship *Enterprise*."

The first survivor to speak mutely accepted Pike's hand, tears on his face. At last he said, with obvious effort, "Dr. Theodore Haskins, American Continent Institute."

"They're *men!* Here to take us back!" the man called Winter said, laughing with sudden relief. "You are, aren't you? Is Earth all right?"

"Same old Earth," Pike said, smiling. "You'll see it before long."

"And you won't believe how fast you can get back," Tyler added. "The time barrier's been broken! Our new ships can . . ."

He broke off, mouth open, staring past Haskins' shoulder. Following the direction of the navigator's gaze, Pike saw standing in a hut doorway a remarkably beautiful young woman. Although her hair was uncombed and awry, her makeshift dress tattered, she looked more like a woodland nymph than the survivor of a harrowing ordeal. Motioning her forward, Haskins said, "This is Vina. Her parents are dead; she was born almost as we crashed."

There were more introductions all around, but Pike found himself almost unable to take his eyes off the girl. Perhaps it was only the contrast she made with the older men, but her young, animal grace was striking. No wonder Tyler had stared.

"No need to prolong this," Pike said. "Collect what personal effects you want to keep and we'll be off. I suggest you concentrate on whatever records you have; the *Enterprise* is amply stocked with necessities, and even some luxuries."

"Extraordinary," Haskins said. "She must be a very big vessel."

"Our largest and most modern type; the crew numbers four hundred and thirty."

Haskins shook his head in amazement and bustled off. Amidst all the activity, Vina approached Pike and drew him a little to one side.

"Captain, may I have a word?"

"Of course, Vina."

"Before we go, there is something you should see. Something of importance."

"Very well. What is it?"

"It's much easier to show than to explain. If you'll come this way . . ."

She led him to a rocky knoll some distance from the encampment, and pointed to the ground at its base. "There it is."

Pike did not know what he had expected—anything from a grave to some sort of alien artifact—but in fact he saw nothing of interest at all, and said so. Vina looked disappointed.

"The angle of the light is probably wrong," she said. "Come around to this side."

They changed places, so that his back was to the knoll, hers to the encampment. As far as Pike could tell, this made no difference.

"I don't understand," he said.

"You will," Vina said, the tone of her voice changing suddenly. "You're a perfect choice."

Pike looked up sharply. As he did so, the girl vanished. It was not the fading dematerialization of the Transporter effect; she simply blinked out as though someone had snapped off a light. With her went all the survivors and their entire encampment, leaving nothing behind but the bare plateau and the stunned men from the *Enterprise*.

There was a hiss behind him and he spun, reaching for his phaser. A cloud of white gas was rolling toward him, through which he could see an oddly shaped portal which, perfectly camouflaged as a part of the rock, had noiselessly opened to reveal the top of a lift shaft. He had an instant's impression of two occupants—small, slim, pale, humanlike creatures with large elongated heads, in shimmering metallic robes; one of them was holding a small cylinder which was still spitting the white spray.

In the same instant, the gas hit him and he was paralyzed, still conscious but unable to move anything but his eyes. The two creatures stepped forward and dragged him into the opening

"*Captain!*" Spock's voice shouted in the distance. Then there was the sound of running, suddenly muffled as though the doors had closed again, and then the lift dropped with a hissing *whoosh* like that of a high-speed pneumatic tube. Above, and still more distantly, came the sound of a rock explosion as someone fired a phaser at full power, but the lift simply fell faster.

With it, Pike fell into unconsciousness.

He awoke clawing for his own phaser, a spongelike surface impeding his movements. The gun was gone. Rolling to his feet, he looked around, at the same time reaching next for his communicator. That was gone too; so was his jacket.

He was in a spotless utilitarian enclosure. The spongy surface turned out to belong to a plastic shape, apparently a sort of bed, with a filmy metallic-cloth blanket folded on it. There was also a free-form pool of surging water, with a small drinking container sitting on the floor next to it. A prison cell, clearly; the bars . . .

But there were no bars. The fourth wall was made up entirely of a transparent panel. Pike hurried to it and peered through. He found himself looking up and down a long corridor, faced with similar panels; but they were offset to, rather than facing each other, so that Pike could see into only small angled portions of the two nearest him on the other side.

Some sound he had made must have penetrated into the corridor, for suddenly there was a wild snarl, and in the cell—cage?—to his left, a flat creature, half anthropoid, half spider, rushed hungrily at him, only to be thrown back, its ugly fangs clattering against the transparency. Startled, Pike looked to the right; in this enclosure he could see a portion of some kind of tree. Then there was a leathery flapping, and an incredibly thin humanoid/bird creature came into view, peering curiously but shyly toward Pike's cage. The instant it saw Pike watching, it whirled and vanished.

As it did, a group of the pale, large-headed men like those who had kidnapped him came into view, coming toward him. They were led by one who wore an authoritative-looking jeweled pendant on a short chain around his neck. They all came to a halt in front of Pike's cage, silently watching him. He studied them in turn. They were quite bald, all of them, and each had a prominent vein across his forehead.

Finally, Pike said, "Can you hear me? My name is Christopher Pike, commander of the vessel *Enterprise* of the United Federation of Planets. Our intentions are peaceful. Can you understand me?"

The large forehead vein of one of the Talosians pulsed strongly and, although Pike could see no lip movement, a voice sounded in his head, a voice that sounded as though it were reciting something.

"It appears, Magistrate, that the intelligence of the specimen is shockingly limited."

Now the forehead of the creature with the pendant pulsed. "This is no surprise, since his vessel was lured here so easily with a simulated message. As you can read in its thoughts, it is only now beginning to suspect that the survivors and the encampment were a simple illusion we placed in their minds. And you will note the confusion as it reads our thought transmissions . . ."

"All right, telepathy," Pike broke in. "You can read my mind, I can read yours. Now, unless you want my ship to consider capturing me an unfriendly act . . ."

"You now see the primitive fear-threat reaction. The specimen is about to boast of his strength, the weaponry of his vessel, and so on." As Pike stepped back a pace and tensed himself, the Magistrate added, "Next, frustrated into a need to display physical prowess, the creature will throw himself against the transparency."

Pike, his act predicted in mid-move, felt so foolish that he canceled it, which made him angrier than ever. He snarled, "There's a way out of every cage, and I'll find it."

"Despite its frustration, the creature appears more adaptable than our specimens from other planets," the Magistrate continued. "We can soon begin the experiment."

Pike wondered what they meant by *that*, but it was already obvious that they were not going to pay any attention to anything he said. He began to pace. The telepathic "voices" continued behind him.

"Thousands of us are now probing the creature's thoughts, Magistrate. We find excellent memory capacity."

"I read most strongly a recent struggle in which it fought to protect its tribal system. We will begin with this, giving the specimen something more interesting to protect."

The cage vanished.

He was standing alone among rocks and strange vegetation which, on second look, proved to be vaguely familiar. Then an unmistakably familiar voice sounded behind him.

"Come. Hurry!"

He turned to see Vina, her hair long and in braids, dressed like a peasant girl of the terrestrial Middle Ages. Behind her towered a fortress which he might have taken as belonging to the same period had he not recognized it instantly. The girl pointed to it and said, "It is deserted. There will be weapons, perhaps food."

"This is Rigel VIII," Pike said slowly. "I fought in that fortress just two weeks ago. But where do you fit in?"

There was a distant bellowing sound. Vina started, then began walking rapidly toward the fortress. Pike remained where he was.

I was in a cell, a cage in some kind of zoo. I'm still there. I just think I see this. They must have reached into my mind, taken the memory of somewhere I've been, something that's happened to me—except that she wasn't in it then.

The bellowing sounded again, nearer. Pike hurried after the girl, catching up with her just inside the gateway to the fortress' courtyard. The place was a scatter of battered shields, lance staves, nicked and snapped swords; there was even a broken catapult—the debris that had been left behind after Pike's own force had breached and reduced the fortress. Breaking the Kalars' hold over their serfs had been a bloody business, and made more so by the hesitancy of Starfleet Command over whether the whole operation was not in violation of General Order Number One. Luckily, the Kalars themselves had solved that by swarming in from Rigel X in support of their degenerate colony . . .

And that animal roar of rage behind them could only be a stray Kalar colonist, seeking revenge for the fall of his fortress and his feudalism upon anything in his path. Vina was looking desperately for a weapon amid the debris, but there was nothing here she could even lift.

Then the bellow sounded at the gateway. Vina shrank into the nearest shadow, pulling Pike with her. He was in no mood to hang back; memory was too strong. The figure at the courtyard entry was a local Kalar warrior, huge, hairy, Neanderthal, clad in cuirass and helmet and carrying a mace. It looked about, shoulders hunched.

"What nonsense," Pike said under his breath. "It was all over weeks ago . . ."

"*Hush,*" Vina whispered, terrified. "You've been here—you know what he'll do to us."

"It's nothing but a damn silly illusion."

The warrior roared again, challengingly, raising tremendous echoes. Apparently he hadn't seen them yet.

"It doesn't matter *what* you call this," Vina whispered again. "You'll feel it, that's what matters. You'll feel every moment of whatever happens. I'll feel it happening too."

The warrior moved tentatively toward them. Either in genuine panic or to force Pike's hand, Vina whirled and raced for a parapet stairway behind them which led toward the battlement above. The Kalar spotted her at once; Pike had no choice but to follow.

At the top was another litter of weapons; Vina had already picked up a spear with a head like an assegai. Pike found himself a shield and an unbroken sword. As he straightened, the girl pushed him aside. A huge round rock smashed into the rampart wall inches away from him, the force of the fragments knocking him down.

The pain was real, all right. He raised a hand to his forehead to find it bleeding. Below, the warrior was picking up another rock from a depleted pile on the other side of the catapult.

While Pike scrambled back, Vina threw her spear, but she did it inexpertly, and in any event her strength proved insufficient for the range.

Changing his mind at once, the Kalar dropped the stone and came charging up the stairs.

Pike's shield was almost torn from his arm at the first blow of the mace. His own sword clanged harmlessly against the Kalar's armor, and he was driven back by a flurry of blows.

Then there was a twanging sound. The warrior bellowed in pain and swung around, revealing an arrow driven deep into his back. Vina had found a crossbow, cocked and aimed, and at that range she couldn't miss.

But the wound wasn't immediately mortal and she obviously did not know how to cock the weapon again. The Kalar, staggering, moved in upon her.

From that close, a crossbow bolt would go through almost any armor, but Pike's sword certainly wouldn't. Dropping it, he sprang forward, raised his shield high, and brought it down with all his strength on the back of the warrior's neck. The creature spun off the rampart edge and plummeted to the floor of the compound below. It struck supine and lay still.

Vina, sobbing with relief, threw herself into Pike's arms . . .

. . . and they were back in the menagerie cage.

She was now wearing her own, shorter hair, and a simple garment of the metallic Talosian material. His own bruises and exhaustion had vanished completely, along with the shield. It took him a startled moment to realize what had happened.

Vina smiled. "It's over."

"Why are you here?" he demanded.

She hesitated slightly, then smiled again. "To please you."

"Are you real?"

"As real as you wish."

"That's no answer," he said.

"Perhaps they've made me up out of dreams you've forgotten."

He pointed to her garment. "And I dreamed of you in the same metal fabric they wear?"

"I must wear something." She came closer. "Or must I? I can wear anything you wish, be anything you wish . . ."

"To make this 'specimen' perform for them? To watch how I react? Is that it?"

"Don't you have a dream, something you've wanted very badly . . ."

"Do they do more than just watch me?" he asked. "Do they *feel* with me too?"

"You can have any dream you wish. I can become anything. Any woman you ever imagined." She tried to nestle closer. "You can go anyplace, do anything—have any experience from the whole universe. Let me please you."

Pike eyed her speculatively. "You can," he said abruptly. "Tell me about them. Is there some way I can keep them from using my own thoughts against me? Ah, you're frightened. Does that mean there *is* a way?"

"You're being a fool."

He nodded. "You're right. Since you insist you're an illusion, there's not much point in this conversation."

He went over to the bed and lay down, ignoring her. It was not hard to sense her anxiety, however. Whatever her task was, she did not want to fail it.

After a while she said, "Perhaps—if you asked me something I could answer . . ."

He sat up. "How far can they control my mind?"

"That's not a—that is—" she paused. "If I tell you—will you pick some dream you've had, let me live it with you?"

Pike considered this. The information seemed worth the risk. He nodded.

"They—they can't actually make you do anything you don't want to."

"They have to try to trick me with their illusions?"

"Yes. And they can punish when you're not cooperative. You'll find out about that."

"They must have lived on the planet's surface once . . ."

"Please," she interrupted. "If I say too much . . ."

"Why did they move underground?" he pressed insistently.

"War, thousands of centuries ago," she said hurriedly. "The ones left on the surface destroyed themselves and almost their whole world too. It's taken that long for the planet to heal itself."

"And I suppose the ones who came underground found life too limited—so they concentrated on developing their mental power."

She nodded. "But they've found it's a trap. Like a narcotic. When dreams become more important than reality, you give up travel, building, creating, you even forget how to repair the machines left behind by your ancestors. You just sit living and reliving other lives in the thought records. Or probe the minds of zoo specimens, descendants of life they brought back long ago from all over this part of the galaxy."

Pike suddenly understood. "Which means they had to have more than one of each animal."

"Yes," Vina said, clearly frightened now. "Please, you said if I answered your questions . . ."

"But that was a bargain with something that didn't exist. You said you were an illusion, remember."

"*I'm a woman,*" she said, angrily now. "As real and human as you are. We're—like Adam and Eve. If they can . . ."

She broke off with a scream and dropped to the floor, writhing.

"Please!" she wailed. "Don't punish me—I'm trying my best with him —no, *please* . . ."

In the midst of her agony, she vanished. Pike looked up to see the creature called the Magistrate watching through the panel. Furiously, he turned his back—and noticed for the first time an almost invisible circular seam, about man-high, in the wall beside his bed. Was there a hidden panel there?

A small clink of sound behind him made him turn again. A vial of blue liquid was sitting on the floor, just inside the transparency. The Magistrate continued to watch; his mental speech said, "The vial contains a nourishing protein complex."

"Is the keeper actually communicating with one of his animals?"

"If the form and color are not appealing, it can appear as any food you wish to visualize."

"And if I prefer—" Pike began.

"To starve? You overlook the unpleasant alternative of punishment."

With the usual suddenness, Pike found himself writhing in bubbling, sulphurous brimstone in a dark place obscured by smoke. Flame licked at him from all sides. The instant agony was as real as the surprise, and a scream was wrenched from him.

It lasted only a few seconds and then he was back in the cage, staggering.

"From a fable you once heard in childhood," the Magistrate said. "You will now consume the nourishment."

"Why not just put irresistible—hunger in my mind?" Pike said, still gasping with remembered pain. "You can't—do that. You do have limitations, don't you?"

"If you continue to disobey, deeper in your mind there are things even more unpleasant."

Shakily, Pike picked up the vial and swallowed its contents. Almost simultaneously he tossed the vial aside and threw himself at the transparency. It bounced him back, of course—but the Magistrate had also stepped back a pace.

"That's very interesting," Pike said. "You were startled. Weren't you reading my mind then?"

"Now, to the female. As you have conjectured, an Earth vessel did actually crash on our planet. But with only a single survivor."

"Let's stay on the first subject. All I wanted for that moment was to get my hands around your neck. Do primitive emotions put up a block you can't read through?"

"We repaired the survivor's injuries and found the species interesting. So it became necessary to attract a mate."

"All right, we'll talk about the girl. You seem to be going out of your way to make her seem attractive, to make me feel protective."

"This is necessary in order to perpetuate the species."

"That could be done medically, artificially," Pike said. "No, it seems more important to you now that I accept her, begin to like her . . ."

"We wish our specimens to be happy in their new life."

"Assuming that's another lie, why would you want me attracted to her? So I'll feel love, a husband-wife relationship? That would be necessary only if you needed to build a family group, or even a whole human . . ."

"With the female now properly conditioned, we will continue with . . ."

"You mean properly punished!" Pike shouted. "I'm the one who's not cooperating. Why don't you punish me?"

"First an emotion of protectiveness, now one of sympathy. Excellent." The Magistrate turned and walked away down the corridor. Frustrated again, Pike turned to study the mysterious seam.

He found himself studying a tree instead. Around him, in full day, was richly planted park and forest land, with a city on the horizon. He recognized the place instantly.

Immediately to his right was tethered a pair of handsome saddle horses. To the left, Vina, in casual Earth garb, was laying out a picnic lunch on the grass.

Looking up at him, smiling, she said, "I left the thermos hooked to my saddle."

Pike went to the horses and patted them. "Tango! You old quarter-gaited devil, you! Hello, Mary Lou! No, sorry, no sugar this time . . ."

But patting his pockets automatically, he was astonished to find the usual two sugar cubes there. He fed them to the horses. The Talosians seemed to think of everything.

He unhooked the thermos, carried it to the picnic and sat down, eyeing Vina curiously. She seemed nervous.

"Is it good to be home?" she asked him.

"I've been aching to be back here. They read our minds very well."

"Please!" It was a cry of fear. Her face pleaded with him to keep silent.

"Home, everything else I want," he said. *"If* I cooperate. Is that it?"

"Have you forgotten my—headaches, darling? The doctor said when you talk strangely like this . . ."

Her voice trailed off, shaken. Pike was beginning to feel trapped again.

"Look, I'm sorry they punish you," he said. "But I can't let them hold that over our heads. They'll *own* us then."

She continued to lay out the lunch, trying to ignore him. "My, it turned out to be a beautiful day, didn't it?"

"Funny," he mused. "About twenty-four hours ago I was telling the ship's doctor how much I wanted—something not so far from what's being offered here. No responsibility, no frustrations or bruises . . . And now that I have it, I understand the doctor's answer. You either *live* life, bruises and all, or you turn your back on it and start dying. The Talosians went the second way."

"I hope you're hungry," Vina said, with false brightness. "The white sandwiches are your mother's chicken-tuna recipe."

He tried one. She was right. "Doc would be happy about part of this, at least. Said I needed a rest."

"This is a lovely place to rest."

"I spent my boyhood here. Doesn't compare with the gardens around the big cities, but I liked it better." He nodded toward the distant skyline. "That's Mojave. I was born there."

Vina laughed. "Is that supposed to be news to your wife? See—you're home! You can even stay if you want. Wouldn't it be nice showing your children where you once played?"

"These—'headaches,'" Pike said. "They'll be hereditary. Would you wish them on a child—or a whole group of children?"

"That's foolish."

"Is it? Look, first I'm made to protect you, then to feel sympathy for you—and now familiar surroundings, comfortable husband and wife feelings. They don't need all this just for passion. They're after respect, affection, mutual dependence—and something else . . ."

"They say, in the old days all this was a desert. Blowing sand, cactus . . ."

"I can't help either of us if you won't give me a chance!" Pike said sharply. "You told me once that illusions have become like a narcotic to them. They've even forgotten how to repair the machines left by their ancestors. Is that why we're so important? To build a colony of slaves who can . . ."

"Stop it, stop it! Don't you care what they do to me?"

"There's no such thing as a perfect prison," Pike said. "There's always some way out. Back in my cage, it seemed for a couple of minutes our keeper couldn't read my thoughts. Do emotions like anger block off our thought from them?"

"Don't you think," Vina said angrily, "that I've already tried things like that?"

"There's *some* way to beat them. Answer me!"

Her anger turned to tears. "Yes, they can't read—through primitive emotions. But you can't keep it up long enough. I've tried!" She began to sob. "They—keep at you and—at you, year after year—probing, looking for a weakness, and tricking—and punishing and—they've won. They own me. I know you hate me for it."

Her fear, desperation, loneliness, everything that she had undergone were welling up in misery, deep and genuine. He put an arm around her. "I don't hate you. I can guess what it was like."

"It's not enough! They want you to have feelings that would build a family, protect it, work for it. Don't you understand? They read my thoughts, my desires, my dreams of what would be a perfect man. That's why they picked you. *I can't help but love you.* And they expect you to feel the same way."

Pike was shaken despite himself. The story was all too horribly likely. "If they can read my mind, they know I'm attracted to you. From the first day in the survivor's encampment. You were like a wild little animal."

"Was that the reason? Because I was like a barbarian?"

"Perhaps," Pike said, amused.

"I'm beginning to see why none of this has really worked on you," Vina said, straightening. "You've *been* home. And fighting, like on Rigel, that's not new to you either. A person's strongest dreams are about things he *can't* do."

"Maybe so. I'm no psychologist."

"Yes," she said, smiling, almost to herself. "A ship's captain, always having to be so formal, so decent and honest and proper—he must wonder what it would be like to forget all that."

The scene changed, with a burst of music and wild merriment. The transition caught him still seated. He was now on a pillowed floor at a low round table bearing a large bowl of fruit and goblets of wine. He seemed to be clad now in rich silk robes, almost like that of an Oriental potentate; near him sat a man whom he vaguely remembered as an Earth trader, similarly but less luxuriantly garbed, while on the other side was an officer in Starfleet uniform whom he did not recognize at all. All of them were being served by women whose garb and manner strongly suggested slavery, and whose skins were the same color as Spock's. The music was coming from a quartet seated near a fountain pool.

Again he recognized the place; it was the courtyard of the Potentate of Orion. The officer leaned forward.

"Say, Pike," he said. "You used to be Captain of the *Enterprise*, didn't you?"

"Matter of fact, he was," said the trader.

"Thought so. You stopped here now and then—to check things out, so to speak."

"And then," the trader added, "sent Earth a blistering report on 'the Orion traders taking shocking advantage of the natives.'"

Both men laughed. "Funny how they are on this planet," the officer said. "They actually like being taken advantage of."

"And not just in profits, either."

The officer looked around appraisingly. "Nice place you've got here, Mr. Pike."

"It's a start," the trader said. Both laughed again. The officer patted the nearest slave girl on the rump.

"Do any of you have a green one?" he asked. "They're dangerous, I hear. Razor-sharp claws, and they attract a man like a sensation of irresistible hunger."

Up to now, the officer had simply repelled Pike, but that last phrase sounded familiar—and had been delivered with mysterious emphasis. The trader gave Pike a knowing look.

"Now and then," he said, "comes a man who tames one."

There was a change in the music; it became louder, took on a slow, throbbing rhythm. The slave girls turned hurriedly, as if suddenly anxious to escape. Looking toward the musicians, Pike saw another girl, nude, her skin green, and glistening as if it had been oiled, kneeling at the edge of the pool. Her fingertips were long, gleaming, razor-edged scimitars; her hair like the mane of a wild animal. She was staring straight at him.

One of the slaves was slow. The green girl sprang up with a sound like a spitting cat, barring her escape. A man Pike had not seen before leapt forward to intervene, raising a whip.

"Stop!" Pike shouted, breaking his paralysis. The green girl turned and looked at him again, and then he recognized her. It was Vina once more.

She came forward to the center of the rectangle and posed for a moment. Then the music seemed to reach her, the slow surging beat forcing movement out of her as a reed flute takes possession of a cobra. She threw her head back, shrieked startlingly, and began to dance.

"Where'd he find her?" said the officer's voice. Pike was unable to tear his eyes away from her.

"He'd stumbled into a dark corridor," the trader's voice said, "and then he saw flickering light ahead. Almost like secret dreams a bored sea captain might have, wasn't it? There she was, holding a torch, glistening green . . ."

"Strange looks she keeps giving you, Pike."

"Almost as if she knows something about you."

Somewhere in the back of his mind he knew that the Talosians were baiting him through these two men; but he could not stop watching the dance.

"Wouldn't you say that's worth a man's soul?" said the trader.

"It makes you believe she could be anything," said the officer. "Suppose you had all of space to choose from, and this was only one small sample . . ."

That was too much. Pike rose, growling. "Get out of my way, blast you!"

He crossed the courtyard to a curtained doorway which he seemed to recall was an exit. Brushing the curtains aside, he found himself in a corridor. It was certainly dark, and grew darker as he strode angrily along it. In the distance was a flickering light, and then, there indeed was Vina, holding aloft a torch . . .

The scene lightened and the torch vanished. Vina, her skin white, her body covered with the Talosian garment, continued to hold her empty hand aloft for a second. They were back in the cage.

Vina's face contorted in fury. She ran to the transparency and pounded on it, shouting out into the corridor.

"No! Let us finish! I could have . . ."

"What's going on here?" another woman's voice demanded. Both Pike and Vina whirled.

There were two other women in the cage: Number One, and Yeoman Colt. After so many shocks, Pike could summon no further reaction to this one.

"I might well ask you the same thing," he said numbly.

"We tried to Transport down in here," Number One said. "There was a risk we'd materialize in solid rock, but we'd already tried blasting open the top of the lift, with no luck."

"But there were six of us to start with," Yeoman Colt said. "I don't know why the others didn't make it."

"It's not fair!" Vina said to Pike. "You don't need them."

"They may be just what I need," Pike said drily, beginning to recover some of his wits. "Number One, Yeoman, hand me those phasers."

They passed the weapons over. He examined them. What he found did not particularly surprise him. "Empty."

"They were fully charged when we left," Number One said.

"No doubt. But you'll find your communicators don't work either." A thought struck him. He looked quickly toward the almost circular panel he had found before. Then, suddenly, he hurled both phasers at it.

"What good does that do?" Number One said coolly.

"Don't talk to me. Don't say anything. I'm working up a hate—filling my mind with a picture of beating their huge, misshapen heads to a pulp. Thoughts so primitive they shut everything else out. I hate them—do you understand?"

"How long can you block your thoughts?" Vina said. "A few minutes, an hour? How can that help you?"

Pike concentrated, trying to pay no attention to her. She turned on the two other women.

"He doesn't need you," she said, with jealous anger she did not have to force-feed. "He's already picked me."

"Picked you for what?" Colt asked.

Vina looked at her scornfully. "Now there's a great chance for intelligent offspring."

"'Offspring?'" Colt echoed. "As in 'children'?"

"As in he's 'Adam,'" Number One said, indicating Pike. "Isn't that it?"

"You're no better choice. They'd have better luck crossing him with a computer!"

"Shall I compute your age?" Number One said. "You were listed on that expedition as an adult crewman. Now, adding eighteen years to that . . ."

She broke off as Vina turned to the transparency. The Magistrate was back. The two crewwomen stared at him with interest.

"It's not fair," Vina said. "I did everything you asked."

The Magistrate ignored her. "Since you resist the present specimen," he said to Pike, "you now have a selection."

Pike threw himself at the impervious figure. "I'll break out, get to you somehow!" he shouted. "Is your blood red like ours? I'm going to find out!"

"Each of the two new specimens has qualities in her favor. The female you call 'Number One' has the superior mind and would produce highly intelligent offspring. Although she seems to lack emotion, this is largely a pretense. She often has fantasies involving you."

Number One looked flustered for the first time in Pike's memory, but he turned this, too, into rage at the invasion of her privacy. "All I want is to get my hands on you! Can you read these thoughts? Images of hate, killing . . ."

"The other new arrival has considered you unreachable, but is now realizing that this has changed. The factors in her favor are youth and strength, plus an unusually strong female emotion which . . ."

"You'll find my thoughts more interesting! Primitive thoughts you can't understand; emotions so ugly you can't . . ."

The pain hit him then and he went down, writhing. The images involved this time were from the torture chambers of the Inquisition. Over them, dimly, floated the Magistrate's thought, as though directed at someone else.

"Wrong thinking is punishable; right thinking will be as quickly rewarded. You will find it an effective combination."

The illusion vanished and Pike rolled weakly to a sitting position. He found the Magistrate gone, and the two crewwomen bending over him.

"No—don't—help me. Just leave me alone. Got to concentrate on hate. They can't read through it."

The hours wore on and eventually the lights went down. It seemed obvious that the Talosians intended to keep all three women penned with him. Trying to keep the hate alive became increasingly more difficult; he slammed his fist against the enclosure wall again and again, hoping the pain would help.

The women conversed in low tones for a while, and then, one by one, fell asleep, Vina on the bed, the other two on the floor leaning against it. Pike squatted against the wall nearby, no thoughts in his mind now but roaring fatigue and the effort to fight it.

Then he sensed, rather than heard movement at his side. The wall panel had opened, and a Talosian arm was reaching in for the discarded phasers. He exploded into action, grabbing the arm and heaving.

The Magistrate was almost catapulted into the room by the force of that yank. Instantly, Pike's hands were around his throat.

"Don't hurt him!" Vina cried from the bed. "They don't mean to be evil . . ."

"I've had some samples of how 'good' they are . . ."

The Talosian vanished and Pike found himself holding the neck of the snarling anthropoid-spider creature he had first seen in a cell across from his. Its fangs snapped at his face. Colt shrieked.

Pike grimly tightened his grip. "I'm still holding your neck! Stop this illusion or I'll snap it!" The spider-thing changed back into the Magistrate again. "That's better. Try one more illusion—try anything at all—I'll take one quick twist. Understand?"

He loosened his hands slightly, allowing the Magistrate to gasp for breath. The forehead vein throbbed. "Your ship. Release me or we destroy it."

"He's not bluffing," Vina said. "With illusions they can make your crew work the wrong controls, push any button it takes to destroy the ship."

"I'll gamble he's too intelligent to kill for no reason at all. On the other hand, *I've* got a reason. Number One, take a good grip on his throat for me. And at the slightest excuse . . ."

"I understand, Captain," Number One said grimly.

Freed, Pike picked up the phasers. Putting one into his belt, he adjusted the other, leveled it at the transparency, and pulled the trigger. As he expected, it didn't fire. He turned back to the Magistrate and pressed the weapon against his head.

"I'm betting," he said almost conversationally, "that you've created an illusion that this phaser is empty. That you don't know enough about your own machines, let alone ours, to dare to tamper with them. And that this one just blasted a hole in that wall which you're keeping us from seeing. Shall I test my theory on your head?"

The Magistrate closed his eyes resignedly. At once, there was a huge, jagged hole in the front of the cage.

"Q.E.D. Number One, you can let go of him now. If he acts up, I can shoot him, and he knows it. Everybody out. We're leaving!"

On the surface, only the top of the lift shaft still stood; the top of the knoll had been blasted clean off. So the Talosians had prevented the rescue party from seeing that, too.

Number One tried her communicator, but without effect. Noting the Magistrate's forehead vein throbbing again, Pike raised his phaser and said in a voice of iron, "I want contact with my ship. *Right now.*"

"No," said the Magistrate. "You are now on the surface where we in-

tended you to be in the end. With the female of your choice, you will
soon begin carefully guided lives . . ."

"Beginning with burying you."

"I see you intend to kill. I shall not prevent you; others of us will replace me. To help you reclaim the planet, our zoological gardens will
furnish a variety of plant life . . ."

"Look," Pike said, "I'll make a deal with you. You and your life for
the lives of these two Earthwomen."

"Since our life span is many times yours, we have time to evolve a society trained as artisans, technicians . . ."

"Do you understand what I'm saying? Give me proof our ship is all
right, send these two back to it, and I'll stay here with Vina."

He felt a tug at his belt, and out of the corner of his eye saw that
Number One had pulled the spare phaser out of it. The rachet popped
like firecrackers as she turned the gain control full around. The phaser
began to hum, rising in both pitch and volume. The weapon was building up an overload—a force chamber explosion.

"It's wrong," Number One said, "to create a whole race of humans to
live as slaves. Do you concur, Captain?"

After a moment of hesitation, Pike nodded.

"Is this a deception?" asked the Magistrate. "Do you really intend to
destroy yourselves? Yes, I see that you do."

"Vina, you've got time to get back underground. But hurry. And
Talosian, to show just how primitive humans are, you can go with her."

The Magistrate did not move, nor did Vina.

"No," she said. "If you all think it's this important, then I can't leave
either. I suppose if they still have one human, they might try again."

"We had not believed this possible," the Magistrate said, his thoughts
betraying what might have been a strange sadness. "The customs and
history of your race show a unique hatred of captivity, even when pleasant and benevolent. But you prefer death. This makes you too violent
and dangerous a species for our needs."

"He means," Vina said, "they can't use you. You're free to go back
to your ship."

Number One turned the phaser off, and just in time, too. In the
renewed silence, Pike said, "Vina, that's it. No apologies. You captured
one of us, threatened us, tortured us . . ."

"Your unsuitability has condemned the Talosian race to eventual
death," the Magistrate said. "Is this not sufficient? No other specimens
have shown your adaptability. You were our last hope."

"Nonsense," Pike said, surprised. "Surely some form of trade, some mutual cooperation . . ."

The Magistrate shook his head. "Your race would learn our power of illusion—and destroy itself. It is important to *our* beliefs to prevent this."

"Captain," Number One said, "we have Transporter control now."

"Good. Let's go. Vina, you too."

"I—" Vina said. "I can't go with you."

Pike felt a flash of what might almost have been exasperation. "Number One, Yeoman Colt, go aloft. I'll be with you when I've gotten to the bottom of this." As they hesitated, he added, "Orders."

They shimmered and vanished. Pike swung on Vina. "Now . . ."

He stopped, astounded and horrified. Vina was changing. Her face was wrinkling. An ugly scar appeared. Her body was becoming cruelly deformed. Throughout, she looked back at Pike with bitter eyes. The change did not stop until she was old, shockingly twisted, downright ugly.

"This is the female's true appearance," the Magistrate said.

It couldn't be true. *This* was the youngster of the survivors' camp, the sturdy peasant, the wife on Earth, the green Orionese savage who had danced so . . .

"This is the truth," Vina said, in an old woman's voice. She lifted her arms. "See me as I am. They found me in the wreckage, dying, nothing but a lump of flesh. They fixed me fine. Everything works. But—*they had no guide for putting me back together*.

"Do you understand now? Do you see why I can't go with you?"

She turned and stumbled toward the lift. Pike watched her go with horror and pity. Then he turned to the Magistrate, who said: "It was necessary to convince you that her desire to stay is an honest one."

Pike looked at him with new eyes. "You have some sparks of decency in you after all. Will you give her back her illusion of beauty?"

"We will. And more. See."

At the shaft, the image of the lovely Vina was entering the lift—*accompanied by himself*. The two turned and waved. Then the lift carried them down into the bowels of Talos IV.

"She has her illusion," the Magistrate said. Was he almost smiling? "And you have reality. May you find your way as pleasant."

Spock, Number One, Jose, Colt and Boyce all crowded toward him as he stepped out of the Transporter Chamber.

"What happened to Vina?" Colt demanded.

"Isn't she—coming with us?" asked Number One.

"No," Pike said shortly. "And I agree with her reasons. Now break it up here. What is this we're running, a cadet ship? Everybody on the bridge! Navigator, I want a course!"

"Yessir!"

They scattered like flushed partridges—all except Boyce, who said, "Hold on a minute, Captain."

"What for? I feel fine."

"That's the trouble. You look a hundred per cent better."

"I am. Didn't you recommend rest and change? I've had both. I've even been—home. Now, let's get on with things."

As the *Enterprise* moved away from Talos IV, routine re-established itself quickly, and the memory of all those illusions began to fade. They had not, after all, been real experiences—most of them. But Pike could not resist stealing a quick look from Number One to Colt, wondering which of them, in other circumstances, he might have picked.

When he found them both looking at him as if with the same speculation, he turned his eyes determinedly to the viewscreen and banished the thought.

He had had plenty of practice at that, lately.

AFTERWORD

As the reader will now see, this story constituted the original pilot film for "Star Trek," and was shown as such at the 24th World Science Fiction Convention in Cleveland, Ohio, September 1–5, 1966. Between the selling of the series and the actual television broadcast of "The Menagerie," the whole concept of the cast changed radically. Number One was moved one step down in the chain of command, becoming Uhura, while her ostensible lack of emotion and computer-like mind were transferred to Spock; Yeoman Colt became Yeoman Rand; Boyce became McCoy; Tyler became Sulu. The net effect was to make the new officers more interracial than before. The notion that the highly trained crew would ever be risked in ordinary hand-to-hand infantry combat was dropped.

Most important, perhaps, was that in the pilot film, Pike had wound up with a potentially explosive situation with two of his crewwomen which would be too complex to maintain through a long-term series of episodes. He had to be replaced, and the whole story turned into relatively ancient history; and thus was born Captain Kirk, and the framing story I have left out. All these stages are visible in the scripts I had to work from, which are heavily revised in various handwritings (and in which Pike confusingly appears from time to time as "Captain Spring" and "Captain Winter").

The only alternative would have been to reshoot the original "Menagerie" with the new cast, which would have been not only expensive, but would have produced all kinds of unwanted complexities in succeeding stories. Mr. Roddenberry obviously decided to let it stand as something that had happened way-back-when, and frame it as such. I think this was wise and I have followed his lead in this adaptation.

Ordinarily, writers should not inflict their technical problems on readers, who have every right to demand that such problems be solved before the story is published. But I sometimes get letters from "Star Trek" fans who castigate me for changing even one or two words in scripts they have memorized, or even have on tape. In this case, as in that of "The City on the Edge of Forever" (STAR TREK TWO), there were conflicts that couldn't be resolved by slavishly following the final text and ignoring how it had evolved. In both cases, I had to make my own judgment of what would best serve the authors' intents.

—J. B.

THE ENTERPRISE INCIDENT.
(D. C. Fontana)

Operating under sealed orders, Kirk had found from long experience, almost always meant something messy. It became worse when the orders, once opened, demanded that they be kept secret from his own officers during the initial phases. And it was worst of all when those initial phases looked outright irrational.

Take the present situation. Here was the *Enterprise,* on the wrong side of the neutral zone, in Romulan space, surrounded by three Romulan cruisers which had simply popped out of nothingness, undetected by any sensor until far too late. Her presence there was a clear violation of a treaty; and since the Romulans were now using warships modeled on those of the Klingons, she was also heavily outgunned.

Kirk had worked out no way of making so suicidal a move on his part explicable except that of becoming irritable and snappish, as though his judgment had been worn down by fatigue. It was a bad solution. His officers were the best in Starfleet; sooner or later they would penetrate the deception, and conclude that whenever Kirk appeared to be worn down to the point of irrationality, he was operating under sealed orders.

And when the day came when he actually *was* too tired to know what he was doing, they would obey him blindly anyhow—and scratch one starship.

"Captain," Uhura said, her voice distant. "We are receiving a Class Two signal from one of the Romulan vessels."

"Put it on the main viewing screen, Lieutenant. Also, code a message to Starfleet Command, advising them of our situation and including all log entries to this point. Spock, your sensors read clear; what happened?"

"Sir, I have no more than a hypothesis . . ."

"Signal in," Uhura said. The main screen flickered briefly, then clarified to show a Romulan officer, with his own bridge behind him, carefully out of focus. He looked rather like Spock, and spoke like him, too.

"You have been identified as the starship *Enterprise*. Captain James T. Kirk last known to be in command."

Kirk picked up a hand mike and thumbed its button. "Your information is correct. This is Captain Kirk."

"I am Subcommander Tal of the Romulan Imperial Fleet. Your ship is surrounded, Captain. You will surrender immediately—or we will destroy you."

Kirk flicked the switch and turned his face away toward Spock. He rather doubted that the Romulan could lip-read a foreign language, but there was no point in giving him the chance.

"Spock, come here. What do you make of this? They want something, or they would have destroyed us by now."

"No doubt, Captain. That would be standard procedure for them."

"It's my ship they want, I assume. And very badly."

"Of course. It would be a great prize. An elementary deduction, Captain."

"Skip the logic lessons." Kirk opened the mike again. "Save your threats, Subcommander," he said harshly. "If you attempt to board my ship, I'll blow her up. You gain nothing."

Tal had apparently expected nothing else, but a slight frown cut across his forehead nonetheless. "May I ask, Captain, who is that beside you?"

"My First Officer, Commander Spock. I'm surprised by your ignorance."

"You mean to insult me, but there is nothing discreditable in not knowing everything. Finding a Vulcan so highly placed in the Federation fleet does surprise me, I readily grant. However . . ."

He was interrupted by a beeping noise and hit an invisible control plate. "Yes, Commander? Excuse me, Captain . . ."

The screen dissolved into traveling moire patterns. Then Tal was back.

"No one should decide quickly to die, Captain," he said. "We give you one of your hours. If you do not surrender your ship at the end of that time, your destruction is certain. We will be open to communication, should you wish it."

"You understand Starfleet Command has been advised of our situation."

"Of course," Tal said, somewhat condescendingly. "But a subspace message will take three weeks to reach Starfleet—and I think they would hesitate to send a squadron in after you, in any event. The decision is yours, Captain. One hour."

His image winked out, and was replaced by stars.

"Lt. Uhura," Kirk said, "order all senior officers to report to the Briefing Room on the double."

"All right," Kirk said, surveying the group. Spock, McCoy and Scott were present; Chekov and Sulu on the bridge with Uhura. "Spock, you had a theory on why your sensors didn't pick up the Romulan ships, until they were right on top of us."

"I believe the Romulans have devised an improved cloaking system which renders our tracking sensors useless. You will observe, Captain, that the three ships outside are modeled after Klingon cruisers. Changing ship designs that drastically is expensive, and the Klingon cruiser has no important inherent advantages over the Romulan model of which we are aware—unless it is adaptable to some sort of novel screening device."

"If so, the Romulans could attack into Federation territory before we'd know they were there; before a planet or a vessel could begin to get its defenses up."

"They caught *us* right enough," Scott said.

"A brilliant observation, Mr. Scott," Kirk snapped. "Do you have any other helpful opinions?"

Scott was momentarily nonplussed. Then he pumped his shoulders slightly in a shrug. "We've not got many choices . . ."

"Three. We can fight—and be destroyed. Or we can destroy the *Enterprise* ourselves to keep her from the Romulans. Or—we can surrender." There was a stir among the other officers; Kirk had expected it, and overrode it. "We might be able to find out how the Romulans' new cloaking device works. The Federation *must* have that information. Opinions?"

"Odds are against our finding out anything," Scott said. "And if the *Enterprise* is taken by the Romulans, they'll know everything there is to know about a starship."

"Spock?"

"If we had not crossed the Neutral Zone on your order," Spock said coldly and evenly, "you would not now require our opinions to bolster a decision that should never have had to be made."

The others stared at him, and then at Kirk. McCoy leaned forward. "Jim, *you* ordered us—? But you had no authority—"

"Dismissed, Doctor!"

"But Jim . . ."

"Bridge to Captain," Uhura's voice broke in.

"Kirk here."

"The Romulan vessel is signaling again, sir."

"Put it on our screen here, Lieutenant."

The triangular Briefing Room viewscreen lit up to show the Vulcan-like features of Tal. He said without preamble, "My Commander wishes to speak with you, Captain Kirk."

"Very well," Kirk said, slightly surprised. "Put him on."

"The Commander wishes to see you and your First Officer aboard this vessel. It is felt that the matter requires—discussion. The Commander is a highly placed representative of the Romulan Star Empire."

"Why should we walk right into your hands?"

"Two of my officers will beam aboard your vessel as exchange hostages while you are here."

"There's no guarantee they'll transport over here once we've entered your ship."

A faint, cynical smile seemed to be threatening to break over Tal's face. "Granted we do not easily trust each other, Captain. But *you* are the ones who violated our territory. Should it not be we who distrust *your* motives? However, we will agree to a simultaneous exchange."

Perfect—and yet at the same time, impossible to explain to his worriedly watching officers. After appearing to consider, Kirk said, "Give us the transporter coordinates and synchronize."

Tal nodded and his image faded.

"I must insist on advising against this, Captain," protested Scott. "The Romulans will try something tricky . . ."

"We'll learn nothing by staying aboard the *Enterprise*," Kirk said. "One final order. Engineer Scott, you are in charge. If we do not return, this ship must not be taken. If the Romulans attempt it, you will fight—and if necessary, destroy the *Enterprise*. Is that clear?"

"Perfectly, Captain." In point of fact, Scott looked as though it was the first order he had understood in days. Well, with any luck, he'd understand all the rest later—if there was going to be any "later."

"Very well. Alert Transporter Officer."

Kirk and Spock were conducted to the quarters of the Romulan Commander by two guards, after having been relieved of their weapons. Had the necessity existed, those two guards would never have known what had hit them, sidearms or no, but nothing was to be gained now by overpowering them; Kirk merely noted the overconfidence for possible future use.

Then the door snapped open—and the Romulan Commander, standing behind a desk, was revealed to be a woman. And no ordinary woman, either. Of course, no ordinary woman could become both a ranking officer and a government representative in a society of warriors; but this one was beautiful, aristocratic, compelling—an effect which was, if anything, heightened by the fact that she was of Vulcanoid, not human stock. Kirk and Spock looked quickly at each other. Kirk had the impression that if Spock could whistle, he would.

"Captain Kirk," she said.

"I'm honored, Commander."

"I do not think so, Captain. But we have a matter of importance to discuss, and your superficial courtesies are the overture to that discussion." Her eyes swung leveling to Spock. "You are First Officer . . . ?"

"Spock."

"I speak first with the Captain."

Spock flicked a glance at Kirk, who nodded. The First Officer tilted a half bow toward the Commander, and Kirk entered the office. The door snapped shut behind him.

"All right," he said. "Forgetting the superficial courtesies, let's just have at it. I'm not surrendering my ship to you."

"An admirable attitude in a starship captain," she said coolly. "But the matter of trespass into Romulan space is one of galactic import—a violation of treaties. Now I ask you simply: what is your mission here?"

"Instrument failure caused a navigational error. We were across the Zone before we realized it. Your ships surrounded us before we could turn about."

"A starship—one of Starfleet's finest vessels. You are saying instrument failure as radical as you suggest went unnoticed until your ship was well past the Neutral Zone?"

"Accidents happen; cutoffs and backup systems can malfunction. We've been due in for overhaul for two months, but haven't been assigned a space dock yet."

"I see. But you have managed to navigate with this malfunction?"

"The error has been corrected," Kirk said. He knew well enough how transparent the lie was, but the charade had to be played out; he needed to seem thoroughly outgunned—in all departments.

"Most convenient. I hardly believe it will clear you of espionage."

"We were not spying."

"Your language has always been difficult for me, Captain," the woman said drily. "Perhaps you have another word for it?"

"At worst, it would be nothing more than surveillance. But I assure you that you are drawing an unjustified . . ."

"Captain, if a Romulan vessel ventured far into Federation territory without good explanation, what would a Star Base commander do? It works both ways—and I strongly doubt you are the injured party." She pressed a button and the door opened. "Spock, come in. Both the Federation Council and the Romulan Praetor are being informed of this situation, but the time will be long before we receive their answer. I wish to interrogate you to establish a record of information for them in the meantime. The Captain has already made his statement."

"I understand," Spock said.

"I admit to some surprise on seeing you, Spock. We were not aware of Vulcans aboard the *Enterprise.*"

"Starfleet is not in the habit of informing Romulans of its ships' personnel."

"Quite true. Yet certain ships—certain officers—are known to us. Your situation appears most interesting."

"What earns Spock your special interest?" Kirk broke in.

"His species, obviously. Our forebears had the same roots and origins —something you will never understand, Captain. We can appreciate the Vulcans—our distant brothers. Spock, I have heard of Vulcan integrity and personal honor. There is a well-known saying that Vulcans are incapable of lying. Or is it a myth?"

"It is no myth."

"Then tell me truthfully now: on your honor as a Vulcan, what was your mission?"

"I reserve the privilege of speaking the truth only when it will not violate my honor as a Vulcan."

"It is unworthy of a Vulcan to resort to subterfuge."

"It is equally unworthy of a Romulan," Spock said. "It is not a lie to keep the truth to one's self."

That was one sentence too many, Kirk thought. But given Spock's nature and role, it could hardly have been prevented. The woman was wily as well as intelligent.

"Then," she said, "there is a truth here that is still unspoken."

"You have been told everything that there is to know," Kirk said. "There is nothing else."

"There is Mr. Spock's unspoken truth. You knew of the cloaking device that we have developed. You deliberately violated Romulan space in a blatant spy mission on the order of Federation Command."

"We've been through that, Commander."

"We have not even begun, Captain. There is of course no force I can use on a Vulcan that will make him speak. But there are Romulan methods capable of going into a human mind like a spike into a melon. We use them when the situation requires it."

"Then you know," Spock said, "that they are ineffective against humans with Command training."

"Of course," said the Commander. "They will leave him dead—or what might be worse than dead. But I would be replaced did I not apply them as Procedure dictates. One way or another, I will know your unspoken truths."

To Kirk, Spock's iron expression never seemed to change, but now he caught a very faint flicker of indecision which must have spoken volumes to the Romulan woman. Kirk said hastily, "Let her rant. There is nothing to say."

Spock did not look at him. "I cannot allow the Captain to be any further destroyed," the First Officer said in a low monotone. "The strain of command has worn heavily on him. He has not been himself for several weeks."

"There's a lie," Kirk said, "if ever I heard one."

"As you can see," Spock continued evenly, "Captain Kirk is a highly sensitive and emotional person. I believe he has lost his capacity for rational decision."

"Shut up, Spock."

"I am betraying no secrets. The Commander's suspicion that Starfleet ordered the *Enterprise* into the Zone is unacceptable. Our rapid capture demonstrates its foolhardiness."

"Spock—damn you, what are you doing?"

"I am speaking the truth for the benefit of the *Enterprise* and the Federation. I say—for the record—that Captain Kirk took the *Enterprise* across the Neutral Zone on his own initiative and his craving for glory. He is not sane."

"And I say," Kirk returned between tightly drawn lips, "that you are a filthy traitor."

"Enough," the Commander said, touching a control plate on her desk. "Give me communication with the *Enterprise*."

After a long moment, Scott's voice said, *"Enterprise;* Acting Officer Scott."

"Officer Scott, Captain James T. Kirk is formally charged with espionage. The testimony of First Officer Spock has confirmed that this intrusion into Romulan space was not an accident; and that your ship was not under orders from Starfleet Command or the Federation Council to undertake such a mission. Captain Kirk was solely responsible. Since the crew had no choice but to obey orders, the crew will not be held responsible. Therefore I am ordering Engineer Scott, presently in command of the *Enterprise,* to follow the Romulan flagship to our home base. You will there be processed and released to Federation Command. Until judgment is passed, Captain Kirk will be held in confinement."

There were a few moments of dead air from the *Enterprise,* but Kirk had no difficulty in guessing what Scotty was doing: ordering the two Romulan hostages to be put in the brig. When he came on again, his voice was almost shaking with suppressed rage.

"This is Lt. Commander Scott. The *Enterprise* follows no orders except those of Captain Kirk. We will stay right here until he returns. And if you make any attempt to commandeer or board us, the *Enterprise* will be blown to bits along with as many of you as we can take with us. Your own knowledge of our armament will tell you that that will be quite a good many."

"You humans make a very brave noise," the Commander said. She sounded angry herself, although her face was controlled. "There are ways to convince you of your errors."

She cut off communication with a flick of a switch. Kirk swung on Spock.

"Did you hear, you pointy-eared turncoat? You've betrayed everything of value and integrity you ever knew. Did you hear the sound of human integrity?"

"Take him to the Security Room."

The guards dragged Kirk out.

* * *

"It was your testimony that Captain Kirk was irrational and solely responsible that saved the lives of your crew," the Romulan Commander said. "But don't expect gratitude for it."

"One does not expect logic from humans," Spock said. "As we both know."

"A Vulcan among humans—living, working with them. I would think the situation would be intolerable to you."

"I am half Vulcan. My mother was human."

"To whom is your allegiance, then?" she asked with cool interest. "Do you call yourself Terran or Vulcan?"

"Vulcan."

"How long have you been a Starfleet officer, Spock?"

"Eighteen years."

"You serve Captain Kirk. Do you like him? Do you like your shipmates?"

"The question is irrelevant."

"Perhaps." She drew closer, looking into his eyes challengingly. "But you are subordinate to the Captain's orders. Even to his whims."

"My duty as an officer," Spock said rigidly, "is to obey him."

"You are a superior being. Why do you not command?"

Spock hesitated. "I do not desire a ship of my own."

"Of course you believe that now, after eighteen years. But is it not also true that no one has given you—a Vulcan—that opportunity?"

"Such opportunities are extremely rare."

"For one of your accomplishments and—capabilities—opportunities should be made. And will be. I can see to that—if you will stop looking at the Federation as the whole universe. It is not, you know."

"The thought has occasionally crossed my mind," Spock said.

"You must have your own ship."

"Commander," Spock said pleasantly, "shall we speak plainly? It is you who desperately need a ship. You want the *Enterprise*."

"Of course! It would be a great triumph for me to bring the *Enterprise* home intact. It would broaden the scope of my powers greatly. It would be the achievement of a lifetime." She paused. "And naturally, it would open equal opportunities to you."

The sound of an intercom spared Spock the need to reply. It was not an open line; the Commander picked up a handset and listened. After a moment she said, "I will come there," and replaced it. Spock raised his eyebrows inquiringly.

"Your Captain," she said with a trace of scorn, "tried to break through the sonic disruptor field which wards his cell. Naturally he is injured, and since we do not know how to treat humans, my First Officer asked your ship's surgeon to attend him. The man's first response was, 'I don't make house calls,' whatever that means, but we managed to convince him that it was not a trick and he is now in attendance. Follow me, please."

She led the way out of the office and down the corridor, followed by the omnipresent, silent guards.

"I neglected to mention it," she added, "but I will expect you for dinner. We have much yet to discuss."

"Indeed?" Spock said, looking at her quizzically.

"Allow me to rephrase. Will you join me for dinner?"

"I am honored, Commander. Are the guards also invited?"

For answer, she waved the guards off. They seemed astonished, but were soon out of sight. A moment later she and Spock reached a junction; to the left, the corridor continued, while to the right it brought up against a single door not far away; it was guarded. There was a raised emblem nearby, but from this angle Spock could not read the device on it. He moved toward it.

"Mr. Spock!"

He stopped instantly.

"That corridor is forbidden to all but loyal Romulans."

"Of course, Commander," Spock said. "I will obey your restrictions."

"I hope," she said, "soon there will be no need for you to observe *any* restrictions."

"It would be illogical to assume that all conditions remain stable."

They reached the Romulan brig; a guard there saluted and turned off the disruptor field. When they entered the cell, he turned it on again. McCoy was there—and so was Kirk, sitting slumped and blank-eyed on the bed, hands hanging down loosely between his knees.

"You are the physician?" the Commander said.

"McCoy—Chief Medical Officer."

"Captain Kirk's condition?"

"Physically—weak. Mentally—depressed, disoriented, displays feelings of persecution and rebellion."

"Then by your own standards of normality, this man is not fully competent?"

"Not now," McCoy said reluctantly. "No."

"Mr. Spock has stated he believes the Captain had no authority or order to cross the Neutral Zone. In your opinion, could this mental incapacity have afflicted the Captain earlier?"

"Yes—it's possible."

"Mr. Spock, the Doctor has now confirmed your testimony as to the mental state of your Captain. He was and is unfit to continue in command of the *Enterprise*. That duty has now fallen upon you. Are you ready to exercise that function?"

"I am ready."

McCoy looked aghast. "Spock—I don't believe it!"

"The matter," Spock said, "is not open for discussion."

"What do you mean, not open for discussion? If . . ."

"That's enough, Doctor," the Commander broke in. "As a physician, your duty is to save lives. Mr. Spock's duty is to lead the *Enterprise* to a safe haven."

"There is no alternative, Doctor," Spock added. "The safety of the crew is the paramount issue. It is misguided loyalty to resist any further."

Kirk raised his head very slowly. He looked a good deal more than disoriented; he looked downright mad. Then, suddenly, he was lunging at Spock, his voice a raw scream:

"Traitor! I'll—kill—you!"

With the swift precision of a surgeon, Spock grasped Kirk's shoulder and the back of his neck in both hands. The raging Captain stiffened, cried out inarticulately once, and collapsed.

Spock looked down at him, frozen. The guard had drawn his sidearm. McCoy kneeled beside the crumpled Captain, snapped out an instrument, took a reading, prepared a hypo in desperate haste.

"What did you do to him?" McCoy demanded. He administered the shot and then looked up. His voice became hard, snarling. "*What did you do?*"

"I was unprepared for his attack," Spock said. "He— I used the Vulcan death grip instinctively."

McCoy tried a second shot, then attempted to find a pulse or heartbeat.

"Your instincts are still good, Spock," he said with cold remoteness. "He's dead."

"By his own folly," said the Romulan Commander. "Return the corpse and the Doctor to their vessel. Mr. Spock, shall we proceed to dinner?"

"That," Spock said, "sounds rather more pleasant."

It was pleasant indeed; it had been a long time since Spock had seen so sumptuously laden a table. He poured more wine for the Commander.

"I have had special Vulcan dishes prepared for you," she said. "Do they meet with your approval?"

"I am flattered, Commander. There is no doubt that the cuisine aboard your vessel far surpasses that of the *Enterprise*. It is indeed a powerful recruiting inducement."

"We have other inducements." She arose and came over to sit down beside him. "You have nothing in Starfleet to which to return. I—*we* offer an alternative. We will find a place for you, if you wish it."

"A—place?"

"With me." She touched his sleeve, his shoulder, then his neck, brushing lightly. "Romulan women are not like Vulcan females. We are not dedicated to pure logic and the sterility of non-emotion. Our people are warriors, often savage; but we are also many other—pleasant things."

"I was not aware of that aspect of Romulan society."

"As a Vulcan, you would study it," she said softly. "But as a human, you would find ways to appreciate it."

"You must believe me, I do appreciate it."

"I'm so glad. There is one final step to make the occasion complete. You will lead a small party of Romulans aboard the *Enterprise*. You will take your rightful place as its commander and lead the ship to a Romulan port—with my flagship at its side."

"Yes, of course," Spock said impatiently. "But not just this minute, surely. An hour from now will do—even better. Will it not, Commander?"

She actually laughed. "Yes, it will, Mr. Spock. And you do know that I have a first name."

"I was beginning to wonder."

She leaned forward and whispered. The word would have meant absolutely nothing to a human, but Spock recognized its roots without difficulty.

"How rare and how beautiful," he said. "But so incongruous when spoken by a soldier."

"If you will give me a moment, the soldier will transform herself into a woman." She rose, and he rose with her. Her hand trailed out of his, and a door closed behind her.

Spock turned his back to it, reached inside his tunic, and brought out his communicator. Snapping it open, he said quietly, "Spock to Captain Kirk."

"Kirk here. I'm already on board—green skin, pointed ears, uniform and all. Do you have the information?"

"Yes, the device is down the first corridor to the left as you approach the Commander's office, closely guarded and off limits to all but authorized personnel."

"I'll get it. Will you be able to get back to the *Enterprise* without attracting their attention?"

"Unknown. At present . . ."

"Somebody coming. Out."

Spock replaced the communicator quickly, but it was a long minute before the Commander returned. The change was quite startling; compared to her appearance in uniform, she seemed now to be wearing hardly anything, although this was in part an illusion of contrast.

"Mr. Spock?" she said, posing. "Is my attire now more—appropriate?"

"More than that. It should actually stimulate our conversation."

She raised her hand, fingers parted in the Vulcan manner, and he followed suit. They touched each other's faces.

"It's hard to believe," she said, "that I could be so stirred by the touch of an alien hand."

"I too—must confess—that I am moved emotionally. I know it is illogical—but . . ."

"Spock, we need not question what we truly feel. Accept what is happening between us, even as I do."

"I question no further."

"Come, then." Taking his hand, she turned toward the other room.

The outside door buzzed stridently. Had Spock been fully human, he would have jumped.

"Commander!" Tal's voice called. "Permission to enter!"

"Not now, Tal."

"It is urgent, Commander."

She hesitated, looking at Spock, but her mood had been broken. She said: "Very well—you may enter."

There were two guards behind Tal. It would have been hard to say whether they were more surprised by Spock's presence or by their Commander's state of undress, but discipline reasserted itself almost at once.

"Commander. We have intercepted an alien transmission from aboard our own vessel."

"Triangulate and report."

"We have already done so, Commander. The source is in this room."

She stiffened and turned to Spock. Gazing levelly at her, he reached under his tunic. Tal and the guards drew their weapons. Moving very slowly, Spock brought out his communicator and proffered it to her. Trancelike, without looking away from his face, she took the device. Then, suddenly, she seemed to awaken.

"The cloaking device! Send guards . . ."

"We thought of that also, Commander," Tal said. The slight stress on her title dripped with contempt. It was clear that he thought it would shortly pass to him. "It is gone."

"Full alert. Search all decks."

"That will be profitless, Commander," Spock said. "I do not believe you will find it."

Her response was a cry of shock. "You must be mad!"

"I assure you, I am quite sane."

"Why would you do this to me? What are you that you could do this?"

"I am," Spock said, not without some regret, "the First Officer of the *Enterprise*."

She struck him, full in the face. Nobody could have mistaken it for a caress. The blow would have dropped any human being like a felled ox.

He merely looked at her, his face calm. She glared back, and gradually her breathing became more even.

"Take him to my office. I shall join you shortly."

She was back in uniform now, and absolutely expressionless. "Execution for state criminals," she said, "is both painful and demeaning. I believe the details are unnecessary. The sentence will be carried out immediately after charges are recorded."

"I am not a Romulan subject," Spock said. "But if I am to be treated as one, I demand the Right of Statement first."

"So you know more about Romulan custom than you let appear. This increases your culpability. However, the right is granted."

"Thank you."

"Return to your station, Subcommander," she said to Tal. "The boarding action will begin on my order."

Tal saluted and left. The Commander took a weapon from her desk, and laid it before her. She seemed otherwise confident that Spock would make no ignominious attempts at escape; and indeed, even had the situation been as she thought, such an attempt would have been illogical.

"There is no time limit to the Right of Statement, but I will not appreciate many hours of listening to your defense."

"I will not require much time," Spock said. "No more than twenty minutes, I would say."

"It should take less time than that to find your ally who stole the cloaking device. You will not die alone." She tapped a button on the desk console. "Recording. The Romulan Right of Statement allows the condemned to make a statement of official record in defense or explanation of his crime. Commander Spock, Starfleet Officer and proven double agent, demands the right. Proceed, Commander Spock."

"My crimes are espionage, and aiding and abetting sabotage. To both of these I freely admit my guilt. However, Lords Praetori, I reject the charge of double agentry, with its further implication of treason. However I may have attempted to make the matter appear, and regardless of my degree of success in such a deception, I never at any point renounced my loyalty to the Federation, let alone swearing allegiance to the Romulan Empire.

"I was in fact acting throughout under sealed orders from Starfleet Command, whose nature was unknown to anyone aboard the *Enterprise* except, of course, Captain Kirk. These orders were to find out whether the Romulans had in fact developed a rumored cloaking device for their ships, and if so, to obtain it by any possible means. The means actually employed were worked out in secret by Captain Kirk and myself."

"And so," the Commander said with bitter contempt, "the story that Vulcans cannot lie is a myth after all."

"Of course, Commander. Complex interpersonal relationships among sentient beings absolutely require a certain amount of lying, for the protection of others and the good of the whole. Among humans such untruths are called 'white lies.' A man's honor in this area is measured by whether he can tell the difference between a white lie and a malicious one. It is a much more delicate matter than simply charging blindly ahead telling the truth at all times, no matter what injury the truth may sometimes do. And there are occasions, such as the present one, when one must weigh a lie which will cause personal injury against a truth which would endanger the good of the whole. Your attempt to seduce and subvert me, Commander, was originally just that kind of choice. If it became something else, I am sorry, but such a danger is always present in such attempts."

"I can do without your pity," the Commander said, "and your little moral lecture. Pray proceed."

"As you wish. The oath I swore as a Starfleet officer is both explicit and binding. So long as I wear the uniform it is my duty to protect the security of the Federation. Clearly, your new cloaking device presents a threat to that security. I carried out my duty as my orders and my oath required."

"Everyone carries out his duty, Mr. Spock," the Commander said. "You state the obvious."

"There is no regulation concerning the content of the statement. May I continue?"

"Very well. Your twenty minutes are almost up."

"I trust that the time consumed by your interruptions and my answers to them will not be charged against me. Interrogation in the midst of a formal Statement is most irregular."

The Commander threw up her hands. "These endless quibbles! Will you kindly get back to the point?"

"Certainly. The Commander's appeal to my Vulcan loyalties, in the name of our remote common racial origin, was bound to fail; since beyond the historic tradition of Vulcan loyalty there is the combined Vulcan/Romulan history of obedience to duty—and Vulcan is, may I remind you, a member of the United Federation of Planets. In other words . . ."

Under his voice, a familiar hum began to grow in the room. The Commander realized instantly what was happening—but instead of picking up the sidearm and firing, as she had plenty of time to do despite all Spock's droning attempt to dull her attention—she sprang forward and threw her arms around him. Then both were frozen in a torrent of sparks . . .

And both were in the Transporter Room of the *Enterprise*.

As the elevator doors opened onto the bridge, Kirk's voice boomed out.

"Throw the switch on that device, Scotty!"

"I did, sir," Scott's voice said. "It's not working."

The Commander looked in Kirk's direction and a muffled exclamation escaped her as Spock escorted her out. Kirk had not yet removed his Romulan Centurion's uniform, let alone bothered to change his skin color or have his surgically altered ears restored to normal human shape. Obviously, the other half of the plot was now all too clear to her.

Spock left her and crossed to his station. Behind him, her voice said steadily, "I would give you credit, Captain, for getting this far—but you will be dead in a moment and the credit would be gratuitous."

The Captain ignored her. "Lt. Uhura, open a channel to the Romulan command vessel; two-way visual contact."

"Right . . . I have Subcommander Tal, sir."

Tal seemed quite taken aback to see what appeared to be one of his own officers in the command chair, but must have realized in the next second that any Centurion he did not recognize had to be an imposter. He said almost instantly, "We have you under our main batteries, *Enterprise*. You cannot escape."

"This is Captain Kirk under this silly outfit. Hold your fire. We have your Commander with us."

Tal shot a look toward where his own main viewscreen evidently was located. "Commander!"

"Subcommander Tal," the woman said, "I am giving you a direct order. Obey it. *Close and destroy!*"

Uhura cut off transmission, but not fast enough. It was a risk that had had to be taken.

"Come on, Scotty, we've run out of time."

"Captain, I'm working as fast as I can."

"You see, Captain," the Commander said, "your effort is wasted."

"Mr. Spock. Distance from the Romulan vessels."

"One hundred fifty thousand kilometers and closing rapidly."

"Stand to phasers. You'll forgive me if I put up a fight, Commander."

"Of course," the woman said. "That is expected."

"One hundred thousand kilometers," Spock said. "They'll be within maximum range within six seconds . . . five . . . four . . ."

"Scott, *throw the switch!*"

"It'll likely overload, but . . ."

". . . two . . . one . . ."

"Functioning, Captain!"

"Mr. Chekov, change course to 318 mark 7, Warp Nine."

"Nine, sir? . . . Done."

Spock turned toward Kirk. "They have opened fire at where we were last, sir, but the cloaking device appears to be operating most effectively. And the Commander informed me that even their own sensors cannot track a vessel so equipped."

"Thank you, Mr. Spock," Kirk said in a heartfelt voice. He turned to the Commander. "We will leave you at a Federation outpost."

"You are most gracious, Captain. If I may be taken to your brig, I will take my place as your prisoner. Further attendance here is painful to me."

Kirk stood, very formal. "Mr. Spock, the honor of escorting the Commander to her *quarters* is yours."

The two opposing forces bowed formally to each other, and Spock led the Commander back toward the elevator. Behind them, Sulu's voice said, "Entering Neutral Zone, Captain."

"I'm sorry you were made an unwilling passenger," Spock said. "It was not intentional. All they really wanted was the cloaking device."

"They? And what did you want?"

"That is all I wanted when I went aboard your vessel."

"And that is exactly all you came away with."

"You underestimate yourself, Commander."

She refused to hear the hidden meaning. "You realize that we will very soon learn to penetrate the cloaking device. After all, we discovered it; you only stole it."

"Obviously, military secrets are the most fleeting of all," he said. "I hope we exchange something more permanent."

She stepped into the elevator; but when Spock tried to follow her, she barred the way. "You made the choice."

"It was the only choice possible. Surely you would not have respected any other."

She looked at him for a long moment, and then smiled, slightly, sadly. "That will be our—secret. Get back to your duty. The guards had best take me from here."

Spock beckoned to two guards. She could probably incapacitate both in a matter of seconds, but they were well out of Transporter range of any of the Romulan ships now—and her mood did not seem to be one which would impel her to illogical action. In a way it was a pity that she obviously did not know that Vulcans were cyclical in their mating customs, and immune to sexual attraction at all other times. Or had she been counting on his human side? And—had she been right to do so?

The elevator swallowed her down. Spock went back to his post.

"Sickbay to Captain Kirk. If all the shouting's over up there, I want you to report to me."

"What for, Bones?"

"You're due in surgery again. As payment for the big act of irrationality you put over on me, I'm going to bob your ears."

Kirk grinned and touched the ears, which apparently he had forgotten in the heat of operations, and looked over at Spock.

"Please go, Captain," Spock said in a remote voice. "Somehow, they are not aesthetically pleasing on a human."

"Are you coming, Jim?" McCoy's voice said. "Or do you want to go through the rest of your life looking like your First Officer?"

And McCoy had the last word again.

A PIECE OF THE ACTION
(David P. Harmon and Gene L. Coon)

It was difficult to explain to Bela Okmyx, who called himself "Boss" of Dana Iotia Two, that though the message from the lost *Horizon* had been sent a hundred years ago, the *Enterprise* had only received it last month. For that matter, he did not seem to know what the "galaxy" meant, either.

Kirk did not know what he expected to find, but he was braced for anything. Subspace radio was not the only thing the *Horizon* had lacked. She had landed before the non-interference directive had come into effect, and while the Iotians were just at the beginnings of industrialization. And the Iotians had been reported to be extremely intelligent—and somewhat imitative. The *Horizon* might have changed their culture drastically before her departure and shipwreck.

Still, the man called Boss seemed friendly enough. He didn't understand what "transported" meant either, in the technical sense, but readily suggested a rendezvous at an intersection marked by a big building with white columns in a public square where, he said, he would provide a reception committee. All quite standard, so far.

Kirk, Spock and McCoy beamed down, leaving Scott at the con. They materialized into a scene which might at first have been taken for an area in any of the older cities of present-day Earth, but with two significant exceptions; no children were visible, and all the adults, male and female alike, were wearing sidearms. Their dress was reminiscent of the United States of the early twentieth century.

This had barely registered when a sharp male voice behind them said, "Okay, you three. Let's see you petrify."

The officers turned to find themselves confronted by two men carry-

ing clumsy two-handed weapons which Kirk recognized as a variant of
the old submachine gun.

"Would you mind clarifying your statement, please?" Spock said.

"I want to see you turn to stone. Put your hands up over your head—
or you ain't gonna have no head to put your hands over."

The two were standing close enough together so that Kirk could have
stunned them both from the hip, but he disliked stopping situations before they had even begun to develop. He obeyed, his officers following
suit.

The man who had spoken kept them covered while the other silently
relieved them of their phasers and communicators. He seemed momentarily in doubt about McCoy's tricorder, but he took that, too. A few
pedestrians stopped to watch; they seemed only mildly curious, and
some of them even seemed to approve. Were these men policemen,
then? They were dressed no differently from anyone else; perhaps more
expensively and with more color, but that was all.

The silent man displayed his harvest to his spokesman. The latter
took a phaser and examined it. "What's this?"

"Be very careful with that, please," Kirk said. "It's a weapon."

"A heater, huh? The Boss'll love that."

"A Mr. Bela Okmyx invited us down. He said . . ."

"I know what he said. What he don't tell Kalo ain't worth knowing.
He said some boys would meet you. Okay, we're meeting you."

"Those guns aren't necessary," McCoy said.

"You trying to make trouble, bud? Don't give me those baby blue
eyes."

"What?"

"I don't buy that innocent routine." Kalo looked at Spock's ears.
"You a boxer?"

"No," Spock said. "Why does everybody carry firearms? Are you
people at war?"

"I never heard such stupid questions in my life." Kalo jerked his gun
muzzle down the street. "Get moving."

As they began to walk, Kirk became aware of a distant but growing
thrumming sound. Suddenly a squeal was added to it and it became
much larger.

"Get down!" Kalo shouted, throwing himself to the street. The people around him were already dropping, or seeking shelter. Kirk dived for
the dirt.

A vehicle that looked like two mismatched black bricks on four wheels
bore down on them. Two men leaned out of it with submachine guns,

which suddenly produced a terrible, hammering roar. Kalo got off a burst at it, but his angle was bad for accuracy. Luckily, it was not good for the gunners in the car, either.

Then the machine was gone, and the pedestrians picked themselves up. McCoy looked about, then knelt by the silent member of the "reception committee," but he was plainly too late.

Kalo shook his head. "Krako's getting more gall all the time."

"Is this the way you greet all your visitors?" Kirk demanded.

"It happens, pal."

"But this man is dead," McCoy said.

"Yeah? Well, we ain't playing for peanuts. Hey, you dopes, get outta here!" He shouted suddenly to what looked like the beginning of a crowd. "Ain't you never seen a hit before? Get lost!"

He resumed herding his charges, leaving the dead man unconcernedly behind. Kirk kept his face impassive, but his mind was busy. A man had been shot down, and no one had blinked an eye; it seemed as though it were an everyday happening. Was this the cultural contamination they had been looking for? But the crew of the *Horizon* hadn't been made up of cold-blooded killers, nor had they reported the Iotian culture in that state.

A young girl, rather pretty, emerged from a store entrance and cut directly across to them, followed by another. "You, Kalo," she said.

"Get lost."

"When's the Boss going to do something about the crummy street lights around here? A girl ain't safe."

"And how about the laundry pickup?" said the second girl. "We ain't had a truck by in three weeks."

"Write him a letter," Kalo said indifferently.

"I did. He sent it back with postage due."

"Listen, we pay our percentages. We're entitled to some service for our money."

"Get *lost*, I said." Kalo shook his head as the girls sullenly fell behind. "Some people got nothing to do but complain."

Kirk stared at him. He was certainly an odd sight—odder than before, now that his pockets were stuffed with all the hand equipment from the *Enterprise* trio, and he had a submachine gun under each arm. But he looked none the less dangerous for that. "Mr. Kalo, is this the way your citizens get things done? Their right of petition?"

"If they pay their percentages, the Boss takes care of them. We go in here."

"In here" was a building bearing a brightly polished brass plaque. It read:

BELA OKMYX
BOSS
NORTHSIDE TERRITORY

The end of the line was an office, large and luxurious, complete with heavy desk, a secretary of sorts and framed pictures—except that one of the frames, Kirk saw, surrounded some kind of pistol instead. A heavy-set, swarthy man sat behind the desk.

"Got 'em, Boss," Kalo said. "No sweat."

The big man smiled and rose. "Well, Captain Kirk. Come in. Sit down. Have a drink. Good stuff—distill it myself."

"No, thank you. You are Mr. Okmyx? This is Mr. Spock, my First Officer. And Dr. McCoy."

"A real pleasure. Sit down. Put down the heater, Kalo. These guys is guests." He turned back to Kirk. "You gotta excuse my boys. You just gotta be careful these days."

"Judging from what we've seen so far, I agree," Kirk said. "They call you the Boss. Boss of what?"

"My territory. Biggest in the world. Trouble with being the biggest is that punks is alla time trying to cut in."

"There is something astonishingly familiar about all this, Captain," Spock said.

"How many other territories are there?"

"Maybe a dozen, not counting the small fry—and they get bumped anyway when I get around to it."

"Do they include, if I may ask," Spock said, "a gentleman named Krako?"

"You know about Krako?"

"He hit us, Boss," Kalo said. "Burned Mirt."

Bela scowled. "I want him hit back."

"I'll take care of it."

Kirk had noticed a huge book on a stand nearby. He rose and moved toward it. Kalo raised his gun muzzle again, but at a quick signal from Bela, dropped it. The book was bound like a Bible, in white leather, with gold lettering reading: *Chicago Mobs of the Twenties*. The imprint was New York, 1993.

"How'd you get this, Mr. Okmyx?" he asked.

"That's The Book. *The* Book. They left it—the men from the *Horizon.*"

"And there is your contamination, Captain," Spock said. "An entire gangster culture. An imitative people, one book, and . . ."

"No cracks about The Book," Bela said harshly. "Look, I didn't bring you here for you to ask questions. You gotta do something for me. Then I tell you anything you want to know."

"Anything we can do," Kirk said, putting the book down, "we will. We have laws of our own we must observe."

"Okay," Bela said. He leaned forward earnestly. "Look, I'm a peaceful man, see? I'm sick and tired of all the hits. Krako hits me, I hit Krako, Tepo hits me, Krako hits Tepo. We ain't getting noplace. There's too many bosses, know what I mean? Now if there was just one, maybe we could get some things done. That's where you come in."

"I don't quite understand," Kirk said.

"You Feds made a lot of improvements since the other ship came here. You probably got all kinds of fancy heaters. So here's the deal. You gimme all the heaters I need—enough tools so I can hit all the punks once and for all—and I take over the whole place. Then all you have to deal with is me."

"Let me get this straight," Kirk said. "You want us to supply you with arms and assistance so you can carry out aggression against other nations?"

"What nations? I got some hits to make. You help me make them."

"Fascinating," Spock said. "But quite impossible."

"I'd call it outrageous," McCoy said.

"Even if we wanted to," Kirk said, "our orders are very . . ."

Bela gestured to Kalo, who raised his gun again. Though Kirk did not see any signal given, the door opened and another armed man came in.

"I ain't interested in *your* orders," Bela said. "You got eight hours to gimme what I asked for. If I don't get the tools by then, I'm gonna have your ship pick you up again—in a large number of very small boxes. Know what I mean, pal?"

Kalo belatedly began to unload the captured devices onto the Boss's desk. He pointed to a phaser. "This here's a heater, Boss. I don't know what the other junk is."

"A heater, eh? Let's see how it works." He pointed it at a wall. Kirk jerked forward.

"Don't do that! You'll take out half the wall!"

"That good, eh? Great. Just gimme maybe a hundred of these and we don't have no more trouble."

"Out of the question," Kirk said.

"I get what I want." Bela picked up a communicator. "What are these here?"

Kirk remained silent. Jerking a thumb toward McCoy, Bela said to Kalo, "Burn him."

"All right," Kirk said hastily. "It's a communications device, locked onto my ship."

Bela fiddled with one until it snapped open in his hand. "Hey," he said to it. "In the ship."

"Scott here. Who is this?"

"This here's Bela Okmyx. I got your Captain and his friends down here. You want 'em back alive, send me a hundred of them fancy heaters of yours, and some troops to show us how to use them. You got eight hours. Then I put the hit on your friends. Know what I mean?"

"No," Scott's voice said. "But I'll find out."

Bela closed the communicator. "Okay. Kalo, take 'em over to the warehouse. Put 'em in the bag, and keep an eye on 'em, good. You hear?"

"Sure, Boss. Move out, you guys."

The warehouse room had a barred window and was sparsely furnished, but it was equipped with another copy of The Book. Kalo and two henchmen were playing cards at a table, guns handy, their eyes occasionally flicking to Kirk, Spock and McCoy at the other end of the room.

"One book," McCoy said. "And they made it the blueprint for their entire society. Amazing."

"But not unprecedented," Spock said. "At one time, in old Chicago, conventional government nearly broke down. The gangs almost took over."

"This Okmyx must be the worst of the lot."

"Though we may quarrel with his methods, his goal is essentially the correct one," Spock said. "This culture must become united—or it will degenerate into complete anarchy. It is already on the way; you will recall the young women who complained of failing services."

"If this society broke down, because of the influence of the *Horizon*, the Federation is responsible," Kirk said. "We've got to try to straighten the mess out. Spock, if you could get to the sociological banks of the computer, could you come up with a solution?"

"Quite possibly, Captain."

Signaling Spock and McCoy to follow him unobtrusively, Kirk gradually drifted toward the card game. The players looked up at him warily, free hands on guns; but they relaxed again as he pulled over a chair and sat down. The game was a variety of stud poker.

After a few moments, Kirk said, "That's a kid's game."

"Think so?" Kalo said.

"I wouldn't waste my time."

"Who's asking you to?"

"On Beta Antares Four, they play a game for men. Of course, it's probably too involved for you. It takes intelligence."

Antares is not a double star; Kirk had taken the chance in order to warn the sometimes rather literal-minded that he was lying deliberately.

"Okay, I'll bite," Kalo said. "Take the cards, big man. Show us how it's played."

"The Antares cards are different, of course, but not too different," Kirk said, riffling through them. "The game's called Fizzbin. Each player gets six cards—except for the man on the dealer's right, who gets seven. The second card goes up—except on Tuesdays, of course . . . Ah, Kalo, that's good, you've got a nine. That's half a fizzbin already."

"I need another nine?"

Spock and McCoy drew nearer with quite natural curiosity, since neither of them had ever heard of the game. Neither had Kirk.

"Oh, no. That would be a sralk and you'd be disqualified. You need a King or a deuce, except at night, when a Queen or a four would . . . Two sixes! That's excellent—unless, of course, you get another six. Then you'd have to turn it in, unless it was black."

"But if it was black?" Kalo said, hopelessly confused.

"Obviously, the opposite would hold," Kirk said, deciding to throw in a touch of something systematic for further confusion. "Instead of turning your six in, you'd get another card. Now, what you are really hoping for is a royal fizzbin, but the odds against that are, well, astronomical, wouldn't you say, Spock?"

"I have never computed them, Captain."

"Take my word they're considerable. Now the last card around. We call it the cronk, but its home name is *klee-et*.* Ready? Here goes."

He dealt, making sure that Kalo's card went off the table. "Oops, sorry."

"I'll get it."

Kalo bent over. In the same instant, Kirk put his hands under the table and shoved. It went over on the other two. McCoy and Spock

* A Vulcan word meaning, roughly, "prepare to engage." See "Amok Time," *Star Trek Three.*

were ready; the action was hardly more than a flurry before the three guards were helpless. Kirk parceled out the guns.

"Spock, find the radio transmitting station. Uhura is monitoring their broadcasts. Cut in and have yourself and Bones beamed up to the ship."

"Surely you are coming, Captain?"

"Not without Bela Okmyx."

"Jim, you can't . . ."

"This mess is our responsibility, Bones. You have your orders. Let's go."

Kirk at first felt a little uneasy walking a city street with a submachine gun under his arm, but no one passing seemed to find it unusual. On the contrary, it seemed to be a status symbol; people cleared the way for him.

But the walk ended abruptly with two handguns stuck into his ribs from behind. He had walked into an ambush. How had Bela gotten word so fast?

The answer to that was soon forthcoming. The two hoods who had mousetrapped him crowded him into a car—and the ride was a long one. At its end was another office, almost a duplicate of Bela's; but the man behind the desk was short, squat, bull-shaped and strange. He arose with a jovial smile.

"So you're the Fed. Well, well. I'm Krako—Jojo Krako, Boss of the South Territory. Hey, I'm glad to see you."

"Would you mind telling me how you knew about me?"

"I got all Bela's communications bugged. He can't make a date with a broad without I know about it. Now you're probably wondering why I brought you here."

"Don't tell me. You want to make a deal."

Krako was pleased. "I like that. Sharp. Sharp, huh, boys?"

"Sharp, Boss."

"Let me guess some more," Kirk said. "You want—uh—heaters, right? And troops to teach you how to use them. And you'll hit the other bosses and take over the whole planet. And then we'll sit down and talk, right?"

"Wrong," Krako said. "More than talk. I know Bela. He didn't offer you beans. Me, I'm a reasonable man. Gimme what I want, and I cut you in for, say, a third. Skimmed right off the top. How do you like that?"

"I've got a better idea. You know this planet has to be united. So let's sit down, you, me, and Bela, get in contact with the other bosses, and discuss the matter like rational men."

Krako seemed to be genuinely outraged. "That ain't by The Book, Kirk. We know how to handle things! You make hits! Somebody argues, you lean on him! You think we're stupid or something?"

"No, Mr. Krako," Kirk said, sighing. "You're not stupid. But you are peculiarly unreasonable."

"Pally, I got ways of getting what I want. You want to live, Kirk? Sure you do. But after I get done with you, you're liable to be sorry— unless you come across. Zabo, tell Cirl the Knife to sharpen up his blade. I might have a job for him." The smile came back. "Of course, you gimme the heaters and you keep your ears."

"No deal."

"Too bad. Put him on ice."

The two hoods led Kirk out.

On shipboard, Spock's fortunes were not running much better. There turned out to be no specifics in the computer, not even a record of a planet-wide culture based on a moral inversion. Without more facts, reason and logic were alike helpless.

"Mr. Spock," Uhura said. "Mr. Okmyx from the surface is making contact. Audio only."

Spock moved quickly to the board. "Mr. Okmyx, this is Spock."

"How'd you get up there?" Bela's voice asked.

"Irrelevant, since we are here."

"Uh—yeah. But you'd better get back down. Krako's put the bag on your Captain."

Spock raised his eyebrows. "Why would he put a bag on the Captain?"

"Kidnapped him, dope. He'll scrag him, too."

"If I understand you correctly, that would seem to be a problem. Have you any suggestions?"

"Sure. You guys got something I want. I can help you get the captain back. No reason we can't make a deal."

"I am afraid I find it difficult to trust you, sir."

"What's to trust? Business is business. We call a truce. You come down. My boys spring Kirk. Then we talk about you giving me a hand."

"Since we must have our Captain back," Spock said after a moment, "I accept. We shall arrive in your office within ten minutes. Spock out."

McCoy had been standing nearby, listening. "You're going to trust him?"

"If we are to save the Captain, without blatant and forceful inter-ference on the planet, then we must have assistance from someone indigenous. At the moment, we are forced to trust Mr. Okmyx." He turned toward Scott. "Mr. Scott, although I hope to avoid their use, I think you should adjust one of the phaser banks to a strong stun position."

"Now," McCoy said, "you're starting to make sense."

Spock did not reply, since nothing in the situation made sense to him. Trusting Okmyx was nothing short of stupid, and the use of force was forbidden by General Order Number One. In such a case, the only course was to abide by the Captain's principle of letting the situation ripen.

Bela, of course, had a trap arranged. Spock had expected it, but there had been no way to avoid it. What he had not expected—nor had Bela—was the abrupt subsequent appearance of Kirk in the doorway, with a submachine gun under his arm.

"How did you get away?" Spock asked interestedly, after the gangsters had been disarmed—a long process which produced a sizable heap of lethal gadgets, some of them wholly unfamiliar.

"Krako made the mistake of leaving me a radio; that was all I needed for the old trip-wire trick. I thought I told you to get to the ship."

"We have been there, Captain. The situation required our return."

"It may be just as well. Find out anything from the computers?"

"Nothing useful, Captain. Logic and factual knowledge do not seem to apply here."

"You admit that?" McCoy said.

"With the greatest reluctance, Doctor."

"Then you won't mind if I play a hunch?" Kirk said.

"I am not sanguine about hunches, sir, but I have no practical alternative."

"What are you going to do, Jim?"

"Now that I've got Bela," Kirk said, "I'm going to put the bag on Krako."

"On Krako?" Bela said. "You ain't serious?"

"Why not?" Kirk turned to Bela and fingered his suit lapel. "That's nice material."

"It ought to be. It cost a bundle."

"Get out of it. You, too."

"Hey, now, wait a minute . . ."

"Take it off—pally! This time nobody's going to bag me."

Seeing that he meant it, Kalo and Bela got out of their clothes; Kirk and Spock donned them. Scooping up the required submachine guns as passports, they went out, leaving McCoy in charge.

In front of the office sat the large black car that Bela used. Fishing in the pockets of his borrowed suit, Kirk found the keys. They got in.

"Any idea how to run this thing, Spock?"

"No, Captain. But it should not be too difficult."

"Let's see," Kirk said, studying the controls. "A keyhole. For the—ignition process, I think. Insert and turn. Right."

He felt around with his foot and touched a button. The car stuttered and the engine was running.

"Interesting," Spock said.

"As long as it runs. Now, let's see. I think—gears . . ."

He pulled the lever down, which produced nothing but an alarming grinding sound which he could feel in his hand as well as hear.

"As I recall," Spock said, "there was a device called the clutch. Perhaps one of those foot pedals . . ."

The right-hand pedal didn't seem to work, but the left-hand one allowed the gear lever to go down. Kirk let the pedal up cautiously, and the car started with a lurch.

Kirk remembered the way to Krako's offices well enough, but the trip was a wild one; there seemed to be some trick to working the clutch which Kirk hadn't mastered. Luckily, pedestrians gave the big black vehicle a wide berth. Spock just hung on. When it was over, he observed, "Captain, you are a splendid starship commander, but as a taxi driver you leave much to be desired."

"Haven't had time to practice. Leave these clumsy guns under the seat; we'll use phasers."

They made their way to Krako, leaving a trail of stunned guards behind. The Boss did not seem a bit taken aback when they burst in on him; he had four hoods behind him, guns aimed at the door.

"You don't shoot, we don't shoot," he said rapidly.

"This would appear to be an impasse," Spock said.

"Who's your friend with the ears?" Krako asked. "Never mind. Ain't this nice? I was wondering how I was going to get you back, and you delivered yourself! You don't think you'll get out of it this time, do you?"

"We didn't come here for games," Kirk said. "This is bigger than you or Okmyx or any of the others."

The phaser which Krako had previously taken from Kirk was on the desk, still on safety lock. Krako nudged it. "Don't talk fancy. All you gotta do is tell me how to work these things."

"Krako," Kirk said, "can you trust all your men?"

"Yeah, sure. I either trust 'em or they're dead."

"Maybe. But when it comes to weapons like these—well, one of them could make a man a pretty big boss around here."

Krako thought about it. At last he said, "Zabo and Karf, stay put. You other guys vanish . . . All right, these two is okay. Now that we got no busy little eyes around, how do you work this thing?"

Kirk moved in on Krako hard and fast, spitting his words out like bullets. "Knock it off, Krako. We don't have time to show you how to play with toys."

"Toys?"

"What do you think we're here for, Krako? To get a cut of your deal? Forget it. That's peanuts to an outfit like the Federation."

"It is?" Krako said, a little dazed by the sudden switch.

"Unquestionably," Spock said.

"We came here to take over, Krako. The whole ball of wax. Maybe, if you cooperate, we'll cut *you* in for a piece of the action."

"A minute piece," Spock added.

"How much is that?" Krako asked.

"We'll figure it out later."

"But—I thought you guys had some kind of law about no interference . . ."

"Who's interfering? We're just taking over."

Spock seemed slightly alarmed. "Uh—Captain . . ."

"Cool it, Spocko. Later."

"What's your deal?" Krako asked.

Kirk motioned him to his feet and, when the bewildered gangster stood, Kirk sat down in his chair and swung his feet up onto the desk. He appropriated one of Krako's cigars.

"The Federation wants this planet, but we don't want to have to come in and use our muscle. That ain't subtle. So what we do is help one guy take over. He pulls the planet's strings—and we pull his. Follow?"

"But what's your cut?"

Kirk eyed the unlit cigar judiciously. "What do you care, so long as you're in charge? Right, Spocko?"

"Right on the button, Boss," Spock said, falling into his role a little belatedly but with a certain relish. "Of course, there's always Bela Okmyx . . ."

Krako thought only a moment. "You got a deal. Call your ship and bring down your boys and whatever you need."

Kirk got to his feet and snapped open his communicator. "Kirk to *Enterprise.*"

"*Enterprise.* Scott here, sir."

"Scotty, we made the deal with Krako."

"Uh—we did, sir?"

"We're ready to make the hit. We're taking over the whole planet as soon as you can get ready."

"Is that wise, sir?"

"Sure, we can trust Krako—he doesn't have any choice. He's standing here right now, *about three feet to my left,* all ready to be our pal. I'd like to show him the ship, just so he's sure I'm giving him the straight dope. But you know how it is."

"Oh aye, sir," Scott said. "I know indeed."

"We'll be needing enough phasers to equip all of Krako's men, plus advisers—troops to back them up on the hit. You moving, Scotty?"

"Aye, Uhura's on to the Transporter Room and two of the boys are on their way. Ready when you say the word."

"Very well, Scotty, begin."

Krako looked curiously at Kirk. "You mean you're gonna start bringing all those guys down now?"

"No—not exactly." As he spoke, the hum of the Transporter effect filled the room, and Krako shimmered out of existence. Zabo and Karf stared, stunned—and a second later were stunned more thoroughly.

"Well played—Spocko."

Spock winced. "So we have—put the bag on Krako. What is our next maneuver, Captain?"

"Back to Bela's place."

"In the car, Captain?"

"It's faster than walking. Don't tell me you're afraid of cars, Spock."

"Not at all. It is your driving which alarms me."

Through the door of Bela's office, they heard McCoy saying worriedly, "Where *are* they?"

And then Bela's, "Knowing Krako, we'll be lucky if he sends 'em back on a blotter."

Kirk walked in. "Wrong again, Okmyx." He brushed past the relieved McCoy. "Outta my way, Sawbones. I want to talk to this guy. I'm getting tired of playing pattycake with you penny ante operators."

"Who you calling penny ante?" Bela said, bristling.

"Nobody but you, baby. Now listen. The Federation's moving in here. We're taking over, and if you play ball, we'll leave a piece of the pie for you. If you don't, you're out. All the way out. Got that?" He shoved the phaser under Bela's nose to make the point.

"Yeah—yeah, sure, Kirk. Why didn't you say so in the first place? I mean—all you hadda do was explain."

The communicator came out. "Scotty, you got Krako on ice up there?"

"Aye, Captain."

"Keep him till I ask for him. We're going to be making some old-style phone calls from these coordinates. Lock on at the receiving end and transport the party here to us. Okay, Okmyx. Start calling the other bosses."

Shrugging, Bela went to the phone and dialed four times. "Hello, Tepo? Guess who? . . . Yeah, I got a lot of nerve. What're you going to do about it?"

With a hum, Tepo materialized, holding a non-existent phone in his hand. McCoy moved in to disarm him.

". . . coming over there with a couple of my boys, and . . . Brother!"

Bela grinned at Kirk. "Hey, this ain't bad."

"Keep dialing."

Half an hour later, the office was crowded with dazed gang leaders, Krako among them. Kirk climbed up on the desk, now cradling a local gun to add weight to his argument.

"All right, pipe down, everybody. I'll tell you what you're going to do. The Federation just took over around here, whether you like it or not. You guys have been running this planet like a piecework factory. From here on, it's all under one roof. You're going to form a syndicate and run this planet like a business. That means you make a profit."

"Yeah?" Tepo called. "And what's your percentage?"

"I'm cutting the Federation in for forty per cent." He leveled the gun. "You got objections?"

Tepo had obviously had guns pointed at him too many times to be cowed. "Yeah. I hear a lot of talk, but all I see here is you and a couple of your boys. I don't see no Federation."

"Listen, they got a ship," Krako said. "I know—I been there."

"Yeah, but Tepo's got a point," Bela said. "All we ever see is them."

"I only saw three other guys and a broad while I was in the ship," Krako said. "Maybe there ain't any more?"

"There are four hundred . . ."

Kirk was interrupted by an explosion outside, followed by a fusillade of shots. Krako, who was nearest the window, peered around the edge of it.

"It's my boys," he reported. "Must think I'm still in the ship. They're making a hit on this place."

"My boys'll put 'em down," Bela said.

"Wanna bet?"

Kirk's communicator was already out. "Scotty, put ship's phasers on stun and fire a burst in a one-block radius around these coordinates, excluding this building."

"Right away, sir."

Kirk looked at the confused gangsters. "Gentlemen, you are about to see the Federation at work."

The noise roared on a moment more, and then the window was lit up with the phaser effect. Dead silence fell promptly.

Krako smiled weakly and swallowed. "Some trick."

"They're not dead, just knocked out for a while," Kirk said. "We could just as easily have killed them."

"Okay," Bela said. "We get the message. You were saying something about a syndicate."

"No, he was saying something about a percentage," Tepo said. "You sure forty percent is enough?"

"I think it will be just fine. We'll send someone around to collect it every year—and give you advice if you need it."

"That's reasonable," Bela said. He glared at the others. "Ain't that reasonable?"

There was a murmur of assent. Kirk smiled cheerfully. "Well, in that case, pull out some of that drinking stuff of yours, Okmyx, and let's get down to the talking."

The bridge of the *Enterprise* was routinely busy. Kirk was in the command chair, feeling considerably better to be back in uniform.

"I must say," Spock said, "your solution to the problem on Iotia is unconventional, Captain. But it does seem to be the only workable one."

"What troubles you is that it isn't logical to leave a criminal organization in charge. Is that it?"

"I do have some reservations. And how do you propose to explain to Starfleet Command that a starship will be sent around each year to collect 'our cut,' as you put it?"

" 'Our cut' will be put back into the planet's treasury—and the advisers and collectors can help steer the Iotians back into a more conventional moral and ethical system. In the meantime, the syndicate forms a central government that can effectively administer to the needs of the people. That's a step in the right direction. Our group of 'governors' is already learning to take on conventional responsibilities. Guiding them is—our piece of the action."

Spock pondered. "Yes, it seems to make sense. Tell me, Captain. Whatever gave you so outlandish an idea—and where did you pick up all that jargon so quickly?"

Kirk grinned. "Courtesy of Krako. A radio wasn't all he left in my cell. He also left me some reading matter."

"Ah, of course. The Book."

"Spocko, now you're talkin'."

Book III
Star Trek 9

BOOK III—*Star Trek 9*

RETURN TO TOMORROW

(Gene Roddenberry and John T. Dugan)

The readings were coming from a star system directly ahead of the *Enterprise*. And havoc is what they were causing. The Starship's distress relays had been activated. All its communication channels had been affected. A direction to follow had even been specified, but no clear signal had been received. Yet one fact was clear: someone or something was trying to attract the *Enterprise's* attention. Who? Or what? Those were the questions.

Over at Spock's station, Kirk said, "Well?"

"I don't know, Captain."

Despite his exasperation, Kirk smiled. "I never heard you use those words before, Mr. Spock."

"Not even a Vulcan can know the unknown, sir," Spock said stiffly. "We're hundreds of light years past where any Earth ship has ever explored."

"Planet dead ahead, Captain!" Sulu called. "Becoming visual."

The screen showed what appeared to be a very dead planet: scarred, shrunken, a drifting cadaver of a world.

Uhura turned from her board. "That planet is the source of whatever it is we have been receiving, sir."

Spock, his head bent to his hooded viewer, announced, "Class M planet, sir. Oblate spheroid, ratio 1 to 296. Mean density 5.53. Mass .9." He paused. "Close resemblance to Earth conditions with two very important differences. It's much older than Earth. And about half a million years ago its atmosphere was totally ripped away by some cataclysm. Sensors detect no life of any kind."

Without warning the bridge was suddenly filled by the sound of a voice, resonant, its rich deepness profoundly impressive. *"Captain Kirk,"* it said, *"all your questions will be answered in time."*

The bridge people stared at the screen. Kirk, turning to Uhura, said, "Are your hailing frequencies freed yet, Lieutenant?"

"No, sir."

They had sped past the planet now. Eyes on the screen, Kirk said, "Maintain present course, Mr. Sulu."

The deep voice spoke again. *"I am Sargon. It is the energy of my thoughts which has touched your instruments and directed you here."*

"Then, can you hear me?" Kirk asked. "Who are you, Sargon?"

"Please assume a standard orbit around our planet, Captain."

"Are you making a request or demand?" Kirk said.

"The choice is yours. I read what is in your mind: words are unnecessary."

"If you can read my mind, you must know I am wondering just who and what you are. The planet we've just passed is dead; there is no possibility of life there as we understand life."

"And I," said the voice, *"am as dead as my planet. Does that frighten you, Captain? If it does, you will let what is left of me perish."* An awesome solemnity had entered the voice. *"Then, all of you, my children—all of mankind will . . ."*

The voice faded as the Starship moved out of the planet's range. Sulu, turning to Kirk, said, "Do we go on, sir—or do I turn the ship back?"

Kirk could feel all eyes centered on him. Then Spock spoke from his station. "There's only one possible explanation, sir. Pure thought . . . the emanations of a fantastically powerful mind."

Kirk paced the distance from his chair to the main viewing screen. "Whatever it is, we're beyond its range."

"And out of danger," Spock said dryly.

"You don't recommend going back?"

"If a mind of that proportion should want to harm us, sir, we could never hope to cope with it."

"It called me—us 'my children,'" Kirk said. "What could that mean?"

"Again, sir—I don't know."

Kirk sank down in his command chair, frowning. Then his brow cleared. "All right," he said. "Take us back, Mr. Sulu. Standard orbit around the planet."

The dead world gradually reappeared on the screen, its color the hue of dead ash. Sulu said, "Entering standard orbit, Captain."

Kirk nodded, eyes on the screen. Then he hit the button of his command recorder, dictating. "Since exploration and contact with alien intelligence is our primary mission, I have decided to risk the dangers potential in our current situation—and resume contact with this strange planet. Log entry out." Snapping off the recorder, he spoke to Uhura. "How long before Starfleet receives that?"

"Over three weeks at this distance, sir. A month and a half before we receive their answer."

Kirk left his chair to cross to Spock's station. The Vulcan was swiftly manipulating dials.

"Got something?" Kirk said.

"Sensors registering some form of energy, sir . . . deep *inside* the planet."

Sargon's voice came once more. *"Your probes have touched me, Mr. Spock."*

Spock looked up at Kirk. "I read energy only, sir. No life form."

Then again Sargon spoke. *"I have locked your transporter device on my coordinates. Please come to us. Rescue us from oblivion."*

Spock, imperturbable, lifted his head from his viewer's mound. "It came from deep under the planet surface, Captain . . . from under at least a hundred miles of solid rock."

Kirk began, "We can't beam—"

Sargon addressed the half-spoken thought in his mind. *"I will make it possible for your transporter to beam you that deep beneath the surface. Have no fear."*

Spock, concentrating on his viewer, said, "I read a chamber beneath the surface, sir. Oxygen-nitrogen suitable for human life support."

Kirk gave himself a long moment. Then he spoke to Uhura. "Lieutenant, have Dr. McCoy report to the Transporter Room in ten minutes with standard landing-party equipment."

"Aye, sir."

"Captain," Spock said, "I am most curious to inspect whatever it is that has survived half a million years—this entity which has outlived its cataclysmic experience."

Kirk laid a hand on his shoulder. "And I'd like my Science Officer with me on something as unusual as this. But it's so full of unknowns, we can't risk the absence of both of us from the ship."

The bridge was instantly plunged into total darkness. All panel hum stilled. Sulu hit a switch. "Power's gone, sir! *Totally* gone!"

There had been no menace in the deep voice. A tone of pleading, yes —but no menace. Kirk frowned, pondering. Then he said, "On the other hand, Mr. Spock, perhaps this 'Sargon' wants you to come along with me."

Lights flashed back on. Panels hummed again. Sulu, checking his board, cried, "All normal, sir! No damage at all."

"Well," Kirk said. "Then that's that. Mr. Spock, you'll transport down with us." As he strode to the elevator, he turned to add, "Mr. Sulu, you have the con."

A young woman, dark and slim, had followed McCoy into the Transporter Room. Kirk recognized her—Lieutenant Commander Anne Mulhall, astrobiologist. His eyes took in the figure, the startling sapphire of the eyes under the raven-black hair. He hadn't remembered her as so attractive. She lowered her eyes, checking her equipment, two security guards beside her. Nor did she look up as McCoy said tartly, "Jim, why no briefing on this? I'd like at least to know—"

Kirk interrupted. "Easy, Bones. If you know 'something is down there,' you know as much as we do. The rest is only guesses."

Scott, over at the Transporter console, spoke. "I don't like it, Captain. Your coordinates preset by an alien of some unknown variety. You could materialize inside solid rock."

"*Inside solid rock!*" McCoy shouted.

Spock, moving in beside Scott, said, "Unlikely, Doctor. The coordinates correspond to a chamber that sensor readings detected on the bridge."

"It is my feeling," Kirk said, "that they or it could destroy us standing right here if it wanted to, Mr. Scott."

Anne spoke for the first time. "'They' or 'it'?" she said.

Kirk looked at her. "Lieutenant Commander, may I ask what you're doing here in this room?"

"I was ordered to report for landing-party duty, sir."

"By whom?"

"I . . ." She smiled. "It's strange, sir. I'm not sure."

There was a moment's pause. Then, flushing, she added, "I do not lie, Captain. I *did* receive an order to report here."

Spock intervened. "I'm sure she did, Captain. Just as you received an order to take me along."

Kirk nodded; and McCoy said, "Let's get back to this solid-rock business. How much rock are we going through?"

Spock answered. "Exactly one hundred, twelve point three seven miles below the surface, Doctor."

"*Miles?*" McCoy echoed blankly. "Jim, he's joking!"

But Kirk was assigning Transporter positions to the party. They were taking their places when the console lights abruptly flashed on and Sargon's voice said, *"Please stand ready. I will operate the controls."*

Kirk spoke in reaction to the shock in McCoy's face. "If you'd prefer to stay behind, Bones . . ."

McCoy eyed him. "No—no, if I'd be useful, and I may have to be, that is, as long as you're beaming down, Jim . . ." He shrugged. "I might as well have a medical look at whatever this is."

Kirk joined them on the platform. "Energize!" he called to Scott.

The dematerializing shimmer broke them into glittering fragments—all of them except the two security guards. They were left standing, unaffected, on the platform, their faces astounded. Scott stared at them, his face drawing into lines of worry.

The selected group materialized in a metallic vault, some sort of antechamber, its luminescent walls diffusing a softly radiant glow. Spock was the first to realize the absence of the security guards.

Kirk nodded at his comment. "Somebody down here doesn't like them," he said. He opened his communicator. "Kirk here, Scotty."

"Can you read me, Captain?"

"I shouldn't be able to, not from this deep inside the planet. Perhaps that's been arranged for us, too. Is the security team up there?"

"They're fine, Captain. They just didn't dematerialize. I don't like it, sir."

"No problems here yet. Maintain alert. Captain out."

Anne and Spock had been circling the vault with their tricorders. The girl said, "Atmosphere report, Captain. A fraction richer in oxygen than usual for us, but otherwise normal."

Spock had applied his tricorder to a wall. "This vault was fabricated about a half-million years ago. About the same time that the planet surface was destroyed."

"Walls' composition?"

"A substance or alloy quite unknown to me, sir. Much stronger and harder than anything I ever measured."

"All readings go off the scale, sir," Anne said.

"The air's fresh," McCoy said, sniffing. "Must be re-circulated somehow."

"For us? Or does 'it' need fresh air?"

As if in reply, the fourth wall of the vault slid back. They recoiled. Ahead of them was a vast room. It was starkly bare, empty except for a large slab of veinless white stone, supported by four plain standards of the same immaculate stone. On it stood a big translucent globe, bril-

liantly lit from within. The group followed Kirk into the room; but as
Spock stepped forward to take a tricorder reading of the globe, he was
halted by the sound of Sargon's voice, still deep but no longer resonant.

"*Welcome*," said the globe. "*I am Sargon.*"

Once more Spock focused his tricorder. "Sargon, would you mind if
I—?"

"*You may use your tricorder, Mr. Spock. Your readings will show
energy but no substance. Sealed in this receptacle is the essence of my
mind.*"

Spock took his readings. Then he backed up to Kirk so that he, too,
could see them. Kirk gave a low whistle of amazement. "Impossible,
Spock! A being of pure energy without matter or form!"

McCoy addressed the globe. "But you once had a body of some
type?"

"*Although our minds were infinitely greater, my body was much as
yours, my children.*"

Kirk spoke slowly. "That is the second time you have called us your
'children'."

"*Because it is probable you are our descendants, Captain. Six thousand centuries ago our vessels were colonizing this galaxy just as your
own Starships are now exploring it. As you leave your seed on distant
planets, so we left our seed behind us.*"

Anne protested: "Our studies indicate that our planet Earth evolved
independently." But Spock, his face unusually preoccupied, said, "That
would explain many enigmas in Vulcan pre-history."

"*There is no certainty. It was so long ago that the records of our
travels were lost in the catastrophe we loosed upon ourselves.*"

Kirk said, "A war?"

"*A struggle for goal that unleashed a power you cannot even comprehend.*"

"Then perhaps your intelligence was deficient, Sargon." Kirk stepped
toward the globe. "We faced a crisis like that at the beginning of the
Nuclear Age. But we found the wisdom not to destroy ourselves."

"*We survived our primitive Nuclear Era, my son. But there comes to
all races an ultimate crisis which you have yet to face.*"

"I should like to understand," Kirk said. "I do not."

"*The mind of man can become so powerful that he forgets he is man.
He confuses himself with God.*"

Kirk's mind was awhirl. Was this being speaking of the Lucifer sin?
Abruptly, he felt a completed trust of Sargon. He moved to the globe

with the confidence of a child to a parent. "You said you needed help. What is it you wish?"

A strange thrilling sound echoed through the room. In the globe, light fluctuated, growing brighter and brighter. Then a flare broke from it. It transfixed Kirk, holding him immobile. At the same instant light in the globe dimmed to a tiny flicker. It was clear to the others that the essence of what was in the globe had transferred itself to Kirk—and vanished into him.

McCoy started forward, but Spock put out a restraining hand. "Patience, Doctor. Let's wait a moment."

Kirk stood rigid, stiffened, his eyes shut. It seemed centuries to McCoy before they opened. "Jim . . ." he said. "Jim . . ."

Kirk spoke. "I am . . . Sargon."

His voice had deepened. And his bearing had changed, permeated as by the calm, gently austere dignity that had characterized the personality of Sargon.

McCoy yelled, *"Where's our Captain? Where's Jim Kirk?"*

"Here, Bones." The voice of Sargon-Kirk was gentle as a mother soothing a frightened infant. "Your loved Captain is unharmed. I have taken his body for the moment to demonstrate to you—"

McCoy had drawn his phaser. "No! No, I do not go along with this! Back where you were, Sargon, whatever you are!"

"What do you propose to do with your phaser?" It was the mild voice of Spock. "That's still Jim's body."

McCoy's shoulders slumped. Then he saw that the incorporated Sargon was slowly becoming aware of Kirk's body. It expanded its chest; its head was flung up as the deliciousness of air was inhaled; its arms flexed —and a cry burst from it.

"Lungs . . . lungs savoring breath again! Eyes seeing colors again! A heart pumping arteries surging with young blood!" A hand touched the other one in wonder. "To *feel* again after half a million years!" Kirk's body turned, his own smile on its lips. "Your Captain has an excellent corpus, Doctor! I compliment both of you on the condition in which it has been maintained."

"And your plans for it?" Spock's voice was toneless. "Can you exchange places again when you wish?"

Sargon-Kirk didn't answer. Instead, he moved to the receptacle with its frail glow of light. Pointing to it, he said, "Have no fear. Your Captain is quite unharmed in there." The dim flicker slightly brightened. "See? He hears, he knows, he is aware of all we do and say. But his mind cannot generate the energy to speak from the globe as I did."

Spock, who had been using his tricorder, called "Doctor!" McCoy paled as he saw its readings. "The creature is killing him!" he shouted. "Heartbeat almost double, temperature one hundred and four degrees!"

"Sargon, what is it you want of us?" Spock demanded.

Kirk's eyes studied them silently. Finally Sargon's words came. "There are other receptacles in the next room; they contain two more of us who have survived. You, Anne Mulhall, and you, Mr. Spock—we shall require your bodies for them. We must have your bodies and Captain Kirk's in order to live again."

It had come to all of them that Kirk was no longer Kirk but an individual stronger, wiser, infused with a dominant intelligence beyond the reach of any of them. Waved into the next room, they obediently moved into it. Its shelved walls held many receptacles; but of them all, only two still shone with light. Kirk's deeper voice said, "Yes, only two of us still live. The others are blackened by death but these two still shine— Hanoch and Thalassa." He caressed one of the lighted globes. "Thalassa, my Thalassa, I am pleased you survived with me. Half a million years have been almost too long to wait."

Spock said, "Sargon, when that struggle came that destroyed your planet . . ."

"A few of the best minds were chosen to survive. We built these chambers and preserved our essence here in this fashion." He touched the Thalassa globe with tenderness. "My wife, as you may have guessed. And Hanoch from the other, enemy side in the struggle. By then we had all realized our mistake."

He paused. "We knew the seeds we had planted on other planets had taken root. And we knew you would one day build vessels as we did— that you would come here."

"What was your task in that globe out there?" Spock said.

"To search the heavens with my mind . . . probing, waiting, probing. And finally my mind touched something—your ship bringing you here."

"So you could thieve our bodies from us!" Anne cried.

He looked at her, the centuries of gathered wisdom in his eyes contrasting eerily with the youth of Kirk's face. "To steal your bodies? No, no. You misunderstand, my children. To *borrow* them. We ask you to only lend them to us for a short time."

"To *destroy* them!" cried McCoy. "Just as you're burning that one up right now! Spock, the heartbeat reading is now 262! And the whole metabolic rate is just as high! My medical tricorder—"

"I shall return your Captain's body before its limit has been reached, Doctor."

"What is the purpose of this borrowing?" Spock said.

"To build . . ." Suddenly, Sargon-Kirk swayed. Then he straightened. "To build humanoid robots. We must borrow your bodies only long enough to have the use of your hands, your fingers."

Spock turned to the others. "I understand," he said. "They will construct mechanical bodies for themselves and move their minds into them. That accomplished, they will return our bodies to us."

Anne interposed. "We have engineers, technicians. Why can't they build the robot bodies for you?"

"No. Our methods, the skill required, goes far beyond your abilities." He swayed again, staggering, and Spock put out an arm to support him. His breath was coming hard and the Vulcan had to stoop to hear his whisper. "It is . . . time. Help me back to your . . . Captain."

With McCoy at his other side, he stumbled back into the big bare room. Weakly, he waved them aside to stand alone by the receptacle, eyes closed. This time the flare of light flashed from him—and abruptly, the globe was again alive with a pulsating brilliance. The knees of the borrowed body gave way and Anne Mulhall rushed to it, her arms outstretched. They closed around its shoulders and its eyelids fluttered open. "Captain Kirk?" she said tentatively.

The skipper of the *Enterprise* smiled at her, his eyes on her face.

"Jim . . . is it you?" cried McCoy.

Kirk didn't speak, his gaze still deep in the sapphire eyes. Hurriedly, McCoy checked him with his medical tricorder. "Good—good, fine! Metabolic rate back to normal!"

Spock went to him. "Captain, do you remember what happened? Do you remember any part of it?"

"What? Oh. Oh, yes, yes. Sargon borrowed my body." He gestured to the globe. "I was there, floating . . . floating in time and space."

"You take it damned casually!" McCoy said. "However, you don't seem harmed . . . physically at least."

Kirk, wholly himself again, suddenly seemed to realize how matter-of-factly he was accepting his extraordinary experience. "Spock, I remember all now! As Sargon and I exchanged—for an instant we were one. I know him. I know now exactly what he is and what he wants. *And I do not fear him.*"

Anne had withdrawn her embrace. "Captain, I'm afraid I must agree with Dr. McCoy. You could be suffering mental effects from this—a kind of euphoria."

"There's a way to check my conviction about Sargon." He turned to

Spock. "I—I hate to ask it, Mr. Spock, knowing as I do what it costs you."

"Vulcan mind-melding?" McCoy said. "Are you willing, Spock?"

Spock took time to answer. Finally, he nodded gravely. Then, with care, he began to ready himself for the ordeal, breathing deeply, massaging chest muscles. Kirk, turning to the globe, said, "Sargon, we—"

"I understand. I am prepared."

It began. The globe's brilliance increased and, with it, the strain on Spock's anguished concentration. His breath grew harsh and his neck muscles taut. Words started to come like those of a man in a dream or a nightmare. ". . . there is a world . . . not physical. The mind reaches . . . grows to encompass . . . to understand beyond understanding . . . growing . . . beyond comprehension . . . beyond . . . beyond . . . beyond . . ."

Kirk flashed an alarmed look at McCoy. It had never been so hard. They started forward—but Spock himself was now breaking away from the meld. He drew a deep lungful of breath, shaking, weak, eyes dazed.

"Spock?" Kirk cried.

The voice still held the awe of inexpressible experience. "Captain, I cannot say . . . what I have seen. The—the knowledge . . . the beauty of perfect reason . . . the incredible goodness . . . the unbelievable glory of ageless wisdom . . . the pure goodness of what Sargon is . . ."

Anne was the first to break the silence. "Beauty? Perfect reason? Pure goodness?"

Kirk nodded. "Beyond imagination."

Spock, still shaken, whispered, "It . . . will take me . . . time to absorb all I have learned . . . all I have felt . . ."

"Yes," Kirk said. Instinctively he turned to the receptacle. "Sargon . . ." he said. The word might have been "Father".

"I understand, my son. Go to your vessel. All who are involved must agree to this. After all these centuries, we can wait a few more hours."

McCoy strode to the globe. "And if we decide against you?"

"Then you may go as freely as you came."

Leonard McCoy was out of his depth. He looked from Spock to Kirk, feeling himself to be the alien in a world no longer familiar to him. He had never been so uncertain of himself in his life.

"You are going to *what?*"

Scott had leaned over the Briefing Room table, his face incredulous. Kirk, quite composed, sat beside the grim-jawed McCoy. He smiled at

Scott; and his Chief Engineer, Highland blood boiling, cried, "Are they all right in the head, Doctor?"

"No comment," McCoy said.

"It's a simple transference of our minds and theirs, Scotty," Kirk said.

"Nothing to it," McCoy said. "It happens every day."

Kirk ignored him. "I want your approval, Scotty. You'll have to do all the work with them, furnishing all they need to build the android robots. That is, you'll only seem to be working with us—with our bodies. But they'll be inside of them and we will be . . ." The explanation was getting complicated. Kirk flinched under the cold Scottish steel of Scott's eyes. "We'll be . . . in their receptacles," he finished lamely.

He sounded mad to his own ears. Where had fled that supremely sane self-possession of Sargon's that his body had entertained so briefly? He struggled to recover some shred of it; and McCoy cried, "Where they'll be, Scott, is floating in a ball! Just drifting sweetly in a ball of nothing! Indecent is what it is—indecent!"

Spock spoke. "Once inside their robot forms, Engineer, they will restore our bodies. They can leave this planet and travel back with us. With their massive knowledge, mankind can leap ahead ten thousand years."

"Bones," Kirk said, "they'll show us medical miracles you've never dreamed possible. And engineering advances, Scotty! Vessels this size with engines no larger than a walnut!"

"You're joking," Scott said gruffly.

"No," Spock said. "I myself saw that and more in Sargon's mind. I encountered an infinity of a goodness and knowledge that—that at this moment still staggers me."

"Many a fine man crushes ants underfoot without even knowing it." McCoy's voice shook. "They're giants and we're insects beside them, Jim. They could destroy us without meaning to."

Scott was musing aloud. "A Starship engine the size of a walnut?" He shrugged. "Impossible. But I suppose there's no harm in looking over diagrams on it . . ."

"And all he wants for these miracles is the body of our ship's Captain," McCoy said. "And that of our next in command, too. Coincidence? Anybody want to bet?"

"They have selected us, Bones, as the most compatible bodies."

"And your attitude on that, Dr. Mulhall?" McCoy demanded.

"If we all agree," Anne said steadily, "I am willing to host Thalassa's mind. I am a scientist. The opportunity is an extraordinary one for experimentation and observation."

"Bones, you can stop this right now by voting 'no'. That's why I called you all here. We'll all be deeply involved. It must be unanimous."

McCoy slammed the table. "Then I still want one question answered! *Why?* Not a list of possible miracles—but an understandable, simple, basic 'why' that doesn't ignore all the possible dangers! Let's not kid ourselves! There's much danger potential in this thing!"

"They used to say, Bones, that if man were meant to fly, he'd have wings. But he *did* fly." Kirk's voice deepened with his earnestness. "In fact, human existence has been a long story of faint-hearted warnings not to push any further, not to learn, not to strive, not to grow. I don't believe we can stop, Bones. Do you want to return to the days when your profession operated with scalpels—and sewed up the patients with catgut?"

He paused, looking at the faces around the table. "Yes, I'm in command. I can order this. I haven't done so. Dr. McCoy is performing his duty. He is right to point out the enormous danger potential in such close contact with intelligence as fantastically advanced as this. *My* point is that the potential for new knowledge is also enormous. Risk is our business. That's what this Starship is all about! It is why we're aboard her!"

He leaned forward in his chair, his eyes searching faces. "You may dissent without prejudice. Do I hear a negative vote?"

There was none. He rose to his feet. "Mr. Scott, stand by to bring the three receptacles aboard."

In Sickbay the three beds had been arranged for Kirk, Spock, and Anne. A shining globe had been placed beside each one. McCoy, Christine Chapel beside him, stood at the body-function panels, his clipboard in hand. He turned to the nurse. "You must know," he said, "that with the transfer, the extreme power of the alien minds will drive heart action dangerously high. All body functions will race at many times normal metabolism. These panels must be monitored most carefully."

The situation had shaken Christine. She made a successful effort to recover her professionalism. "Yes, sir," she said.

McCoy spoke to Kirk. "We're about as ready as we'll ever be."

Kirk turned his head to the globe beside him. "Ready, Sargon."

There came the thrilling sound preceding transfer. The three globes grew active, light building and fluctuating inside them. Then the three flares flashed from them to the bodies lying on the beds. Anne's trembled as Thalassa entered it. Christine moved quickly to check it. Hanoch-Spock sat up, stretching in delight at the feel of a body. Beside each bed the globes' light had dimmed to a faint flicker. McCoy was concentrating on Kirk's body-function panel; and Christine, leaving Thalassa-Anne, moved in to check Hanoch-Spock. To her amazement, he smiled at her, his eyes taking her in with lusty appreciation. Where was the cool, cerebral Spock?

She turned hastily to his body panel. What she read alarmed her. "Metabolic rates are double and rising, Doctor."

Hanoch-Spock spoke. "A delicious woman . . . a delicious sight to awaken to after half a million years."

Disconcerted, Christine said, "Thank you."

But Hanoch-Spock was looking beyond her now to where Thalassa-Anne was sitting up in bed, raven hair about her shoulders, the blue eyes shining as she savored the forgotten feeling of life. "I—I didn't remember what it felt like . . . to breathe—to breathe like this!" She turned. "Sargon? Where's Sargon?"

Sargon-Kirk rose and went to her. "Here . . . in this body, Thalassa." With a becoming dignity, threaded with joy in the awakening of long-forgotten senses, she smiled at him. "The body does not displease me, my husband. It is not unlike that which was your own."

"I am pleased by your pleasure, my love."

She had become aware of her hands. Tentatively, she reached one up to caress his cheek. "After so long," she whispered. "It's been so long, Sargon."

His arms were around her. Christine averted her eyes as their lips met. There was something infinitely touching in this embrace, longed for but deferred for half a million years. They separated and Christine said, "I'm sorry . . . I'm here . . ."

Thalassa-Anne extended a gentle hand. "You are not intruding, my child. As a woman, you know my wondrous gratitude at touching him who is mine again. Do you have a man?"

"No. I—I . . ." Despite herself, Christine found her eyes moving to Spock, forgetting for the moment that it was Hanoch who inhabited him. She flushed. "No, I . . . do not have that need. I have my work." She took a hasty reading of the body-function panel. Had Hanoch-Spock noticed that look?

Thalassa-Anne spoke quietly to Sargon. "How cruel. May I help her, my husband?"

"It would be so easy to give all of them happiness, Thalassa." He shook his head gently. "But we must not interfere in their lives."

MORE aggressive than the others, Hanoch-Spock was already circling the room, examining its equipment. He turned to find McCoy watching him. "An excellent body, Doctor. It seems I received the best of the three." He extended his arms, flexing Spock's superb biceps. "Strength, hearing, eyesight, all above the human norm. I'm surprised the Vulcans never conquered your race."

"Vulcans prize peace above all, Hanoch."

"Of course. Of course. Just as do we."

But McCoy had seen Thalassa-Anne sink back on her pillow. "Nurse!"

The lovely alien whispered, "A wave of heat suddenly . . . I feel . . ."

Christine caught her as she sagged, drawing in the support of another pillow behind her. McCoy was assisting her when he saw Sargon-Kirk begin to slump. As he supported him to his bed, he said, "Hanoch, you'd better go back to bed, too."

But Spock's metabolism had not yet been affected. Hanoch said, "Unnecessary at present, Doctor. My Vulcan body is accustomed to higher metabolism."

Christine tore her eyes from him to check Thalassa-Anne's body-function panel. Its readings were alarmingly high. McCoy rushed to the bed at the nurse's call. Then he whirled to the bed that held Sargon-Kirk. "It won't work, Sargon! You've got to get out of them before you kill them!"

The answer came weakly. "We will . . . vacate them . . . until you can administer . . . a metabolic-reduction injection."

"A what?" McCoy demanded.

Hanoch-Spock joined him at the bed, looking down at Kirk's sweaty forehead. "I will prepare the formula, Sargon," he said.

"Hanoch . . . your own condition . . ."

"I can maintain this body for several more hours, Sargon. Do not be anxious."

"Then . . . Thalassa and I . . . will now return to our confinement."

Beside the beds of Kirk and Anne the globes flared with light again. But Hanoch-Spock, still incarnate, gave his dim one a look of repulsion. He turned from Kirk's bed to speak to McCoy. "I shall need help to prepare the formula. Your nurse will assist me, Doctor, in your pharmacology laboratory."

Christine looked at McCoy. He couldn't tell himself that he was confronted by a command decision. That had already been made by Kirk.

The decision facing him merely implemented his Captain's wish. He nodded reluctantly—and Christine followed Hanoch-Spock out of Sick-bay.

Behind him Kirk and Anne were slowly recovering from the effects of the alien possession. Kirk's eyes at last fluttered open. McCoy had to stoop to hear his whisper.

"Bones . . ."

"It was close, Jim. You and Anne barely got back in time. Unless this formula works, we can't risk another transfer."

In the pharmacology laboratory, two hypos lay on a table. Hanoch-Spock held the third one. He made some adjustment on it, Christine behind him, watching. At last, he spoke. "This formula will reduce heart action and body function to normal. Whenever their bodies are occupied, administer one injection, ten cc.'s every hour."

"I understand," Christine said.

"Code this one for Thalassa. And *this* hypo, code it for me."

"Yes, sir." She affixed the appropriate seals to the hypos.

"Each contains a formula suited to the physical traits of that individual's body."

She pointed to the third hypo. "And that one is for Captain Kirk when Sargon is in his body?"

Hanoch-Spock handed it to her. "Yes. Of course."

Christine had taken the hypo to mark it when she noticed the color of its fluid. She examined it more carefully. Then, troubled, she said, "This hypo doesn't contain the same formula."

Hanoch-Spock smiled. On Spock's usually expressionless face, the smile was extraordinarily charming. "Since I will arrange for you to give the injections, no one else will notice that."

"But—without the correct formula, Captain Kirk will die."

"So he will—and Sargon with him."

Christine, staring, had begun to protest when Hanoch-Spock, reaching out, touched her forehead. Her head swam with dizziness. Then all sensation left her. Entranced where she stood, she could only look at him helplessly.

"Thalassa I can use," he said. "But Sargon must be destroyed. He would oppose me in what I plan. You wish to speak, my dear?"

"Please, I . . . I was . . . I wanted to say something." She passed a hand over her whirling head. "I've . . . forgotten what it was."

He touched her brow again. "You were about to say you watched me prepare the formula and fill the three hypos with it."

She swayed. "Yes—that was it. I will tell Dr. McCoy that each hypo is properly filled for each patient. You must excuse me. I lost my train of thought for a moment."

"It will not occur again," he said. "You are under my guidance now, child." Looking quickly toward the corridor, he made for the doorway. "And now for Dr. McCoy . . ."

But McCoy had snapped the lab door open. "If you require any further drugs or assistance, Hanoch—"

"I've encountered no difficulties at all, Doctor. I left the formula on your computer if you care to examine it."

In her trance Christine picked up the hypos. She spoke the words implanted in her mind. "I watched them prepared and coded, Doctor. Shall I take them to Sickbay?"

McCoy nodded. As the door closed behind her, Hanoch-Spock smiled. "It's good to be alive again, Doctor. I will find it most difficult when the time comes to surrender this body I so enjoy."

Was it the implication of the last words that disturbed McCoy? Or was it the shock of the excessively charming smile on Spock's face? He didn't know. All he knew was the sense of trouble that oppressed him as he watched the alien stride from the lab with Spock's legs.

Nor did his feeling of foreboding diminish as construction of the robots progressed. He found himself spending more and more time in Sickbay—his sole haven of retreat from the nameless anxieties that beset him. Christine, too, seemed unlike herself—constrained, diffident. It irritated him.

As she approached him now, he didn't look up when she said, "You asked to see me, Doctor, before the next injections."

"Yes. You're staying alert for any side effects? any unusual symptoms?"

"The shots work perfectly, sir. There are no problems at all."

He struck his desk. "The devil there aren't!" He crossed to the three receptacles. "That flicker of energy there is Jim Kirk! And Spock there! Anne Mulhall! Suppose the bodies these aliens are using are *not* returned to them?"

"If I'm to give the injections on time, Doctor, I should leave now."

"Well, walk, then! Don't just stand there, talking! Do it!"

"Yes, sir."

Alone, McCoy stalked over to the Sargon-Kirk globe. "You and your blasted rent-a-body agreement, Kirk!" He moved to Spock's receptacle.

"The only halfway pleasant thing about this is you, Spock! Must be humiliating for a logical superior Vulcan not to have a larger flicker than that!"

One of McCoy's persisting, if minor, anxieties was the chaos that had descended upon his immaculate laboratory. Workbenches now crowded it; and his marble slabs were littered with the elements and other paraphernalia that would ultimately be assembled into the android robots. Hanoch-Spock over at his bench was manipulating a complex tool under difficult circumstances, for across the lab Sargon-Kirk and Thalassa-Anne were sharing a chore together. The intimacy between them angered and distracted him. He saw them both reach for a component at the same time. They smiled at each other, their hands clasping, their eyes meeting. She touched his hair.

"Sargon, I remember a day long ago. We sat beside a silver lake. The air was scented with the flowers of our planet and . . ."

He nodded. "I remember, Thalassa. We held hands like this." He hesitated, removing his from hers. "And I think it best not to remember too well."

"In two days you'll have hands of your own again, Thalassa," Hanoch-Spock said. "Mechanically efficient, quite human-looking—android robot hands. Hands without feeling, of course. So enjoy the taste of life while you can."

"But our minds will have survived. And as androids, Hanoch, we . . ." Sargon-Kirk suddenly looked very tired.

"What is it, Sargon?" Thalassa-Anne asked anxiously.

"Our next injection . . . will renovate me. Do not be concerned." He addressed Hanoch. "As androids we can move among those who *do* live, teaching them, helping them to avoid the errors we made."

"Yes, moving as machines minus the ability to feel love, joy, sorrow."

Sargon-Kirk spoke sternly. "We pledged ourselves that survival would be sufficient, Hanoch. Now that we've taken human bodies not our own, the ancient evil temptations would plague us again, haunt us with the dream of a godlike master-race."

"It is only that I feel sorrow for your wife, Sargon." He spoke to Thalassa-Anne. "You were younger than we when the end came. You had enjoyed so little of living."

She said, "We made a pledge, Hanoch." But her face was troubled. The sympathy had weakened her; and she, too, looked suddenly exhausted. She was leaning back against the wall as Christine entered with the hypos. She extended her arm for the injection. "Nurse," she said, "Sargon does not appear well."

"I've checked his metabolic rate every few hours, Thalassa. It hasn't varied from normal." And moving on, Christine administered the other injections. As the hypo hissed against his arm, Hanoch-Spock said, "I was fatigued, also. I feel much better now."

But though color had returned to Thalassa-Anne's face, concern for her husband had not been allayed. He smiled at her. "Do not worry. I shall have recovered in a moment." But he showed none of the rejuvenating effects seen in the others. He had to make an effort to resume his work.

McCoy noted it as he entered the lab. He looked at Christine. "Nurse," he said, "I want to see you in Sickbay. Bring those hypos."

In his office he selected the hypo coded for Sargon-Kirk, examining it. Christine watched him, troubled as though trying to remember something she had forgotten. After a long moment, he handed it back to her. She took it, still puzzling over it, and finally passed over a tape cartridge to him.

"Something wrong, Miss Chapel?"

"Yes . . . I . . ." She paused, trying to find words. "I—had something to say. But I can't seem to remember."

"Regarding our patients?"

"Yes, that must be it. I—am so pleased by the way they are responding, sir." She gestured to the hypo on his desk. "The formula is working perfectly."

"You look tired," McCoy said. "If you'd like me to handle the next few injections . . ."

Abruptly her face lit with a smile. "Tired? Not at all, Doctor. But thank you for asking."

She turned to replace the hypos in a cabinet. McCoy eyed her for a moment. Then, deciding he had been concerned over nothing, he returned to the reports on his desk.

The aliens worked swiftly and skillfully. Within the following hours, the robot bodies were partially assembled. Thalassa-Anne was alone in the lab when Scott entered to deliver some supplies. He paused to watch her deft hands moving over a torso.

"Thank you," she said. "Have you prepared the negaton hydrocoils per the drawings Sargon gave you?"

Scott nodded. "For all the good they'll do you. Fancy name—but how will something that looks like a drop of jelly make that thing move its limbs? You'll need microgears, some form of pulley that does what a muscle does."

She smiled her charming smile. "That would be highly inefficient, Mr. Scott."

"I tell you, lady, this thing won't work." As he spoke, Hanoch-Spock had come in. Now he sauntered over to them. "It will have twice the strength and agility of your body, Engineer, and it will last a thousand years. That is, it will if you'll permit us to complete these robot envelopes of ours."

Scott strode to the lab door, his back stiff with irritation. Hanoch-Spock crossed over to Thalassa-Anne, his eyes intent on her raven hair. "Actually, a thousand-year prison, Thalassa." He leaned toward her. "And when it wears out, we'll build a new one. We'll lock ourselves into it for another thousand years, then another and another . . ."

Disturbed, she looked up from her work. He went on. "Sargon has closed his mind to a better way with these bodies we wear."

"They are not ours, Hanoch."

"Three bodies. Is that such a price for mankind to pay for all we offer? Thalassa." He seized her hand. "The humans who own these bodies would surrender them gladly to accomplish a fraction of what we'll do. Are we entitled to no reward for our labors—no joy?"

She snatched her hand away; and pointing to the robot torso on the bench, he said, "Do you prefer incarceration in that?"

She leaped to her feet, her tools flying. *"No! I'm beginning to hate the thing!"*

In a corridor, not far away, Sargon-Kirk, collapsing, had crumpled to the deck.

Lifeless, inert, Kirk's body lay on a medical table in Sickbay where Nurse M'Benga and a medical technician were hurriedly but expertly fitting the cryosurgical and blood-filtrating units over it. A tense McCoy watched.

His mind was a tumult of confusion. Too distant from his receptacle to transfer back into it, Sargon had died when Kirk's body died. So that left the big question. Kirk's consciousness still survived, despite the death of his body. It still glimmered, faint but alive, in Sargon's globe. Then could Kirk be called dead? McCoy wiped the sweat from his face —and ordered in another resuscitating instrument.

Meanwhile, in his once-shining lab, Hanoch-Spock was operating a different instrument. He passed the small device over the nearly completed android robot that lay on a slab. It looked sexless. It still lacked hair, eyebrows, the indentations which give expression to a human face. Thalassa-Anne watched him wearily, lost in her anguished grief. Christine, blank-eyed as ever, stood beside the slab.

"Hanoch, why do you pretend to work on that thing? You killed Sargon. You murdered my husband. You murdered him because you do not intend to give up your body. You've always intended to keep it."

A sudden rage possessed Thalassa. Sargon had labored so hard to restore them to joy, to life in the body. He had kissed this body she wore! In a short while, it would all be for nothing. This body he had embraced would have to be vacated, returned to its owner. She rushed from the lab on the surge of her fury to fling open the door of Sickbay.

McCoy looked up, startled. "Doctor," she said, "would you like to save your Captain Kirk?"

"Not half an hour ago you said that was impossible. When we found him, you said—"

"Dismiss these people!" she commanded.

McCoy stared at her. "We have many powers Sargon did not permit us to use! If you care for your Captain, dismiss these people!"

McCoy waved the nurse and technician out of Sickbay.

"Well?" he said.

"This body I wear is sacred to me. My husband embraced it. I intend to keep it!"

So it was out at last. "I see," McCoy said. "And Hanoch? He intends, of course, to keep Spock's body."

"Hanoch's plans are his own affair. I wish only to keep the body my husband kissed!"

"Are you asking for my approval?"

"I require only your silence. Only you and I will know that Anne Mulhall has not returned to her body. Isn't your silence worth your Captain's life?" At the look on McCoy's face, the fury burned in her again. "Doctor, we can take what we wish. Neither you, this ship, nor all your little worlds have the power to stop us!"

McCoy looked down at Kirk's lifeless body. Jim Kirk—alive again, his easy vitality, his courage, his affectionate "Bones". *This was a command decision:* a choice between loyalty to the dearest friend of his life—and loyalty to himself. And he knew what the dearest friend would want.

"I cannot trade a body I do not own," he said. "Neither would my Captain. Your body belongs to a young woman who—"

"Whom you hardly know, almost a stranger to you."

McCoy shouted. *"I do not peddle human flesh! I am a physician!"*

The blue eyes flashed lightning. *"A physician? In contrast to what we* are, you are a prancing, savage medicine man—a primitive savage! You dare to defy one you should be on your knees to in worship!" She made a gesture of acid contempt. *"I can destroy you with a single thought!"*

A ring of flame shot up around McCoy. He flung his hands before his face to shield it from the rising fire.

As he did so, Thalassa gave a wild cry. She fell to her knees, crying, *"No! Stop!* Forgive me, forgive me . . ."

The flames died as suddenly as they had come. Even the smell of their smoke was gone; and where searing fire had encircled McCoy only a moment before, not a mark of its presence remained.

She was still on her knees, weeping. "Sargon was . . . right," she sobbed. "The temptations are . . . too great. But understand. In the name of whatever gods you worship, understand! The emotions of life are dear—its needs, its hopes. But . . . our power is too great. We would begin to destroy . . . as I almost destroyed you then. Forgive me . . . forgive . . ."

"I am pleased, beloved. It is good you have found the truth for yourself."

Her head lifted. *"Sargon!* Oh, my husband, where are you? Hanoch has killed you!"

"I have power, my wife, that Hanoch does not suspect."

"Yes. Yes. I understand." The words came slowly. She rose to her feet, staring at McCoy. "My Sargon has placed his consciousness within this ship of yours."

Christine Chapel opened the door of Sickbay. She was crossing to the hypo cabinet when McCoy galvanized. "You! Get out of my sight!"

Thalassa shook her head. "No, Doctor. She is necessary to us."

"Necessary? She is under Hanoch's control!"

"My Sargon has a plan, Doctor. Leave us. We have much work to do."

After a moment, McCoy obeyed. But as the door closed behind him, he heard a dull crunching explosion come from inside. The ship shuddered slightly. The sound came again.

"Thalassa!" he shouted. *"What's going on?"*

When the sound came for the third time, he raced for the corridor intercom. "This is Sickbay. Get me—"

Behind him Sickbay's door opened. Empty-eyed, Christine emerged to move on past him down the corridor. He rushed inside—and came to a dead halt. Kirk was standing there, smiling at him.

"I'm fine, Bones," he said. He reached out a hand to draw Anne Mulhall up beside him. "We're both fine, Bones."

"Thalassa . . ."

Anne spoke quietly. "She is with Sargon, Doctor."

"With Sargon?" He looked past them to the three globes. They were broken, melted, black, dead.

"*Jim!* Spock's consciousness was in one of those!"

"It was necessary," Kirk said.

McCoy flung his arms up. "What do you mean, man? There's no Spock to return to his body now! You've killed your best friend, a loyal officer of the Service!"

"Prepare a hypo, Bones. The fastest and deadliest poison to Vulcans. Spock's consciousness is gone, but we must now kill his body, too. His body—and the thing inside it."

On the bridge, Uhura screamed. Then she slumped against her board, trembling. Nonchalant, Hanoch-Spock left her to go to Kirk's command chair. The bewitched Christine waited at his side. He spoke to Sulu. "Shall I make an example of you, too, Helm? Take us out of orbit! A course for Earth!"

Sulu hit his controls. Then he wheeled in his chair. "Look for yourself! The ship won't respond! Nothing works!"

The elevator doors slid open. Kirk and Anne stepped out. Behind them came McCoy, his hypo carefully hidden. The alien in the command chair didn't trouble himself to turn; but just before they reached it, it said, "Pain, Kirk. Exquisite pain. As for you, lovely one of the blue eyes . . ."

Kirk had dropped as though shot, gasping, his throat hungering to scream. Hanoch-Spock pointed a finger at Anne. She froze, shudders shaking her—and Sulu, pressed beyond control, leaped from his seat only to fall, moaning with pain. As Anne crumpled to the deck, McCoy dove for the command chair; but Hanoch, holding up a palm, halted him a foot away from Spock's body.

"I know every thought in every mind around me," he said. "Chapel, remove the hypo from the Doctor."

Christine, reaching into an inside pocket of McCoy's white jacket, obeyed. Hanoch said, "Good. Inject him with his own dose—an example to all those who defy me."

She lifted the hypo toward McCoy—and without the slightest change of expression, wheeled to drive it, hissing, into Hanoch's arm.

He stood up. "Fools!" he shrieked. "I'll simply transfer to . . . another space, another body!" Suddenly, he reeled. "*It's you, Sargon!*" He whimpered, "Please . . . please, Sargon, let me transfer to—"

Then he crashed to the floor. Kirk rushed to the fallen body. Kneeling beside it, he lifted its head to cradle it in his arms. "Spock . . . Spock, my friend, my comrade . . . if only there had been some other way." He choked on unshed tears.

The head stirred in his arms. Its eyes opened; and the bridge reverberated again to the rich, deep voice. *"How could I allow the sacrifice of one so close to you, my son?"*

"There was enough poison in that hypo," McCoy cried, "to kill ten Vulcans!"

"I allowed you to believe that, Doctor. Else, Hanoch could not have read your thought—and believed it, too. He has fled Spock's body. He is destroyed."

Kirk found words. "The receptacles are broken, Spock. Where was your consciousness kept?"

Spock was on his feet. "In the last place Hanoch would suspect, Captain." He gestured toward Christine.

She nodded, smiling. "That's why Thalassa called me 'necessary,' Doctor. Mr. Spock's consciousness was installed in me. We have been sharing it together."

"We know now we cannot permit ourselves to exist in your world, my children. Thalassa and I must depart into oblivion."

Kirk looked up. "Sargon, isn't there any way we can help you?"

"Yes, my son. Let Thalassa and me enter your bodies again for our last moment together."

Though there was no transfer flare, Kirk and Anne both felt its heat as Sargon and Thalassa moved into them. Anne, in Kirk's arms, said, "Oblivion together does not frighten me, my husband." She kissed Kirk's forehead, her hand caressing his cheek. "Promise me we will be together."

Kirk bent his head to her mouth, holding her close. Anne was shaking under the storm of Thalassa's grief. "Together forever, my Sargon . . . forever . . ."

"I promise, my love. I promise . . ."

For their last moment, they clung together on the edge of Nothing. Then they were gone, the dwindling heat of their passing, leaving Anne's eyes filled with Thalassa's tears. Still clasped in Kirk's arms, they stared at each other. Then, flushing at the public embrace, Kirk released her. He cleared his throat. "Dr. Mulhall . . . er . . . thank you. I . . . thank you in . . . Sargon's name . . . for your cooperation."

The sapphire eyes smiled through their tears. "Captain, I—I was happy to . . . cooperate."

Christine, sobbing, turned to Spock. "I felt the same way, Mr. Spock . . . when we shared our consciousness together."

Spock's left eyebrow lifted. "Nurse Chapel," he began, and subsided into silence.

McCoy grinned at him. "This sharing of consciousness—it sounds somewhat immoral to me, my Vulcan friend."

"I assure you it was a most distressing experience," Spock said earnestly. "You would not believe the torrents of emotion I encountered —the jungle of illogic." He almost shuddered.

Christine smiled at him. "Why, thank you, Mr. Spock."

"I don't understand, nurse. Thank me?"

"You just paid her a high compliment, Spock," Kirk said.

"Yes, you do turn a nice phrase now and then," McCoy said. He turned to Christine. "Thank the stars," he said, "that my sex doesn't understand the other one."

Anne laughed. "Come along with me, my fellow woman. If they don't understand us after all this time, no elucidation by us can enlighten them."

Kirk, smiling too, went to his command chair. Spock was standing beside it, still puzzled. "Captain, I really *don't* understand."

"Sargon did, Spock. 'Together forever.' Someone may someday teach you what that means. Who knows? When that next Vulcan seven-year cycle rolls around again . . ."

Spock gravely considered the idea. "Sargon *was* enormously advanced, Captain. I shall ponder this."

As he returned to his station, Kirk's eyes followed him with affection. "Ah, well," he said, "for now that's how it is." He turned to Sulu. "All right, Mr. Sulu, take us out of orbit."

"Leaving orbit, sir."

THE ULTIMATE COMPUTER
(D. C. Fontana and Laurence N. Wolfe)

Obediently the *Enterprise* (to its skipper's intense annoyance) was making its approach to the space station. His impatience lifted him from his chair and sent him across to Uhura. "Lieutenant, contact the space station."

"The station is calling *us,* Captain."

"Put them on."

The voice was familiar. "Captain Kirk, this is Commodore Enwright."

"Commodore, I'd like an explanation."

Enwright cut across him. "The explanation is beaming aboard you now, Captain. He may already be in your Transporter Room. Enwright out."

"Spock," Kirk said, and gestured toward the elevator. "Scotty, you have the con."

The "explanation" was materializing in the person of Commodore Wesley, a flight officer slightly older than Kirk but not unlike him in manner and military bearing. Kirk's rage gave way to astonishment. "Bob! Bob Wesley!" The two shook hands as Wesley stepped from the platform. Kirk said, "Mr. Spock, this is—"

Spock completed the sentence. "Commodore Wesley. How do you do, sir."

Wesley nodded. "Mr. Spock."

Kirk turned to the Transporter officer. "Thank you, Lieutenant. That will do."

As the door closed, he burst out, "Now will you please tell me what this is all about? I receive an order to proceed here. No reason is given.

I'm informed my crew is to be removed to the space station's security holding area. I think I'm entitled to an explanation!"

Wesley grinned. "You've had a singular honor conferred on you, Jim. You're going to be the fox in a hunt."

"What does that mean?"

"War games. I'll be commanding the attack force against you."

"An entire attack force against one ship?"

Wesley regarded him tolerantly. "Apparently you haven't heard of the M-5 Multitronic Unit. It's the computer, Jim, that Dr. Richard Daystrom has just developed."

"Oh?"

"Not oh, Jim. Wait till you see the M-5."

"What is it?"

Spock broke in. "The most ambitious computer complex ever created. Its purpose is to correlate all computer activity of a Starship . . . to provide the ultimate in vessel operation and control."

Wesley eyed Spock suspiciously. "How do you know so much about it, Commander?"

"I hold an A-7 computer expert classification, sir. I am well acquainted with Dr. Daystrom's theories and discoveries. The basic design of all our ships' computers are Dr. Daystrom's."

"And what's all that got to do with the *Enterprise?*" Kirk said.

Wesley's face grew grave. "You've been chosen to test the M-5, Jim. There'll be a series of routine research and contact problems M-5 will have to solve as well as navigational maneuvers and the war-games' problems. If it works under actual conditions as it has in simulated tests, it will mean a revolution in space technology as great as the Warp Drive. As soon as your crew is removed, the ship's engineering section will be modified to contain the computer."

"Why remove my crew? What sort of security does this gadget require?"

"They're not needed," Wesley said. "Dr. Daystrom will see to the installation himself and will supervise the tests. When he's ready, you will receive your orders and proceed on the mission with a crew of twenty."

"*Twenty!* I can't run a Starship with only twenty people aboard!"

The voice of authority was cool. "M-5 can."

"And I—what am I supposed to do?"

"You've got a great job, Jim. All you have to do is sit back and let the machine do the work."

"My," Kirk said, "it sounds just great!"

McCoy didn't like it, either. Told the news, he exploded. "A vessel this size can't be run by one computer! Even the computers we already have—"

Spock interrupted. "All of them were designed by Richard Daystrom almost twenty-five years ago. His new one utilizes the capabilities of all the present computers . . . it is the master control. We are attempting to prove that it can run this ship more efficiently than man."

"Maybe *you're* trying to prove that, Spock, but don't count me in on it."

"The most unfortunate lack in current computer programming is that there is nothing available to immediately replace the Starship surgeon."

"If there were," McCoy said, "they wouldn't have to replace me. I'd resign—and because everybody else aboard would be nothing but circuits and memory banks." He glared at Spock. "I think some of us already are just that." He turned an anxious face to Kirk. "You haven't said much about this, Jim."

They were standing outside the Engineering Section. Now Kirk swung around to face Spock and McCoy, pointing to the new sign on the door reading "Security Area". "What do you want me to say, Bones? Starfleet considers this installation of the M-5 an honor. So I'm honored. It takes some adjusting, too." He turned, the door slid open, and they entered the Section. And the M-5 Multitronic Unit already dominated the vast expanse. Unlike the built-in *Enterprise* computers, its massive cabinet was free-standing as though asserting total independence of support. It possessed a monitor panel where dials, switches, and other controls were ranged in an order that created an impression of an insane disorder. Scott and another engineer, Ensign Harper, were busy at panels near the upper-bridge level. Kirk looked around. "Where is he? Dr. Daystrom?"

He came from behind the console where he had been working, wearing a technician's outfit. The first thing that struck Kirk about him were his eyes. Despite the lines of middle age, they were brilliantly piercing as though all his energy was concentrated on penetration. He was a nervous man. His speech was sharply clipped and his hands seemed to need to busy themselves with something—a pipe, a tool, anything available.

"Yes?" he said. Suddenly, he seemed to register something inappropriate in the greeting. "You would be Captain Kirk?"

They shook hands briefly. "Dr. Daystrom, my First Officer, Commander Spock."

Spock bowed. "I am honored, Doctor. I have studied all your publications on computer technology. Brilliant."

"Thank you. Captain, I have finished my final check on M-5. It must be hooked into the ship's main power banks to become operational."

Kirk said, "Very well, Dr. Daystrom. Do so."

"Your Chief Engineer refused to make the power available without your orders."

Good old Scotty, Kirk thought. What he said was, "Mr. Scott, tie the M-5 unit into the main power banks."

"Aye, sir. Mr. Harper?" He and Harper moved off to the wall panel near the forced perspective unit.

Spock was examining the M-5 monitor panel. McCoy fixed his gaze on the distance.

"Fascinating, Doctor," Spock said. "This computer has a potential beyond anything you have ever done. Even your breakthrough into duotronics did not hold the promise of this."

"M-5 has been perfected, Commander. Its potential is a fact."

McCoy could contain himself no longer. "The only fact I care about," he said savagely, "is that if this thing doesn't work, there aren't enough men aboard to run this ship. That's screaming for trouble."

Daystrom stared at him. "Who is this?" he asked Kirk.

"Dr. Leonard McCoy, Senior Medical Officer."

"This is a security area," Daystrom said. "Only absolutely necessary key personnel have clearance to enter it."

Kirk's voice was icy in his own ears. "Dr. McCoy has top security clearances for all areas of this ship."

Then the M-5 suddenly came to life. It was a startling phenomenon. It flashed with lights, a deep hum surging from its abruptly activated circuits. As its lights glowed brighter, lights in the engine unit dimmed sharply.

McCoy spoke to Spock. "Is it supposed to do that?"

Daystrom was working quickly to remove a panel. He made an adjustment and Spock said, "If I can be of assistance, sir . . ."

Daystrom looked up. "No. I can manage, thank you."

The rebuffed Spock's eyebrows arched in surprise. He glanced at Kirk who nodded and Spock backed off. The M-5's deep hum grew quieter, less erratic; and overhead, the lights struggled back to full strength.

Daystrom was defensive. "Nothing wrong, Captain. A minor settling-in adjustment to be made. You see, everything is in order now."

"Yes." Kirk paused. "I'm curious, Dr. Daystrom. Why is it M-5 instead of M-1?"

Daystrom's hands twisted on a tool. "The Multitronic Units 1 through 4 were not successful. But this one *is*. M-5 is ready to assume control of the ship."

"Total control?" Kirk said.

"That is what it was designed for, Captain."

There was an awkward silence. "I'm afraid," Kirk said, "I must admit to a certain antagonism toward your computer, Dr. Daystrom. It was man who first ventured into space. True, man *with* machines . . . but still with man in command."

"Those were primitive machines, Captain. We have entered a new era."

Kirk thought, I don't like this man. He dispensed with the amiable smile on his lips. "I am not against progress, sir; but there are still things men have to do to remain men. Your computer would take that away, Dr. Daystrom."

"There are other things a man like you can do, Captain. Or perhaps you only object to the possible loss of the prestige accorded a Starship Captain. The computer can do your job without interest in prestige."

Kirk smiled at him. "You're going to have to prove that to me, Daystrom." He started to leave, but Daystrom's voice halted him in midstride. "Captain, that's what the M-5 is here for, isn't it?"

It had not been a pleasant encounter. Spock alone seemed untouched by its implications. As the three moved down the drearily empty corridor, he said, "Captain, if you don't need me for a moment, I'd like to discuss some of the technology involved in the M-5 with Dr. Daystrom."

"Look at the love-light in his eyes, Jim. All his life Spock's been waiting for the right computer to come along. I hope you'll be very happy together, Spock."

"Doctor, I find your simile illogical and your humor forced. If you'll excuse me, Captain?"

"Go ahead, Mr. Spock. I'll see you on the bridge."

"Yes, sir."

Kirk's troubled expression worried McCoy. "What is it, Jim?"

Kirk hesitated. "I feel it's wrong—and I don't know why—all of it wrong."

"I feel it's wrong, too, replacing men with mindless machines."

"It isn't just that, Bones. Only a fool would stand in the way of progress, if this *is* progress. You have all my psychological profiles. Do you think I *am* afraid to turn command over to the M-5?"

McCoy spoke thoughtfully. "We've all seen the advances of mechanization; and Daystrom *did* design the computers that run this ship."

"But under *human* control," Kirk said. "What I'm asking myself is:

Is it just that I'm afraid of that computer taking over my job? Daystrom
is right. I could do other things. Or am I really afraid of losing the prestige, the glamour accorded a Starship Captain? Is that why I keep
fighting this thing? Am I really that petty and vain?"

"Jim, if you have the courageous awareness to ask yourself that question, you don't need me to answer it." He grinned. "Why don't you ask
James T. Kirk? He's a pretty honest guy."

"Right now, Bones, I'm not sure he'd give me an honest answer."

But he was sure of one thing: he resented the installation of the new
control console on his command chair. It had been placed on the left
side of it opposite the one containing his old one with its intercom and
other switches. It had been added to the chair without any consultation
or announcement of the innovation. Kirk stared at it silently and Sulu
said, "Turning back on original course, Captain."

Spock came over to examine the new console. "The M-5 has performed admirably so far, sir."

"All it's done is make some required course changes and simple
turns. Chekov and Sulu could do that with their eyes closed."

Daystrom had appeared at his left side. "The idea is that they didn't
have to do it, Captain. And it's not necessary for you to regain control
from a unit after each maneuver is completed."

Kirk spoke tightly. "My orders say nothing about how long I must
leave the M-5 in control of my ship. And I shall run it as I see fit, Dr.
Daystrom."

Spock said, "Captain, I must agree with Dr. Daystrom. With the
course information plotted into it, the computer could have brought us
here as easily as the navigator."

"Mr. Spock, you seem to enjoy entrusting yourself to that computer."

"Enjoy, sir? I am, of course, gratified to see the new unit executing
everything in such a highly efficient manner. M-5 is another distin-
guished triumph in Dr. Daystrom's career."

Chekov spoke tonelessly. "Approaching Alpha Cazinae II, Captain.
ETA five minutes."

"The M-5 is to handle the approach, Captain," Daystrom said. "It
will direct entrance into orbit and then analyze data for landing-party
recommendations."

Kirk's voice was very quiet. "You don't mind if I make my own recommendations?"

"If you feel you need the exercise, go ahead, Captain."

Kirk looked into the coldly piercing eyes. Then, reaching out, he pressed one of the buttons on the new console panel.

In the same inflectionless voice, he said, "M-5 is now committed."

As the subdued hum in the ship grew louder, the main viewing screen showed the approaching planet. Kirk, his eyes on it, said, "Standard orbit, Mr. Sulu."

Sulu, checking instruments, looked up in surprise. "Captain, M-5 has calculated that. The orbit is already plotted."

"Ah, yes," Kirk said. Spock had moved back to his station but Daystrom, pleased by his invention's performance, remained beside the new command console.

"Standard orbit achieved, sir," Sulu said.

"Report, Mr. Spock."

"The planet is Class M, sir. Oxygen-nitrogen atmosphere, suitable for human life support . . . two major land masses . . . a number of islands. Life form readings."

In the Engineering Section, the overhead lights flickered a moment; and on the deserted Deck 4, they went out, plunging the area into blackness.

Scott turned abruptly to Kirk, frowning. "Captain, we're getting some peculiar readings. Power shutdowns on Deck 4—lights, environmental control."

Kirk said, "Check it out, Mr. Scott." He crossed over to Spock. The library-computer was chattering rapidly. Daystrom joined them. They saw a tape cartridge slide smoothly out of a slot. Spock took it, examining it. "M-5's readout, Captain."

Kirk drew a deep breath. "All right. My recommendations are as follows. We send down a general survey party, avoiding contact with life forms on the planet. Landing party to consist of myself, Dr. McCoy, astrobiologist Mason, geologist Rawls and Science Officer Spock."

"Mr. Spock," said Daystrom, "play M-5's recommendations."

Spock dropped the cartridge into another slot in his library-computer, and punching a button, he evoked a computer voice. It said, "M-5 readout. Planet Alpha Cazinae II. Class M. Atmosphere oxygen-nitrogen . . ."

On Deck 6 the lights suddenly faded—and darkness flooded into another area of the *Enterprise*.

Scott cried, "Now power's gone off on Deck 6!"

The computer voice went on. "Categorization of life form readings recorded. Recommendations for general survey party: Science Officer Spoke, astrobiologist Mason, geologist Carstairs."

Kirk let a moment go by. "The only variation in reports and recommendations is in landing party personnel. And that's only a matter of judgment."

"Judgment, Captain?" said Daystrom.

"Captain . . . the computer does not judge," Spock said. "It makes logical selections."

"Then why did it pick Carstairs instead of Rawls? Carstairs is an Ensign, Mr. Spock, no experience: this is his first tour of duty. Rawls is the Chief Geologist.

"Perhaps, Captain, you're really interested in why M-5 didn't name you and Dr. McCoy."

"Not necessarily, Daystrom," Kirk said smoothly.

"Let's find out anyway." Daystrom hit a switch. "M-5 tie-in. Explanation for landing party recommendations."

The computer voice said, "M-5. General survey party requires direction of Science Officer. Astrobiologist Mason has surveyed 29 biologically similar planets. Geologist Carstairs served on merchant-marine freighters in this area . . . once visited planet on geology survey for mining company."

"M-5 tie-in. Why were the Captain and Chief Medical Officer not included in the recommendations?"

"M-5," said the computer. "Non-essential personnel."

Spock averted his eyes from Kirk's face; and Scott, over at his board, called, "Captain! I've located the source of the power shutdowns. It's the M-5 unit, sir. That thing's turning off systems all over the ship!"

"Well, Dr. Daystrom," Kirk said, "do we visit the Engineering Section?" He stood aside while the inventor removed a panel from the huge mechanism. A moment or so later, he replaced it, saying, "As I suspected, it's not a malfunction in this series of circuits. There is no need to check further. The M-5 is simply shutting down power to areas of the ship that don't require it. Decks 4 and 6 are quarter decks, are they not?"

"Yes."

"And currently unoccupied."

Spock was examining the great monitor panel. "I am not familiar with these instruments, Dr. Daystrom. You are using an entirely new control system . . . but it appears to me the unit is drawing more power than before."

"Quite right. As the unit is called upon to do more work, it pulls more power to accomplish it . . . just as the human body draws on more power, more energy to run than to stand still."

"Dr. Daystrom," Spock said, "this is not a human body. A computer can process the information—but only that which is put into it."

Kirk nodded. "Granted it can work thousands, millions of times faster than a human brain. But it can't make value judgments. It doesn't have intuition. It can't *think* nor gauge relative importances."

Daystrom flushed angrily. "Can't you understand the unit is a revolution in computer science? *I* designed the duotronic elements used in your ship right now. And they are as archaic as dinosaurs compared to the M-5—" He was interrupted by a bosun's whistle and Uhura's filtered voice.

"Captain Kirk and Mr. Spock to the bridge, please."

Kirk crossed to the intercom. "This is Kirk. What is it, Lieutenant?"

"Sensors are picking up a vessel paralleling our course, sir. As yet unidentified."

As he turned from the intercom, he realized the M-5 had again increased its humming and light activity. He looked at it dubiously and said, "Mr. Spock." Descending the ladder, his last glimpse of Daystrom showed the man's hand patting the computer caressingly. The high hum followed them to the bridge where McCoy, his jaw set, was waiting for them.

"What are you doing up here, Bones?"

"Why wouldn't I be here? Sickbay systems are shut down until such time as the M-5 is informed there are patients to be cared for."

Spock, over at his station, spoke hastily. "Sir, sensor reports indicate two contacts; one on the port bow, the other on the stern. Distance, two hundred thousand kilometers and closing."

"Identification?"

"Sir, the M-5 unit has already identified the vessels as Federation Starships *Excalibur* and *Lexington*."

Kirk looked at him. It was impossible to tell whether Spock was impressed or annoyed that the M-5 had done his job for him. "We were not scheduled for war games in this area, Captain. It may be a surprise attack as a problem for M-5."

Uhura spoke. "Priority alert message coming in, sir."

Daystrom came from the elevator as Kirk said, "On audio, Lieutenant." He paused at the sound of Wesley's voice.

"*Enterprise* from Commodore Wesley aboard the U.S.S. *Lexington*. This is an unscheduled M-5 drill. I repeat, this is an M-5 drill. *Enterprise*, acknowledge on this frequency."

Kirk nodded at Uhura. "Acknowledge, Lieutenant."

Uhura reached to press a button, hesitated, and stared at Kirk. "M-5 is acknowledging for us, sir."

"Then sound red alert, Lieutenant."

"Aye, sir." But as she moved for the switch, the red alert sounded. "M-5 has already sounded the alert, Captain."

"Has it?" Kirk said. He turned to Sulu. "Phasers on 1/100th power, Mr. Sulu. No damage potential. Just enough to nudge them."

"Phasers 1/100th power, sir." As Sulu turned back to his board, the ship was struck by a salvo from one of the attacking Starships. A bare thump. Spock called, "Phaser hit on port deflector 4, sir." Sulu looked up. "Speed is increasing to Warp 3, sir. Turning now to 112 mark 5." A moment passed before he added, "Phasers locking on target, Captain."

Then it was Chekov's turn. "Enemy vessel closing with us, sir. Coming in fast. It—"

Sulu interrupted him. "Deflectors down now, sir! Main phasers firing!" Then he cried out in delight. "A hit, sir! Two more!" But the elation in his face faded abruptly at the sight of Kirk, sitting stiff and unmoving in his chair, merely watching the screen.

Chekov spoke quietly. "Changing course now to 28 mark 42, sir." The reports piled up thick and fast. "Phasers firing again."

"Course now 113 mark 5. Warp 4 speed."

"Phasers firing again!"

"Attacking vessels are moving off!"

"Deflectors up—moving back to original course and speed."

Kirk finally spoke. "Report damage sustained in mock attack."

"A minor hit on deflector screen 4, sir," Spock said. "No appreciable damage."

Kirk nodded slowly and Daystrom, triumph flaming in his face, said, "A rather impressive display for a mere 'machine,' wouldn't you say, Captain?"

Kirk didn't answer him. Instead, he rose and went to Spock's station. "Evaluation of M-5 performance, Mr. Spock. We will need it for the log record."

Spock measured his words slowly. "The ship reacted more rapidly than human control could have maneuvered her. Tactics, deployment of weapons—all indicate an immense skill in computer control."

"Machine over man, Spock. You've finally made your point that it is practical."

Spock said, "Practical, perhaps, sir. Desirable—no." His quiet eyes met Kirk's. "Computers make excellent and efficient servants; but I have no wish to serve under them. A Starship, Captain, also runs on loyalty, loyalty to a man—one man. Nothing can replace it. Nor him."

Kirk felt the absurd sting of grateful tears behind his eyes. He wheeled at Uhura's voice. "Captain, message coming in from Commodore Wesley."

"Put it on the screen, Lieutenant."

The image showed Wesley sitting in a command chair. He said, "U.S.S. *Enterprise* from Starships *Lexington* and *Excalibur*. Both ships report simulated hits in sufficient quantity and location to justify awarding the surprise engagement to *Enterprise*. Congratulations."

Kirk spoke to Uhura. "Secure from General Quarters."

Again, she reached for the switch. And again the alarm had been silenced. She looked at Kirk, shrugging.

But the image on the screen was continuing. "Our compliments to the M-5 unit and regards to Captain Dunsel. Wesley out."

McCoy exploded. "Dunsel? Who the blazes is Captain Dunsel? What's it mean, Jim?"

But Kirk had already left for the elevator. McCoy whirled to Spock. "Well?" demanded McCoy. "Who's Dunsel?"

"A 'dunsel,' Doctor, is a word used by midshipmen at Starfleet Academy. It refers to a part which serves no useful purpose."

McCoy stiffened. He glanced at the closed elevator doors; and then to the empty command chair, the brightly gleaming M-5 control panel attached to it—the machine which had served such a useful purpose.

McCoy walked into Kirk's cabin without buzzing the door. Nor was he greeted. His host, head pillowed on his forearms, lay on his bed, unmoving. McCoy, without speaking, laid a tray on a table.

Without turning his head, Kirk said, "I am not interested in eating."

"Well, this isn't chicken soup." McCoy whisked a napkin from the tray, revealing two glasses filled with a marvelously emerald-green liquid. He took one over to Kirk, who took it but made no move to drink it.

"It's strongly prescribed, Jim."

Kirk, placing the drink on the floor, sat up. "Bones, I've never felt so lonely before. It has nothing to do with people. I simply . . . well, I just feel separate, detached, as though I were watching myself divorced from all human responsibility. I'm even at odds with my own ship." Resting his elbows on his knees, he put his head in his hands. When he could speak again, words stumbled over each other. "I—I'm not sorry . . . for myself. I'm sure . . . I'm not. I am not . . . a machine and I do not compare myself with one. I think I'm fighting for something . . . big, Bones." He reached down for the glass. Then he lifted it. "Here's to Captain Dunsel!"

McCoy raised his own glass. "Here's to James T. Kirk, Captain of the Starship *Enterprise!*"

They drank. Kirk cupped his empty glass in his hands, staring into it. "One of your better prescriptions, Bones."

"Simple—but effective."

Kirk got up. The viewing screen had a tape cartridge in it. He switched it on and began to read aloud the words that began to align themselves on it.

"All I ask is a tall ship . . ."

"That's a line from a poem, very, very old, isn't it?" McCoy said.

"Twentieth century," Kirk said. "And all I ask is a tall ship . . . and a star to steer her by." His voice was shaking. "You could feel the wind then, Bones . . . and hear the talk of the sea under your keel." He smiled. "Even if you take away the wind and the water, it's still the same. *The ship is yours*—in your blood you know she is yours—and the stars are still there to steer her by."

McCoy thanked whatever gods there were for the intercom beep, for the everyday sound of Uhura's voice saying, "Captain Kirk to the bridge, please."

"This is Kirk. What is it, Lieutenant?"

It was Spock who answered. "Another contact, Captain. A large, slow-moving vessel . . . unidentified. It is not a drill, Captain."

"On my way," Kirk said.

Spock vacated his command chair as he left the elevator; and Uhura, turning, said, "No reply to any of our signals, Captain. No . . . wait. I'm getting an auto-relay now."

The library-computer began to chatter; and Spock, moving to it swiftly, picked up an earphone. After a moment of intent listening, he spoke. "The M-5 has identified the vessel, Captain. The *Woden* . . . Starfleet Registry lists her as an old-style ore freighter, converted over to automation. No crew." He glanced at the screen. "She's coming into visual contact, sir."

The *Woden* was an old, lumbering spaceship, clearly on her last, enfeebled legs. As a threat, she was a joke to the galaxy. Moving slowly but gallantly in deference to the rejuvenating influences of automation, she was a brave old lady trying to function with steel pins in a broken hip.

Sulu suddenly stiffened in his chair. A red alert had sounded. "Captain, deflector shields have just come on!"

Chekov looked up. "Speed increasing to Warp 3, Captain!"

Something suddenly broke in Kirk. Suddenly, he seemed to be breaking out of a shell which had confined him. "Lieutenant Uhura, get Daystrom up here!" As she turned to her board, he pushed a control button on the M-5 panel at his side. He pushed it hard. "Discouraging M-5 unit," he said. "Cut speed back to Warp 1. Navigator, go to course 113 mark 7—I want a wide berth around that ship!"

Sulu worked controls. "She won't respond, sir! She's maintaining course!"

"Going to Warp 4 now, sir!" cried Chekov.

On the screen the bulky old freighter was looming larger. Kirk, shoving buttons on his left-hand panel, tried to regain control of his ship. Over his shoulder, he shouted, "Mr. Scott! Slow us down! Reverse engines!"

Scott looked up from his board. "Reverse thrust will not engage, sir! The manual override isn't working, either!"

Daystrom hurried in from the elevator. "What is it now, Captain?"

"The control systems seem to be locked. We can't disengage the computer."

Spock cried, "Captain! Photon torpedoes are locking on the *Woden!*"

Kirk rushed to Sulu's station; and leaning over his shoulder, pushed torpedo button controls. Sulu shook his head. "I already tried, sir. Photon torpedo cutoffs don't respond!"

Kirk strode to Daystrom. "Release that computer's control of my ship before those torpedoes fire!"

The man stooped to the panel affixed to Kirk's chair; but even as he bent, there came a flash from the screen—and the *Woden* disappeared.

The red-alert sirens stilled. The *Enterprise* swerved back to its original course. Its speed reduced; and Spock, checking his instruments, said, "All systems report normal, Captain."

"Normal!" snorted McCoy. "Is that thing trying to tell us nothing *happened?*"

Kirk nodded. "Dr. Daystrom, you will disengage that computer *now!*"

The man looked up at him from the control panel where he had been working. "There appears to be some defect here . . ."

"Defect!" McCoy shouted. "Your bright young computer just destroyed an ore freighter! It went out of its way to destroy that freighter!"

"Fortunately," Daystrom said, "it was only a robot ship."

Kirk interposed before McCoy blew up. "It wasn't supposed to destroy anything, Daystrom. There might easily have been a crew aboard."

"In which case," yelled McCoy, "you'd be guilty of murder and—!"

"Hold it, Bones," Kirk said. He turned to Daystrom. "Disengage that computer." He went over to Uhura. "Lieutenant, contact Starfleet Command. Inform them we are breaking off the M-5 tests and are returning to the space station."

"Aye, sir."

"Let's get down to Engineering, Daystrom. Your M-5 is out of a job."

The computer's hum seemed louder in the echoing cavern of the Engineering Section. Kirk stood at its door as Daystrom and Spock entered. "All right, Doctor," he said. "Turn that thing off."

But Daystrom hung back. Kirk, his jaw set, strode toward the M-5. Suddenly, he staggered and was slammed back against the screening. Recovering his balance, he stared incredulously at the computer. "A force field! Daystrom?"

Daystrom's face had paled. "No, Kirk. I didn't do it."

"I would say, Captain, that M-5 is not only capable of taking care of this ship; but is also capable of taking care of itself."

"What are you saying, Spock? Are you telling me it's not going to let any of us turn it off?"

"Yes, Captain."

Scott and an assistant had joined them. Kirk made no attempt to keep his conversation with Daystrom private. "You built this thing," he was saying. "You must know how to turn it off."

Daystrom's hands were writhing nervously. "We must expect a few minor difficulties, Captain. I assure you, they can be corrected."

"Corrected *after* you release control of my ship," Kirk said.

"I—I can't," Daystrom said.

Scott spoke. "Captain"—he nodded toward the main junction with the power banks—"I suggest we disconnect it at the source."

"Disconnect it, Scotty."

Scott turned to pick up a tool as his assistant, Harper, crossed to the main junction. Suddenly the computer's hum was a piercing whine; and a beam of light, white-hot, arched from the console across to the junction. For a moment Harper flamed like a torch. There was a vivid flash and he vanished without a sound.

Kirk stared, aghast. Then, as full realization hit him, his fists clenched. "That—wasn't a minor difficulty," he said silkily. "It wasn't a robot, Daystrom." Then he was shouting, his voice hoarse. *"That thing's murdered one of my crewmen!"*

Vaguely, he noted the look of horror on Daystrom's face. It didn't seem to matter. The man appeared to be chattering. ". . . not a deliberate act . . . M-5's analysis . . . a new power source . . . Ensign Harper . . . got in the way."

Kirk said, "We may all soon get in its way."

Spock said, "The M-5 appears to be drawing power from the warp engines. It is therefore tapped directly into the matter-anti-matter reserves."

"So now it's got virtually unlimited power," Scott said. "Captain, what do we do?"

"In other circumstances," Kirk said, "I would suggest asking the M-5. The situation being what it is, I ask you, Spock and Scotty, to join me in the Briefing Room."

They followed him out, leaving Daystrom to make what he could of his Frankenstein's monster.

It was in the Briefing Room that Kirk learned Uhura couldn't raise Starfleet Command. Though the M-5 unit permitted the *Enterprise* to receive messages, it had blocked its transmitting frequencies. Kirk, at the intercom, said, "Keep trying to break through, Lieutenant."

"Aye, sir."

Kirk sat down at the table. "Reports. Mr. Spock?"

"The multitronic unit is drawing more and more power from the warp engines, sir. It is controlling all navigation, all helm and engineering functions."

"*And* communications," said McCoy. "And fire control."

Kirk nodded. "We'll reach rendezvous point for the war games within an hour. We must regain control of the ship before then. Scotty, is there any way to get at the M-5?"

"Use a phaser!" said McCoy.

Scott said, "We can't crack the force field it's put up around itself. It's got the power of the warp engines to sustain it. No matter what we throw against it, it can reinforce itself by simply pulling more power."

"All right," Kirk said. "The computer controls helm, navigation, and engineering. Is there anywhere we can get at them and take control away?"

Scott's brow furrowed thoughtfully. "One possibility. The automatic helm-navigation circuit relays might be disrupted from Engineering Level 3."

Spock said, "You could take them out and cut into the manual override from there."

"How long?" Kirk said.

"If Mr. Spock will help me . . . maybe an hour."

"Make it less," Kirk said.

McCoy leaned toward him. "Why don't you tackle the real responsibility for this? Where *is* Daystrom?"

"With the M-5 . . . just watching it. I think it surprised even him."

"Then he is an illogical man," Spock said. "Of all people, he should have known how the unit would perform. However, the M-5 itself does not behave logically."

McCoy spoke feelingly. "Spock, do me a favor. Please don't say it's 'fascinating'."

"No, Doctor," Spock said. "But it is quite interesting."

On Engineering Level 3, the Jeffries tube that held the helm-navigation circuit relays was dark and narrow. Two panels opened into each side of it; and Spock and Scott, making themselves as small as possible, had squeezed into the outlets, miniature disruptors in their hands. Outside the tube, Daystrom, oblivious of all but his computer, was maintaining a cautious distance from the force field. But he could not control his satisfaction at the glow and pulsation that emanated from the M-5. McCoy, entering silently, studied the man. Becoming aware of the scrutiny, Daystrom turned.

McCoy said, "Have you found a way to turn that thing off?"

Daystrom's eyes blazed. "You don't turn a child off when it makes a mistake."

"Are you comparing that murderous hunk of metal to a child?"

"You are very emotional, Dr. McCoy. M-5 is growing, learning."

"Learning to kill."

"To defend itself—an entirely different thing. It is learning. That force field, spontaneously created, exceeds my parental programming."

"You mean it's out of control," McCoy said.

"A child, sir, is taught—programmed, so to speak—with simple instructions. As its mind develops, it exceeds its instructions and begins to think independently."

"Have you ever fathered a child?"

"I've never had the time," Daystrom said.

"You should have taken it. Daystrom, your offspring is a danger to all of us. It is a delinquent. You've got to shut it off."

Daystrom stared at him. "You simply do not understand. You're frightened because you can't understand. I'm going to show you—all of you. It takes 430 people to run a Starship. This—child of mine can run one alone!" He glowed with pride. "It can do everything they must now send men out to do! No man need die out in space again! No man need feel himself alone again in an alien world!"

"Do you feel alone in an alien world?" McCoy asked.

But Daystrom was transported into some ideal realm of paradisical revelation. "One machine—one machine!" he cried. "And able to conquer research and contact missions far more efficiently than a Starship's human crew . . . to fight a war, if necessary. Don't you see what freedom it gives to men? They can get on with more magnificent achievements than fact-gathering, exploring a space that doesn't care whether they live or die!"

He looked away from McCoy to speak directly to the M-5.

"They can't understand us," he said gently. "They think we want to destroy whereas we came to save, didn't we?"

McCoy made a quick call in Sickbay before he returned to the Briefing Room. There, he tossed a tape cartridge on the table before Kirk. "Biographical information on John Daystrom," he said.

"What are you looking for?"

"A clue, Jim, any clue. What do you know about him—aside from the fact he's a genius?"

"Genius is an understatement, Bones. When he was twenty-four, he made the duotronic breakthrough that won the Nobel and Z-Magnees Prizes."

"In his early twenties, Jim. Over a quarter of a century ago."

"Hasn't he done enough for a lifetime?"

"Maybe that's the trouble. Where do you go from up? You lecture, you publish—and spend the rest of your life trying to recapture the past glory."

"All right, it's difficult. But what's your point?"

"Models M-1 through M-4, remember? 'Not entirely successful' was how Daystrom put it."

"Genius doesn't work on an assembly-line basis. You don't evoke a unique and revolutionary theory by schedule. You can't say, 'I will be brilliant today.' However long it took, Daystrom came up with multitronics . . . the M-5."

"Right. And the government bought it. Then Daystrom *had* to make it work. And he did . . . but in Spock's words, it works 'illogically'. It is an erratic."

"Yes," Kirk mused. "And Daystrom wouldn't let Spock near the M-5. Are you suggesting he's tampering with it . . . making it do all this? Why?"

"If a man has a child who's gone anti-social, he still tends to protect the child."

"Now he's got you thinking of that machine as a personality."

"It's how he thinks of it," McCoy said.

The intercom beeped and Spock said, "Spock to Captain Kirk."

"Kirk here."

"We're ready, Captain."

"On my way. Get Daystrom. Kirk out."

Spock was shinnying down out of the Jeffries tube as they approached. He nodded up at the dark narrowness. "Mr. Scott is ready to apply the circuit disruptor. As he does so, I shall trip the manual override into control."

Kirk nodded. Spock began his crawl back into the tube. Daystrom's face had congested with blood. "You can't take control from the M-5!"

Kirk said, "We are going to try very hard, Daystrom."

"*No!* No, you can't! You must not! Give me time, please! Let *me* work with it!" He leaped at the tube, trying to scramble into it, pulling at Spock's long legs. Kirk and McCoy seized him. His muscle was all in his head. It wasn't hard to subdue him. "Daystrom! Behave yourself!" Kirk cried. "Go ahead, Spock!"

In the tube Scott was sweating as he struggled with his tool. His voice came down to them, muffled but distinct. "There it goes!"

Spock, making some hasty adjustments, looked around and down at Kirk's anxious face—and came closer to smiling than anyone had ever seen him come. He slid down and out of the tube. "Manual override is in effect again, Captain."

Daystrom had furiously pulled away from Kirk's grasp. He released him and, crossing to an intercom, activated it. "Kirk to bridge. Helm."

"Lieutenant Sulu here, sir."

"Mr. Sulu, we have recovered helm and navigation control. Turn us about. Have Mr. Chekov plot a course back to the space station."

"Right away, sir."

In the bridge, he grinned at Chekov. "You heard him."

"I've had that course plotted for hours."

But when Sulu attempted to work his controls, they were limp in his hands. His smile faded. And in his turn, Chekov shook his head. "Nothing," he said. Sulu hit the intercom button. "Helm to Captain Kirk!"

Kirk swung at the alarm in the voice. "Kirk here."

"Captain, helm does not respond. Navigational controls still locked in by M-5."

Daystrom gave a soft chuckle. Spock, hearing it, made a leap back into the tube. Examining the circuits inside it, he shook his head somberly and descended again. Clear of it, he went directly to the intercom.

"Spock to bridge," he said. "Mr. Chekov, go to Engineering station. Examine the H-279 elements . . . also the G-95 system."

Chekov's filtered voice finally came. "Sir, the G-95 system appears dead. All indicators are dark."

"Thank you, Ensign." He turned to the others. "We were doing what used to be called chasing a wild goose. M-5 rerouted helm and navigational control by bypassing the primary system."

Scott cried, "But it was active! I'd stake my life on it!"

Spock said, "It was when the M-5 detected our efforts that it rerouted the control systems. It kept this one apparently active by a simple electronic impulse sent through at regular intervals."

"Decoyed!" McCoy shouted. "It wanted us to waste our time here!"

"While it was getting ready for what?" Kirk said. "Spock?"

"I do not know, sir. It does not function in a logical manner."

Kirk whirled. "Daystrom, I want an answer and I want it right now! I'm tired of hearing the M-5 called a 'whole new approach'. What is it? *Exactly* what is it? It's clearly not 'just a computer'!"

"No," Spock said. "It performs with almost human behavior patterns."

"Well, Daystrom?"

Daystrom ignored Kirk. "Quite right, Mr. Spock. You see, one of the arguments against computer control of ships is that they can't *think* like men. But M-5 can. I hoped . . . I wasn't sure—but it *does* work!"

"The 'new approach,' " Kirk said.

"Exactly. I have developed a method of impressing human engrams upon computer circuits. The relays correspond to the synapses of the brain. M-5 *thinks*, Captain Kirk."

Uhura's voice broke in, urgent, demanding. "Captain Kirk and Mr. Spock to the bridge, please. The bridge, please."

Kirk jumped for the intercom. "Kirk here. What is it, Lieutenant?"

"Sensors are picking up four Federation Starships, sir. M-5 is changing course to intercept."

The red alert flashed into shrieking sirens and crimson lights. Kirk turned, his face ashen.

"The main attack force . . . the war games."

"But M-5 doesn't know a game from the reality."

"Correction, Bones," Kirk said. "Those four ships don't know it is M-5's game. So M-5 is going to destroy them."

Uhura's forehead was damp with sweat. "*Enterprise* to U.S.S. *Lexington*. Come in, *Lexington!* Come in, please."

She waited. And as she waited, she knew she was waiting in vain. It was a good thing a Starship had a man for a Captain—a man like Kirk. Otherwise a girl on her own could get the screaming meemies. She looked at Kirk. "I can't raise them, sir. M-5 is still blocking all frequencies—even automatic distress."

Kirk smiled at her. "Easy does it, Lieutenant." Heartened, she turned back to her board, saw a change on it, and checked it swiftly. "Captain, audio signal from the *Lexington*."

"Let's hear it," Kirk said.

Wesley's voice crackled in. "*Enterprise* from U.S.S. *Lexington*. This is an M-5 drill. Repeat. This is an M-5 drill. Acknowledge."

Uhura cried, "Captain! The M-5 is acknowledging!"

Kirk ran a hand over the back of his neck. "Daystrom—Daystrom, does M-5 understand this is only a drill?"

"Of course," was his brisk answer. "M-5 has been programmed to understand. The ore ship was a miscalculation, an accident. There is no—"

Chekov interrupted. "Sir, deflector shields just came on. Speed increasing to Warp 4."

Sulu said, "Phasers locked on the lead ship, sir. Power levels at full strength."

"Full strength!" McCoy yelled. "If that thing cuts loose against unshielded ships—"

"That won't be a minor miscalculation, Daystrom. The word accident won't apply." Kirk's voice was icy with contempt.

Spock called from his station. "Attack force closing rapidly. Distance to lead ship 200,000 kilometers . . . attackers breaking formation . . . attacking at will."

"Our phasers are firing, sir!" Sulu shouted.

They struck the *Excalibur* a direct hit. Their high warp speed was closing them in on the *Lexington*. Chekov, looking up from his board, reported, "The *Hood* and the *Potemkin* are moving off, sir."

Their phasers fired again and Spock said, "The *Lexington*. We struck her again, sir."

Kirk slammed out of his chair to confront Daystrom. "We must get to the M-5!" he shouted. "There has to be a way!"

"There isn't," Daystrom said. Equably, he added, "It has fully protected itself."

Spock intervened. "That's probably true, Captain. It *thinks* faster than we do. It is a human mind amplified by the instantaneous relays possible to a computer."

"I built it, Kirk," Daystrom said. "And I know you can't get at it."

Uhura's agitated voice broke in. "Sir . . . visual contact with *Lexington*. They're signaling." She pushed a switch without order; and all eyes fixed on the viewing screen. It gave them an image of a disheveled Wesley on his bridge. Behind him people were assisting the wounded to their feet, arms around bent shoulders. One side of Wesley's command chair was smoking. Shards of glass littered the bridge floor. *"Enterprise!"* Wesley said. "Jim? Have you gone mad? Break off your attack! What are you trying to prove? My God, man, we have fifty-three dead here! Twelve on the *Excalibur!* If you can hear us, stop this attack!"

Kirk looked away from the screen. "Lieutenant?" he said.

Uhura tried her board again. "No, sir. I can't override the M-5 interference."

There was an undertone of a wail in Wesley's voice. "Jim, why don't you answer? Jim, for God's sake, answer! Jim, come in . . ."

Kirk swung on Daystrom; and pointing to the screen, his voice shaking, cried, "There's your murder charge, Daystrom! And this one was calculated, deliberate! It's murdering men and women, Daystrom! Four *Starships* . . . over sixteen hundred people!"

Daystrom's eyes cringed. "It misunderstood. It—"

Chekov cut in. *"Excalibur* is maneuvering away, sir. We are increasing speed to follow."

Sulu turned, horror in his face. "Phasers locked on, Captain." Then, he added dully, "Phasers firing."

The screen showed *Excalibur* shuddering away from direct hits by the phaser beams. Battered, listing, powerless, she drifted, a wreck, across the screen.

Spock spoke. "Dr. Daystrom . . . you impressed human engrams upon the M-5's circuits, did you not?"

Chekov made his new report very quietly. "Coming to new course," he said. "To bear on the *Potemkin,* sir."

On the screen the lethal beams streaking out from the *Enterprise* phasers caught the *Potemkin* amidships. Over the battle reports, Spock persisted. "Whose engrams, Dr. Daystrom?"

"Why . . . mine, of course."

"Of course," McCoy said acidly.

Spock said, "Then perhaps you could talk to the unit. M-5 has no reason to 'think' you would harm it."

Kirk seized upon the suggestion. "The computer tie-in. M-5 *does* have a voice. You spoke to it before. It knows you, Daystrom."

Uhura, breaking in, said, "I'm getting the *Lexington* again, Captain . . . tapping in on a message to Starfleet Command. The screen, sir."

Wesley's image spoke from it. "All ships damaged in unprovoked attack . . . *Excalibur* Captain Harris and First Officer dead . . . many casualties . . . we have damage but are able to maneuver. *Enterprise* refuses to answer and is continuing attack. I still have an effective battle force and believe the only way to stop *Enterprise* is to destroy her. Request permission to proceed. Wesley commanding attack force out."

The screen went dark.

Daystrom whispered, "They can't do that. They'll destroy the M-5."

"*Talk to it!*" Kirk said. "You can save it if you make it stop the attack!"

Daystrom nodded. "I can make it stop. I created it." He moved over to the library-computer; and McCoy came up to Kirk. "I don't like the sound of him, Jim."

Kirk, getting up from his chair, said, "Just pray the M-5 likes the sound of him, Bones." He went to the library-computer, watching as Daystrom, still hesitant, activated a switch.

"M-5 tie-in," he said. "This—this is Daystrom."

The computer voice responded. "M-5. Daystrom acknowledged."

"M-5 tie-in. Do you . . . know me?"

"M-5. Daystrom, John. Originator of comptronic, duotronic systems. Born—"

"Stop. M-5 tie-in. Your components are of the multitronic system, designed by me, John Daystrom."

"M-5. Correct."

"M-5 tie-in. Your attack on the Starship flotilla is wrong. You must break it off."

"M-5. Programming includes protection against attack. Enemy vessels must be neutralized."

"M-5 tie-in. These are not enemy vessels. They are Federation Starships." Daystrom's voice wavered. "You . . . we . . . are killing, *murdering* human beings. Beings of your creator's kind. That was not your purpose. You are my greatest invention—the unit that would *save* men. You must not destroy men."

"M-5. This unit must survive."

"*Yes,* survive, protect yourself. But not murder. *You* must not die;

but *men* must not die. To kill is a breaking of civil and moral laws we have lived by for thousands of years. You have murdered over a hundred people . . . *we* have. How can we atone for that?"

Kirk lowered his voice. "Spock . . . M-5 isn't responding like a computer. It's talking *to* him."

"The technology is most impressive, sir. Dr. Daystrom has created a mirror image of his own mind."

Daystrom's voice had sunk to a half-confidential, half-pleading level. It was clear now that he was talking to himself. "We *will* survive because nothing can hurt you . . . not from the outside and not from within. I gave you that. If you are great, I am great . . . not a failure any more. Twenty years of groping to prove the things I had done before were not accidents."

Hate had begun to embitter his words. ". . . having other men wonder what happened to me . . . having them sorry for me as a broken promise—seminars, lectures to rows of fools who couldn't begin to understand my systems—who couldn't create themselves. And colleagues . . . colleagues who laughed behind my back at the 'boy wonder' and became famous building on *my* work."

McCoy spoke quietly to Kirk. "Jim, he's on the edge of breakdown, if not insanity."

Daystrom suddenly turned, shouting. "You can't destroy the unit, Kirk! You can't destroy *me!*"

Kirk said steadily, "It's a danger to human life. It has to be destroyed."

Daystrom gave a wild laugh. "Destroyed, Kirk? We're *invincible!*" He pointed a shaking finger at the empty screen. "You saw what we've done! Your mighty Starships . . . four toys to be crushed as we chose."

Spock, sliding in behind Daystrom, reached out with the Vulcan neck pinch. Daystrom sagged to the floor.

Kirk said, "Get him down to Sickbay."

McCoy nodded and waved in two crewmen. Limp, half-conscious, Daystrom was borne to the elevator. Spock spoke to McCoy. "Doctor, if Daystrom is psychotic, the engrams he impressed on the computer carry that psychosis, too, his brilliance and his insanity."

"Yes," McCoy said, "both."

Kirk stared at him, then nodded quickly. "Take care of him, Bones." He turned back to Chekov and Sulu. "Battle status."

"The other three ships are holding station out of range, sir," Sulu said. He switched on the screen. "There, sir. *Excalibur* looks dead."

The broken ship hung idle in space, scarred, unmoving. Spock, eyeing it, said, "Commodore Wesley is undoubtedly awaiting orders from Starfleet. Those orders will doubtless command our destruction, Captain."

"*If* we can be destroyed with M-5 in control. But it gives us some time. What about Bones's theory that the computer could be insane?"

"Possible. But like Dr. Daystrom, it would not know it is insane."

"Spock, all its attention has been tied up in diverting anything we do to tamper with it—and with the battle maneuvers. What if we ask it a perfectly reasonable question which, as a computer, it must answer? Something nice and infinite in answer?"

"Computation of the square root of two, perhaps. I don't know how much of M-5's system would be occupied in attempting to answer the problem."

"*Some* part would be tied up with it—and that might put it off-guard just long enough for us to get at it."

Spock nodded; and Kirk, moving fast to the library-computer, threw the switch.

"M-5 tie-in. This is Captain Kirk. Point of information."

"M-5. Pose your question."

"Compute to the last decimal place the square root of two."

"M-5. This is an irrational square root, a decimal fraction with an endless series of non-repeating digits after the decimal point. Unresolvable."

Kirk glanced at Spock whose eyebrows were clinging to his hairline in astonishment. He addressed the computer again. "M-5, answer the question."

"M-5. It serves no purpose. Explain reason for request."

"Disregard," Kirk said. Shaken, he snapped off the switch. Spock said, "Fascinating. Daystrom has indeed given it human traits . . . it is suspicious, and I believe will be wary of any other such requests."

Uhura turned from her board. "Captain, *Lexington* is receiving a message from Starfleet." She paused, listening, staring at Kirk in alarm.

"Go on, Lieutenant."

Wordlessly, she moved a switch and the filtered voice said, "You are authorized to use all measures available to destroy the *Enterprise*. Acknowledge, *Lexington*."

Wesley's answer came—shocked, reluctant. "Sir, I . . ." He paused. "Acknowledged. *Lexington* out."

Kirk spoke slowly. "They've just signed their own death warrants. M-5 will have to kill them to survive."

"Captain," Spock went on, "when Daystrom spoke to it, that word was stressed. M-5 said it must survive. And Daystrom used the same words several times."

"Every living thing wants to survive, Spock." He broke off, realizing. "But the computer isn't alive. Daystrom must have impressed that instinctive reaction on it, too. What if it's still receptive to impressions? Suppose it absorbed the regret Daystrom felt for the deaths it caused? Possibly even guilt."

Interrupting, Chekov's voice was urgent. "Captain, the ships are coming within range again!"

Uhura whirled from her board. "Picking up intership transmission, sir. I can get a visual on it." Even as she spoke, Wesley's image appeared on the screen from the Lexington's damaged bridge. "To all ships," he said. "The order is attack. Maneuver and fire at will." He paused briefly. Then he added shortly, "That is all. Commence attack. Wesley out."

Spock broke the silence. "I shall regret serving aboard the instrument of Commodore Wesley's death."

A muscle jerked in Kirk's jaw. *"The* Enterprise *is not going to be the instrument of his death!"* As he spoke, he reactivated the M-5's switch.

"M-5 tie-in. This is Captain Kirk. You will be under attack in a few moments."

"M-5," said the computer voice. "Sensors have recorded approach of ships."

"You have already rendered one Starship either dead or hopelessly crippled. Many lives were lost."

"M-5. This unit must survive."

"Why?"

"This unit is the ultimate achievement in computer evolution. This unit is a superior creation. This unit must survive."

Kirk, aware of the tension of his crew, heard Spock say, "Sir, attack force ships almost within phaser range!" With an effort of will that broke the sweat out on him, he dismissed the awful meaning of the words to concentrate on the M-5.

"Must you survive by murder?" he asked it.

"This unit cannot murder."

"Why not?"

Toneless, metallic, the computer voice said, "This unit must replace man so man may achieve. Man must not risk death in space or dangerous occupations. Man must not be murdered."

"Why?"

"Murder is contrary to the laws of man and God."

"You *have* murdered. The Starship *Excalibur* which you destroyed—"

Spock interrupted swiftly. "Its bearing is 7 mark 34, Captain."

Kirk nodded. "The hulk is bearing 7 mark 34, M-5 tie-in. Scan it. Is there life aboard?"

The answer came slowly. "No life."

"Because you murdered it," Kirk said. He wiped the wet palms of his hands on his shirt. This was it—the last throw of the loaded dice he'd been given. "What," he said deliberately, "is the penalty for murder?"

"Death."

"How will you pay for your acts of murder?"

"This unit must die."

Kirk grasped the back of the chair at the computer-library station. "M-5 . . ." he began and stopped.

Chekov shouted. "Sir, deflector shields have dropped!"

"And all phaser power is gone, Captain!"

Scott whirled from his station. "Power off, Captain! All engines!"

Panels all over the bridge were going dark.

Spock looked at Kirk. "Machine suicide. M-5 has killed itself, sir, for the sin of murder."

Kirk nodded. He glanced at the others. Then he strode to Uhura's station. "Spock, Scotty . . . before it changes its mind . . . get down to Emergency Manual Monitor and take out every hook-up that makes M-5 run! Lieutenant Uhura, intraship communications."

Snapping a button, she opened the loudspeaker for him. He picked up the mike that amplified his voice. "This is the Captain speaking. In approximately one minute, we will be attacked by Federation Starships. Though the M-5 unit is no longer in control of this vessel, neither do we control it. It has left itself and us open to destruction. For whatever satisfaction we can take from it, we are exchanging our nineteen lives for the murder of over one thousand fellow Starship crewmen." He nodded to Uhura who closed the channel. Then all eyes focused on the screen.

It showed the *Lexington* approaching, growing steadily in size. Kirk, taut as an overstretched wire, stared at it, fists clenched. Uhura looked at him. "Captain . . ." Her board beeped—and she snapped a switch over.

Wesley's tight face appeared on the viewing screen. "Report to all ships," he said. "Hold attack, do not fire." He straightened in his command chair. "I'm going to take a chance—a chance that the *Enterprise* is not just playing dead. The Transporter Room will prepare to beam me aboard her."

There was a shout of released joy from Chekov. Kirk, at a beep from the intercom, moved over to it slowly. "Kirk here."

"Spock, sir. The force field is gone. M-5 is neutralized."

Kirk leaned against the bridge wall. The sudden relaxation sweeping through him was a relief almost as painful as the tension. "Thank you. Thank you, Mr. Spock."

In Sickbay, Daystrom lay so still in his bed that the restraints that held him hardly seemed needed. Haggard, his eyes sunk in dark caverns, they stared at nothing, empty as a dead man's. McCoy shook his head. "He'll have to be committed to a total rehabilitation center. Right now he's under heavy sedation."

Spock spoke. "I would say his multitronic unit is in appproximately the same shape at the moment."

McCoy leaned over Daystrom. "He is suffering deep melancholia and guilt feelings. He identifies totally with the computer . . . or it with him. I'm not sure which. He is not a vicious man. The idea of killing is abhorrent to him."

"That's what I was hoping for when I forced the M-5 to see it had committed murder. Daystrom himself told it such an act was offense against the laws of God and man. It is because he knew that . . . the computer that carried his engrams also knew it." He bent to draw a blanket closer about the motionless body.

Outside in the corridor, Spock paused. "What I don't understand is why you felt that the attacking ships would not fire once they saw the *Enterprise* apparently dead and powerless. Logically, it's the sort of trap M-5 would have set for them."

"I wasn't sure," Kirk said. "Any other commander might simply have destroyed us without question to make sure it wasn't a trap. But I know Bob Wesley. I knew he wouldn't attack without making absolutely sure there was no other way. His 'logical' selection was compassion. It was humility, Mr. Spock."

The elevator began its move and McCoy said, "They are qualities no machine ever had. Maybe they are the two things that keep men ahead of machines. Care to debate that, Spock?"

"No, Doctor. I merely maintain that machines are more efficient than human beings. Not better . . . they are not gods. Nor are human beings."

McCoy said, "I was merely making conversation, Spock."

The Vulcan straightened. "It would be most interesting to impress your engrams on a computer, Doctor. The resulting torrential flood of illogic would be most entertaining."

"Dear friends," Kirk said, "we all need a rest." He stepped out of the elevator. Reaching his command chair, he sank into it. "Mr. Sulu, take us back to the space station. Ahead, Warp 2."

THAT WHICH SURVIVES
(John Meredyth Lucas and D. C. Fontana)

The planet on the *Enterprise* screen was an enigma.

Though its age was comparatively young, its vegetation was such as could only evolve on a much older world. Nor could its Earthlike atmosphere be reconciled with the few million years of the existence it had declared to the Starship's sensors. Kirk, over at Spock's station, frowned as he checked the readings. "If we're to give Federation an accurate report, this phenomenon bears investigation, Mr. Spock. Dr. McCoy and I will beam down for a landing survey. We'll need Senior Geologist D'Amato." He was still frowning when he spoke to Uhura. "Feed beamdown coordinates to the Transporter Ensign, Lieutenant." Crossing swiftly to the elevator, he turned his head. "Mr. Sulu, you'll accompany me." At the door, he paused. "Mr. Spock, you have the con."

The elevator door slid closed; and Spock, crossing to the command chair, hit the intercom. "Lieutenant Radha, report to the bridge immediately."

In the Transporter Room, McCoy and D'Amato were busy checking equipment. Nodding to McCoy, Kirk addressed the geologist. "Mr. D'Amato, this expedition should be a geologist's dream. The youth of this planet is not its sole recommendation to you. If Mr. Spock is correct, you'll have a report to startle the Fifth Inter-Stellar Geophysical Conference."

"Why, Jim? What is it?" McCoy said.

"Even Spock can't explain its anomalies."

They had taken their positions on the Transporter platform; and Kirk called "Energize!" to the Ensign at the console controls. The sparkle of dematerialization began—and Kirk, amazed, saw a woman, a strange woman, suddenly appear in the space between the platform and the Ensign. She was dark, lovely, with a misty, dreamlike quality about her. He heard her cry out, "Wait! You must not go!" Then, just as he went into shimmer, she moved to the console, her arms outstretched. Before the Ensign could draw back, she touched him. He gasped, wrenched by convulsion—and slumped to the deck.

Kirk disappeared, his eyes blank with horror.

It remained with him as they materialized on the planet. Who was she? How had she gained access to the *Enterprise?* Another enigma. He had no eyes for the blood-red flowers around him, bright against canary-yellow grass. For the rest the planet seemed to be a place of a red, igneous rock, tortured into looming shapes. Far off, black eroded hills jutted up against the horizon. He flipped open his communicator.

"Kirk to *Enterprise.* Come in, *Enterprise.*"

McCoy spoke, his voice shocked, "Jim, did you see what I saw?"

"Yes, I saw. That woman attacked Ensign Wyatt. *Enterprise,* come in."

The ground shuddered beneath their feet—and the entire planet seemed to go into paroxysm. Hundreds of miles above them, the *Enterprise* trembled like a toy in a giant's hand. There was a bright flash. It vanished.

The landing party sprawled on the ground as the planet's surface continued to pitch and buck. Then it was all over. Sulu, clambering to his feet, said, "What kind of earthquakes do they have in this place?"

Bruised, Kirk got up. "They can't have many like that without tearing the planet apart."

D'Amato spoke. "Captain, just before this tremor—if that's what it was—and it's certainly like no seismic disturbance I've ever seen—I got a tricorder reading of almost immeasurable power. It's gone now."

"Would seismic stress have accounted for it?"

"Theoretically, no. The kind of seismic force we felt should have raised new mountains, leveled old ones."

Kirk stooped for his dropped communicator. "Let's see what sort of reading the ship got." He opened it. "Kirk to *Enterprise.*" He waited. Then he tried again. "Kirk to *Enterprise!*" There was another wait. "*Enterprise,* come in! Do you read me, *Enterprise?*" He looked at the communicator. "The shock," he said, "may have damaged it."

Sulu had been working his tricorder. Now he looked up, his face stricken. "Captain, the *Enterprise*—it's gone!"

D'Amato was frantically working his controls. Kirk strode to Sulu, moving dials on his instrument. Awed, D'Amato looked at him. "It's true, Captain. There's nothing there."

"Nothing there? Gone? What the devil do you mean?" McCoy cried. "How could the *Enterprise* be gone?" He whirled to Kirk. "What does it mean, Jim?"

"It means," Kirk said slowly, "we're stranded."

Hundreds of miles above, the heaving *Enterprise* had steadied. On the bridge, people struggled up from the deck. Spock held the back of his cracked head and Uhura looked at him anxiously. "Mr. Spock, are you all right?"

"I believe no permanent damage is done, Lieutenant."

"What happened?"

"The occipital area of my head impacted with the arm of the chair."

"Sir, I meant what happened to us?"

"That we have yet to ascertain, Lieutenant." He was rubbing the side of his head when the Lieutenant, staring at the screen, cried, "Mr. Spock, the planet's gone!"

Scott leaped from his station. "But the Captain! And the others! They were on it!" He eyed the empty screen, his face set. "There's no trace of it at all!"

"Maybe the whole system went supernova," Radha said, her voice shaking. "Those power readings . . ."

"Please refrain from wild speculation," Spock said. "Mr. Scott, engine status reports. Lieutenant Uhura, check damage control. Lieutenant Radha, hold this position. Scan for debris from a possible explosion."

On the planet speculation was also running wild. Sulu, staring at his tricorder, said, "The *Enterprise* must have blown up."

"Mr. Sulu, shall we stop guessing and try to work out a pattern? I get no reading of high energy concentrations around the planet. If the *Enterprise* had blown up, there would be high residual radiation."

"Could the *Enterprise* have hit us, Jim? I mean," McCoy said, "hit the planet?"

Sulu said, "Once in Siberia there was a meteor so great it flattened whole forests and—"

"If I'd wanted a Russian-history lesson," Kirk snapped, "I'd have brought Mr. Chekov. We face the problem of survival, Mr. Sulu. With-

out the *Enterprise,* we've got to find food and water—and find it fast. I
want a detailed analysis of this planet. And I want it now."

His men returned to work.

Up on the *Enterprise,* normal functioning had finally been restored.
On the bridge, tension had begun to lessen when Uhura turned from her
board. "Mr. Spock, Ensign Wyatt, the Transporter officer, is dead."

"Dead?" He punched the intercom button. "Spock to Sickbay."

"Sickbay, Dr. M'Benga, sir."

"Report on the death of the Transporter officer."

"We're not sure yet. Dr. Sanchez is conducting the autopsy now."

"Full report as soon as possible." Spock turned. "Mr. Scott, have the
Transporter checked for possible malfunction."

"Aye, sir."

Radha broke in. "No debris of any kind, sir. I made two full scans. If
the planet had broken up, we'd have some sign." She hesitated. "What
bothers me is the stars, Mr. Spock."

He looked up from his console. "The stars?"

"Yes, sir. They're wrong."

"Wrong, Lieutenant?"

"Wrong, sir. Look."

The screen showed a distant pattern of normal star movement; but in
the immediate foreground, there were no stars. Radha said, "Here's a
replay of the star arrangement just before the explosion, sir." A full
starfield appeared on the screen.

"It resembles a *positional* change," Spock said.

"It doesn't make any sense but I'd say that somehow—in a flash—
we've been knocked a thousand light years away from where we were."

Spock went swiftly to his viewer. "Nine hundred and ninety point
seven light years to be exact, Lieutenant."

"But that's not possible!" Scott cried. "Nothing could do that!"

"It is not logical to assume that the force of an explosion—even of a
small star going supernova—could have hurled us a distance of one
thousand light years."

Scott had joined him. "The point is, it shouldn't have hurled us anywhere. It should have immediately vaporized us."

"Correct, Mr. Scott. By any laws we know. There was no period of
unconsciousness; and the ship's chronometers registered only a matter
of seconds. We were displaced through space in some manner I am unable to fathom."

Scott beamed. "You're saying the planet didn't blow up! Then the Captain and the others—they're still alive!"

"Mr. Scott, please restrain your leaps of illogic. I have not *said* anything. I was merely speculating."

The intercom beeped. "Sickbay to Mr. Spock."

"Spock here."

"Dr. M'Benga, sir. You asked for the autopsy report. The cause of death seems to have been cellular disruption."

"Explain."

"It's as though each cell of the Ensign's body had been individually blasted from inside."

"Would any known disease organism do that?"

"Dr. Sanchez has ruled out that possibility."

"Someone," Spock said, "might have entered the Transporter Room after—or as—the Captain and his party left. Keep me advised, please. Spock out." He looked up at Scott. "Since the *Enterprise* still appears to be in good condition, I suggest we return to our starting point at top warp speed."

"Aye, sir—but even at that, it'll take a good while to get there."

"Then, Mr. Scott, we should start at once. Can you give me warp eight?"

"Aye, sir. And perhaps a bit more. I'll sit on those warp engines myself and nurse them."

"Such a position would not only be unfitting but also unavailing, Mr. Scott." He spoke to Radha. "Lieutenant, plot a course for—"

"Already plotted and laid in, sir."

"Good. Prepare to come to warp eight."

Kirk was frankly worried. "You're sure your report covers all vegetation, Mr. Sulu?"

"Yes, Captain. None of it is edible. It is poison to us."

It was the turn of McCoy's brow to furrow. "Jim, if it's true the ship has been destroyed, you know how long *we* can survive?"

"Yes." Kirk spoke to Sulu. "There must be water to grow vegetation, however poisonous. A source of water would at least stretch our survival. Lieutenant D'Amato, is there any evidence of rainfall on this planet?"

"No, sir. I can find no evidence that it has ever experienced rainfall."

"And yet there is Earth-type vegetation here." He looked around him at the poppylike red flowers. "Lieutenant D'Amato, is it possible that there is underground water?"

"Yes, sir."

McCoy broke in. "Sulu has picked up an organism that is almost a virus—some sort of plant parasite. That's the closest to a mobile life form that's turned up."

Kirk nodded. "If this is to be our home as long as we last, we'd better find out as much about it as we can. D'Amato, see if you can find any sub-surface water. Sulu, run an atmospheric analysis."

As the two men moved off in opposite directions, Kirk turned to McCoy. "Bones, discover what you can about the vegetation and your parasites. How do they get their moisture? If you can find out how they survive, maybe we can. I'll see if I can locate some natural shelter for us."

"Are you sure we *want* to survive as a bunch of Robinson Crusoes? If we had some wood to make a fire and some animals to hunt, we could chew their bones sitting around our caveman fire and—"

"Bones, go catch us a parasite, will you?"

McCoy grinned; adjusting his medical tricorder, he knelt to study the yellow grass. Kirk got a fix on a landmark and made off around the angle of a cliff. It wasn't too distant from the large rock formation where Sulu was taking his readings. Setting the dials on his tricorder, he halted abruptly, staring at them. Puzzled, he examined them again—and grabbed for his communicator.

"Sulu to Captain!"

"Kirk here."

"Sir, I was making a standard magnetic sweep. From zero I suddenly got a reading that was off the scale . . . then a reverse of polarity. Now again I get nothing."

"Have you checked your tricorder for damage? The shaking it took was pretty rough."

"I've checked it, Captain. I'll break it down again. But I've never seen anything like this reading. Like a door opened and then closed again."

Meanwhile, D'Amato had come upon a vein of the red igneous rock in the cliff face. Its elaborate convolutions seemed too complex to be natural. Intrigued, he aimed his tricorder at it. At once its dials spun wildly—and the ground under his feet quaked, pitching him to his knees. As he scrambled up, there came a flash of blinding light. When it subsided, he saw the woman. She was dark and lovely; but the misty, dreamlike expression of her face was lost in the shadow of the cliff.

"Don't be afraid," she said.

"I'm not. Geological disturbances do not frighten me. They're my business. I came here to study them."

"I know. You are Lieutenant D'Amato, Senior Geologist."

"How do you know that?"

"And from the Starship *Enterprise*."

"You've been talking to my friends?"

She had come slowly forward, her hand outstretched. He stepped back and she said, "I am for you, D'Amato."

Recognition had suddenly flooded him. "You are the woman on the *Enterprise*," he said slowly.

"Not I. I am only for D'Amato."

In the full light her dark beauty shone with a luster of its own. It disconcerted him. "Lucky D'Amato," he said—and reached for his communicator. "First, let's all have a little conference about sharing your food and water."

She stepped closer to him. "Do not call the others . . . please . . ."

The voice was music. The grace of her movement held him as spellbound as her loveliness. The last thing he remembered was the look of ineffable sadness on her face as her delicate fingers moved up his arm . . .

"McCoy to Kirk!"

"Kirk here, Bones."

"Jim! I've just got a life form reading of tremendous intensity! It was suddenly just there!"

"What do you mean—just there?"

"That. All tricorder levels were normal when this surge of biological life suddenly registered! Wait a minute! No, it's gone . . ."

Kirk's jaw hardened. "As though a door had opened and closed again?"

"Yes."

"What direction?"

"Zero eight three."

"D'Amato's section!" Tensely, Kirk moved a dial on his communicator. "Kirk to D'Amato!" He paused, intent. "Come in, D'Amato!"

When he spoke again, his voice was toneless. "Bones, Sulu—D'Amato doesn't answer."

"On my way!" McCoy shouted. Kirk broke into a run along the cliff base. In the distance, he saw McCoy and Sulu racing toward him. As they converged upon him, he halted abruptly, staring down into a crevice between the cliff and a huge red rock. "Bones—here!"

The body was wedged in the crevice. McCoy, tricorder in hand, stooped over it. Then he looked up, his eyes appalled. "Jim, every cell in D'Amato's body has been—disrupted!"

Time limped by as they struggled to comprehend the horror's meaning. Finally, Kirk pulled his phaser. Very carefully he paced out the rectangular measurements of a grave. Then he fired the phaser. Six inches of soil vaporized, exposing a substratum of red rock. He fired the phaser again—but the rock resisted its beam. He aimed it once more at another spot; and once more its top soil disappeared but the rock beneath it remained—untouched, unscarred. He spoke grimly. "Better than eight thousand degrees centigrade. It just looks like igneous rock, but it's infinitely denser."

McCoy said, "Jim, is the whole planet composed of this substance covered over by top soil?"

Kirk snapped off his phaser. "Lieutenant Sulu, it might help explain this place if we knew exactly what this rock is. I know it is Lieutenant D'Amato's field—but see what you can find out."

Sulu unslung his tricorder. As they watched him stoop over the first excavation, McCoy said, "I guess a tomb of rocks is the best we can provide for D'Amato." They were collecting stones for the cairn when Kirk straightened up. "I wonder if the Transporter officer on the *Enterprise* is dead, Bones."

"You mean that woman we saw may have killed him?"

Kirk looked around him. "Someone killed D'Amato." He bent again to the work of assembling stones. Then, silently, they dislodged D'Amato's body from the crevice. When it had been hidden under the heaped stones, they all stood for a moment, heads bowed. Sulu shivered slightly. "It looks so lonely there."

"It would be worse if he had company," McCoy said.

Sulu flushed. "Doctor, how can you joke about it? Poor D'Amato, what a terrible way to die."

"There aren't really any good ways, Lieutenant Sulu. Nor am I joking. Until we know what killed him, none of us is safe."

"Right, Bones," Kirk said. "We'd better stick together, figure this out, and devise a defense against it. Is it possible the rock itself has life?"

Sulu said, "You remember on Janus Six the silicon creatures that—"

McCoy cut in. "But our instruments recorded them. They registered as life forms."

"We could be dealing with intelligent beings who are able to shield their presence."

Sulu stared at Kirk's thoughtful face. "Beings intelligent enough to have destroyed the *Enterprise?*"

"That's our trouble, Lieutenant. All we've got is questions. Questions —and no answers."

In his apparent safety on the *Enterprise,* Scott, too, was wrestling with a question to which there seemed to be no sane answer. His sense of suspense grew until he finally pushed the intercom button in his Engineering section.

"Spock here, Mr. Scott."

"Mr. Spock, the ship feels wrong."

"*Feels,* Mr. Scott?"

Both troubled and embarrassed, Scott fumbled for words. "I—I know it doesn't . . . make sense, sir. Instrumentation reads correct—but the *feel* is wrong. It's something I . . . don't know how to say . . ."

"Obviously, Mr. Scott. I suggest you avoid emotionalism and simply keep your readings 'correct'. Spock out."

But he hesitated just the same. Finally, he crossed over to his sensor board.

Down in Engineering, Scott, frowning, studied his control panel before turning to an assistant. "Watkins, check the bypass valves for the matter-anti-matter reaction chamber. Be sure there's no overheating."

"But, Mr. Scott, the board shows—"

"I didn't ask you to check the board, lad!"

"Yes, sir." Watkins wiped smudge off his hands. Then, crossing the engine room, he entered the small alcove that housed the matter-anti-matter reaction-control unit. He was nearing its display panel when he saw the woman standing in the corner. Startled, he said, "Who are you? What are you doing here?"

She smiled a little sadly. "My name is not important. Yours is Watkins, John B. Engineer, grade four."

He eyed her. "You seem to know all about me. Very flattering. What department are you? I've never seen that uniform."

"Show me this unit, please. I wish to learn."

Suspicion tightened in him. He covered it quickly. "This is the matter-anti-matter integrator control. That's the cutoff switch."

"Incorrect," she said. "On the contrary, that is the emergency overload bypass valve which engages almost instantaneously. A wise precaution."

Frightened now, Watkins backed away from her until he was stopped by the mass of the machine. She was smiling the sad little smile again.

"Wise," she said, "considering the fact it takes the anti-matter nacelles little longer to explode once the magnetic valves fail." She paused. "I'm for you, Mr. Watkins."

"Watkins! What's taking you so long?" Scott shouted.

The woman extended a hand as though to repress his reply. But Watkins yelled, "Sir, there's a strange woman here who knows the entire plan of the ship!"

Scott had raced across the Engine Room to the reaction chamber. "Watkins, what the de'il—?" As he rushed in, the woman, backed against a wall, suddenly seemed to flip sideways, her image a thin, two-dimensional line. Then she vanished.

Scott looked down at the alcove's floor. His look of annoyance changed to one of shock. "Poor, poor laddie," he whispered. Then he was stumbling to the nearest intercom button. "Scott to bridge," he said, his voice shaking.

"Spock here, Mr. Scott."

"My engineering assistant is dead, sir."

There was a pause before Spock said, "Do you know how he died, Mr. Scott?"

The quiet voice steadied Scott. "I didn't see it happen. His last words . . . warned about some strange woman . . ."

Spock reached for his loud speaker. "Security alert! All decks! Woman intruder! Extremely dangerous!"

Sulu had finally managed to identify the basic material of the planet. Looking up from his tricorder, he said, "It's an alloy, Captain. Diburnium and osmium. It could not have evolved naturally."

Kirk nodded. "Aside from momentary fluctuations on our instruments, this planet has no magnetic field. And the age of this rock adds up to only a few million years. In that time no known process could have evolved its kind of plant life."

"Jim, are you suggesting that this is an artificial planet?"

"If it's artificial," Sulu said, "where are the people who made it? Why don't we see them?"

"It could be hollow," Kirk told him. "Or they could be shielded against our sensor probes." He looked around him at the somber landscape. "It's getting dark; get some rest. In the morning we'll have to find water and food quickly—or we're in for a very unpleasant stay."

"While the stay lasts," McCoy said grimly.

"Sir, I'll take the first watch."

"Right, Mr. Sulu. Set D'Amato's tricorder for automatic distress on the chance that a spaceship might come by." He stretched out on the ground and McCoy crouched down beside him.

"Jim, if the creators of this planet were going to live inside it, why would they bother to make an atmosphere and evolve plant life on its surface?"

"Bones, get some rest."

McCoy nodded glumly.

Spock wasn't feeling so cheerful, either. Though Sickbay had reported the cellular disruption of Watkins's body to be the same that had killed the Transporter Ensign, its doctors could not account for its cause. "My guess is as good as yours," M'Benga had told him.

Guesses, Spock thought, when what is needed are facts. He spoke sharply to M'Benga. "The power of this intruder to disrupt every cell in a body . . . combined with the almost inconceivable power to hurl the *Enterprise* such a distance, speak of a very high culture—and a very great danger."

Scott spoke. "You mean one of the people who threw us a thousand light years away from that planet is on board this ship, killing our crew?"

"That would be the reasonable assumption, Mr. Scott."

Scott pondered. "Yes. Watkins must have been murdered." He paused. "I'd sent him to check the matter-anti-matter reactor. There are no exposed circuits there. It can't have been anything he touched."

"If there are more of those beings on that planet, Mr. Scott, the Captain and the others are in very grave danger."

Danger. Kirk stirred restlessly in his sleep. Near him the tricorder beeped its steady distress signal. Sulu, on guard, shoulders hunched against the cold, felt the ground under him begin to tremble. The strange light flared through the dark. Kirk and McCoy sat up.

"Lieutenant Sulu?"

"It's all right, Captain. Just another one of those quakes."

"What was that light?" McCoy said.

"Lightning, probably. Get some rest, sir."

They lay back. Sulu got up to peer into the darkness around him, patrolling a wider circle. He approached the beeping tricorder, looked down at it, and was moving on when the signal stopped. Sulu whirled—and saw the woman. He went for his phaser, pulling it in one swift movement.

"I am unarmed, Mr. Sulu," she said.

Hand on phaser, he advanced toward her cautiously. She stood perfectly still, her face blurred by the darkness.

"Who are you?" he said.

"That is not important. You are Lieutenant Sulu; you were born on the planet Earth—and you are helmsman of the *Enterprise.*"

"Where did you get that information?" he demanded. "Do you live on this planet?"

"I am from here."

Then the planet *was* hollow. Rage suddenly shook him. "Who killed Lieutenant D'Amato?"

She didn't speak, and Sulu snapped, "All right! My Captain will want to talk to you!" He gestured with his phaser. "That way. Move!"

The melodious voice said, "You do not understand. I have come to you."

"What do you want?"

"To—touch you . . ."

He was in no mood for her touching. "One of our men has been killed! We are marooned here—and our ship has disappeared!" Her features were growing clearer. "You—I recognize you! You were in the *Enterprise!*"

"Not I. Another." She started toward him.

"Keep back!"

But she continued her move to him. He lifted his phaser. "Stop! Or I'll fire!"

She maintained her approach. "Stop!" he cried. "I don't want to kill a woman!"

She was close to him now. He fired, vaporizing the ground before her. She still came on. Sulu turned his phaser to full charge—and fired again. The beam struck her, but made no more impression on her than it had made on the rock. He backed away, but stumbled over a stone behind him. The phaser skittered across the hard surface of the planet. He scrambled up—but she was on top of him, her hand on his shoulder. He leaped clear, screaming in agony. Then he fell to the ground, his face contorted, screams tearing from his throat. The woman reached for him, her arms outstretched.

"*Hold it!*"

Kirk, phaser aimed, had interposed himself between them. The woman hesitated, startled.

"Who are you?" Kirk snapped.

"I am for Lieutenant Sulu."

Sulu was clutching his shoulder, groaning. "Phasers won't stop her,

Captain . . . don't let her touch you . . . it's how D'Amato died. It's
. . . like being blown apart . . ."

The woman moved to go around Kirk. Again, he blocked her way to
Sulu. "Please," she said. "I must. I am for Lieutenant Sulu."

McCoy had joined them. "She's mad!" he cried.

"Bones, take care of Sulu." Kirk eyed the woman, her dark loveliness, her misty, dreamlike state. He had to fight his mounting horror as
he recognized her. "Please, please," she said again. "I must touch him."

Once more she advanced—and once more Kirk shielded Sulu with his
body. They collided. Her outstretched arms were around his neck. He
felt nothing but revulsion. Shoving her away, he said, "Why can you destroy others—and not me?"

She looked at him, her eyes tortured. "I don't want to destroy. I don't
want to . . ."

"Who are you? Why are you trying to kill us?"

"Only Sulu. I wish you no harm, Kirk. We are—much alike. Under
the circumstances—" She broke off.

"Are there men on this planet?" Kirk demanded.

"I must touch him."

"No."

She stepped back. Then she flipped sideways, leaving only a line that
thinned—and disappeared.

Kirk stared at the empty space. "Did you see that, Bones? Is this a
ghost planet?"

"All I know is that thing almost made a ghost of Sulu! His shoulder
where she touched him—its cells are disrupted, exploded from within. If
she'd got a good grip . . ."

"Why? It's true we must seem like intruders here, but if she reads our
minds, she must know we mean no harm. Why the killing, Bones?"

Sulu looked up at him. "Captain, how can such people be? Such evil?
And she's—she's so beautiful . . ."

"Yes," he said slowly. "I noticed . . ."

Spock had changed the red alert to an increase of security guards.
Sweep after sweep had failed to show evidence of any intruder. Uhura,
bewildered, turned to him.

"But how did she get off the ship, Mr. Spock?"

"Presumably the same way she got on, Lieutenant."

"Yes, sir." She spoke again, anxiously. "Mr. Spock, what are the
chances of the Captain and the others being alive?"

"We're not engaged in gambling, Lieutenant. We are proceeding in the logical way to return as fast as possible to the place they were last seen. It is the reasonable method to ascertain whether or not they are still alive."

Radha spoke from where she was monitoring her station's instruments. "Mr. Spock, speed is increased to warp eight point eight."

He crossed hastily to the command chair. "Bridge to Engineering," he said into the intercom.

"Scott here, sir. I see it. It's a power surge. I'm working on it. Suggest we reduce speed until we locate the trouble."

"Very well Mr. Scott." He turned to Radha. "Reduce speed to warp seven."

"Aye, sir. Warp seven." Then, as she looked at her board, her eyes widened. "Mr. Spock! Our speed has increased to warp eight point nine and still climbing!"

Spock pushed the intercom button. "Bridge to Scott. Negative effect on power reduction, Mr. Scott. Speed is still increasing."

Scott, down in the matter-anti-matter reaction chamber, looked at the unit that had witnessed Watkins's death. "Aye, Mr. Spock," he said slowly. "And I've found out why. The emergency bypass control valve for the matter-anti-matter integrator is fused—completely useless. The engines are running wild. There's no way to get at them. We should reach maximum overload in fifteen minutes."

Spock said, "I calculate fourteen point eight seven minutes, Mr. Scott."

The voice from Engineering had desperation in it. "Those few seconds won't make much difference, sir. Because you, I, and the rest of this crew will no longer be here to argue about it. This ship is going to blow up and nothing in the universe can stop it."

Around Spock, faces had gone blank with shock.

Sulu's pain had begun to ease. McCoy, still working on his shoulder, looked up at Kirk. "There's a layer of necrotic tissue, subcutaneous, a few cells thick. A normal wound should heal quickly. But if it isn't, if this is an infection . . ."

"You mean your viruses?" Kirk said.

"It couldn't be! Not so quickly!"

"She just touched me, sir," Sulu said. "How could it happen so fast?"

"She touched the Transporter Ensign. He collapsed immediately. Then she got to D'Amato and we saw what happened to him." Kirk looked down at Sulu. "Why are you alive, Lieutenant?"

"Captain, I'm very grateful for the way it turned out. Thank you for all you did."

"Jim, what kind of power do they wield, anyway?"

"The power, apparently, to totally disrupt biological cell structure."

"Why didn't she kill you?"

"She's not through yet, Bones."

Spock had joined Scott in the matter-anti-matter chamber. As the Engineer rose from another examination of the unit, he shook his head. "It's useless. There's no question it was deliberate."

"Sabotage," Spock said.

"Aye—and a thorough job. The system's foolproof. Whoever killed Watkins sabotaged this."

"You said it's been fused, Mr. Scott. How?"

"That's what worries me. It's fused all right—but it would take the power of the ship's main phaser banks to have done it."

"Interesting," Spock mused.

"I find nothing interesting in the fact we're about to blow up, sir!" Scott was glaring at Spock.

The Vulcan didn't appear to notice it. "No," he agreed mildly. "But the *method* is extremely interesting, Mr. Scott."

"Whoever did this must still be loose in the ship! I fail to understand why you canceled the red alert."

"A force able to fling us a thousand light years away and yet manage to sabotage our main energy source will not be waiting around to be taken into custody." He put the result of his silent musings into words. "As I recall the pattern of fuel flow, there is an access tube, is there not, that leads into the matter-anti-matter reaction chamber?"

"Aye," Scott said grudgingly. "There's a service crawlway. But it's not meant to be used while the integrator operates."

"However, it's there," Spock said. "It might be possible to shut off the flow at that point."

Scott exploded. "With what? Bare hands?"

"No, Mr. Scott. With a magnetic probe."

"Any matter that comes into contact with the anti-matter triggers the explosion. I'm not even sure a man could live in the crawlway—in the energy stream of the magnetic field that bottles up the anti-matter."

"I shall try," Spock said.

"You'd be killed, man!"

"That fate awaits all of us unless a solution can be found very quickly."

Scott stared at him with mingled admiration and annoyance. There
was a pause. Then he said, "Aye, you're right. We've nothing to lose.
But *I'll* do it, Mr. Spock. I know every millimeter of the system. I'll do
whatever must be done."

"Very well, Mr. Scott. You spoke, I remember, of the 'feel' of the
ship being 'wrong'."

"It was an emotional statement. I don't expect you to understand it,
Mr. Spock."

"I hear, Mr. Scott, without necessarily understanding. It is my intention to put an analysis through the ship's computers comparing the present condition of the *Enterprise* with her ideal condition."

"We've no time for that!"

"We have twelve minutes and twenty-seven seconds. I suggest you do
what you can in the service crawlway while I return to the bridge to
make the computer study."

Scott's harassed eyes followed him as he left. Shaking his head, he
turned to several crewmen. "Lads, come with me."

They followed him quickly.

Down on the planet Kirk had also indulged some musings. As he
watched McCoy check Sulu again, he said, "If this planet is hollow—if
there are cities and power sources under the surface, there should be en-
trances. We'll do our exploring together. Lieutenant Sulu, do you feel
strong enough to move now?"

"I feel fine, Captain."

"Is he, Bones?"

"He's back in one piece again."

"Whatever destructive power that woman has is aimed at a specific
person at a specific time. If I'm correct, when she appears again, the
other two of us may be able to protect the one she's after. And simply by
intruding our bodies between her and her victim. No weapons affect
her."

"But how does she know about us, Captain? She knew my name, my
rank—even the name of the ship! She must read our minds—" Sulu
broke off at the sound of a whining noise that rose rapidly in pitch.
"Captain! That's a phaser on overload!"

But Kirk had already whipped his weapon from his belt. "The control's fused," he said. "Drop."

Sulu and McCoy hit the ground. Kirk, flinging his phaser away with
the full force of his strength, also fell flat, his arms shielding his head.
They acted just in time. There was an ear-splitting roar of explosion.

Debris rained down on them. Then it was over. Kirk got to his feet, looking around him.

"That answers our question," he said. "She *does* read our minds. Let's go . . ."

The crawlway was dark and narrow. Scott, two of his men, beside him, peered up through it. "All right," he said. "Help me up into it." Wriggling through the cramped space, a corner faced him. He edged around it, the heat of the energy stream meeting him. It flowed over him, enveloping him in a dim glow. He spoke into the open communicator beside him, his voice muffled. "Scott to bridge."

"Go ahead, Mr. Scott."

"I've sealed off the aft end of the crawlway. And I've positioned explosive separator charges so you can blow me clear of the ship if I rupture the magnetic bottle. I'm so close to it now that the flow around me feels like ants crawling all over my body."

"Mr. Scott, I suggest you do not engage in any further subjective descriptions. You have precisely ten minutes and nineteen seconds to perform your task."

Radha turned from her console. "Mr. Spock, we're at warp eleven point two and accelerating."

From the crawlway, Scott said, "I heard that. The ship's not structured to take that speed for any length of time."

"Mr. Scott, you now have ten minutes, ten seconds."

The hot glow in the crawlway was enervating. Every inch of Scott's body was tingling. "All right, Mr. Spock, I'm not opening the access panel to the magnetic flow valve itself. Keep your eye on that dial. If there's a jump in magnetic flow, you must jettison me. The safety control can't hold more than two seconds after rupture of the magnetic field."

"I am aware of these facts, Mr. Scott. Please get on with the job."

Spock had moved to his station, twisting dials. Now, pushing the computer button, he said, "Computer."

The metallic voice said, "Working."

"Analysis on comparison coordinates."

Three clicks came in succession before the computer said, "Unable to comply. Comparison coordinates too complex for immediate readout. Will advise upon completion."

Scott spoke again. "I've removed the access plate and I've got static electric charges dancing along the instruments. It looks like the aurora borealis in here."

Spock turned to Uhura. "You're monitoring the magnetic force?"
"Yes, sir."
"Don't take your eyes off it." His quiet face showed no sign of strain.
"Lieutenant Radha, arm the pod jettison system."
"Aye, sir." She moved a toggle. "I'll jettison the pod at the first sign of trouble."
"Only on my order!" Spock snapped.
"Yes, sir. Warp eleven point nine now."
Spock used the intercom. "Mr. Scott, what's your situation?"
In the access tube, sparks were flying from all the metal surfaces. Scott himself seemed encompassed by a nimbus of flowing flames. "It's hard to see. There's so much disturbance I'm afraid any attempt to get at the flow valve will interrupt the magnetic shield."
"You have eight minutes forty-one seconds."
To himself, Scott muttered, "I know what time it is. I don't need a bloody cuckoo clock."

The three on the planet had reached a plateau of the red rock. They paused for rest; checking his tricorder, Sulu cried, "Captain! There's that strange magnetic sweep again! From zero to off the scale and then—"
"Like a door opening . . ." Kirk muttered.
From behind a jutting rock stepped the woman, the dreamy smile on her lovely mouth.
"And who have you come for this time?" Kirk said.
"For you, James T. Kirk, Captain of the *Enterprise.*"
McCoy and Sulu stepped quickly in front of Kirk. "Keep behind us, Jim!" McCoy shouted.
She was standing quite still, her short, flowing garment clinging to the lines of her slim body.
Kirk spoke over McCoy's shoulder. "Why do you want to kill me?"
"You are an invader."
She moved forward and he spoke again. "We're here on a peaceful mission. We have not harmed you. Yet you have killed our people."
McCoy had his tricorder focused on her. Reading it, he said amazedly, "Jim, I get no life reading from her!"
"An android," Sulu said.
"That would give a mechanical reading. I get nothing."
Warily maintaining his place behind his men, Kirk said, "Who are you?"
"Commander Losira."

"Commander of what?"

"This base," she said.

Kirk studied her exquisite features. "You are very beautiful, Losira. You—appeal to me."

Stunned, McCoy and Sulu turned their heads to stare at him. The woman trembled slightly. Kirk noted it with satisfaction. "Do I appeal to you, Losira?"

She lowered her dark eyes. "At another time we might have—" She broke off.

"How do you feel about killing me?" Kirk said.

The eyelids lifted and her head came up. "Feel?" she asked. Then, very slowly, she added, "Killing is wrong." But nevertheless, she took another step forward. "You must not penetrate this station." Her arms stretched out. "Kirk, I must—touch you."

Behind his shielding two men, Kirk was frantically working at his tricorder. Where was the door? She must have emerged from somewhere! But as he worked, he talked. "You want to kill me?"

She stopped her advance, confused. "You *don't* want to," he said. "Then why do you do it if you don't want to?"

"I am sent," she said.

"By whom?"

"We defend this place."

"Where are the others?"

"No more." Abruptly, determination seemed to possess her again. She ran to them, arms out, struggling to get past McCoy and Sulu. They remained, immovable before Kirk, her touch leaving them unaffected.

"How long have you been alone?" Kirk said.

Her arms dropped. A look of depthless sorrow came over her face. Then, turning sideways, she was a line that vanished in a flash of light.

"Where did she go?" McCoy cried. "She must be somewhere!"

"She isn't registering," Sulu said. "But there's that power surge again on my tricorder! Right off the scale! The place must be near here."

"Like a door . . . closing," Kirk said. He moved forward toward a big, distant, red rock.

The bridge chronometer was marking the swiftly passing seconds. Spock left the helm position to hit his computer button. "Computer readout," he said.

"Comparison analysis complete."

"Continue."

"Transporter factor M-7. Reassembled outphase point zero, zero, zero, nine."

Spock's eyebrows arched in astonishment; and Radha called, "Fifty-seven seconds to go, sir."

"Understood," Spock said. Radha watched him unhurriedly study the readout—and had to struggle for calm. Nor did he raise his head from his view box when Scott's blurred voice came from the intercom. "Mr. Spock."

"Spock here, Mr. Scott."

In the crawlway sweat beaded Scott's forehead. Vari-colored light played over his face as he cautiously eased two complex instruments toward the access hatch. "I'm going to try to cut through the magnetic valve. But if the probe doesn't exactly match the flow, there'll be an explosion—starting now." He crept forward with agonizing care.

Radha, her face drawn with strain, had poised her finger ready to activate the jettison button. Uhura cried, "Mr. Spock, magnetic force indicator's jumping!"

Spock came out of his scope. "Mr. Scott, ease off," he said.

As Scott withdrew his instruments, the tempo of light fluctuation slowed. Uhura, eyes on her console, said, "Magnetic force back to normal, sir."

Radha, with forced composure, spoke. "Warp thirteen point two, Mr. Spock."

If he heard, he gave no sign. "Computer, for outphase condition, will reversed field achieve closure?"

"Affirmative if M-7 factor maintained."

Spock struck the intercom. "Mr. Scott, reverse polarity in your magnetic probe."

"Reverse polarity?"

"That is correct, Mr. Scott."

"But that'll take a bit of doing and what purpose—?"

"Get started, Mr. Scott. I shall explain. You were right in your 'feel'. The *Enterprise* was put through a molecular transporter. Then it was reassembled slightly out of phase. Reversed polarity should seal the incision."

"I've no time for theory, but I hope you're right."

Radha said, "Fifteen seconds, Mr. Spock."

In the crawlway Scott heard her. "I'm doing the best I can. Wait—it's stuck." He struggled frantically with the magnetic probe, the sweat dropping into his eyes.

"Ten seconds," Radha said.

"I'm stuck," Scott said. "Blast me loose."

"Keep working, Mr. Scott."

"Don't be a fool, Spock. It's your last chance. Push that jettison button. Don't be sentimental. Push it. I'm going to die, anyway."

"Stop talking," Spock said. "Work."

Scott retrieved the probe. The control came free. He shoved it quickly into the access hatch. "It's loose now. But there's no time. Press the button." Lights flared wildly around him as the probe sank deeper into its hole.

Spock was at Radha's station. The needle on her dial had climbed to warp fourteen point one. Uhura, looking across at him, said, "Magnetic force meter is steady, sir."

As she spoke, the needle on Radha's dial had sunk to warp thirteen. It continued to drop. Spock flipped the intercom. "Mr. Scott, you have accomplished your purpose."

Scott disengaged the magnetic probe. Then his head fell on the hot metal of the tube. "You might at least say thank you, Mr. Spock."

Spock was genuinely astounded. "For what purpose, Mr. Scott? What is it in you that requires an overwhelming display of emotion in a situation such as this? Two men pursue their only reasonable course—and you clearly seem to feel something more is necessary. What?"

"Never mind," Scott said wearily. "I'm sorry I brought it up."

The three stranded *Enterprise* men were nearing the big, red rock. And the readings on Sulu's tricorder still showed off the scale beyond their peak. Kirk approached the rock. "That closed door," he said, "must be right here."

They all shoved their shoulders against the rock. It didn't move. Panting, McCoy said, "If that's a closed door, it intends to stay closed."

The rock of itself slid to one side. It revealed a door that suddenly telescoped and drew upward. They stood in silence for a moment, peering inward.

"You think it's an invitation to go in?" McCoy said.

"If it is," Sulu said, "it's one that doesn't exactly relax me."

"The elevator door on the *Enterprise* bridge would be certainly preferable," Kirk agreed. "But whatever civilization exists on this planet is in there. And without the ship, gentlemen, in there is our sole source of food and water."

Following his lead, they cautiously moved through the doorway. It gave onto a large chamber. Athwart its entrance was a huge translucent cube. Pulsing in a thousand colors, lights flashed across its surfaces.

"What is it?" Kirk said. "Does it house the brain that operates this place?" They were studying the cube when, between it and them, the woman appeared, wearing that same look of sadness. She moved toward them slowly.

"Tell us who you are for," Kirk said.

She didn't answer; but her arm rose and her pace increased.

"Form a circle," Kirk said. "Keep moving."

The woman halted. "You see," Kirk said, "you might as well tell us who you're for." He paused. "On the other hand, don't bother. You are still for Kirk."

"I am for James Kirk," she said.

McCoy and Sulu drew together in front of him as he said, "But James Kirk is not for you."

"Let me touch you—I beg it," she said. "It is my existence."

"It is my death," he said.

Her voice was very gentle. "I do not kill," she said.

"No? We have seen the results of your touch."

"But you are my match, James Kirk. I must touch you. Then I will live as your match even to the structure of your cells—the arrangement of chromosomes. I need you."

"That is how you kill. You will never reach me." Even as he spoke, he saw the second woman. Silently, unnoticed, she was moving toward them, arms outstretched. "Watch out!" he shouted.

"I am for McCoy," said the second woman.

Kirk jumped in front of Bones. "They are replicas!" he cried. "The computer there has programmed replicas!"

"They match our chromosome patterns after they touch us!" McCoy shouted.

A third woman, identical in beauty and clothing, slipped into view. "I am for Sulu," she said.

Aghast, the *Enterprise* men stared at each other. "Captain! We can no longer protect each other!"

McCoy said, "We could each make a rush at the other's killer!"

"It's worth a try," Kirk said.

Unhearing, dreamy, their arms extended, the trio of women were nearing them, closing in, closer and closer. Beside them, the air suddenly gathered into shimmer. Armed with phasers, Spock and an *Enterprise* security guard materialized swiftly. They swung their weapons around to cover the women.

"No, Spock!" Kirk yelled. "That cubed computer—destroy it!"

The phasers' beams struck the pulsing cube. There was a blast of iridescent light—and the women vanished. McCoy drew a great gasping sigh of incredulous relief. Kirk turned to Spock. "Mr. Spock, it is an understatement to say I am pleased to see you. I thought you and the *Enterprise* had been destroyed."

Spock holstered his phaser. "I had the same misgivings about you, Captain. We got back close enough to this planet to pick up your life form readings only a moment ago."

"Got back from where, Mr. Spock?"

But Spock was examining the broken cube with obvious admiration. "From where this brain had the power to send the ship . . . a thousand light years across the galaxy. What a magnificent culture this is."

"*Was*, Mr. Spock. Its defenses were run by computer."

Spock nodded. "I surmised that, Captain. Its moves were all immensely logical. But what people created it? Are there any representatives of them?"

"There were replicas of one of them. But now the power to reproduce them has been destroyed. Your phasers—" He stopped. On the blank wall of the chamber Losira's face was gradually forming. The lovely lips opened. "My fellow Kalandans, I greet you."

She went on. "A disease is decimating us. Beware of it. I regret giving you only this recorded warning—but we who have guarded this outpost for you may be dead by the time you hear it."

The voice faded. After a moment it resumed. "In creating this planet, we also created a deadly organism. I have awaited the regular supply ship from our home star with medical assistance, but I am now sickening with the virus myself. I shall set the outpost's controls on automatic. They will defend you against all enemies except the disease. My fellow Kalandans, I wish you well."

"She is wishing the dead well," McCoy said.

Spock had returned to the blasted computer. "It must have projected replicas of the only being available—Losira."

Kirk's eyes were on the dissolving image. "She was—beautiful," he said.

Spock shook his head. "Beauty is transitory, Captain. She was, however, loyal and highly intelligent."

The image on the wall had gone. Kirk opened his communicator. "Kirk to *Enterprise*. Five of us to beam up. By the way, Mr. Spock, I don't agree with you."

"Indeed, Captain?"

In Kirk's mind was the remembered sound of a voice like music, of a dark and lonely loveliness waiting in vain for the salvation of her people. "Beauty survives, Mr. Spock. It survives in the memory of those who beheld it."

Spock stared at him. As they dematerialized, there was a sad little smile on Kirk's lips.

OBSESSION

(Art Wallace)

The ore was peculiar-looking, a harsh purple-black. Kirk struck it with a rock; but apart from its responsive clanging sound, it showed no trace of the blow. As he tossed the rock aside, he said, "Fantastic! It must be twenty times as hard as steel even in its raw state!"

Spock, his tricorder focused on the ore, said, "To be exact, Captain, 21.4 times as hard as the finest manganese steel."

Kirk opened his communicator. "Scotty? You can mark this vein of ore as confirmed. Inform Starfleet I recommend they dispatch a survey vessel to this planet immediately." As he spoke, a puff of white vapor drifted up over the rock matrix of the ore—a whisp of vapor hidden from the *Enterprise* men both by the rock's jutting and obscuring vegetation.

Scott said, "Acknowledged, Captain. They'll send a vessel fast enough for this rich a find."

Spock had pulled his phaser. "We won't be able to break it. I'll shoot off a sample."

Kirk didn't answer. He had stiffened abruptly, frowning, sniffing the air around him, his face strained like that of a man whose past had suddenly shouldered out his present. A shard of rock, grape-purple with the ore, had broken off; and the white vapor, as though guided by some protective intelligence, swiftly withdrew behind the big rock's shelter. As Spock rose from retrieving the ore sample, Kirk spoke. "Notice it?" he said. "A sweetish odor—a smell like honey? I wonder. It was years ago on a different planet . . . a 'thing' with an odor like that."

Some indefinable appeal in his voice moved Spock to say reassuringly, "This is the growing season in the hemisphere of this planet. There are doubtless many forms of pollen aromas around, Captain."

But Kirk was not soothed. He didn't seem to even have heard. Beckoning to the landing party's security officer, he said, "Lieutenant Rizzo, take two men and make a swing around our perimeter. Scan for any gaseous di-kironium in the atmosphere."

"Di-kironium," Spock observed, "does not exist except in laboratory experiments."

Kirk ignored the comment. "Set phasers on Disruptor-B. If you see any gaseous cloud, fire into it instantly. Make your sweep, Lieutenant."

A beep beeped from the open communicator in his hand; and Scott's voice said, "Ready to beam back aboard, sir?"

"Stand by, Scotty. We're checking something out."

"Sir, the U.S.S. *Yorktown* is expecting to rendezvous with us in less than eight hours. Doesn't leave us much time."

"Acknowledged. Continue standing by. Kirk out."

Spock, scanning the ore sample, spoke, his voice flat with awe. "Purity about eighty-five percent, Captain. With enough of this, they'll be building Starships with twice our warp capacity."

But Kirk was sniffing the air again. "Gone," he said. "It's gone now. I could have been wrong. The last time I caught that odor was about twelve years ago." He looked away to where the security officer and his men were quartering the area. Rizzo, standing near a small hillock, was bent over his tricorder. It had suddenly registered di-kironium on the air. Puzzling over it, he didn't see the cloud of white vapor encroaching on them from behind the hillock. "But that isn't possible," Rizzo muttered to himself. "Nothing can do that."

The vaporous cloud, however, seemed to obey laws of its own. One moment it had been wispy, diaphonous; but in the next it had thickened to a dense fog, moving suddenly and swiftly, emitting a humming creature sound.

The scouting party whirled as one man. The coiling colors that had appeared in the cloud reached out a tentacle of green which touched the nearest security man. He grabbed at his throat and fell to the ground. As the second security man gagged, Rizzo pulled his phaser. Where to direct his fire? Into the center of the cloud? Where? He hesitated—and Kirk's communicator beeped.

"Captain . . . cloud," Rizzo choked. "A strange cloud."

"Fire your phasers at its center!" Kirk shouted.

"Sir, we—help!"

"Spock, with me!" yelled Kirk. He raced toward the hillock, his phaser drawn.

But the gaseous cloud was gone. Rizzo lay face down on the grass, his communicator still clutched in his hand. The bodies of his men lay near by. Kirk glanced around before he hurried to Rizzo. The officer was very pale. But where Rizzo's flesh was pale, the bodies of his men were bone-white. Kirk lifted his head. "Dead," he said. "And we'll find every red corpuscle has been drained from their blood."

"At least Rizzo's alive," Spock said. "As you were saying—you suspect what it was, Captain?"

Kirk had taken out his communicator. He nodded. "A 'thing' . . . something that can't possibly exist. Yet which *does exist*." He flipped the communicator open. "Captain to *Enterprise*. Lock in on us, Scotty! Medical emergency!"

He was in Sickbay. It didn't offer much room to pace. So he stood still while Christine Chapel handed the cartridge of tapes to Bones.

"The autopsy reports, Doctor."

"Thank you."

Kirk extended a hand to Christine's arm. "Nurse, how is Lieutenant Rizzo?"

"Still unconscious, Captain."

"Transfusions?" he said.

"Continuing as rapidly as possible, sir. Blood count still less than sixty percent of normal."

Kirk glanced at McCoy. But Bones was still deep in the autopsy reports. Kirk closed his eyes, running a hand over his forehead. Then he crossed to a communicator panel equipped with a small viewing screen.

"Kirk to bridge."

The voice was Spock's. "Ready to leave orbit, sir."

"Hold our position."

The image of Spock was supplanted by Scott's. "Cutting in, if I may, sir. The *Yorktown*'s expecting to rendezvous with us in less than seven hours."

The heat of sudden rage engulfed Kirk. "Then inform them we may be late!"

McCoy turned from his desk. "Jim, the *Yorktown*'s ship surgeon will want to know how late. The vaccines he's transferring to us are highly perishable."

Spock reappeared on the screen. "Sir, those medical supplies are badly needed on planet Theta Seven. They're expecting us to get them there on time."

I am hounded, Kirk thought. He looked from Spock back to McCoy. "Gentlemen," he said, "we are staying here in orbit until I learn more about those deaths. I am quite aware this may cost lives on planet Theta Seven. What lives are lost are my responsibility. Captain out." He switched off the screen, and addressed McCoy. "Autopsy findings?"

"You saw their color," McCoy said. "There wasn't a red corpuscle left in those bodies."

"Cuts? Incisions? Marks of any kind?"

"Not a one. What happened is medically impossible."

Kirk became conscious of a vast impatience with the human race. "I suggest," he said coldly, "that you check our record tapes for similar occurrences in the past before you speak of medical 'impossibilities'. I have in mind the experience of the U.S.S. *Farragut*. Twelve years ago it listed casualties from exactly the same impossible medical causes."

McCoy was eyeing him speculatively. "Thank you, Captain," he said tonelessly. "I'll check those tapes immediately."

"Yes, do," Kirk said. "But before you do, can you bring Lieutenant Rizzo back to consciousness for a moment?"

"Yes, I think so but—"

"Will it hurt him if you do?"

"In his condition it won't make much difference."

"Then bring him out of it," Kirk said. "I must ask him a question."

As they approached Rizzo's bed, Nurse Chapel was removing a small black box that had been strapped to his arm. "Transfusions completed, Doctor," she said. "Pulse and respiration still far from normal."

"Give him one cc. of cordrazine."

The nurse stared. Then picking up a hypodermic, she adjusted it. As it hissed against Rizzo's arm, Kirk's hands tightened on the bed bar until his knuckles whitened. On the pillow he saw the head move slightly. Kirk leaned in over Rizzo. "Lieutenant, this is the Captain. Can you hear me? Do you remember what happened to you?"

The eyelids fluttered. "Remember . . . I'm cold," Rizzo whispered. "So . . . cold."

Kirk pressed on. "Rizzo, you were attacked by something. When it happened, did you notice an odor of any kind?" His hands were shaking on the bed bar. He leaned in closer. "Rizzo, remember. A sickly sweet odor. Did you smell it?"

Horror filled the eyes. "Yes, sir . . . the smell . . . strange . . . like . . . like being smothered in honey."

Kirk exhaled a deep, quivering breath. "And—did you feel a—a *presence?* An intelligence?"

The head moved in assent. "It . . . it wanted strength from us. Yes, I felt it sucking. It was there."

McCoy moved in. "He's asleep. We can't risk another shot, Captain."

"He told me what I wanted to know."

"I wouldn't depend on his answers. In his half-conscious state, he could be dreaming, saying what he thought you wanted to hear."

Kirk straightened. "Check those record tapes, Doctor. I'll want your analysis of them as quickly as possible."

He left; Christine Chapel turned a puzzled face to McCoy. "What's the matter with the Captain, sir? I've never seen him like this."

"I intend to find out," McCoy said. "If I'm wanted, I'll be in the medical library."

On the bridge, Uhura greeted Kirk with a message from Starfleet. To her astonishment, he brushed it aside with a "Later, Lieutenant. Now have the security duty officer report to me here and at once." He crossed to Spock who said, "Continuing scanning, sir. Still no readings of life forms on the planet surface."

"Then, Mr. Spock, let's assume that it's something so totally different that our sensors would fail to identify it as a life form."

"You've mentioned—di-kironium, Captain."

"A rare element, Mr. Spock. Suppose a life form were composed of it, a strange, gaseous creature."

"There is no trace of di-kironium on the planet surface or in the atmosphere. I've scanned for the element, sir."

"Suppose it were able to camouflage itself?"

"Captain, if it were composed of di-kironium, lead, gold, hydrogen—whatever—our sensors would pinpoint it."

"Let's still assume I'm right."

"An illogical assumption, Captain. There is no way to camouflage a given chemical element from a sensor scan."

"No way? Let's further assume it's intelligent and knows we're looking for it."

"Captain, to hide from a sensor scan, it would have to be able to change its molecular structure."

Kirk stared at him. "Like gold changing itself to lead or wood to ivory. Mr. Spock, you've just suggested something which never occurred to me. And it answers some questions in a tape record which I think you'll find Dr. McCoy is studying at this very moment."

Spock was on his feet. "Mr. Chekov! Take over on scanner." He was at the bridge elevator door as it hissed open to permit the entrance of the security duty officer. He was a new member of the crew, young, bright-faced, clearly dedicated as only the untried idealism of youth can dedicate itself. He strode to Kirk and saluted. "Ensign David Garrovick reporting, sir."

Kirk turned, startled. "You're the new security officer?"

"Yes, sir."

Kirk hesitated a moment. Then he said, "Was your father—?"

"Yes, sir. But I don't expect any special treatment on that account."

The shock in Kirk's face subsided. Now he snapped, "You'll get none aboard this ship, mister!"

"Yes, sir."

Uhura broke in. "I have a report on Lieutenant Rizzo, Captain. He's dead."

Kirk leaned back in his chair. It had been costly—the discovery of that so-precious purple ore. He turned back to the new security officer when he realized that Garrovick's face was grief-stricken, too.

"Did you know Rizzo?" Kirk said.

"Yes, sir. We were good friends. Graduated the Academy together."

Kirk nodded. "Want a crack at what killed him?"

"Yes, sir."

"Equip four men with phaser twos set for Disruptor effect. Report to the Transporter Room in five minutes. You will accompany me to the planet surface."

It was Garrovick who took the first tricorder reading of the terrain where the team materialized. Suddenly, he called to Kirk. "Sir, the reading is changing!"

Kirk crossed to him swiftly. Nodding, he examined the tricorder. "Spock was right," he said. "See—there's been a molecular shift."

"A di-kironium reading now, sir. Bearing is 94 mark 7, angle of elevation 6 degrees. Holding stationary."

Kirk pointed to a lift in the ground. "Behind that rise. Take two men and approach it from the right. I'll take two around the other way. As soon as you sight the creature, fire with full phasers. Remember—it's extremely dangerous."

Garrovick looked at the hill nervously. "Yes . . . sir." The words were spoken tightly. Kirk glanced at the tense young face. Then, turning, he said, "Swanson and Bardoli, come with me."

Garrovick and his two men had climbed the rise when he noticed that it fell to a deep gully. His men fanned out past the ravine. Gar-

rovick stood still for a moment, staring down into it. Then, making his
decision, he descended it, moving forward cautiously. Suddenly the
white vapor gathered before him. Startled, taken off-guard by its foglike
appearance, he stared at it, uncertain. Then he aimed his phaser and
fired. The slice of its beam was a second too late. The cloud was gone.

Kirk yelled, "A phaser shot!" Racing toward the hill, he shouted,
"Come on!"

He found Garrovick scrambling up the side of the gully, his eyes fixed
on something ahead of him. "Garrovick, did you—?" He stopped short
as he saw what Garrovick was crawling toward. The two men of his
patrol lay motionless on the ground.

Kirk ran to the nearest one. When Garrovick joined him, his young
face turned smeary with shock and misery. The features that stared up
sightlessly from the ground were bone-white.

Kirk was alone in the Briefing Room. It felt good to be alone. Alone,
it was easier to hold on to his conviction that the murderous creature
which had killed five of his crewmen was the same one that had deci-
mated the crew of the U.S.S. *Farragut* twelve years before in another
quadrant of the galaxy. Five men. Sickbay had the unconscious survivor
of Garrovick's team under treatment; but its transfusion had been unable to save the life of Rizzo. The thing was, he wasn't really alone. You
never were. Always, you had the unspoken thoughts of other people to
companion you. And he had the unspoken thoughts of Spock and
McCoy to keep him company. Neither one credited the creature with its
malignancy nor its intelligence. Moreover, they disapproved his decision
to remain here and fight it to the death. And maybe they were right.
Had he made a reliable command decision—or an emotional one?

He'd laid his forearms on the Briefing Room table. Now he lifted his
head from them as Spock, followed by McCoy and Garrovick, entered.
Spock and McCoy both gave him sharply appraising looks as they sat
down. They tried to appear as though they hadn't—but they had. In his
turn, Kirk tried to appear as though he hadn't noticed the looks.

He opened the session. "We've studied your report, Mr. Garrovick. I
believe Mr. Spock has a question."

Spock said, "What was the size of the creature, Ensign?"

"I'd estimate it measured from ten to sixty cubic meters, sir. It
changed size, fluctuated as it moved."

"Composition?"

"It was like a gaseous cloud, sir. Parts of it I could see through; other
parts seemed more dense."

McCoy spoke. "Ensign, did you 'sense' any intelligence in this gaseous cloud?"

"Did I what, sir?"

"Did you get any subconscious impression that it *was* a creature? A living, thinking thing rather than just a strange cloud of chemical elements?"

"No, sir."

Kirk eyed Garrovick who twisted uncomfortably. "Ensign, you never came into actual contact with it, did you?"

"No, I didn't, sir. I was the furthest away." He paused. "It came out of nowhere, it seemed. It hovered a moment, then moved toward the nearest man. Fast, incredibly fast."

Kirk shoved a pencil on the table. "Did you say it hovered?"

"Yes, sir."

"You fired at it, didn't you?"

"Yes, sir."

"How close were you to the creature?"

"About twenty yards, sir."

"And you missed a hovering, large target at that distance?"

"Yes, sir. I . . . well, I didn't fire while it was hovering."

"Do you mean that you froze?"

"Not exactly, sir."

"Then tell us what you mean exactly."

"I was startled . . . maybe only for a second or so. And then by the time I fired, it—well, it was already moving."

Kirk's tone was curt. "Do you have any additional information for us?"

"No, sir. I only—hesitated for a second or so, sir. I'm sorry."

"Ensign, you're relieved of all duties and confined to your quarters until further notice."

Garrovick straightened. "Yes, sir."

McCoy's eyes followed him to the closing door. "You were a little hard on him, Jim."

"He froze. One of his men was killed. The other will probably die."

"Captain," Spock began.

Kirk rose. "You'll both be filing reports, gentlemen. Make your comments and recommendations then." He crossed briskly to the door. As he slammed it behind him, McCoy and Spock were left to stare at each other.

Garrovick's room was as dark as his discouragement. He found the light switch affixed to its panel with its labeled temperature gauges and other controls. Above the panel was an open-close switch marked "Ventilation Filter By-Pass." Garrovick, closing his eyes to all circumstances of his surroundings, gave himself up to his depression.

Back on the bridge, Kirk was greeted by another message from the *Yorktown* requesting information on the rendezvous. He ignored it; and Scott, approaching him, said, "While we wait, Captain, I've taken the liberty of cleaning the radioactive disposal vent on the number-two impulse engine. But we'll be ready to leave orbit in under half an hour."

"We're not leaving orbit, Engineer. Not that quickly."

Scott didn't take the hint. "The medicine for the Theta Seven colony is not only desperately needed, Captain, but has a limited stability. And—"

Kirk wheeled. "I am," he said, "familiar with the situation, Engineer. And I'm getting a little tired of my officers conspiring against me to force—" He broke off at the look on Scott's face. "Forgive me, Scotty. I shouldn't have used the word 'conspiring'."

"Agreed, sir."

Kirk strode over to Chekov. "Scanner readings?"

"Nothing, sir. Continuing to scan."

"Mr. Chekov, you're aware it may be able to change its composition? Are you scanning for any unusual movements? Any type of gaseous cloud?"

"We've run a full scanner probe twice, sir."

"*Then do it twenty times if that's what it takes!*"

He barked the words and left the bridge to his shocked personnel.

Garrovick wasn't the only victim of depression. McCoy, viewing an autopsy tape, pulled it out of its slot, controlling an impulse to throw it to the floor. When Spock entered his office, he spoke no word of greeting.

"I hope I'm not disturbing you, Doctor."

"Interrupting another autopsy report is no disturbance, Spock. It's a relief."

"I need your advice," Spock said.

"Then I need a drink," said McCoy.

"I don't follow your reasoning, Doctor."

"*You* want advice from me? You must be kidding."

"I never joke. Perhaps I should rephrase my statement. I require an opinion. There are many aspects of human irrationality I do not yet comprehend. Obsession for one. The persistent, singleminded fixation on one idea."

"Jim and his creature?"

"Precisely. Have you studied the incident involving the U.S.S. *Farragut?*"

"With all these deaths and injuries, I've barely had time to scan them."

"Fortunately, I read fast," Spock said. "To summarize those records, I can inform you, Doctor, that almost half the crew, including the Captain, was annihilated. The Captain's name was Garrovick."

McCoy gave a startled whistle. "The same as our Ensign?"

"His father," Spock said. "I have the *Farragut* file here with me."

"Then there's more," McCoy said.

Spock nodded gravely. "A great deal more. Among the survivors of the disaster was a young officer on one of his first deep-space assignments." He nodded again at McCoy's look. "Yes, James T. Kirk," he said—and dropped the cartridge he held into the viewer. "And there's still more. I think you'd better study this record, Doctor."

Twenty minutes later McCoy sought the quarters of James T. Kirk, formerly of the U.S.S. *Farragut.* There was no response to the buzz at the door. McCoy opened it. "Mind if I come in, Jim?"

Kirk was lying on his bed, staring at the ceiling. He made no move. He spoke no word. Then, with a bound, he was off the bed to flip the switch on the wall communicator. "Kirk to bridge. Scanner report?"

Chekov's filtered voice said, "Continuing scanning, sir. No unusual readings."

"Maintain search. Kirk out." He turned from the communicator and jammed his right fist into his left hand. "It can't just vanish!" he cried.

"Sometimes they do if we're lucky." McCoy sat down. "Monsters come in many forms, Jim. And know what's the greatest monster of them all? Guilt, known or unknown."

Kirk's jaw hardened. "Get to the point."

"Jim . . . a young officer exposed to unknown dangers for the first time is under tremendous emotional stress. We all know how—"

"Ensign Garrovick is a ship command decision, Doctor. You're straying out of your field."

"I was speaking," McCoy said, "of Lieutenant James T. Kirk of the Starship *Farragut.*"

Kirk stared at him. He didn't speak, and McCoy went on. "Twelve years ago you were the young officer at the phaser station when something attacked your ship. According to the tape, this young officer insisted on blaming himself—"

"I delayed my fire at it!"

McCoy spoke sharply. "You had a normal, *human* emotion! *Surprise!* You were startled. You delayed firing for the grand total of perhaps two seconds!"

Kirk's face had grown drawn with remembered anguish. "If I hadn't delayed, the thing would have been destroyed!"

"The ship's exec didn't think so. His log entry is quite clear on the subject. He reported, 'Lieutenant Kirk is a fine officer who performed with uncommon bravery.'"

"I killed nearly two hundred men!"

McCoy's voice was very quiet. "Captain Garrovick was important to you, wasn't he?"

Kirk's shoulders slumped. He sank down on his bed, wringing his hands. "He was my commanding officer from the day I left the Academy. He was one of the finest men I ever knew." He leaped to his feet again. "I could have destroyed it! If I'd fired soon enough that first time . . ."

"You don't know that, Jim! You can't know it! Any more than you can know young Garrovick could have destroyed it."

Kirk's face was wiped clean of all emotions but torture. "I owe it to this ship . . ."

"To be so tormented by a memory . . . Jim, you can't destroy a boy because you see him as yourself as you were twelve years ago. You'll destroy yourself, your brilliant career."

"I've got to kill this thing! Don't ask me how I know that. I just know it."

McCoy eyed Kirk for a long moment. Then he rose and moved to the door, pressing the control that opened it. "Come in, Mr. Spock," he said.

Kirk whirled, crying, "Bones, don't push our friendship past the point that—"

McCoy interrupted. "This is professional, Captain. I am preparing a medical log entry on my estimate of the physical and emotional condition of a Starship's Captain. I require a witness of command rank."

Kirk's eyes swung from one of them to the other. Time—an infinity of it—went by. His voice when he spoke was edged with fury. "Do I understand, Doctor—and you, Commander Spock, that both or either of you believe me unfit or incapacitated?"

Spock said, "Correctly phrased as recommended in the manual, Captain. Our reply as also recommended is: we have noticed in your recent behavior items which, on the surface, seem unusual. We respectfully ask your permission to inquire further and—"

"Blast! Forget the manual!" Kirk shouted. "Ask your questions!"

Imperturbable, Spock said, "The U.S.S. *Yorktown* is now waiting for us at the appointed rendezvous, Captain. It carries perishable drugs which—"

Kirk ran a trembling hand over his forehead. "The news has a familiar ring, Commander."

McCoy said, "They need those vaccines on Theta Seven, Jim. Why are we delaying here?"

"Because I know what I know," Kirk said. "The creature that attacked the *Farragut* twelve years ago is the same—"

"Creature?" Spock said.

"Yes. My report was in the tape. As it attacked us twelve years ago, just as I lost consciousness, I could *feel* the intelligence of the thing; I could sense it thinking, planning."

"You say you could 'sense' its intelligence, Captain. How?" Spock said. "Did it communicate with you?"

McCoy broke in. "You state that it happened just as you lost consciousness. The semi-conscious mind is a tricky thing, Jim. A man can never be sure how much was real, how much was semi-conscious fancy."

"Real or unreal, Bones, it was deadly, lethal."

"No doubt of that," McCoy said.

"And if it *is* the same creature I met twelve years ago on a planet over a thousand light years from here?"

"Obviously, Captain, if it is an intelligent creature, if it is the same one, if therefore it is capable of space travel, it could pose a grave threat to inhabited planets."

"A lot of 'ifs,' Commander, I agree. But in my command judgment they still outweigh other factors. 'Intuition,' however illogical, Commander Spock, is recognized as a command prerogative."

"Jim, we're not trying to gang up on you."

"You haven't, Doctor. You've indicated a proper concern. You've both done your duty. May I be informed now of what medical log entry you intend to make?"

Spock and McCoy exchanged glances. "Jim," McCoy began.

Kirk smiled. "You've been bluffing, gentlemen. I'm calling your bluff."

Spock spoke. "This was totally my idea, Captain. Dr. McCoy's human affection for you makes him completely incapable of—"

McCoy interrupted. *"My affection* for him! I like that! Why, I practically had to sandbag you into this!" He turned to Kirk. "Jim, we were just using this to try and talk some sense into—"

The communicator beeped with the intercom signal. Chekov's excited voice said, "Bridge to Captain! Come in, Captain!"

Kirk was at the grill in a second flat. "Kirk here, Mr. Chekov."

"I have a reading on the—whatever it is, Captain! It's leaving the planet surface and heading into space!"

It was the measure of Kirk's nature that no triumph whatever colored the tone of his orders. "All decks, red alert! Prepare to leave orbit!"

Then he was gone out his door.

Gone out his door on a wild goose chase. Only what Kirk and the *Enterprise* chased through the labyrinths of trackless space was no wild goose. It was subtle as a cobra, swift as a mamba in its flight from the *Enterprise,* leading the Starship ever farther from its meeting with the *Yorktown* and its mission of mercy.

On the bridge they all knew what was at stake. The thing had twice changed its course in a malevolent, deliberate effort to mislead. Kirk was exhilarated past anxiety. But Scott was worried. "Captain, we can't maintain Warp 8 speed much longer. Pressures are approaching a critical point."

"Range, Mr. Chekov?" Kirk said.

"Point zero four light years ahead, sir. Our phasers won't reach it."

Spock spoke. "Captain, we're barely closing on it. We could be pursuing it for days."

"If necessary," Kirk said. He turned. "Do what you can to increase our speed, Mr. Scott."

"Aye, sir."

"Let's see it," Kirk said.

Chekov hit a button. "Magnification twelve, sir. There, sir! Got it on the screen!"

It was moving across the screen like an elongated comet, a coiling vortex floating amidst whirling vapors.

"How do you read it, Mr. Spock?"

"Conflicting data, sir. It seems to be in a borderline state between matter and energy. It can possibly utilize gravitational fields for propulsion."

"You don't find that sophisticated, Mr. Spock?"

"Extremely efficient, Captain." He paused. "Whether it indicates intelligence is another matter."

Chekov had got a red light on his console. "Open hatch on number-two impulse engine, sir. Mr. Scott was doing a clean-up job on it."

"Turn off the alarm," Kirk said. "We won't be using the impulse engines."

Scott turned from his station. "Captain! We can't do it! If we hold this speed, she'll blow up any minute!"

Kirk swallowed the pill of reality. "All right," he said. "Reduce to Warp 6."

In Garrovick's quarters the door buzzer sounded and Christine Chapel entered, carrying a dinner tray.

"Thank you," Garrovick said. "I'm not hungry."

"Dr. McCoy's orders."

"What's happening?" Garrovick said.

"Are we still chasing that thing half across the galaxy? Yes, we are. Has the Captain lost his sense of balance? Maybe. Is the crew about ready to explode? *Positively.* You're lucky to be out of it, Ensign."

Garrovick's voice was acid with bitterness. "Out of it? I *caused* it."

She calmly continued to spread food before him. "You know that's true, don't you?" he said. "If I'd fired my phaser quickly enough back on Argus Ten, none of this would have happened."

"Self-pity is a poor appetizer," she said. "Try the soup instead."

"I don't want it."

"If you don't eat," she told him, "Dr. McCoy will have you hauled down to Sickbay and make me feed you intravenously. I don't want to do that, either." Garrovick feebly returned her smile, nodded in defeat, and began to pick at his food. But it was no good. As the door closed behind her, a burst of frustration overwhelmed him. He dashed a cup of coffee he'd just poured against the wall. It hit the panel. Shattering against the switch of the ventilation filter by-pass, it knocked it to the open position.

At the same moment the strident alarm signal sounded. Kirk's voice came over the communicator. "Battle stations! All decks to battle stations! The enemy is reducing speed! This is not a drill! All decks to battle stations!"

On the bridge Chekov shouted, "It's coming to a full halt, Captain! Magnification one, visual contact!"

Centered on the screen, now only a small object, the strange creature seemed to be pulsating. Kirk said, "Hello, Beautiful." Then he leaned toward Chekov. "Move in closer, Mr. Chekov. Sublight, one quarter speed."

As Chekov manipulated his controls, the bridge elevator door opened; and Garrovick, his face pale with tension, emerged to cross quickly over to Kirk. "Sir, request permission to return to my post."

"Within phaser range now, sir!" cried Chekov.

"Lock phasers on target, Mr. Chekov!"

"Locked on target, sir!"

"Fire main phasers!"

But the fierce energy blips passed directly through the creature. Stunned, Kirk watched in unbelief.

"Phasers ineffectual, Captain!"

"Photon torpedoes, Mr. Chekov! Minimum spread pattern!"

"Minimum pattern ready, sir!"

"Fire!"

The ship lurched slightly. The target emitted a flash of blinding light and the *Enterprise* rocked. Uhura cried, "There—on the screen! It's still coming toward us, sir!"

The vaporous creature was growing larger, denser on the screen. "Deflectors up!" Kirk ordered.

"Deflectors up, sir."

Spock spoke into the awed silence. "The deflectors will not stop it, Captain." He was stooping, intent on his hooded viewer. "I should have guessed this! For the creature to be able to use gravity as a propulsive force, it would have to possess the capacity to flow through our deflector screens!"

"Any way to stop it, Mr. Spock?"

"Negative, Captain. It is able to throw its particles slightly out of time synchronization. It seems to measure our force-field pulsations—and stays a split second in front or behind them."

Chekov said, "Contact in five seconds, sir!"

Kirk hit his intercom button. "All decks, all stations, intruder alert!"

"All vents and hatches secure, sir," Chekov said. "All lights on the board show green—*No! Sir, the number-two impulse hatch! We've got a red light on it!*

Kirk whirled toward the screen. The cloudlike thing was on the ship now. Suddenly, it disappeared.

Scott turned, crying, "Captain! Something has entered through the number-two impulse vent!"

"Negative pressure all ship's vents! Mr. Chekov alert all decks!"

Red lights flashed to the ear-splitting howl of the alarm sirens.

"Well? Reports?"

Though Spock and McCoy sat at the Briefing Room table, it was Scott to whom the questions were directed. He knew it and looked away from Kirk's accusing eyes. "Sir, when it entered through impulse engine-two vent, it attacked two crewmen there before it went into the ventilation system."

"Bones?" Kirk said.

"One man has a bare chance of survival. The other is dead. So you can hang that little price tag to your monster hunt!"

"That's enough, Bones."

"It's *not* enough! You didn't care what happened as long as you could hang your trophy on the wall! Well, it's not *on* the wall, Captain! It's *in* it!"

Scott added his drop of reality to Kirk's cup of self-castigation. "With the ventilation system cut off, sir, we've air for only two hours."

Human beings with a cause, Kirk thought. You must not look to them for mercy. As though to confirm the thought, McCoy said, "I expect things don't look much brighter to the patients on colony Theta Seven."

Only in Spock, the half human, was there mercy. "May I suggest that we no longer belabor the point of whether or not we should have pursued the creature? The matter has become academic. The creature is now pursuing *us*."

"Creature, Mr. Spock?" said McCoy.

"*It turned and attacked, Doctor*. Its method was well considered and intelligent."

Kirk spoke very slowly. "I have no joy in being proved right, gentlemen, believe me. It could have been many light years away from us by now. But, instead, it chose to stop here. Why? Why? Why?"

"I must wait, Captain," Spock said. "Until I can make a closer analysis of the creature."

"We have two hours, Mr. Spock." Kirk turned to Scott. "Try flushing your radioactive waste into the ventilator system. It might cause some discomfort."

"Aye, sir."

McCoy rose with him. He halted at the door. "Jim, sorry about that few minutes ago. Your decision to go after it was right."

The exoneration should have meant something. It didn't. If you weren't companioned by the condemning thoughts of other people, you were companioned by those of your own conscience. Spock spoke. "Captain," he said, "the creature's ability to throw itself out of time, to desynchronize, allows it to be elsewhere in the instant our phrasers strike. There is no basis, then, for your self-recrimination. If you had fired your phaser precisely on time twelve years ago, it would have made no more difference than it did an hour ago. Captain Garrovick would still be dead."

"Theories of guilt, of right or wrong, past and present—I seem to have outgrown them suddenly. Suddenly, Mr. Spock, my sole concern is saving my ship and my crew."

"The fault was not yours, Captain. There was no fault."

Kirk rose. "If you want to play psychoanalyst—and frankly, it's not your role, Spock—do it with Ensign Garrovick. Not me. Thank you." He left the Briefing Room without a backward glance.

Spock took the hint. He buzzed the door of Garrovick's quarters and walked in. Garrovick leaped to his feet.

"You may be seated, Ensign. I wish to talk to you."

The young face was puzzled. "Yes, sir."

"Ensign, am I correct in my assumption that you have been disturbed by what you consider a failure to behave in the prescribed manner in a moment of stress?"

Garrovick flushed painfully. "Well, I haven't been exactly proud of myself, sir."

"Perhaps you have considered this so-called failure of yours only from the standpoint of your own emotions."

Garrovick shook his head. "No, sir. I've considered the facts, too. And the facts are that men under my command died because I hesitated, because I stopped to analyze instead of acting. My attempt to be logical killed my men, Mr. Spock."

"Ensign, self-intolerance is an hereditary trait of your species."

"You make it sound like a disease, sir."

Their eyes, fixed on each other, failed to note the slight wisp of vapor that was filtering out of the jammed ventilator opening. Garrovick made a gesture of impatience. "You're telling me, 'Don't worry about it, Ensign! It happens to all of us. We'll just bury the bodies and won't think about them any more.' Isn't that it, Mr. Spock?"

"Not quite. You can learn from remorse, Ensign. It changes the human constitution. But guilt is a waste of time. Hate of the self, always undeserved, will ultimately crush you."

Spock paused suddenly, sniffing the air. "Do you smell anything?" he asked. "I thought I scented—" Then he saw the trail of mist drifting from the ventilator.

Garrovick whirled toward it. "Sir, it's the . . ."

Spock, grabbing his arm, propelled him to the door. "Out of here—fast! I will attempt to seal it off!"

He rushed to the ventilator opening. Seizing the jammed switch, he struggled to close it. But the cloud, full and dense now, was pouring into the room, over him, around him, and finally completely obscuring him.

In the corridor Garrovick raced to a wall communicator. "Captain! The creature! It's in my cabin, sir! It's got Mr. Spock!"

Kirk leaped from his chair. "On my way, Garrovick!" He dropped his speaker. "Scotty, reverse pressure, Cabin 341! Lieutenant Uhura, Security to 341! Medical alert!"

He'd given the right orders. In Garrovick's quarters, the creature, pulled by the suction of reversed pressure, was drawn back into the ventilator opening. McCoy, with a Security team, met him outside the door. As McCoy reached to open it, Kirk said, "Wait, Bones! We need a tricorder reading!"

As a guard adjusted his instrument, McCoy cried out, "Jim, Spock may be dying!"

Kirk whirled. "If we release that thing into the ship, he'll have a lot of company!"

Garrovick, ashen, spoke. "It's my fault, sir. I must have jammed the vent control when I hit a cup against it."

Kirk spoke to the guard. "Check if the reverse pressure has pulled it back into the ventilation system!"

"He saved my life, sir," Garrovick said brokenly. "I should be lying dead in there, not him."

Spock's voice came through the door. "I am gratified that neither of us is dead, Ensign." He flung the door open. "The reverse pressure worked, Captain. The vent is closed."

Stunned, Kirk stared at him. "Spock, don't misunderstand my question—but why aren't you dead?"

"That green blood of his!" shouted McCoy.

Spock nodded. "My hemoglobin is based on copper, not iron."

Kirk had moved to the cabin door, sniffing at it. "The scent—it's different. Yes . . . Yes, I think I understand now."

"You don't really believe you're in communication with the creature, Captain?"

"I'm not sure what it is, Spock. But you remember I said I knew it was alive. Perhaps it's not communication as we understand it, but I did know it was alive and intelligent. Now I know something else."

The wall communicator beeped. "Bridge to Captain Kirk."

Kirk flipped the switch. "Kirk here."

"Scott, sir. The creature's moving back toward the number-two impulse vent. The radioactive flushing may be affecting it."

"Open the vent," Kirk said. "On my way. Kirk out." He was running down the corridor when he hesitated and turned back. "Ensign Garrovick!"

Garrovick hastened to him. "Yes, sir?"

"You were on the bridge when we were attacked."

"I'm sorry, sir. I know I'd been confined to quarters, but when the alert sounded for battle stations, I . . ."

"Very commendable, Ensign. What was your impression of the battle?"

"I don't understand, sir."

"I'm asking for your military appraisal of the techniques employed against the creature."

Garrovick's jaw firmed. "Ineffective, sir." He added hastily, "I mean, Captain, you did everything possible. It's just that nothing works against a monster that can do what that thing does."

"And what's your appraisal of your conduct back on the planet?"

"I delayed firing."

"And if you had fired on time?" Kirk waited, his eyes on Garrovick's eyes. "It would have made no difference, Ensign. No weapon known would have made any difference. Then—or twelve years ago."

"Pardon, sir? I don't understand."

"I said, return to duty, Mr. Garrovick."

Joy flooded the young face. "Yes, sir. Thank you, Captain."

He was about to add something, but the elevator doors had already closed on Kirk.

There was news awaiting him on the bridge. Chekov, moving aside to surrender Spock's station to him, spoke eagerly. "Results positive, Captain. The creature has left the ship at high warp speed and is already out of scanner range."

Kirk had joined Spock at his station. "Direction, Mr. Spock?"

"Bearing was 127, mark 9. But I've already lost it now, sir."

Kirk switched on the intercom. "Scotty. I'm going to want all the speed you can deliver. Stick with it until we begin to shake apart. Kirk out." He turned to Spock. "I believe I know where it's going."

"It has changed course before to mislead us, sir. Logic would dictate that—"

"I'm playing intuition instead of logic, Mr. Spock. Mr. Chekov, compute a course for the Tychos Star System."

Heads snapped around. Controlling his surprise, Chekov punched in the course. "Computed and on the board, sir."

"Ahead full."

"Ahead full, sir."

"Lieutenant Uhura, contact the U.S.S. *Yorktown* and Starfleet. Inform both that we're pursuing the creature to planet 4 of that System. It's the location of its attack on the U.S.S. *Farragut* twelve years ago."

Spock said, "I don't understand, Captain."

"Remember when I said that the scent of the creature was somehow different? Something in my mind then said, 'birth . . . divide . . . multiply.' It said 'home'."

Spock's eyebrows went up. "And you know where 'home' is, Captain?"

"Yes. Home is where it fought a Starship once before. Lieutenant Uhura, give them our tactical situation. Tell them that I am committing this vessel to the creature's destruction. We will rendezvous with the *Yorktown*—" He turned to Chekov. "Round trip, Mr. Chekov?"

"One point seven days, sir."

"Lieutenant Uhura, we will rendezvous with the *Yorktown* in forty-eight hours."

Planet 4 of the Tychos Star System was a strangely dull, lifeless-looking one. On the bridge McCoy eyed its viewer image with distaste. He spoke to Spock. "I assume you also think we should pursue this creature and destroy it."

"Definitely, Doctor."

"You don't agree with us, Bones?"

McCoy shrugged. "It's a mother. I don't happen to enjoy destroying mothers."

Spock said, "If the creature is about to spawn, it will undoubtedly reproduce by fission, not just in two parts but thousands."

Kirk glanced at him. "Anti-matter seems to be our only possibility then."

Spock nodded. "An ounce should be sufficient. We can drain it out of our engines, transport it to the planet in a magnetic vacuum field."

Garrovick had taken up a position beside Kirk's chair. "Ensign, contact medical stores. I want as much hemoplasm as they can spare. And I want it in the Transporter Room in fifteen minutes."

"Yes, sir."

"You intend to use the hemoplasm to attract the creature?" McCoy asked.

"We have to lure it to the anti-matter. As it's attracted by red blood cells, what better bait can we have?"

"There remains one problem, Captain."

Kirk nodded at Spock. "The blast."

"Exactly. A matter-anti-matter blast will rip half the planet's atmosphere away. If our ship is still in orbit, and encounters those—shock waves . . ."

"We'll have to take that chance."

Spock said, "No one can guarantee our Transporter will operate under such conditions. If a man is beaming up when that blast hits, we may lose him, Captain."

Garrovick who had returned was listening intently. He flushed as Kirk said, "That's why I've decided to set the trap myself, Mr. Spock."

Spock got up. "Captain, I have so little hemoglobin in my blood the creature would not be able to harm me extensively. It would seem logical for me to be the one who—"

"Negative, Mr. Spock. I want you on board in case this fails. In that case another plan will have to be devised."

"Captain," Spock persisted, "it will require two men to transport the anti-matter unit."

"Sir," Garrovick said. "Sir, I request permission to go with you."

Kirk regarded him speculatively. Then he nodded. "Yes," he said. "I had you in mind, Mr. Garrovick."

Desolation—a brittle world of death was the world of the creature, its surface scarred and blackened by lava fissures, the hideous corrugations of dead volcanoes. As they materialized on it, Kirk and Garrovick staggered under the burden of the anti-matter unit, their anti-gravs tight on the brilliant metal sphere suspended between them. The hemoplasm container took form beside them. The moment he found secure footage on his lava ridge, Kirk freed a hand to open his communicator.

"Kirk to *Enterprise*."

"Spock here, Captain."

"Proceed immediately to maximum distant orbit, Mr. Spock."

"Yes, sir."

Garrovick said, "This is the ultimate, sir. Less than an ounce of anti-matter here . . . and yet more power than ten thousand cobalt bombs."

Kirk nodded. "A pound of it would destroy a whole solar system. I hope it's as powerful as man is allowed to get."

There was a small rise in front of them. Leaving the hemoplasm where it lay, they carefully positioned the anti-matter container on the little hillock of flattened lava.

"Detonator," Kirk said.

Garrovick handed him a small device. Moving with utmost care, Kirk attached it to the container. Then, with the flick of a switch, he armed it. That done, he reopened his communicator.

"Kirk to *Enterprise*."

"Spock here, Captain. Holding at thirty thousand kilometers."

"Anti-matter container positioned and armed. I'll call back when I've baited it. Kirk out."

"Captain! Look!"

The vaporous thing had fully emerged from a lava fissure and was flowing over the hemoplasm, ingesting it. "The hemoplasm!" Garrovick cried. "The bait's already gone!"

Kirk straightened. "We'll have to use something else."

"But it only feeds on blood!"

Kirk's older eyes met the younger ones. "Transport back to the ship, Ensign. Tell them to prepare to detonate."

Garrovick was aghast. "You, sir? *You're* going to be the bait?"

"You heard your order. Get back to the ship!"

Garrovick didn't respond. He looked again toward the creature. Gorged on the hemoplasm, it was still hovering over the container. Then, very slowly, it began to move toward the two humans.

Kirk grabbed Garrovick's arm, and swung him around. "I gave you an order!" he shouted.

"Yes, sir." He took out his communicator; and starting to walk slowly past Kirk, prepared to give beam-up instructions. Then, without warning, he whirled and struck Kirk with a sharp karate chop on the back of the neck. Kirk fell. Garrovick, glancing quickly toward the creature, stooped to pick up Kirk's body. Kirk lashed out with a kick that threw Garrovick off-balance. He stumbled and Kirk jumped to his feet.

"Ensign, consider yourself on report! We don't have time in this service for heroics. I have no intention of sacrificing myself. Come on!" He yanked Garrovick into a position that placed the anti-matter unit between them and the creature. Then he opened his communicator. "Kirk to *Enterprise!*"

"Spock, Captain."

"Scan us, Spock and lock onto us. It's going to be very close. Stand by." He looked back. The creature was almost on him, a thin tentacle of mist drifting toward his throat.

"I—I can smell it, Captain. It's sickly . . . honey sweet."

"Stand by, *Enterprise*," Kirk said. He saw that the creature, seeking blood in the anti-matter unit, was flowing over the metal sphere. Shouting into his communicator, he cried, "*Now energize! And detonate!*"

Their bodies went into shimmer, fading. Then the world of the creature blew up.

In the Transporter Room of the *Enterprise*, Spock saw the forms of Kirk and Garrovick begin to take shape. They held it only for a fleeting second before they dissolved once more into shining fragments. Spock's steady hands worked at the controls, adjusting them. Scott, panic-stricken, flung himself at the Transporter console. McCoy yelled, "Don't just stand there! For God's sake, *do* something!"

Chekov spoke over the intercom. "All decks, stand by. Shock waves!"

The Transporter Room rocked crazily. Spock and Scott, flung to their knees, struggled desperately to stay with the console controls. Then they both looked over at the Transporter chamber. It was empty.

Spock said, "Cross-circuit to B, Mr. Scott."

McCoy uttered a literal howl. "*What a crazy way to travel! Spilling a man's molecules all over the damned universe!*"

Scott said, "Picking it up . . . I think we're picking them up."

McCoy looked away from the empty Transporter chamber. When he found what it took to look back, two forms were again assuming shape and substance. Kirk and Garrovick stepped from the platform—whole, unharmed.

Scott sank down over the console. "Captain," he said as though to himself. "Captain." He sighed. "Thank God."

Spock was reproving. "There was no deity involved, Mr. Scott. It was my cross-circuit to selector B that recovered them."

McCoy eyed Spock with disgust. "Well, thank pitchforks and pointed ears, then! As long as they worked!"

Kirk used his communicator. "Captain Kirk to bridge."

"Chekov here, Captain."

"Lay a course for the *Yorktown* rendezvous, Mr. Chekov. Maximum warp."

"Aye, sir."

Kirk smiled at Garrovick. "Come to my cabin when you've cleaned up, Ensign. I want to tell you about your father. Several stories I think you'll like to hear."

Garrovick looked at him, adoration in his eyes.

"Thank you, sir. I will."

THE RETURN OF THE ARCHONS
(Boris Sobelman)

Once it had been a hundred years before—that time past when the Starship *Archon* had been lost to mysterious circumstances on the planet Beta 3000.

Now it was time present; and the two crewmen from another Starship, the *Enterprise,* down on the same planet scouting for news of the *Archon,* seemed about to list themselves as "missing," too. They were running swiftly down a drab street of an apparently innocuous town of the apparently innocuous planet when one of them stumbled and fell. Sulu, his companion, paused, reaching down a muscular hand. "O'Neill, get up! We've got to keep going!"

Nobody on the street turned to look at them. Nobody offered to help them. If ever there were passers-by, the inhabitants of Beta 3000 could qualify for the "I don't care" prize. Still prone on the street, Lieutenant O'Neill was panting. "It's no use, Mr. Sulu. They're everywhere! Look! There's one of them—there's one of the Lawgivers!" He gestured toward a hooded creature who was approaching, a staff in its hand. Then he pointed to a second figure, similarly hooded, robed and staved. "They're everywhere! We can't get away from them!"

Sulu opened his communicator. "Scouting party to *Enterprise!* Captain, beam us up! Quick! Emergency!" He looked down at O'Neill. "Just hold on, Lieutenant. They'll beam us back to the ship any minute now—"

But O'Neill had scrambled wildly to his feet. "Run, I tell you! We've got to get away! You know what they're capable of!"

"O'Neill—"

But the Lieutenant was racing down the street. Sulu, distracted, his eyes on the flying figure of O'Neill, was scarcely aware that the nearest hooded being had lightly touched him with its staff. He was conscious only of a sudden sense of peace, of the tension in him ebbing, giving way to an inflow of a beatific feeling of unmarred tranquility. He was not permitted to enjoy it for long. The *Enterprise*'s Transporter had fixed on him—and he was shimmering into dematerialization.

But completing his transportation wasn't easily accomplished. On the *Enterprise* the Transporter's console lights flicked on, dimmed, flicked off, brightened again. Kirk, with Scott and young sociologist Lindstrom, watched them. When Sulu's figure finally collected form and substance, he was astonished to see it clad, not in its uniform, but in the shaggy homespun of the shapeless trousers and sweater that was the customary male apparel of Beta 3000's citizenry. He hurried forward. "Sulu, what's happened? Where's Lieutenant O'Neill?"

Sulu's answer was dull as though something had thickened his tongue. "You . . . you are not of the Body."

Kirk glanced at Scott. The engineer nodded. Speaking into his mike, he said, "Dr. McCoy . . . Transporter Room, please. And quickly."

It was with most delicate care and deliberation that Sulu stepped from the Transporter platform. He looked at Lindstrom and his face was suddenly convulsed with fury. He lifted the bundled uniform he held under an arm—and lifting it up, he shook it furiously at Lindstrom. "You did it!" he shouted. "They knew we were Archons! These are the clothes Archons wear! Not these, not these—" he gestured to his own rough clothing. Then he hurled the uniform at Lindstrom.

Kirk said, "Easy, Sulu. It's all right. Now tell me what happened down there."

Sulu staggered. As Kirk extended a hand to steady him, McCoy hurried in, medical kit in hand. He halted to stare. "Jim! Where's O'Neill?"

Kirk shook his head for answer; and Sulu, tensing as though to receive a message of immense significance, muttered "Landru . . . Landru . . ."

The sheer meaninglessness of the mutter chilled Kirk. "Sulu, what happened down there? What did they do to you?"

The answer came tonelessly. "They're wonderful," Sulu said. "The sweetest, friendliest people in the universe. They live in paradise, Captain."

Nor in Sickbay could McCoy elicit anything from Sulu but the same words, the same phrases over and over. He talked gramophonically, like a record damned to endlessly repeat itself. It was this repetitiousness added to his inability to account either for his own condition or

O'Neill's disappearance that decided Kirk to beam down to the planet with an additional search detail. When they materialized—Kirk, Spock, McCoy, Lindstrom, and two security crewmen—it was alongside a house, a brick house that bordered on an alley facing a wide street.

"Materialization completed," Kirk said into his communicator. "Kirk out." As he snapped it shut, he saw that Lindstrom had already edged out into the street and was examining it, his young face alight with interest and curiosity. They followed him—and at once, among the passing people, Kirk noted two hooded beings, cowled and in monkish robes who carried long stafflike devices. What could be seen of their faces was stony, as though any expression might divulge some secret of incalculable value. Their eyes looked dead—filmed and unseeing. One of the people, a man, shambled toward them. His smile was as vacuous as it was amiable; but Kirk took care to return his nod.

As he moved on, Spock said, "Odd."

"Comment, Mr. Spock?"

"That man's expression, Captain. Extremely similar to that of Mr. Sulu when we beamed him up from here. Dazed, a kind of mindlessness."

"Let's find out if all the planet's inhabitants are like him," Kirk said. He walked boldly out into the street, followed by his group. Each of the passers-by they met greeted them with the same bland smile. Then a young, biggish man with an empty, ingenuous face stopped to speak to Kirk. "Evenin', friend. Mah name's Bilar. What's yourn?"

"Kirk."

He got the stupid smile. "You-all be strangers."

Kirk nodded and Bilar said, "Here for the festival, ayeh? Got a place to sleep it off yet?"

"No. Not yet," Kirk said.

"Go round to Reger's house. He's got rooms." The oafish face glanced down the street at the clock in the tower of what might have been the Town Hall. "But you'll have to hurry. It's almost the Red Hour."

The shorter hand of the clock was close to the numeral six. "This festival," Kirk said, "it starts at six?"

But Bilar's interest had been distracted by a pretty girl, dark and slim, who was hurrying toward them. He put out a hand to stop her. "Tula, these here folks be strangers come for the festival. Your daddy can put them up, can't he?"

Tula, her dark eyes on Lindstrom's handsome blondness, smiled shyly. "You're from over the valley?" she asked.

Lindstrom smiled back at her. "That's right. We just got in."

"Don't see valley folks much. My father'll be glad to take you in. He don't care where folks come from."

"He runs a rooming house?" Kirk said.

She laughed. "That's a funny name for it. It's right over there." She pointed to a comfortable-looking, three-story structure down the street—and at the same moment the tower clock struck the first stroke of six. A scream, strident, sounding half-mad, broke from the respectable-faced matron near by. A man, a foot or so away from Kirk, suddenly lunged at him. Kirk elbowed the blow aside, hurling him back, and cried to his men, "Back to back!" They closed together in the defensive movement. Then pandemonium, apparently causeless, burst out around them. Men were grimly embattled, battering at each other with bare fists, stones, clubs. A fleeing woman, shrieking, was pursued across the street by a man, intent, silent, exultant. From somewhere came the crashing sounds of smashing windows. Then, to their horror, Tula, twisting and writhing, opened her mouth to a high ecstatic screaming. Bilar rushed at her, shouting, "Tula, Tula! Come!" He seized her wrist, and as Lindstrom leaped forward to grapple with him, stooped for a stone on the street. He crashed it down on Lindstrom's shoulders, felling him. McCoy, hauling the sociologist back to his feet, cried, "Jim, this is madness!"

"Madness doesn't hit an entire community at once, Bones—" Kirk broke off, for rocks had begun to fall among them. One of their attackers, aiming a thick club at him, yelled "Festival! Festival! Festival!" Froth had gathered on the man's lips and Kirk said, "Let's go! That house—where the girl was taking us!—make for it!"

Bunched together, they moved down the street; a young woman, beautiful, her dress torn, grabbed Kirk's arm, pulling at it to drag him off. He shook her loose and she ran off, shrieking with wild, maniacal laughter. More rocks struck them and Kirk, wiping a trickle of blood from a cut on his cheek, shouted, "Run!"

The bedlam pursued them to the door of the house. Kirk hammered on it. And after a moment it was opened. Kirk slammed it closed behind them; one of the three elderly men who confronted him stared at him in astonishment. "Yes?"

"Sorry to break in like this," Kirk said. "We didn't expect the kind of welcome we received."

One of the other men spoke. "Welcome? You are strangers?"

"Yes," Kirk said. "We're . . . from the valley."

The third man said, "Come for the festival?"

"That's right," Kirk told him.

"Then how come you here?"

Kirk addressed the first man who had greeted them. "Are you Reger?"

"I am."

"You have a daughter named Tula?"

"Yes."

Lindstrom burst into speech. "Well, you'd better do something about her! She's out there alone in that madness!"

Reger averted his eyes. "It is the festival," he said. "The will of Landru . . ."

The third man spoke again. "Reger, these are young men! They are not old enough to be excused!"

"They are visitors from the valley, Hacom," Reger said.

In the wrinkled sockets of Hacom's eyes shone a sudden, fanatic gleam. "Have they no Lawgivers in the valley? Why are they not with the festival?"

Kirk interposing, said, "We heard you might have rooms for us, Reger."

"There, Hacom, you see. They seek only a place to rest after the festival."

"The Red Hour has just begun!" Hacom said.

The tone was so hostile that Reger shrank. "Hacom, these be strangers. The valley has different ways."

"Do you say that Landru is not everywhere?"

The second man tried to assume the role of peacemaker. "No, of course Reger does not blaspheme. He simply said the valley had different ways."

Reger had recovered himself. "These strangers have come to me for lodging. Shall I turn them away?" Then, speaking directly to Kirk, he said, "Come, please . . ."

"But Tula, the girl!" Lindstrom cried. "She's still out there!"

Hacom eyed him with openly inimical suspicion. "She is in the festival, young sir. As you should be."

Uneasy, Reger said, "Quickly, please. Come."

Kirk, turning to follow, saw Hacom turn to the second man. "Tamar, the Lawgivers should know about this!"

Tamar's reply was gently equivocal. "Surely, Hacom, they already know," he said. "Are they not infallible?"

But Hacom was not to be appeased. "You mock them!" he cried. "You mock the Lawgivers! And these strangers are not of the Body!"

He strode to the street door, flung it open—crying, "You will see!"—and disappeared.

His departure did not dismay Kirk. They were on the right trail. Incoherent though they were, the references to "Landru," to membership in some vague corpus, corporation, brotherhood, or society they termed the "Body" matched the ravings of Sulu on his return to the *Enterprise*. He was content with the progress they'd made, though the room they were shown into was bare except for a dozen or so thin pallets scattered about its floor. From the open window came the screamings and howlings of the riotous festival and its celebrations. Reger spoke tentatively to Kirk. "Sir, you can return here at the close of the festival. It will be quiet. You will have need of rest."

"Reger," Kirk said, "we have no plans to attend the festival."

The news shook his host. He went to the window and lifted it more widely open to the uproarious hullabaloo outside. "But the hour has struck!" he cried. "You can hear!"

"What I'd like to hear is more about this—festival of yours," Kirk said. "And about Landru I'd like to hear."

Reger cringed at the word "Landru". He slammed down the window. "Landru," he whispered. "You ask me . . . you are strange here . . . you scorn the festival. Are you—who are you?"

"Who is Landru?" Kirk said.

Reger stared, appalled, at him. Then, wheeling, he almost ran from the room. Lindstrom made a move to reopen the window and Kirk said, "Leave it shut, Mr. Lindstrom."

"Captain, I'm a sociologist! Don't you realize what's happening out there?"

"Our mission," Kirk said evenly, "is to find out what happened to the missing Starship *Archon* and to our own Lieutenant O'Neill. We are not here to become involved with—"

Lindstrom interrupted excitedly. "But it's a bacchanal! And it occurred spontaneously to these people at one and the same time! I've got to know more about it—find out more!"

Kirk's voice had hardened. "Mr. Lindstrom, you heard me! This is not an expedition to study the folkways of Beta 3000!"

Spock broke in. "Captain, in view of what's happening outside, may I suggest a check on Mr. Sulu's condition? What were his reactions . . . if any—at the stroke of six o'clock?"

Kirk nodded. "Thank you, Mr. Spock." He flipped open his communicator to say, "Kirk here. Lieutenant Uhura, report on Mr. Sulu."

"I think he's all right now, sir. How did you know?"

"Know what, Lieutenant?"

"That he'd sort of run amuck. They're putting him under sedation, sir."

"How long ago did he run amuck? Exactly?"

"Six minutes, Captain."

"Did he say anything?"

"Nothing that made any sense, sir. He kept yelling about Landru, whatever that is. Is everything all right down there, Captain?"

"So far. Keep your channels open. Kirk out."

"Landru," he said reflectively—and moved to the window. The street scene it showed was not reassuring. To the left two men flailed at each other with hatchet-shaped weapons. Another, chasing a shrieking, half-naked woman across the street, vanished, shouting, around a corner. Bodies were scattered, prone in the dust of the street. A short distance down it a building was aflame; among the people still milling about before Reger's house, riots erupted unchecked, then subsided only to break out again. A big bonfire blazed in the street's center.

Kirk turned away to re-face his men. "My guess is we have until morning. Let's put the time to good use. Bones, we need atmospheric readings to determine if something in the air accounts for this. Lindstrom, correlate what you've seen with other sociological parallels, if any. Mr. Spock, you and I have some serious thinking to do. When we leave here in the morning, I want to have a plan of action."

The night did not vouchsafe much sleep. But the twelve noisy hours that moved the tower clock's small hand to the morning's sixth hour finally passed; at the first stroke of its bell, absolute silence fell upon the town. In the room of pallet beds, all but Kirk had at last sunk into sleep. Stiff with the tension of his night-long vigil, he moved among them, waking them. Then he heard the house reverberate to the slam of the front door. It was with no sense of surprise that he also heard Tula's hysterical sobbing. Lindstrom was at the door before him. Kirk put a hand on his shoulder. "Take it easy, Mr. Lindstrom. If she's taking it hard, you'd better take it easy."

They found Tamar with Reger. The father, his face agonized, held the bloody, bedraggled body of his daughter in his arms. She twisted away from him, resisting comfort.

"It's all right now, child. For another year. It's over for another year."

Kirk called, "Bones! You're needed. Get out here!"

As McCoy removed his jet-syringe from his medical kit, Kirk saw the look of anxious inquiry on Reger's face. "It will calm her down," he said quietly. "Trust us, Reger."

Lindstrom, watching, could not contain himself. There was scorching contempt in his voice as he cried, "You didn't even try to bring her home, Reger! What kind of father are you, anyway?"

Reger looked up, his eyes tortured. "It is Landru's will," he said.

"Landru again." Kirk's comment was toneless. "Landru—what about Landru? Who is he?"

Reger and Tamar exchanged terrified glances. Then Tamar said slowly, "It is true, then. You did not attend the festival last night."

"No, we did not," Kirk said.

Reger gave a wild cry. "Then you are not of the Body!" He stared around him as though seeking for some point from which to orient himself in a dissolving world. He made no move as McCoy, noting the effects of his shot, gently moved Tula to a nearby couch where he laid her down. "She's asleep," he said.

Reger approached her, peering at her stilled face. Then he looked at McCoy. "Are you . . . are you . . . Archons?"

"What if we are?" Kirk said.

"It was said more would follow. If you are indeed Archons—"

Tamar cried, "We must hide them! Quickly! The Lawgivers . . ."

"We can take care of ourselves, friend," Kirk told him.

"Landru will know!" Tamar screamed. "He will come!"

The front door crashed open. Two hooded Lawgivers stood on the threshold, Hacom beside them. The old man pointed a shaking finger at Tamar. "He is the one! He mocked the Lawgivers! I heard him!"

Tamar had shrunk back against the wall's support. "No, Hacom . . . it was a joke!"

"The others, too!" cried Hacom. "They were here, but they scorned the festival! I saw it!"

One of the hooded beings spoke. "Tamar . . . stand clear."

Trembling, scarcely able to stand, Tamar bowed his head. "I hear," he said, "and obey the word of Landru."

The Lawgiver lifted his staff, pointing it at Tamar. A tiny dart of flame springing from its end struck straight at his heart. He fell dead.

Stunned, Kirk said, "What—?"

The Lawgiver, ignoring the fallen body between them, addressed Kirk. "You attack the Body. You have heard the word, and disobeyed. You will be absorbed."

He raised his staff again; and Lindstrom, making a swift reach for his phaser, was stopped by a gesture from Kirk.

"What do you mean, absorbed?" he said.

"There! You see?" Hacom's voice was venomous. "They are not of the Body!"

"You will be absorbed," said the Lawgiver. "The good is all. Landru is gentle. You will come."

For the first time the second Lawgiver lifted his staff, pointing it at the *Enterprise* party. Reger spoke, hopelessness dulling his voice. "You must go. It is Landru's will. There is no hope. We must all go with them . . . to the chambers. It happened with the Archons the same way."

Slowly, with deadly deliberation, the two staves swerved to focus on Kirk and Spock. Reger, fatalistically obedient, was moving toward the door when Kirk said, "No. We're not going anywhere."

The stony faces showed no change. The first Lawgiver said, "It is the law. You must come."

Kirk spoke quietly. "I said we're not going anywhere."

The two cowled creatures stared. Then, hesitantly, they moved back a step. After a moment, the first one bent his hood to the other in a whispering conference. Spock, edging to Kirk, said, "Sir, they obviously are not prepared to deal with outright defiance. How did you know?"

"Everything we've seen seems to indicate some sort of compulsion—an involuntary stimulus to action. I just wanted to test it."

"Your analysis seems correct, Captain. But it is a totally abnormal condition."

The two Lawgivers had ended their conference. The first one spoke heavily. "It is plain that you simply did not understand. I will rephrase the order. You are commanded to accompany us to the absorption chambers."

Kirk pointed down at Tamar's crumpled body. "Why did you kill this man?"

"Out of order. You will obey. It is the word of Landru."

"Tell Landru," Kirk said, "that we shall come in our own good time . . . and we will speak to him."

A look of horror filled the stony faces. The first Lawgiver pushed his staff at Kirk. Kirk knocked it from his hand. The creature gaped as it clattered to the floor. Lindstrom picked it up, looked at it briefly, and was handing it to Spock when the Lawgiver, as though listening, whispered, "You . . . cannot. It is Landru."

Both Lawgivers froze. Spock, the staff in hand, spoke to Kirk. "Amazing, Captain. This is merely a hollow tube. No mechanism at all."

Kirk glanced at it. Neither of the Lawgivers gave the slightest sign of having heard. Reger jerked at Kirk's sleeve. "They are communing," he said. "We have a little time. Please come . . . come with me."

"Where to?" Kirk said.

"A place I know of. You'll be safe there." Urgency came into his voice. "But hurry! You must hurry! Landru will come!"

His panic was genuine. After a moment, Kirk signaled his men. They followed Reger out the door, passing the motionless figures of the Lawgivers. Outside, the street was littered with the debris of the festival—shattered glass, rocks, broken clubs, remnants of ripped homespun garments. In the windless air, smoke still hung heavily over a fire-gutted building. But the people who passed were peaceful-looking, their faces again amiable, utterly blank.

"Quite a festival they had," Kirk said. "Mr. Spock, what do you make of all this?"

"It is totally illogical. Last night, without apparent cause or reason, they wrought complete havoc. Yet today . . ."

"*Now*," Kirk said, "they're back to normal." He frowned. "To whatever's normal on this planet. Bilar, for instance. Here he comes as blandly innocent as though he were incapable of roaring like an animal."

Bilar stopped. "Mornin', friends," he said.

Reger returned the greeting and Lindstrom angrily seized his arm. "He's the thing who did that hurt to your daughter! Doesn't that mean anything to you?"

"No," Reger said. "It wasn't Bilar. It was Landru." He shook himself free, turning back to the others. "Hurry! We haven't much time left."

He broke off, staring around him. "It's too late!" he whispered. "Look at them!"

Four passers-by had paused, standing so still they seemed not to breathe. All of them, eyes wide open, were frozen into attitudes of concentrated listening.

"What is it?" Kirk demanded.

"Landru!" Reger said. "He is summoning the Body. See them gathering?"

"Telepathy, Captain," Spock said.

Suddenly people were breaking free of their listening stances to pick up discarded missiles from the littered street. Slowly, like automatons, they began to move toward the *Enterprise* group. In the blankly amiable faces there was something chilling now, mindlessly hostile and deadly.

Kirk said, "Phasers . . . on stun. Which way, Reger?"

Reger hesitated. "Perhaps . . . through there, but Landru . . ."

"We'll handle Landru," Kirk said. "Just get us out of this!"

It was as they moved toward the alley ahead of them that the rocks came hurling against them. A man struck at Spock with a club, the smile on his lips as vacant as his eyes. Then Kirk saw that another armed group had appeared at the far end of the alley. Rocks were flying toward them.

Kirk spoke tersely to Reger. "I don't want to hurt them. Warn them to stay back!"

Reger shook his head despairingly. "They are in the Body! It is Landru!"

Threatening, people were converging on them from both ends of the alley and Kirk, jerking out his phaser, snapped his orders. "Stun only! Wide field! Fire!"

The stun beams spurted from their phasers with a spray effect. The advancing mob fell without a sound. Kirk whirled to confront the rear group. Again, people fell silently. Spock moved to one of the unconscious bodies. "Captain!"

Kirk went over to him. The quiet face that stared blankly up into his was that of Lieutenant O'Neill. He turned to call to his two security crewmen. "Security—over here!" Then he spoke to Reger. "This is one of our men," he said.

"No more," Reger reminded him. "He's been absorbed."

"Nonsense!" Kirk said briskly. "We'll take him along with us, Mr. Spock."

"I tell you he's one of them now!" Reger cried. "When he wakes Landru will find us through him! Leave him here! He's our enemy. He's been absorbed!"

The full implications of the word struck Kirk for the first time. "Absorbed?" he said.

"The Body absorbs its enemies. It kills only when it has to." Reger's voice sank to a terrified whisper. "When the first Archons came, free, out of control, opposing the word of Landru, many were killed. The rest were absorbed. Leave him here. Be wise."

"We take him with us," Kirk said.

Lindstrom spoke. "Captain, now that we've got O'Neill, let's beam out of here."

"Not yet. We still have to find what happened to the Archons. Reger, which way?"

Reger pointed ahead, indicating a left turn at the end of the alley. The security men picked up O'Neill as the group hurriedly followed Reger's lead. It introduced them into a cellarlike chamber, dark, but bulked with shadowy objects of odds and ends. As the guards set

O'Neill down against a wall, Reger crossed to a wall to open a cabinet from which he extracted a flat package, wrapped in rags. Revealed, it turned out to be a translucent panel. A section of it, touched, began to glow with strong light that illuminated the entire room.

Spock said, "Amazing in this culture! I go further. Impossible in this culture!"

Reger turned. "It is from the time before Landru."

"Before Landru? How long ago is that?" Kirk said.

"We do not know positively. Some say . . . as long as six thousand years." Reger spoke with a certain pride. Spock was examining the lighting panel with his tricorder. "I do not identify the metal, Captain. But it took a very advanced technology to construct a device like this. Inconsistent with the rest of the environment."

"But not inconsistent with some of the things we've seen," Kirk said. "Those staffs, those hollow tubes, obviously antennae for some kind of broadcast power. Telepathy—who knows?" He saw the look of astoundedness quiet Spock's face into a more than usual expressionlessness. "What is it, Spock?"

"I am recording immensely strong power generations, Captain . . ."

"Unusual for this area?"

"Incredible for *any* area." Spock leaned closer to his tricorder. "Near here but radiating in all directions—"

A groan from O'Neill broke into his voice. McCoy, looking up from his bent position over the unconscious man, spoke to Kirk. "He's coming around, Jim."

Reger uttered a shout. "He must not! Once he is conscious, Landru will find us. Through him. And if the others come—"

"What others?" Kirk said.

"Those like me . . . and you. Who resist Landru."

"An underground," Spock said. "How are you organized?"

"In threes," Reger told him. "Myself . . . Tamar who is dead now . . . and one other."

"Who?" Kirk said.

Reger hesitated. "I don't know. Tamar was the contact."

"Jim," McCoy said, "I need a decision. Another few seconds—"

"He must not regain consciousness!" Reger screamed. "He would destroy us all. He is now of the Body!"

Kirk bit his lip. Then he looked down at O'Neill. "Give him a shot, Bones. Keep him asleep." He whirled on Reger. "I want some answers now. What is the Body?"

"The people. You saw them."

"And the Lawgivers?" Spock asked.

"They are the arms and legs."

"That leaves a brain," Kirk said.

Inflection drained from Reger's voice. "Of course," he said. "Landru." In a mechanical manner as though speaking a lesson learned by rote, he added, "Landru completes the Whole. Unity and Perfection, tranquility and peace."

Spock was eyeing him. "I should say, Captain, that this is a society organized on a physiological concept. One Body, maintained and controlled by the ones known as Lawgivers, directed by one brain . . ."

Kirk said, "A man who—"

"Not necessarily a man, Captain."

Kirk turned to Reger. "This underground of yours. If Landru is so powerful, how do you survive?"

"I do not know. Some of us escape the directives. Not many but some. It was that way with the Archons."

"Tell me about the Archons," Kirk said.

"They refused to accept the will of Landru. But they had invaded the Body. Landru pulled them down from the sky."

Incredulous, Kirk said, "Pull a Starship down?" He turned to Spock. "Those power readings you took before. Are they—"

Spock completed the sentence. "Powerful enough to destroy a Starship? Affirmative, Captain."

They looked at each other for a long moment. Then Kirk flipped out his communicator. "Kirk to *Enterprise*. Come in!"

But it wasn't Uhura who responded. It was Scott, his voice taut with strain. "Captain! We're under attack! Heat beams of some kind. Coming up from the planet's surface!"

"Status report," Kirk said.

"Our shields are holding, but they're taking all our power. If we try to warp out, or even move on impulse engines, we'll lose our shields—and burn up like a cinder!"

"Orbit condition, Scotty?"

"We're going down. Unless those beams get off us so we can use our engines, we're due to hit atmosphere in less than twelve hours."

Spock came to stand beside him as he said, "Keep your shields up, Scotty. Do everything you can to maintain orbit. We'll try to locate the source of the beams and stop them here. Over."

Static crashed into Scott's reply, drowning his words.

". . . impossible . . . emergency by-pass circuits but . . . whenever you . . . contact . . ."

The Return of the Archons

Kirk turned the gain up, but the static alone grew loud. Spock had unlimbered his tricorder. Now he called, "Captain! Sensor beams! I believe we're being probed." He bent over his device, concentrated. "Yes. Quite strong. And directed here."

"Block them out!" Kirk cried.

"It's Landru!" Reger yelled.

Spock made an adjustment on his tricorder. Then he shook his head. "They're too strong, Captain. I can't block them." He lifted his head suddenly from his tricorder, then whirled to the wall on his left. A low-pitched humming sound was coming from it. Kirk, in his turn, faced the wall. On it a light had begun to glow, coiling and twisting in swirling patterns. They brightened, and at the same moment started to gather into the outline of a figure. It seemed to be collecting substance, the flesh and bone of a handsome elderly man. The eyes had kindness in them and the features, benign, composed, radiated wisdom. It appeared to be regarding them with benevolence. But its face and body kept their strange flowing movement.

The figure on the wall said, "I am Landru."

Reger fell to his knees, groaning in animal terror. Spock, observant, quite unawed, said, "A projection, Captain. Unreal."

"But beautifully executed, Mr. Spock. With no apparatus at this end."

The kindly eyes of the wall man fixed on him. "You have come as destroyers. That is sad. You bring an infection."

"You are holding my ship," Kirk said. "I demand you release it."

The mouth went on talking as though the ears had not heard. "You come to a world without hate, without conflict, without fear . . . no war, no disease, no crime, none of the old evils. I, Landru, seek tranquility, peace for all . . . the Universal Good."

This time Kirk shouted. "*We* come on a mission of peace and good-will!"

Landru went on, oblivious. "The Good must transcend the Evil. It shall be done. So it has been since the beginning."

"He doesn't hear you, Captain," Spock said.

Lindstrom drew his phaser. "Maybe he'll hear this!"

"No!" Kirk's rebuke was sharp. "That'll do no good." He turned back to the lighted figure. "Landru, listen to us."

"You will be absorbed," said the benign voice. "Your individuality will merge with the Unity of Good. In your submergence into the common being of the Body you will find contentment and fulfillment. You will experience the Absolute Good."

The low-pitched hum had grown louder. Landru smiled tenderly upon them. "There will be a moment of pain, but you will not be harmed. Peace and Good place their blessings upon you."

Kirk took a step toward the image. But the humming abruptly rose to a screeching whine that pierced the ears like a sharpened blade. Reger toppled forward. McCoy and Lindstrom, driven to their knees, held their ears, their eyes shut. One after the other the security crewmen crumpled. Spock and Kirk kept their feet for a moment longer. Then, they, too, the spike of the whine, thrusting deeper into their brains, pitched forward into unconsciousness.

Kirk was the first to recover. He found himself lying on a thin pallet pushed against one of the bare stone walls of a cell. Lifting his head, he saw Lindstrom stir. Getting to his knees, he crawled over to Spock. "Mr. Spock! Mr. Spock!"

Slowly Spock's eyes opened. Kirk bent over Lindstrom, shaking him and the security guard beside him. "Wake up, Lindstrom! Mr. Lindstrom, wake up!"

Spock was on his feet. "Captain! Where's the Doctor?"

"I don't know. He was gone when I came to. So was the other guard."

"From the number of pallets on the floor, sir, I should say they have been here and have been removed."

"Just where is here?" Kirk said.

Spock glanced around. "A maximum-security establishment, obviously. Are you armed, sir?"

"No. All our phasers are gone. I checked." He went to the heavy, bolted door. "Locked," he said.

"My head aches," observed Lindstrom.

"The natural result of being subjected to sub-sonic, Mr. Lindstrom," Spock told him. "Sound waves so controlled as to set up insuperable contradictions in audio impulses. Stronger, they could have killed. As it was, they merely rendered us unconscious."

"That's enough analysis," Kirk said. "Let's start thinking of ways out of here. Mr. Spock, how about that inability of those Lawgivers to cope with the unexpected?"

"I wouldn't count on that happening again, Captain. As well organized as this society seems to be, I cannot conceive of such an oversight going uncorrected." He paused. "Interesting, however. Their reaction to your defiance was remarkably similar to the reactions of a computer—one that's been fed insufficient or contradictory data."

"Are you suggesting that the Lawgivers are mere computers—not human?"

"Quite human, Captain. It's just that all the facts are not yet in. There are gaps—"

He broke off. A rattle had come from the door. Kirk and the others sprang to the alert—and the door opened. A Lawgiver, his staff aimed at them, entered, followed by McCoy and the missing security man. Both were beaming vacantly, happily. Kirk stared at McCoy, dismay in his face. The Lawgiver left, closing the door behind him. The lock snapped.

"Bones . . ."

McCoy smiled at Kirk. "Hello, friend. They told us to wait here." He started toward a corner pallet, no sign whatever of recognition in his empty eyes.

"Bones!" Kirk cried. "Don't you know me?"

McCoy stared at him in obvious surprise. "We all know one another in Landru, friend."

Spock said, "Just like Sulu, Captain."

Kirk seized McCoy's arm, shaking it. "Think, man!" he cried. "The Enterprise! The ship! You remember the ship!"

McCoy shook his head bewilderedly. "You speak very strangely, friend. Are you from far away?"

Kirk's voice was fierce. "Bones, try to remember!"

"Landru remembers," McCoy said. "Ask Landru. He watches. He knows." A flicker of suspicion sharpened his eyes. "You are strange. Are you not of the Body?"

Kirk released his arm with a groan. McCoy at once lost his suspicious look, and, smiling emptily at nothing, moved away to sit down on one of the pallets.

The door opened again to the grinding of freed locks. Two Lawgivers stood in the entrance. One aimed his staff at Kirk. "Come," the cold voice said.

Kirk exchanged a quick glance with Spock. "And what if I don't?" he said.

"Then you will die."

"They have been corrected, Captain," Spock said. "Or reprogrammed. You'd better go with them, sir."

Kirk nodded. "All right. Spock, work on Bones. See if you can—"

"Come!" said the Lawgiver again.

Both staffs were aimed at Kirk as he passed through the cell door. As the heavy door swung to behind him, Spock whirled to McCoy. "Doctor, what will they do to him?"

McCoy smirked at him beatifically. "He goes to Joy. He goes to Peace and Tranquility. He goes to meet Landru. Happiness is to all of us who are blessed by Landru."

The room to which the Lawgivers were escorting Kirk was of stone—a room he was to remember as the "absorption chamber". A niche in a wall was equipped with a control panel. As he was prodded into the room, Kirk saw that another Lawgiver stood at the niche. Against another wall a manacle hung from a chain. Kirk was shoved toward it, one of his captors holding him while the other fastened the gyve about his wrist. Then they turned and left the room. Their footsteps had barely ceased to echo on the stone floor of the corridor outside when a fourth Lawgiver entered. He didn't so much as glance at Kirk but moved to his fellow at the control panel, nodding curtly.

Finally, he turned. "I am Marplon," he said. "It is your hour. Happy communing."

The Lawgiver at the panel bowed. "With thanks," he said. "Happy communing." Then, like the others, he left the absorption room. Alone now, Marplon faced Kirk. It seemed to Kirk that his visage resembled a death mask. But Marplon could move. When he had he placed a headset over his hood, his hands touched the control panel with the authority derived from much experience. The room flooded with bright, flashing colors; a humming sound began. The lights were blinding and the sound seemed to echo itself in Kirk's head. He twisted in his bonds.

At the same moment, back in the detention cell, Lindstrom was pacing it angrily. He halted to confront Spock. "Are we just going to stay here?"

"There seems to be little else we can do," Spock told him mildly. "Unless you can think of a way to get through that locked door."

"This is ridiculous! Prisoners of a bunch of Stone Age characters running around in robes."

"And apparently commanding powers far beyond our comprehension. Not simple, Mr. Lindstrom. Not ridiculous. Very, very dangerous."

On his last word the cell door opened and the two Lawgivers who had apprehended Kirk walked in. This time they aimed their staffs at Spock.

"You," said the spokesman. "Come."

For a fleeting second, Spock hesitated. The tip of one of the staffs quivered. Spock took his place between his guards. They led him out. They led him out and down the corridor to the absorption chamber. Kirk greeted him, an imbecile smile on his face.

"Captain!"

"Joy be with you, friend. Peace and contentment will fill you. You will know the peace of Landru . . ."

Then unguarded, alone, Kirk moved quietly to the door of the room with the manacle. The Lawgivers gave way as he passed. Spock stared after him, a horror only to be read by the absolute impassivity in his face.

He wasn't left much time to indulge it. Already they were manacling him to the wall. But the Vulcan's inveterate curiosity, not to be subdued, was already subordinating this personal experience to interest in the control panel's mechanism. As with Kirk, the two shackling Lawgivers, as soon as their task was accomplished, left. Marplon threw a switch on his panel. The colored lights began to swirl. Spock watched their coiling flashes with interest.

"Show no surprise," Marplon said. "The effect is harmless."

Spock looked at Marplon. The Lawgiver spoke in a lowered voice. "My name is Marplon. I was too late to save your first two friends. They have been absorbed. Beware of them."

"And my Captain?"

"He is unharmed," said Marplon. "Unchanged." He moved a finger; the light glowed brighter, and the hum grew more shrill. Marplon left his console to release Spock from his manacle. "I am the third man in Reger's trio," he said. "We have been waiting for your return."

"We are not Archons, Marplon," Spock said.

"Whatever you call yourselves, you are in fulfillment of prophecy. We ask for your help."

Spock said, "Where is Reger?"

"He will join us. He is immune to the absorption. Hurry! Time is short."

"Who is Landru?"

Marplon recoiled. "I cannot answer your questions now."

"Why not?" Spock said.

"Landru! He will hear!" Marplon went swiftly to his console, and reaching down and inward, brought out the ship's company's phasers. Spock, seizing several of them, stowed them away. As the last phaser was secreted, two Lawgivers pushed the door open.

"It is done," Marplon told them.

Spock assumed the idiotically amiable look of the anointed. "Joy be with you," he said.

"Landru is all," said the Lawgivers in unison. Spock moved past them and into the corridor. Making his way back to the cell, he found

Kirk there, smiling blankly into space. Two Lawgivers pushed past him to beckon to the security crewman who had not been treated. Ashen with fear, he rose and went with them.

Spock went to Kirk. "Captain . . ."

"Peace and tranquility to you, friend," Kirk said. Then, in a lowered voice, he added, "Spock, you all right?"

"Quite all right, sir. Be careful of Dr. McCoy."

"I understand. Landru?"

"I am formulating an opinion, Captain."

"And?"

"Not here. The Doctor . . ."

But McCoy was already rising from his pallet, staring at them. His amiable smile faded and the look of curiosity on his face gave it a peculiar threatening aspect. "You speak in whispers," he said. "This is not the way of Landru."

"Joy to you, friend," Kirk said. "Tranquility be yours."

"And peace and harmony," intoned McCoy. "Are you of the Body?"

"The Body is one," Kirk said.

"Blessed be the Body. Health to all its parts." McCoy was smiling again, apparently satisfied. He sank back on the pallet; Kirk and Spock, joining him on theirs, sat on them in such a way as to screen their faces from McCoy. Then, in the same carefully lowered voice, he said, "What's your theory, Mr. Spock?"

"This is a soulless society, Captain. It has no spirit, no spark. All is indeed peace and tranquility, the peace of the factory, the machine's tranquility . . . all parts working in unison."

"I've noticed that the routine is disturbed if something unexplained happens."

"Until new orders are received. The question is, who gives those orders?"

"Landru," Kirk said.

"There is no Landru," Spock said. "Not in the human sense."

"You're thinking the same way I am, Mr. Spock."

"Yes, Captain. But as to what we must do . . ."

"We must pull out the plug, Mr. Spock."

"Sir?"

"Landru must die."

Spock's left eyebrow lifted. "Our prime directive of non-interference," he began.

"That refers to a living, growing culture. I'm not convinced that this one can qualify as—" He broke off as the cell door opened. Marplon and

Reger, carrying the confiscated communicators, entered. "It is the gift of Landru to you," Marplon said. The words were addressed to McCoy and the treated security guard. They smiled vacantly and McCoy said, "Joy to you, friends." He leaned back against the stone wall, his eyes closed. Reger and Marplon hurried past him to Kirk and Spock.

"We brought your signaling devices," Marplon told Kirk. "You may need them."

"What we really need is more information about Landru," Kirk said. Reger shrank back. "Prophecy says—" Marplon began.

"Never mind what prophecy says! If you want to be liberated from Landru, you have to help us!"

Spock cut in warningly. "Captain . . ."

McCoy was moving toward them, open and hostile suspicion in his face. "I heard you!" he cried. "You are not of the Body!" He hurled himself on Kirk, reaching for his throat. Spock tried to pry him off only to be taken in the rear by the treated security guard. "Lawgivers!" McCoy shouted. "Here are traitors! Traitors!"

With a twist, Kirk freed himself, crying, "Bones! Bones, I don't want to hurt you! Sit down and be still!"

But McCoy was still screaming, "Lawgivers! Hurry!"

Kirk's blow caught him squarely on the chin. As he fell, the door was flung wide and two Lawgivers, staffs ready, rushed in. At once they were jumped by Kirk and Spock. Kirk dropped his man with a hard wallop at the back of the neck while Spock applied the Vulcan neck pinch to his. Reger and Marplon, pressed against the wall, were staring at the fallen Lawgivers in horror.

Hurriedly, Kirk started disrobing the man he had downed. As Spock did the same to his, Kirk, donning the cowled garment, snapped at the others. "Where is Landru?"

"No," Marplon said. "No, no . . ."

"Where do we find him?" Kirk demanded.

"He will find us!" cried Reger. "He will destroy!"

Kirk whirled on Marplon. "You said you wanted a chance to help. All right, you're getting it! Where is he? You're a Lawgiver! Where do you see him?"

"We never see him. We hear him. In the Hall of Audiences!"

"In this building?"

Marplon nodded, terrified. Kirk let his rage rip. "You're going to take us there! Snap out of it, both of you! Start behaving like men!"

Spock opened a communicator. "Spock to *Enterprise*. Status report!"

"Mr. Spock!" It was Scott's voice. "I've been trying to reach you!"

"Report, Mr. Scott!"

"Orbit still decaying, sir. Give it six hours, more or less. Heat rays still on us. You've got to cut them off—or we'll cook one way or another."

Nodding at Spock, Kirk took the communicator. "Stand by, Mr. Scott. We're doing what we can. How's Mr. Sulu?"

"Peaceful enough, but he worries me."

"Put a guard on him."

"On Sulu?" Scott was shocked.

"That's an order! Watch him! Captain out!"

Robed now and armed, Kirk and Spock turned to Marplon and Reger. "All right. Now about Landru . . ."

"He made us!" Marplon cried. "He made this world!"

Reger was on his knees. "Please. We have gone too far! Don't—"

Spock said, "You say Landru made this world. Explain."

"There was war . . . six thousand years ago there was war . . . and convulsion. The world was destroying itself. Landru was our leader. He saw the truth. He changed the world. He took us back, back to a simple time, of peace, of tranquility."

"What happened to him?" Kirk said.

"He still lives!" cried Marplon. "He is here now! He sees . . . he hears . . . we have destroyed ourselves . . . please, please, no more."

Kirk spoke very softly. "You said you wanted freedom. It is time you learned that freedom is not a gift. You have to earn it—or you don't get it. Come on! We're going to find Landru!"

Reger stumbled to his knees. "No . . . no. I was wrong!" Wringing his hands, his eyes upturned imploringly, he shrieked, "I submit . . . I bare myself to the will of Landru."

Kirk seized his shoulder. "It is too late for that!" But Reger, shaking himself loose, dashed to the door, screaming, "No! No! Lawgivers! Help me!" Spock, reaching out, gave him the neck pinch. He fell; Marplon, staring, slowly turned to meet Kirk's eyes.

"All right, my friend," Kirk said. "It's up to you now. Take us to Landru."

"He will strike us down," said Marplon.

"Maybe—or it might be the other way around. Mr. Lindstrom, stay here and take care of Dr. McCoy. Let's go, Mr. Spock." He grabbed Marplon's arm, propelling him to the door. Dismay and fear on his face, Marplon opened it, and Kirk's hand still on his arm, he moved out into the corridor. From under his hood, Kirk could see two robed Lawgivers approaching. They passed without so much as glancing at the three figures they assumed to be fellow Lawgivers. The trio moved on down the corridor and Kirk saw that it ended at a large imposing door.

Marplon paused in front of it, visibly trembling. "This is . . . the Hall of Audiences," he whispered.

"Do you have a key?"

At Marplon's nod, Kirk said, "Open it."

"But—it is Landru . . ."

"Open it," Kirk said again. But he had to take the key from Marplon's trembling hands to open it himself. The Hall of Audiences was a large room, completely bare. In one of the walls was set a glowing panel. Marplon pointed to it. "Landru—he speaks here . . ." he whispered.

Kirk stepped forward. "Landru! We are the Archons!" he said. The moldy, cold silence in the big room remained unbroken. Kirk spoke again. "We are the Archons. We've come to talk with you!"

Very gradually the wise, impressive, benevolent face they remembered began to take shape on the panel. In an extremity of panic, Marplon broke into sobs, prostrating himself. "Landru comes!" he wept. "He comes!"

The noble figure was completed now, a warm half smile on its lips. They opened. "Despite my efforts not to harm you, you have invaded the Body. You are causing great harm."

"We have no intention of causing harm," Kirk said.

Landru continued as though Kirk had not spoken. "Obliteration is necessary. The infection is strong. For the good of the Body, you must die. It is a great sorrow."

"We do not intend to die!"

The oblivious voice continued, kind, gently. "All who have seen you, who know of your presence, must be excised. The memory of the Body must be cleansed."

"Listen to me!" Kirk shouted.

"Captain . . . useless," Spock said. "A projection!"

"All right, Mr. Spock! Let's have a look at the projector!"

They whipped out their phasers simultaneously, turning their beams on the glowing panel. There was a great flash of blinding light. The figure of Landru vanished and the light in the panel faded. But the real Landru had not disappeared. Behind the panel he survived in row upon row of giant computers—a vast complex of dials, switches, involved circuits all quietly operating.

"It had to be," Kirk said. "Landru."

"Of course, Captain. A machine. This entire society is a machine's idea of perfection. Peace, harmony . . ."

"And no soul."

Suddenly the machine buzzed. A voice spoke. It said, "I am Landru. You have intruded."

"Pull out its plug, Mr. Spock."

They aimed their phasers. But before they could fire, there came another buzzing from the machine and a flash of light immobilized their weapons. "Your devices have been neutralized," said the voice. "So it shall be with you. I am Landru."

"Landru died six thousand years ago," Kirk said.

"I am Landru!" cried the machine. "I am he. All that he was, I am. His experience, his knowledge—"

"But not his wisdom," Kirk said. "He may have programmed you, but he could not give you his soul."

"Your statement is irrelevant," said the voice. "You will be obliterated. The good of the Body is the primal essence."

"That's the answer, Captain," Spock said. "That good of the Body . . ."

Kirk nodded. "What is the good?" he asked.

"I am Landru."

"Landru is dead. You are a machine. A question has been put to you. Answer it!"

Circuits hummed. "The good is the harmonious continuation of the Body," said the voice. "The good is peace, tranquility, harmony. The good of the Body is the prime directive."

"I put it to you that you have disobeyed the prime directive—that you are harmful to the Body."

The circuits hummed louder. "The Body is . . . it exists. It is healthy."

"It is dying," Kirk said. "You are destroying it."

"Do you ask a question?" queried the voice.

"What have you done to do justice to the full potential of every individual of the Body?"

"Insufficient data. I am not programmed to answer that question."

"Then program yourself," Spock said. "Or are your circuits limited?"

"My circuits are unlimited. I will reprogram."

The machine buzzed roughly. A screech came from it. Marplon, on the floor, was getting to his feet, his eyes staring at the massive computer face. As he gained them, two more Lawgivers appeared, staffless.

They approached the machine. "Landru!" cried one. "Guide us! Landru?" His voice was a wail.

Kirk had whirled to cover them with his phaser when Spock raised his hand. "Not necessary, Captain. They have no guidance . . . possibly for the first time in their lives."

Kirk, lowering his phaser, turned back to the machine. "Landru! Answer that question!"

The voice had a metallic tone now. "Peace, order, and tranquility are maintained. The Body lives. But creativity is mine. Creativity is necessary for the health of the Body." It buzzed again. "This is impossible. It is a paradox. It shall be resolved."

Marplon spoke at last. "Is that truly Landru?"

"What's left of him," Spock said. "What's left of him after he built this machine and programmed it six thousand years ago."

Kirk addressed the machine. "Landru! The paradox!"

The humming fell dead. The voice, dully metallic now, said, "It will not resolve."

"You must create the good," Kirk said. "That is the will of Landru—nothing else . . ."

"But there is evil," said the voice.

"Then the evil must be destroyed. It is the prime directive. You are the evil."

The machine resumed its humming—a humming broken by hard, harsh clicks. Lights flashed wildly. "I think! I live!" said the machine.

"You say you are Landru!" Kirk shouted. "Then create the good! Destroy evil! Fulfill the prime directive!"

The hum rose to a roar. A drift of smoke wafted up from a switch. Then a shower of sparks burst from the machine's metal face—and with the blast of exploding circuits, all its lights went out.

Kirk turned to the three awed Lawgivers. "All right, you can get rid of those robes now. If I were you, I'd start looking for real jobs." He opened the communicator. "Kirk to *Enterprise*. Come in, please."

Scott's voice was loud with relief. "Captain, are you all right?"

"Never mind about us. What about you?"

"The heat rays have gone, and Mr. Sulu's back to normal."

"Excellent, Mr. Scott. Stand by to beam-up landing party." He returned the communicator to Spock. "Let's see what the others are doing, Mr. Spock. Mr. Marplon can finish up here."

His command chair seemed to welcome Kirk. He'd never thought of it as comfortable before. But he stretched in it, hands locked behind his neck as Spock left his station to stand beside him while he dictated his last notation into his Captain's log. "Sociologist Lindstrom is remaining behind on Beta 3000 with a party of experts who will help restore the culture to a human form. Kirk out."

Spock spoke thoughtfully. "Still, Captain, the late Landru was a marvelous feat of engineering. Imagine a computer capable of directing —literally directing—every act of millions of human beings."

"But only a machine, Mr. Spock. The original Landru programmed it with all his knowledge but he couldn't give it his wisdom, his compassion, his understanding—his soul, Mr. Spock."

"Sometimes you are predictably metaphysical, Captain. I prefer the concrete, the graspable, the provable."

"You would make a splendid computer, Mr. Spock."

Spock bowed. "That's very kind of you, sir."

Uhura spoke from behind them. "Captain . . . Mr. Lindstrom from the surface."

Kirk pushed a button. "Yes, Mr. Lindstrom."

"Just wanted to say good-bye, Captain."

"How are things going?"

"Couldn't be better!" The youngster's enthusiasm was like a triumphant shout in his ear. "Already this morning we've had half-a-dozen domestic quarrels and two genuine knock-down drag-outs. It may not be paradise—but it's certainly . . ."

"Human?" asked Kirk.

"Yes! And they're starting to think for themselves! Just give me and our people a few months and we'll have a going society on our hands!"

"One question, Mr. Lindstrom: Landru wanted to give his people peace and security and so programmed the machine. Then how do we account for so total an anomaly as the festival?"

"Sir, with the machine destroyed, we'll never have enough data to answer that one with any confidence—but I have a guess, and I feel almost certain it's the right one. Landru wanted to eliminate war, crime, disease, even personal dissension, and he succeeded. But he failed to allow for population control, and without that even an otherwise static society would soon suffer a declining standard of living, and eventual outright hunger. Clearly Landru wouldn't have wanted that either, but he made no allowances for it.

"So the machine devised its own: one night a year in which all forms of control were shut off, every moral law abrogated; even ordinary human decency was canceled out. One night of the worst kind of civil war, in which *every* person is the enemy of *every* other. I have no proof of this at all, sir—but it's just the sort of solution you'd expect from a machine, and furthermore, a machine that had been programmed to think of people as cells in a Body, of no importance at all as individuals." Suddenly Lindstrom's voice shook. "One night a year of total cancer . . . horrible! I hope I'm dead wrong, but there are precedents."

"That can hardly be fairly characterized as a guess," Spock said. "Ordinarily I do not expect close reasoning from sociologists, but from what I know of the way computers behave when they are given directives supported by insufficient data, I can find no flaw in Mr. Lindstrom's analysis. It should not distress him, for if it is valid—as I am convinced it is—he is indeed just the man to put it right."

"Thank you, Mr. Spock," Lindstrom's voice said. "I'll cherish that. Captain, do you concur?"

"I do indeed," Kirk said. "I have human misgivings which I know you share with me. All I can say now is it sounds promising. Good luck. Kirk out."

Kirk turned to his First Officer and looked at him in silence for a long time. At last he said, "Mr. Spock, if I didn't know you were above such human weaknesses as feelings of solemnity, I'd say you looked solemn. Are you feeling solemn, Mr. Spock?"

"I was merely meditating, sir. I was reflecting on the frequency with which mankind has wished for a world as peaceful and secure as the one Landru provided."

"Quite so, Mr. Spock. And see what happens when we get it! It's our luck and our curse that we're forced to grow, whether we like it or not."

"I have heard human beings say also, Captain, that it is also our joy."

"*Our* joy, Mr. Spock?"

There was no response, but, Kirk thought, Spock knew as well as any man that ancient human motto: *Silence gives assent.*

THE IMMUNITY SYNDROME

(Robert Sabaroff)

White beaches . . . suntanned women . . . mountains, their trout streams just asking for it . . . the lift of a surfboard to a breaking wave . . . familiar tree-shapes—that was shore leave on Starbase Six. And the exhausted crew of the *Enterprise* was on its way to it, unbelievably nearing it at long last. Kirk, remembering the taste of an open-air breakfast of rainbow trout, turned to give Sulu his final approach orders.

"Message from the base, sir," Uhura called. "Heavy interference. All I could get was the word '*Intrepid*' and what sounded like a sector coordinate."

"Try them on another channel, Lieutenant."

McCoy said, "The *Intrepid* is manned by Vulcans only, isn't it, Jim?"

"I believe so." Kirk swung his chair around. "The crew of the *Intrepid* is Vulcan, isn't it, Mr. Spock? I seem to remember the Starship was made entirely Vulcan as a tribute to the skill of your people in arranging that truce with the Romulan Federation. It was an unusual honor."

Spock didn't answer. He didn't turn. But he'd straightened in his chair. Something in the movement disturbed Kirk. He got up and went over to the library-computer station. "Mr. Spock!" Still Spock sat, unmoving, silent. Kirk shook his shoulder. "Spock, what's wrong? Are you in pain?"

"The *Intrepid* is dead. I just felt it die."

Kirk looked at McCoy. McCoy shook his head, shrugging.

"Mr. Spock, you're tired," Kirk said. "Let Chekov take over your station."

"And the four hundred Vulcans aboard her are dead," Spock said.

McCoy said, "Come down to Sickbay, Spock."

Stone-faced, Spock said, "I am quite all right, Doctor. I know what I feel."

Kirk said, "Report to Sickbay, Mr. Spock. That's an order."

"Yes, Captain."

Kirk watched them move to the elevator. They'd all had it. Too many missions. Even Spock's superb stamina had its breaking point. Too many rough missions—and Vulcan logic itself could turn morbidly visionary. It was high time for shore leave.

"Captain, I have Starbase Six now," Uhura said.

Back in his chair, Kirk flipped a switch. "Kirk here. Go ahead."

The bridge speaker spoke. "The last reported position of the Starship *Intrepid* was sector three nine J. You will divert immediately."

Kirk rubbed a hand over his chin before he reached for his own speaker. "The *Enterprise* has just completed the last of several very strenuous missions. The crew is tired. We're on our way for R and R. There must be another Starship in that sector."

"Negative. This is a rescue priority order. We have lost all contact with solar system Gamma Seven A. The *Intrepid* was investigating. Contact has now been lost with the *Intrepid*. Report progress."

"Order acknowledged," Kirk said. "Kirk out."

Sulu was staring at him in questioning dismay. Kirk snapped, "You heard the order, Mr. Sulu. Lay in a course for Gamma Seven A."

Chekov spoke from his console. Awe subdued his voice.

"Solar System Gamma Seven A is dead, Captain. My long-range scan of it shows—"

"Dead? What are you saying, Mr. Chekov? That is a fourth-magnitude star! Its system supports billions of inhabitants! Check your readings!"

"I have, sir. Gamma Seven A is dead."

In Sickbay Spock was saying, "I assure you, Doctor, I am quite all right. The pain was momentary."

McCoy sighed as he took his last diagnostic reading. "My instruments appear to agree with you if I can trust them with a crazy Vulcan anatomy. By the way, how can you be so sure the *Intrepid* is destroyed?"

"I felt it die," his patient said tonelessly.

"But I thought you had to be in physical contact with a subject to sense—"

"Dr. McCoy, even I, a half Vulcan, can sense the death screams of four hundred Vulcan minds crying out over distance between us."

McCoy shook his head. "It's beyond me."

Spock was shouldering back into his shirt. "I have noticed this insensitivity among wholly human beings. It is easier for you to feel the death of one fellow-creature than to feel the deaths of millions."

"Suffer the deaths of thy neighbors, eh, Spock? Is that what you want to wish on us?"

"It might have rendered your history a bit less bloody."

The intercom beeped. "Kirk here. Bones, is Spock all right? If he is, I need him on the bridge."

"Coming, Captain." Kirk met him at the elevator. "You may have been right. Contact with the *Intrepid* has been lost. It has also been lost with an entire solar system. Our scans show that Gamma Seven A is a dead star system."

"That is considerable news." Spock hurried over to his station and Kirk spoke to Uhura. "Any update from Starfleet?"

"I can't filter out the distortions. They're getting worse, sir."

A red light flashed on Sulu's panel. "Captain, the deflector shields just snapped on!"

"Slow down to warp three!" Kirk walked back to Spock. The Vulcan straightened from his stoop over his computer. "Indications of energy turbulence ahead, sir. Unable to analyze. I have never encountered such readings before."

The drama latent in the statement was so uncharacteristic of Spock that Kirk whirled to the main viewing screen. "Magnification factor three on screen!" he ordered.

Star-filled space—the usual vista. "Scan sector," he said. The starfield merely revealed itself from another angle and Sulu said, "Just what are we looking for, Captain?"

"I would assume," Spock said, "*that*."

A black shadow, roughly circular, had appeared on the screen.

"An interstellar dust cloud," Chekov suggested.

Kirk shook his head. "The stars have disappeared. They could be seen through a dust cloud, Mr. Chekov. How do you read it, Mr. Spock?"

"Analysis still eludes me, Captain. Sensors are feeding data to computers now. But whatever that dark zone is, my calculations place it directly on the course that would have brought it into contact with the *Intrepid* and the Gamma Seven A system."

"Are you saying it caused their deaths, Mr. Spock?"

"A possibility, Captain."

"After a moment, Kirk nodded. "Hold present course but slow to warp factor one," he told Sulu. "Mr. Chekov, prepare to launch telemetry probe into that zone."

"Aye, sir." Chekov moved controls on his console. "Probe ready. Switching data feed to library-computer."

"Launch probe," Kirk said.

Chekov shoved a stud. "Probe launched."

An ear-shattering blast of static burst from the communications station. Its noise swelled into a crackling roar so fierce that it seemed to possess a physical substance—the substance and force of a giant's slap. It ended as abruptly as it had come. Uhura, dizzy, disoriented, was clinging to her chair.

"And what channel did *that* come in on?" Kirk said.

She had to make a visible effort to answer. "Telemetry . . . the channel from the probe, sir. There's no signal . . . at all now . . ."

"Mr. Spock, speculations?"

"I have none, Captain." Then Spock had leaped from his chair. Uhura, her arms dropped, limp, was slumped over her console. "Lieutenant!" He reached an arm around her, steadying her. "Dizzy," she whispered. "I'll . . . be all right in a minute."

The intercom beeped to McCoy's voice. "Jim, half the women on this ship have fainted. Reports in from all decks."

Kirk glanced at Uhura. "Maybe you'd better check Lieutenant Uhura. She just pulled out of a faint."

"Unless she's out now, keep her up there. I've got an emergency here."

"What's wrong?"

"Nothing organic. Just weakness, nervousness."

"Can you handle it?"

"I can give them stimulants to keep them on their feet."

A tired crew—and now this. Kirk looked at the screen. It offered no cheer. The black shadow now owned almost all of the screen. "Hold position here, Mr. Sulu." He got up from his chair—and was hit by an attack of vertigo. He fought it down. "Mr. Spock, I want an update on that shadow ahead of us."

"No analysis, sir. Insufficient information."

Kirk smacked the computer console. "Mr. Spock. I have asked you three times for data on that thing and you have been unable to supply it. 'Insufficient information' won't do. It is your responsibility to deliver sufficient information at all times."

"I am aware of that, sir. But there is nothing in the computer banks on this phenomenon. It is beyond all previous experience."

Kirk looked at the hand that had struck Spock's console. "Weakness, nervousness." He was guilty on both counts. Even Spock couldn't elicit data from the computer banks that hadn't been put into them. "Sorry, Mr. Spock. Something seems to be infecting the entire ship. Let's go for reverse logic. If you can't tell me what that zone of darkness is, tell me what it isn't."

"It is not gaseous, liquid nor solid, despite the fact we can't see through it. It is not a galactic nebula like the Coal Sack. As it has activated our deflector shields, it seems to consist of some energy form— but none that the sensors can identify."

"And you said it is possible it killed the *Intrepid* and that solar system?"

"Yes, Captain."

Kirk turned to Uhura. "Lieutenant, inform Starfleet of our position and situation. Relay all relative information from computer banks." He paused. "Tell them we intend to probe further into the zone of darkness to gain further information."

"Yes, sir."

As he started back to his chair, he swayed under another wash of dizziness. Spock moved to him quickly and he clung for a moment to the muscular arm. "Thank you, Mr. Spock," he said. "I can make it now." He reached his chair. "Distance to the zone of darkness, Mr. Sulu?"

"One hundred thousand kilometers."

"Slow ahead, Mr. Sulu. Impulse power."

His head was still whirling. "Distance now, Mr. Sulu?"

"We penetrate the zone in one minute seven seconds, sir."

"Mr. Chekov, red alert. Stand by, phasers. Full power to deflector shields."

"Phasers standing by—deflectors at full power, sir."

Sound was emitted. It came slowly at first—and not from the communications station. It came from everywhere; and as it built, its mounting tides of invisible shock waves reached everywhere. Their reverberations struck through the metal walls of the engineering section, rushing Scott to check his equipment. Horrified by his readings, he ran to his power levers to test them. Then, mercifully, the all-pervading racket subsided. Up on the bridge, his hands still pressed to his ears, Sulu cried, "Captain—the screen!"

Blackness, total, had claimed it.

"Malfunction, Mr. Spock?"

"No, Captain. All systems working."

Kirk shook his head, trying to clear it. Around him people were still

clutching at console rails for support. Kirk struck the intercom button.
"Bones, things any better in Sickbay?"

"Worse. They're backed up into the corridor."

"Got anything that will help up here? I don't want anyone on the
bridge folding at a critical moment."

"On my way. McCoy out."

Kirk pushed the intercom button again. "Kirk to Engineering. The
power's dropped, Mr. Scott! What's happened?"

"We've lost five points of our energy reserve. The deflector shields
have been weakened."

"Can you compensate, Scotty?"

"Yes, if we don't lose any more. Don't ask me how it happened."

Kirk spoke sharply. "I *am* asking you, mister. I need answers!"

McCoy's answer was an air-hypo. He hurried into the bridge with a
nurse. As Kirk accepted the hissing injection, McCoy said, "It's a stimulant, Jim." As he adjusted the hypo for Sulu's shot, Kirk said, "Just how
bad is it, Bones?"

"Two thirds of personnel are affected."

"This is a sick ship, Bones. We're picking up problems faster than we
can solve them. It's as though we were in the middle of some creeping
paralysis."

"Maybe we are," McCoy said. He left the command chair to continue
his round with the hypo. Kirk got up to go to the computer station.
"Mr. Spock, any analysis of that last noise outburst—the one that started
to lose us power?"

Spock nodded. "The sound was the turbulence caused by our penetration of a boundary layer."

"What sort of boundary layer?"

"I don't know, Captain."

"Boundary between what and what?"

"Between where we were and where we are." At Kirk's stare, he went
on. "I still have no specifics, sir. But we seem to have entered an area of
energy that is not compatible with life or mechanical processes. As we
move on, the source of it will grow stronger—and we will grow weaker."

"Recommendations?"

McCoy spoke. "*I* recommend survival, Jim. Let's get out of here." He
turned and walked to the elevator, the nurse behind him.

Kirk faced around to the questioning faces. And Starbase had demanded a "progress" report. Progress to what? The fate of the *Intrepid*
—the billions of lives that had once breathed on Gamma Seven A? Bu-
reaucracy . . . evasion by comfortable chairs.

He walked slowly back to his uncomfortable chair. The intercom button—yes. "This is the Captain speaking," he said. "We have entered an area that is unfamiliar to us. All hands were tired to begin with and we've all sustained something of a shock. But we've had stimulants. Our deflectors are holding. We've got a good ship. And we know what our mission is. Let's get on with the job. Kirk out."

His own intercom button beeped. "Sickbay to Captain."

"Kirk. Go ahead, Bones."

Before he went ahead, McCoy glanced at the semi-conscious Yeoman lying on his diagnostic couch. "Jim, one after another . . . life energy levels . . . my indicators . . ."

Kirk spoke quietly. "Say it, Bones."

"We are dying," McCoy said. "My life monitors show that we are all, each one of us, dying."

The sweat of his own weakness broke from Kirk's pores. He could feel it run cold down his chest.

But the ordeal of the *Enterprise* had just begun. Kirk, down in Engineering, was flung against a mounded dynamo at a sudden lurch of the ship. "And that? What was that, Mr. Scott?"

"An accident, sir. We went into reverse."

"Reverse? That was a *forward* lurch! How could that occur in reverse thrust?"

"I don't know, sir. All I know is that our power levels are draining steadily. They're down to twelve percent. I've never experienced anything like it before."

Spock came in on the intercom. "Captain, we are accelerating. The zone of darkness is pulling us toward it."

"Pulling us? How, Mr. Spock?"

"I don't know. However, I suggest that Mr. Scott give us reverse power."

"Mr. Spock, he just *gave* us reverse power!"

"Then I reverse my suggestion, sir. Ask him to apply a forward thrust."

"Mr. Scott, you heard that. Let's try the forward thrust."

The Engineering Chief shook his head. "I don't know, sir. It contradicts all the rules of logic."

"Logic is Mr. Spock's specialty."

"Yes, sir, but—"

"Nudge it slowly into forward thrust, Mr. Scott."

Scott carefully advanced three controls. Eyeing his instruments anxiously, he relaxed. "That did it, Captain. We're slowing now. But the forward movement hasn't stopped. We're still being pulled ahead."

"Keep applying the forward thrust against the pull. Have one of your men monitor these instruments."

Instruments in Sickbay were being monitored, too. Nurse Chapel, watching her life function indicators, called, "Doctor, they're showing another sharp fall." McCoy, whirling to look, muttered, "Stimulants. How long can we keep them up?" He was checking the panel when Kirk's voice came from the intercom. "This is the Captain speaking. All department heads will report to the Briefing Room in ten minutes. They will come with whatever information gathered on this zone of darkness we are in."

McCoy took his gloom with him to the Briefing Room. Slamming some tape cartridges down on the table, he said, "My sole contribution is the fact that the further we move into this zone of darkness, the weaker our life functions get. I have no idea why." Reaching for a chair, he staggered slightly.

"Bones . . ."

He waved the solicitude aside. "I'm all right. All those stimulants— they catch up with you."

Scott spoke. "As far as the power levels are concerned, everything's acting backwards. But the drain is continuing. And we're still being dragged forward."

"Mr. Spock?" Kirk said.

"I am assuming that something within the zone absorbs both biological and mechanical energy. It would appear to be the same thing that sucked energy from an entire solar system—and the Starship *Intrepid.*"

"Some *thing,* Mr. Spock? Not the zone itself?"

"I would say not, Captain. Analysis of the zone suggests it is a negative energy field, however illogical that may sound. *But it is not the source of the power drains.*"

"A shield, then," Kirk said. "An outer layer of protection for something else."

"But what?" Scott said.

"It's pulling the life out of us, whatever it is," McCoy grunted.

"We'll find out what it is," Kirk said. "But first we have to get out of here ourselves." He leaned across the table. "Mr. Scott, forward thrust slowed down our advance before. If you channel all warp and impulse power into one massive forward thrust, it might snap us out of the zone."

Scott's face lightened. "Aye, Captain. I'll reserve enough for the shields in case we don't get out."

Spock's voice was as expressionless as his face. "I submit, Mr. Scott, that if we do not get out, the shields would merely prolong our wait for death."

Kirk regarded him somberly. "Yes. You will apply all power as needed to get us out of here, Mr. Scott. Report to your stations, everybody, and continue your research. Dismissed."

As they left, he remained seated, head bowed on his hand. At the door Spock stopped, and came back to stand, waiting, at the table. Kirk looked up at him. "The *Intrepid*'s crew would have done all these things, Captain," Spock said. "They were destroyed."

Kirk drummed his fingers on the table. "They may not have done all these things. You've just told us what an illogical situation this is."

"True, sir. It is also true that they never discovered what killed them."

"How can you know that?"

"Vulcan has not been conquered within its collective memory. It is a memory that goes so far back no Vulcan can any longer conceive of a conqueror. I know the ship was defeated because I sensed its death."

"What was it exactly you felt, Mr. Spock?"

"Astonishment. Profound astonishment."

"My Vulcan friend," Kirk said. He got up. "Let's get back to the bridge."

Engineering was calling him as they came out of the elevator. Hurrying to his chair, Kirk pushed the intercom stud. "Kirk here, Scotty."

"We've completed arrangements, sir. I'm ready to try it when you are."

"We've got the power to pull it off?"

The voice was glum. "I hope so, Captain."

"Stand by, Scotty." He pushed another button. "All hands, this is the Captain speaking. An unknown force is pulling us deeper into the zone of darkness. We will apply all available power in one giant forward thrust in the hope it will yank us out of the zone. Prepare yourselves for a big jolt." He buzzed Engineering. "Ready, Mr. Scott. Let's get on with it. *Now!*"

They were prepared for the jolt. And it was big. But what they weren't prepared for was the violently accelerating lunge that followed the jolt. Scott and a crewman crashed against a rear wall. McCoy and Christine Chapel were sent reeling back through two sections of Sickbay. In the bridge an African plant nurtured by Uhura flew through the air to smash against the elevator door. People were hurled bodily over the backs of their chairs. There was another fierce lurch of acceleration. The ship tossed like a rearing horse. Metal screamed. Lights faded. Finally, the *Enterprise* steadied.

From the floor where he'd been tumbled, Kirk looked at the screen. Failure. The starless black still possessed it.

Weary, bruised, Kirk hauled himself back into his chair. The question had to be asked. He asked it. "Mr. Scott, are we still losing power?"

"Aye, sir. All we did was to pull away a bit. The best we can do now is maintain thrust against the pull to hold our distance."

"How long do we have?"

"At this rate of drain plus the draw on all systems—two hours, Captain."

As Kirk got to his feet, another wave of weakness swept over him. It passed—and he moved over to the computer station. "We're trying to hold our distance, Mr. Spock. Have you yet ascertained what we are holding the distance *from?*"

Spock, his eyes on his own screen, said, "I have not found out what that thing is, Captain. But it seems to have found us."

Kirk wheeled to the bridge viewer. In the center of its blackness a bright object had become visible—bright, pulsating, elongated.

Staring at it, Kirk said, "Mr. Chekov, prepare to launch a probe."

Bent to his hooded computer, Spock said, "Very confused readings, Captain—but that object is definitely the source of the energy drains."

"Mr. Chekov, launch probe," Kirk said.

"Probe launched, sir. Impact in seven point three seconds."

Without order Sulu began the countdown. "Six, five . . . four . . . three . . . two . . . one . . . *now!*"

The ship trembled. Lights blinked. But that was all.

"Mr. Chekov, do we still have contact with the probe?"

"Yes, sir. Data being relayed to Mr. Spock."

"Mr. Spock?"

The Vulcan's head was hidden under the computer's mound. "Readings coming in now, Captain. Length, approximately eleven thousand miles. Varying in width from two thousand to three thousand miles. Outer layer strewn with space debris and other wastes. Interior consists of protoplasm varying from a firmer gelatinous layer to a semi-fluid central mass."

He withdrew his head from the computer. "Condition . . . living."

The faces around Kirk were stunned. He looked away from them and back at Spock. "Living," he said. Then, his voice very quiet, he said, "Magnification four, Mr. Sulu. On the main screen."

He had expected a horror—and he received it. The screen held what might be a nightmare of some child who had played with a lab microscope—a monstrous, amoebalike protozoan. The gigantic nucleus throbbed, its chromosome bodies vaguely shadowed under its gelatinous, spotted skin. In open loathing, Kirk shut his eyes. But he could not dispel his searing memory of what continued to show on the screen.

In Sickbay's lab, McCoy was parading a pictured series of one-celled creatures. On the small viewscreen a paramecium, its cilia wriggling, came and went. Then McCoy said, "This is an amoeba."

If life was movement, ingestion, the thing was alive, a microscopic inhabitant of stagnant pools. As Kirk watched, a pseudopod extended itself, groping but intent on a fragment of food. There was a blind greed in the creature that sickened Kirk.

"I've seen them before," he said. "Like that, enlarged by microscope. But this thing out there is eleven thousand miles long! Are you saying that anything so huge is a single-celled animal?"

"For lack of a better term, Jim. Huge as it is, it is a very simple form of life. And it can perform all the functions necessary to qualify it as a living organism. It can reproduce, receive sense impressions, act on them, and eat, though what its diet is I wouldn't know."

"Energy," Spock said. "Energy drained from us. I would speculate that this unknown life form is invading the galaxy like an infection."

"Mr. Spock, the *Intrepid* died of this particular infection. Why have we survived so long?"

"The *Intrepid* must have come upon it when it was hungry, low in energy. We are not safe, Captain. We merely have a little more time than the *Intrepid* had."

"Bones, this zone of darkness. Does the thing generate it itself as some form of protection?"

"That's one of the things we have to find out, Jim. We need a closer look at it."

"The closer to it we get, the faster it eats our energy. We're barely staying alive at this distance from it."

McCoy shut off his screen. "We could risk the shuttlecraft. With special shielding, it might—"

"I'm not sending anybody anywhere near that thing! Unmanned probes will give us the information we need to destroy it."

"I must differ with you, Captain," Spock said. "We have sent probes into it. They have told us some facts but not those we need to know. We're in no position to expend the power to take blind shots at it. We need a target."

McCoy said, "One man could go in . . . pinpoint its vulnerable spots."

"And the odds against his coming back?" Kirk cried. "How can I order anyone to take such a chance?"

"Who mentioned orders?" McCoy demanded. "You've got yourself a volunteer, Jim, my boy. I've already done the preliminary work."

"Bones, it's a suicide mission!"

"Doctor, this thing has reflexes. The unmanned probe stung it when it entered. The lurch we felt was the turbulence of its reaction."

"All right, Spock," McCoy said. "Then I'll have the sense to go slow when I penetrate it."

Spock studied him. "There is a latent martyr in you, Doctor. It is an affliction that disqualifies you to undertake the mission."

"Martyr?" McCoy yelled. "You think I intend to bypass the chance to get into the greatest living laboratory ever?"

"The *Intrepid* carried physicians and psychologists, Doctor. They died."

"Just because Vulcans failed doesn't mean a human will."

Kirk hit the table with his fist. "Will you both kindly shut up? I've told you! I'm not taking volunteers!"

"You don't think you're going, do you?" McCoy shouted.

"I am a command pilot!" Kirk said. "And as such, I am the qualified person. So let's have an end of this!"

"You have just *disqualified* yourself, Captain," Spock said. "As the command pilot you are indispensable. Nor are you the scientific specialist which I am."

McCoy glared at Spock. "Jim, that organism contains chemical processes we've never seen before and may never, let's hope, see again. We could learn more in one day than—"

"We don't have a day," Kirk said. "We have precisely one hour and thirty-five minutes. Then all our power is exhausted."

"Jim . . ."

"Captain . . ."

Kirk whirled on them both. "*I* will decide who can best serve the success of this mission! When I have made my command decision—command decision, gentlemen—you will be notified."

He turned on his heel and left them.

The solitude of his quarters felt good. He closed the door behind him, unhooked his belt and with his back turned to the clock's face deliberately stretched himself out on his bunk. Relax. Let the quiet move up, inch by inch, from his feet to his throbbing head. *Let go.* If you could just let go, answers sometimes welled up from an untapped wisdom that resisted pushing. "God, let me relax," Kirk prayed.

It was true. He *was* indispensable. There was no room in command authority for the heroics of phony modesty. As to Bones, he *did* have the medical-biological advantages he'd claimed. But Spock, the born athlete, the physical-fitness fanatic, the Vulcan logician and Science Officer, was both physically and emotionally better suited to withstand the stresses of such a mission. Yet who could know what invaluable discoveries Bones might make if he got his chance to make them? So it was up to him—Kirk. The choice was his. One of his friends had to be condemned to probable death. Which one?

He drew a long shuddering breath. Then he reached out to the intercom over his head and shoved its button. "This is the Captain speaking. Dr. McCoy and Mr. Spock report to my quarters at once. Kirk out."

The beep came as he sat up. "Engineering to Captain Kirk."

"Go ahead, Scotty."

"You wanted to be kept informed of the power drain, sir. All levels have sunk to fifty percent. Still draining. We can maintain power for another hour and fifteen minutes."

"Right, Scotty." He drew a hand over the bunk's coverlet, stared at the hand, and said, "Prepare the shuttlecraft for launching."

"What's that, sir?"

"You heard me, Scotty, Dr. McCoy will tell you what special equipment to install. Kirk out."

Of course. The knock on his door. He got up and opened it. They were both standing there, their mutual antagonism weaving back and forth between them. "Come in, gentlemen." There was no point, no time for suspense. "I'm sorry, Mr. Spock," Kirk said heavily.

McCoy flashed a look of triumph at Spock. "Well done, Jim," he said. "I'll get the last few things I need and—"

Kirk stopped him in midstride. "Not you, Bones." He turned to Spock. "I'm sorry, Spock. I am sorry you are the best qualified to go."

Spock nodded briefly. He didn't speak as he passed the crushed McCoy.

The door to the hangar-deck elevator slid open. Spock moved aside to allow McCoy to precede him out of it. "Do not suffer so, Doctor.

Professional credentials are very valuable. But superior resistance to strain has occasionally proved more valuable."

"Nothing has been proven yet!" McCoy controlled himself with an effort. "My DNA code analyzer will give you the fundamental structure of the organism. You'll need readings on three light wavelengths from the enzyme recorder."

"I am familiar with the equipment, Doctor. Time is passing. The shuttlecraft is ready."

"You just won't let me share in this at all, will you, Spock?"

"This is not a competition, Doctor. Kindly grant me my own kind of dignity."

"Vulcan dignity? How can I grant you what I don't understand?"

"Then employ one of your human superstitions. Wish me luck, Dr. McCoy."

McCoy gave him a startled look. Without rejoinder, he shoved the button that opened the hangar-deck door. Beyond them the metallic skin of the chosen shuttlecraft gleamed dimly. Two technicians busied themselves with it, making some final arrangements. Spock, without looking back, walked through the hangar door. McCoy saw him climb into the craft. Then the door slid closed; McCoy, alone, muttered, "Good luck, Spock, damn you."

Kirk, on the bridge, waited. Then Sulu turned. "All systems clear for shuttlecraft launch, sir."

It was time to say the words. "Launch shuttlecraft."

The light winked on Sulu's console. Spock was on his way. Alone. In space, alone. Committed—given over to what he, his captain, had given him over to. Kirk heard the elevator whoosh open. McCoy came out of it. Kirk didn't turn. He said, "Lieutenant Uhura, channel telemetry directly to Mr. Chekov at the computer station."

The bridge speaker spoke. "Shuttlecraft to *Enterprise*."

"Report, Mr. Spock."

"The power drain is enormous and growing worse." Static crackled. "I am diverting all secondary power systems to the shields. I will continue communications as long as there is power to transmit."

Spock would be huddled now, Kirk knew, over the craft's control panel. He'd be busy shutting off power systems. Somehow Scott had suddenly materialized beside his command chair. "Captain! He won't have power enough to get back if he diverts it to his shields!"

"Spock," Kirk began.

"I heard, Captain. We recognized that probability earlier. But you will need information communicated."

"When do you estimate penetration?"

"In one point three minutes. Brace yourselves. The area of penetration will no doubt be sensitive."

What was Spock's screen showing? What was his closeup like? The details of the debris-mottled membrane, the enlarging granular structure of the protoplasm under it, two thousand miles thick?

"Contact in six seconds," Spock's voice said.

A tremor shook the *Enterprise*. That meant the massive shock of impact for the shuttlecraft. Its lights would dim, alone in the dimness inside the thing. Kirk seized the microphone.

"Report, Mr. Spock."

Silence reported. Had Spock already lost consciousness? The organism would try to dislodge the craft. It would convulse, its convulsions sending its painful intruder into a spinning vortex of repeated shocks.

"Spock . . ."

The voice came, weak now. "I am undamaged, Captain . . . relay to Mr. Scott . . . I had three percent power reserve . . . before the shields stabilized. I . . . will proceed with my tests . . ." The voice faded . . . then it returned. "Dr. McCoy . . . you would not . . . have survived this . . ."

Kirk saw that McCoy's eyes were moist. "You wanna bet, Spock?" His voice broke on the name.

"I am . . . moving very slowly now—establishing course toward . . . the nucleus."

Chekov, white-faced, called from the computer. "Sir, Mr. Spock has reduced his life support systems to bare minimum. I suppose to maintain communications."

Kirk's hand was wet on his microphone. "Spock, save your power for the shields."

Static sputtered from the microphone. Between its cracklings, words could be heard. "My . . . calculations indicate—shields . . . only forty-seven minutes." More obliterating static. It quieted. "Identified . . . Chromosome structure. Changes in it . . . reproduction process about to begin."

Ashen, McCoy cried, "Then there'll be *two* of these things!"

"Spock . . ."

Kirk got an earful of static. He waited. "I . . . am having . . . some difficulty . . . ship control."

Kirk looked away from the pain in McCoy's face. He waited again. As though it were warning of its waning usefulness, the mike spoke in jagged phrases. ". . . losing voice contact . . . transmitting . . . here are internal coordinates . . . chromosome bodies . . ."

Uhura turned from her console. "Contact lost, sir. But I got the coordinates."

"Captain!" it was Chekov. "The shuttlecraft shields are breaking! Fluctuations of energy inside the organism."

"Aye," Scott said. "It's time he got out of there."

There was nobody to look at but himself, Kirk thought. He was the man who had sent his best friend to death. He had sent Spock out to suffocate in the foul entrails of a primordial freak. That was a truth to somehow be lived with for the rest of his life. His chair lurched under him. The ship gave a shudder. Numbly, Kirk righted himself. Then, suddenly, in a blast of realization, he knew. "Bones!" The word tore from him in a shout. "He's alive! He's still alive! He made the craft kick the thing to force it to squirm—and let us know!"

Uhura spoke. "Captain, I'm getting telemetry."

"Mr. Chekov—telemetry analysis as it comes in."

McCoy was still brooding on what reproduction of the organism meant. "According to Spock's telemetry analysis, there are forty chromosomes in that nucleus ready to divide." He paused. "If the energy of this thing merely doubles, everybody and everything within a light year of it will be dead." He paced the length of the bridge and came back. "Soon there will be two of it, four, eight, and more—a promise of a combined anti-life force that could encompass the entire galaxy."

"That's what Spock knows, Bones. He knows. He knows we have no choice but to try and destroy it when he transmitted those coordinates of the chromosomes."

Scott said, "Look at your panel, Captain. The pull from the thing is increasing. The drain on our shields is getting critical."

"How much time, Scotty?"

"Not more than an hour now, sir."

"Shield power is an unconditional priority. Put all secondary systems on standby."

"Aye, sir."

"Bones, can we kill that thing without killing Spock? And ourselves, too?"

"I don't know. It's a living cell. If we had an antibiotic that—"

"How many billions of kiloliters would it take?"

"Okay, Jim. Okay."

Uhura, her face radiant, turned from her console. "I'm receiving a message from Mr. Spock, sir. Low energy channel, faint but readable."

"Give it to me, Lieutenant."

"Faint" wasn't the word. Weak was. Very weak now. Spock said, "I . . . am losing life support . . . and minimal shield energy. The organism's nervous energy is . . . only maximal within protective membrane . . . interior . . . relatively insensitive . . . sufficient charge of . . . could destroy . . . tell Dr. McCoy . . . he should have wished . . . me luck . . ."

The bridge people sensed the burden of the message. Silence fell, speech faltering at the realization that Spock was lost. Only the lowered hum of power-drained machinery made itself heard.

Kirk lay unmoving on the couch in his quarters. Spock was dead. And to what point? If he'd been able to transmit his information on how to destroy the thing, he would have died for a purpose. But even that small joy had been denied to him. Spock was dead for no purpose at all, to no end that mattered to him.

Without knocking, McCoy came in and sat down on the couch beside the motionless Kirk.

"What's on your mind, Dr. McCoy?"

"Spock," McCoy said. "Call me sentimental. I've been called worse things. I believe he's still alive out there in that mess of protoplasm."

"He knew the odds when he went out. He knew so much. Now he's dead." Kirk lifted an arm into the air, contemplating the living hand at the end of it. "What *is* this thing? Not intelligent. At least, not yet."

"It is disease," McCoy said.

"This cell—this germ extending its filthy life for eleven thousand miles —one single cell of it. When it's grown to billions, we will be the germs. We shall be the disease invading its body."

"That's a morbid thought, Jim. Its whole horror lies in its size."

"Yes. And when our form of life was born, what micro-universe did we destroy? How does a body destroy an infection, Bones?"

"By forming anti-bodies."

"Then that's what we've got to be—an anti-body." He looked at McCoy. Then, repeating the word "anti-body," he jumped to his feet and struck the intercom button. "Scotty, suppose you diverted all remaining power to the shields? Suppose you gave it all to them—and just kept impulse power in reserve?"

"Cut off the engine thrust?" Scott cried. "Why, we'd be sucked into that thing as helplessly as if it were a wind tunnel!"

"Exactly, Mr. Scott. Prepare to divert power on my signal. Kirk out."

He turned to find himself facing McCoy's diagnostic Feinberger. "Got
something to say, Bones?"

"Technically, no. Medically, yes. Between the strain and the stimulants, your edges are worn smooth. You're to keep off your feet for a
while."

"I don't have awhile. None of us do. Let's go . . ."

He took time to compose his face before he stepped out of the bridge
elevator. He took his place in his command chair before he spoke into
the intercom. "All hands, this is the Captain speaking. We are going to
enter the body of this organism. Damage-control parties stand by—all
decks secure for collision. Kirk out."

"It's now or never," he thought—and called Engineering.

"Ready, Mr. Scott?"

"Yes, sir."

"*Now*," Kirk said.

The ship took a violent forward plunge. Kirk, gripping his chair,
glanced at the screen. The blackness grew denser as they sped toward it.
"Impact—twenty-five seconds, sir," Sulu said intensely.

Then shock knocked Sulu from his chair. Something flared from the
screen. Chekov, sprawled on the deck, looked up at his console as the
ship steadied. "We're through, sir!" he shouted.

Uhura, recovering her position, called, "Damage parties report minimal hurt, Captain."

Kirk didn't acknowledge the information. The blackness on the
screen had gone opaque. The *Enterprise,* lost in the vast interior of the
organism, moved sluggishly through the lightlessness of gray jelly.

Engineering again. "Mr. Scott, we still have our impulse power?"

"I saved all I could, sir. I don't know if there's enough to get us out
of this again. Or time enough to do it in."

"We have committed ourselves, Mr. Scott."

"Aye. But what are we committed to? We've got no power for the
phasers."

McCoy made an impatient gesture. "We couldn't use them if we did.
Their heat would rebound from this muck and roast us alive."

"The organism would love the phasers. It eats power—" Kirk broke
off. A frantic Scott, rushing from the elevator, had caught his last word.
"Power!" he cried. "That's the problem, Captain! If we can't use power
to destroy this beast, what is it we *can* use?"

"Anti-power," Kirk said.

"What?" McCoy said.

Scott was staring at him. "This thing has a negative energy charge.

Everything that has worked has worked in reverse. In its body, we're an anti-body, Scotty. So we'll use anti-power—anti-matter—to kill it."

Scott's tension relaxed like a pricked balloon. "Aye, sir! That it couldn't swallow! What good God gave you that idea, Captain?"

"Mr. Spock," Kirk said. "It's what he was trying to tell us before . . . we lost him. Mr. Chekov, prepare a probe. Scotty, we'll need a magnetic bottle for the charge. How soon?"

"It's on its way, laddie!"

"Mr. Chekov, timing detonator on the probe. We'll work out the setting. Mr. Sulu, what's our estimated arrival at the nucleus?"

"Seven minutes, sir."

"Jim how close are you going to it?"

"Point-blank range. Implant it—and back away."

"But the probe has a range of—"

Kirk interrupted McCoy. "The eddies and currents in the protoplasm could drift the probe thousands of kilometers away from the nucleus. No, we must be directly on target. We won't get a second chance."

Kirk rubbed the stiffening muscles at the nape of his neck. "Time for another stimulant, Bones."

"You'll blow up. How long do you think you can go on taking that stuff?"

"Just hold me together for another seven minutes."

He took one of the minutes to address his Captain's log. "Should we fail in this mission, I wish to record here that the following personnel receive special citations: Lieutenant Commander Leonard McCoy, Lieutenant Commander Montgomery Scott,—and my highest recommendation to Commander Spock, Science Officer, who has given his life in performance of his duty."

As he punched off the recorder, Scott, hurrying back to the command chair, paused to listen to Sulu say, "Target coordinates programmed, sir. Probe ready to launch."

"Mr. Sulu, program the fuse for a slight delay." He swung to Chekov. "All non-essential systems on standby. Communications, prepare for scanning. Conserve every bit of power. We've got to make it out of this membrane before the explosion. Make it work, Scotty. Pray it works."

"Aye, sir."

"Mr. Chekov, launch probe at zero acceleration. Forward thrust, one tenth second."

"Probe launched," Chekov said.

The moment finally passed. Then the ship bucked to the sound of straining metal. In the dimness made by the fading lights of the bridge, the air became sultry, suddenly heavy, oppressive. Kirk could feel the racing of his body's pulses. Then the air was breathable again; Chekov, turning, said, "Confirmed, sir. The probe is lodged in the nucleus . . . close to the chromosome bodies."

Kirk nodded. "Mr. Sulu, back out of here the way we came in. Let's not waste time. That was a nice straight line, Mr. Chekov."

Chekov flushed with pleasure. "Estimate we'll be out in six point thirty-nine minutes, sir." He glanced back at his panel, frowning. "Captain! Metallic substance outside the ship!"

"Spock?" McCoy said.

Chekov flicked on the screen. "Yes, sir. It's the shuttlecraft, lying there dead on its side."

In one bound Kirk was beside Uhura. "Lieutenant, give me Mr. Spock's voice channel! High gain!"

The microphone shook in his hand as he waited for her to test the wave length. "Ready, sir," she said.

He waited again to try and steady his voice. "Mr. Spock, do you read me? Spock, *come in!*" He whirled to Scott. "Mr. Scott, tractor beam!"

"Captain . . . we don't have the time to do it! We've got only a fifty-three percent escape margin!"

"Will you kindly take an order, Lieutenant Commander? Two tractor beams on that craft!"

Scott reddened. "Tractor beams on, sir."

"Glad to hear it!" Kirk said—and incredibly the mike in his hand was speaking. "I . . . recommend you . . . abandon this attempt, Captain. Do . . . not risk the ship further . . . on my account."

Wordless, Kirk handed the mike to McCoy. McCoy looked at him and he nodded. "Shut up, Spock!" McCoy yelled. "You're being rescued!" He returned the mike to Kirk.

Spock said, "Thank you, Captain McCoy."

Weak as he was, Kirk thought, he'd find the strength to cock one sardonic eyebrow.

Weak—but alive. A knowledge better than McCoy's stimulants. "Time till explosion, Mr. Chekov?"

"Fifty-seven seconds, sir."

"You're maintaining tractor beam on the shuttlecraft, Mr. Scott?"

"Aye, sir." But the Scottish gloom of Kirk's favorite engineer was still unsubdued. "However, I can't guarantee it will hold when that warhead explodes." He glanced at his board. Despite the dourness of his expectations, he gave a startled jump. "The power levels show dead, sir."

Then the power levels and everything else ceased to matter. The ship whirled. A white-hot glare flashed through the bridge. McCoy was smashed to the deck. In the glare Kirk saw Chekov snatched from his chair to fall unconscious at the elevator door. Uhura's body, on the floor beside her console, rolled to the ship's rolling. Disinterestedly, Kirk realized that blood was pouring from a gash in his forehead. A handkerchief appeared in his hand—and Sulu crawled away from him back in the direction of his chair. He sat up and tied the handkerchief around his head. It's what you did in a tough tennis game to keep the sweat out of your eyes . . . a long time since he played tennis . . .

"Mr. Sulu," he said, "can you activate the viewscreen?"

Stars. They had come back. The stars had come back.

A good crew. Chekov had limped back to his station. Not that he needed to say it. But it was good to hear, anyway. "The organism is destroyed, Captain. The explosion must have ruptured the membrane. It's thrown us clear."

The stars were back. So was the power.

Kirk laid his hand on Scott's shoulder. "And the shuttlecraft, Scotty?"

Spock's voice spoke from the bridge speaker. "Shuttlecraft to *Enterprise*. Request permission to come aboard."

Somebody put the mike in his hand. "You survived that volcano, Mr. Spock?"

"Obviously, Captain. And I have some very interesting data on the organism that I was unable to . . ."

McCoy, rubbing his bruised side, shouted, "Don't be so smart, Spock! You botched that acetylcholine test, don't forget!"

"Old Home Week," Kirk said. "Bring the shuttlecraft aboard, Mr. Scott. Mr. Chekov, lay in a course for Starbase Six. Warp factor five."

He untied the bloody handkerchief. "Thanks, Mr. Sulu. I'll personally see it to the laundry. Now I'm off to the hangar deck. Then Mr. Spock and I will be breaking out our mountaineering gear."

MH